For Johns

Hoping this takes you

beyond Faulknom Bicycle,

with affection and

friendship,

J. Chy

Presented
to the library
by
John
Simon

WAR
CRIES
OVER
AVENUE
C

Other Books by Jerome Charyn

ONCE UPON A DROSHKY
ON THE DARKENING GREEN
THE MAN WHO GREW YOUNGER
GOING TO JERUSALEM
AMERICAN SCRAPBOOK
EISENHOWER, MY EISENHOWER
THE TAR BABY
BLUE EYES
MARILYN THE WILD
THE EDUCATION OF PATRICK SILVER
THE FRANKLIN SCARE
SECRET ISAAC
THE SEVENTH BABE
THE CATFISH MAN
DARLIN' BILL
PANNA MARIA
PINOCCHIO'S NOSE

WAR CRIES OVER AVENUE C

by
Jerome Charyn

DONALD I. FINE, INC.
New York

Library of Congress Catalogue Card Number: 84–073516

ISBN: 0–917657–30–6
Manufactured in the United States of America

10 9 8 7 6 5 4 3 2 1

This book is printed on acid free paper. The paper in this book
meets the guidelines for permanence and durability of the Committee on
Production Guidelines for Book Longevity of the Council on Library Resources.

To Don Fine,
Warrior in the Wilderness

THE
ALPHABET
BLOCKS

AVENUES A, B, C, and D form a dirty appendage to Manhattan's Lower East Side: these Alphabet Blocks have become Indian country, the land of murder and cocaine. Though there are still pockets of Ukrainians, Russians, Poles, Italians, and Germans on and around Avenue A, such pockets have little bearing on the internal affairs of the new Indian country. The population is still overwhelmingly Catholic, but even the faithful at Mary Help of Christians, when asked about their own Alphabetville, will answer that Christ stopped at Avenue A.

This is more than a neighborhood joke. Come down to

First Avenue and see for yourself. Have an espresso at Johnny's, under the stairs. You're not in Indian country, no matter what your mommy and daddy tell you. They can't judge the terrain from a terrace up in Riverdale. You won't find Dean & Deluca, but First Avenue does have that peculiar rub of Manhattan, that sense of the constant entrepreneur: wealth hiding behind a window, a horde of taxicabs, a Hunan restaurant . . . you'll not feel lonely on First.

Shove a little east to Avenue A, and you begin to smell the moon. The restaurants haven't disappeared. You can pick your own Russian beanery. Sit and have some stuffed cabbage, say that Doris Quinn sent you, Doris from the *Spy*. They'll treat you to golden pancakes, drop a strawberry in your tea, and you'll think that Avenue A was your own fatted calf. The discomfort won't start until after you pay the bill. It has nothing to do with the strawberry. That strawberry was fine. It's a vague terror that's settling in. The traffic seems different out on the street. Cars move slower on Avenue A. You could die whistling and might not meet a Checker cab. You've entered Indian country without even knowing it. The Checkers are much more suspicious than Christ. First Avenue is their cruising line.

The absence of Checker cabs isn't the only sign of Indian country. Christ doesn't ride a Checker cab. But on Avenue A you discover the first Hunan restaurant in New York that failed. Suddenly you can't remember the last drugstore, and you realize how the corner pharmacy is so much a part of your culture, a piece of civilization you've come to expect. There's a Medicaid mill where the drugstore should have been. Instead of the neighborhood pharmacist, a little factory of doctors and dentists, for Alphabetville.

Then there's the legal clinic, with Polish, Spanish, Yiddish, Chinese, Russian, and Italian phrases in the window to announce itself, like the alphabet of the world. Men and women with angry faces sit inside the window, lists of grievances on their laps, long, long scrolls against landlords, husbands, wives, children, mothers, the United States. You hurry past the window, not wanting to appear in the scrolls as the woman who savaged Avenue A.

It's true, A might be just another eccentric avenue. It does have blueberry blintzes and brown bread. But go a little deeper into the district. All the cozy earmarks evaporate on Avenue B. The good burghers have fled from this street. There isn't even the illusion of the ordinary entrepreneur. B wears the colors of a poverty so basic, it has no use for pretense. The furniture stores have no furniture in the windows other than half a loveseat or a broken crib. Alphabetville isn't burdened with any dream of Little San Juan. The bodegas are minimarkets now, with a dumb idea of produce: bushels of potatoes sit unmolested behind the fenced-in doors, as if they were offerings to the gods of Avenue B, who never heard of Spanish or English, never lived in Puerto Rico or around Madison and Fifth, and can only manage the creole of this particular street.

But B is nearly civilization next to C. C has no gods. It's the dark side of an empty closet. The cops wear Batman capes on Avenue C. They aren't celebrating Halloween. It's a message to snipers in the windows that they're not on patrol; it's Indian country, and they're only passing through. Cops without their Batman capes have a habit of getting killed. But don't interpret this as anarchy in an empty closet. Teenage hitmen patrol the street. They protect the district's cocaine dealers and discourage uptown muggers from moving in.

And we shouldn't forget the soldiers of Saigon Sarah, tiger lady of Avenue C. She operates out of an abandoned religious school, a talmud torah that's been converted into a fortress and a private after-hours club. Some of her soldiers are Vietnam vets. Sarah herself was once a nurse in the neighborhood of Saigon. So she says. The tiger lady is a recent acquisition to the street. Are we witnessing the gentrification of Alphabetville? Yours truly visited the talmud torah a month ago and tried to beg an interview with Sarah behind her metal gate. The tiger lady didn't send for her troops. But she was stingy with the *Spy*. I couldn't get her to natter much with me over the metal teeth.

—Saigon, what kind of operation are you running on this street?

9

—A mercy hospital, said the tiger lady.
—But where's the ambulances, if I'm allowed to ask?
—In the tunnels.
I had a look north and south of the talmud torah.
—Tunnels, Saigon?
—Yes, she said. The tunnels under C.

That was her last word to the *Spy*. I had to start rethinking the parameters of that empty closet. Was Sarah an old-fashioned entrepreneur, bringing her expertise to Alphabetville? Only what was she importing and exporting? It wasn't hospital beds.

She hadn't changed the contours of that street. Fences, gates, and boarded windows. An old woman lived in the hull of a refrigerator a block from the fort. None of Saigon's soldiers swept her inside. Is that a doll's hospital in the talmud torah?

And what about Saigon's influence on the eastern frontier, Avenida D? Does she police the uninterrupted line of housing projects that looks like a primitive rockscape on somebody else's moon? I suspect not. Saigon has her own moon to worry about.

D's rockpiles are only a reminder that Alphabetville swallows up the new and the old, turns them into decoration, a stage set for dinosaurs. Connecting with D on the north is the grimmest rock of all: Con Ed's power station, with cribs and catwalks shoving at the sky, and enormous chimneys that lay a black umbrella over this part of Indian country. There's nothing here identifiable with the least of human landscapes. The power station isn't a glimpse of hell. No self-respecting devil would abide such a place. It's land's end, a monolithic energy castle that relates only to itself.

Is it any wonder Christ stopped at Avenue A?

He'd have jumped into the river after C or D and the power station and swum home to Bethlehem.

—Doris Quinn, *Your Manhattan Spy*,
sixth edition.
New York: Gallatin & Peck, $13.95.

SAIGON
SARAH

1

THEY called her tiger lady. No one knew why she'd come to these badlands, this villa of analfabeticos. She didn't sell coca leaves to the turistas. She carried a pair of .45s under her heart. At first they thought she was with the federales, a spy in God's little house. But El Presidente Reagan wasn't smart enough to rent a talmud torah. No, she was a fugitive, one of their own kind. She'd gathered a little army around her, fugitives like herself. A twitching maniac and a Russian bear. And this grab-bag army chased gypsy thieves out of the projects and obliged the Medicaid mills to lower their price. She was the little Hebrew godmother with cacarañas in her face, memories of smallpox. She stole nothing from the shopkeepers. Her cacarañas kept the peace.

But Saigon Sarah was no mystery to herself. She was thirty-two years old, and she'd been engaged to one man for half her life. The man lived with her. He was a wreck with shrapnel in his hair, a twitch named Howard Biedersbill. She'd stolen him from the United States. But she hadn't longed to become an outlaw. She was a simple girl, riddled with pockmarks. She'd been a poetess once. Might even have become the laureate of New Jersey, if God hadn't interfered. She stood near the talmud torah door, remembering Bayonne where she'd been born. All the poetry had gone out of her skull. She couldn't have licked the easiest line onto a scrap of paper. She had nothing but Biedersbill and her .45s, and her fiancé was deeply damaged. He had no skeleton. He was all shrapnel now.

The criollas waved to her from the street. They curtsied in front of her door, left little gifts of plantains and curried eggs. She protected them from all the banditos in the neighborhood. They worshipped her a little. But she was no tiger lady. She was Sarah Fishman of Bengal High. Pockmarks couldn't hurt the Bayonne belle.

Her daddy was pulling at her. "You slut, you miserable slut."

She'd been out all night with Howard Biedersbill, under the bridge. She couldn't expect Howie to have a car at fourteen. He was two years younger than Sarah, but he was a little fucking genius and he'd fallen in love with her and made Sarah a mahogany heart with his own two hands. He was the first boy who seemed fond of her bitten face. The little genius had seduced her under the Bayonne Bridge. It wasn't much as far as seductions go, but it was the first for Sarah. She had to touch the genius and show him what to do; even then it was mostly fumbling, because his hands got lost in her brassiere, the same hands that had manicured the mahogany heart, and Sarah had to disentangle Howie Biedersbill.

But it was the intent that mattered. Howie had stayed the night with her, held his vigil with an elbow in her blouse, and he'd promised never to do such things with another girl. That was enough for the Bayonne belle.

She hadn't sacrificed much of her virginity, because Howie had avoided her underpants in his great confusion and lust, but she still expected to be strangled by her dad who wasn't interested in technicalities. He was a seller of greeting cards and he knew all the rhymes about love.

"In bed the whole stinking night with that Biedersbill boy."

She had to defend Howie's virtue even if she couldn't convince him of her own. "We weren't in bed, dad. We were under the bridge."

But she'd only made it worse. "Yes, that's your troubadour. He doesn't have the decency to bring you into his father's house. He takes you under the bridge where the whole world can see."

Her dad was a genius himself, coming up with a word like *troubadour,* because that's what Howie was, a troubadour stuck in Bayonne, New Jersey, where he'd discovered the fullness of Sarah's chest. But she wasn't surprised about her dad. He often did his own rhymes for the greeting-card companies. He was a salesman and a pieceworker and he had Sarah by the throat.

"The Biedersbill boy will have to marry you."

"Dad, he's only fourteen."

"It means nothing to the Catholics. He'll get a dispensation from his pope."

Her dad understood greeting cards and the United Jewish Appeal, but he was woefully ignorant about the rest of the world.

15

The pope wouldn't marry a fourteen-year-old believer to a pock-marked girl of the Jewish persuasion. Yet she had to humor her dad. His fingers were getting fatter and fatter around her throat.

"Dad, the pope can't act without his cardinals." She knew that much from her classes in government at Bengal High.

She might have worn the old man down if her mom hadn't butted in. "Don't contradict your father, dear."

"Then you telex the pope," she said while her dad tightened his grip. His ears had gone blood red.

"Herman," her mom warned, "it's not worth it. You'll have a stroke."

Herman Fishman, she thought, although she could hardly breathe. That name had an unfortunate melody, and that's why he'd streamlined it on the greeting cards. Her dad was Herman Fish, the greeting-card poet.

> *If the universe went to stone*
> *I wouldn't love you any less.*
> *We'd sit in our stone hats*
> *Until time began to break*
> *And all the crumbling stones could meet.*

That was Sarah's favorite, and she couldn't see how a man who'd written such sensitive lines could have fallen out of love so fast with his own little girl. That was the problem. She'd never been daddy's little girl. She was a stubborn creature and she meant to have Howie Biedersbill if she didn't strangle on her spit.

And then that curious man gave Sarah back the freedom of her windpipe. "Hilma, pack the girl's belongings. She's going out into the street."

Old Hilma went into Sarah's closet and started to scavenge things. She stuffed shoes and hats and Sarah's silk giraffes into one small valise and daddy pitched the valise out the window. "Take your filth and go."

She trudged out to the valise on the lawn. Its clasp had broken in the fall, and her poor brassiere hung over the valise's edge like a punishing sign. She could have cried on the lawn, but she walked the valise back into the house.

Herman and Hilma stood in the stairwell. "Do you promise never to see the Biedersbill boy?"

"Yes, daddy, yes," she bawled behind the safety of her father's windowsills.

"It's not a bluff? You'll give up your troubadour?"

And she did.

She told Howie she'd marry him in two years but she couldn't have relations or meet with him until she moved out of her daddy's house. She'd be eighteen then and could do whatever she liked.

They had this curious betrothal where they couldn't talk or touch. And Howie slipped away from her. His head had gone into supernatural stuff. She went out for the girl's softball team and he got involved with mummies that were supposed to rise from their bandages in ten thousand years. Howie failed all his subjects and dropped out of Bengal High. He left a note in her locker, mentioning he'd gone to Egypt on account of his lust for mummies.

She missed the little genius but her history teacher, Mrs. Sheridan, swore she could have a fine career in spite of the holes in her face. Mrs. Sheridan had been a WAC in World War II. She told Sarah about her exploits with the Women's Army Corps.

"Dearest," Mrs. Sheridan said, "you could be happy as a nurse for the United States."

What did Sarah have on the other side? Days and nights at home with Herman and Hilma. She got into the nursing program at Trenton State. She fooled around with a boy in the library stacks, but she had Howie on her mind. He hadn't even sent her one postcard from Egypt.

The army took her after two years. She studied tropical diseases at Fort McClellan and began drawing lieutenant's pay. No one whispered to her that she was slated for Vietnam. She could have had two weeks in Honolulu, but she decided on Bayonne. It was a mistake to come back in uniform. Her daddy didn't write her a poem. He was silent during dinner. Mama wept.

"What's wrong? I have two careers. I'm a lieutenant and a nurse."

"Only the gentiles would send their daughters into an army camp . . . unless it was a crisis."

"But I worked hard. Can't you say you're glad?"

"I'm glad, I'm glad, I'm glad." Her father left the table and Sarah had nothing but her mother's tears in New Jersey.

She went to Okinawa and loitered there a month. She couldn't meet the sorriest bit of a man on base. She was at a colony of women officers, and when she did discover a man at the PX, the son of a bitch wouldn't have anything to do with a pock-marked lieutenant. Sarah was convinced she'd die in Okinawa without man or marriage. She drank alone in her room, resigned to being a bachelor lieutenant at a nurse's prison, when she was whisked off Okie and flown to the Nam. She arrived at Ton Son Nhut Airport in the rainy season and never got to see Saigon. "It's Whore City," some captain explained. "You can't sit on a chair at the officers' club without getting the crabs." She was ferried to Fort Cayenne, an old Foreign Legion hospital south of Saigon. It was a hospital in the bush, where a few soldiers and civilians lay in a ward with Viet Cong suspects who were interrogated from morning to night.

Sarah was the only nurse on the compound. She directed traffic at the hospital, and it was like being a constant referee, because fights would break out among her medical corpsmen, nasty boys who happened to be heroin addicts and would rather shoot up than attend to hospital business.

Those damn corpsmen were the first soldiers who took an active interest in Sarah. They called her "Lady Round Eyes" and brought her wildflowers when they weren't shooting up.

They didn't have much respect for her rank. The corpsmen kept trying to poke a finger inside her nurse's blouse. They whooped and screamed when she came on the ward. She had to laugh in her own stinking heart how she'd become Raquel Welch to a gang of hospital monkeys.

The corpsmen carried bowie knives under their medical gowns, and when they got together they'd lick the knives and look at Sarah until they had a mess of blood on their tongues. She wasn't going to take that kind of shit from her own corpsmen. She ran to the weapons sergeant and said to him in plainest English: "Either fuck me, kill me, or outfit me, because I'm not moving from this spot."

The weapons sergeant gave her the last two .45s from his private collection, and Sarah wore them under her belt. No one came down from Saigon to scream at her. Why should the generals worry about a nurse in the bush with two .45s?

The corpsmen didn't cut their tongues so much. The .45s took away some of their enthusiasm. They stumbled on the ward with burnt-out eyes and Sarah had to put them to bed.

She cursed the Women's Army. She'd been assigned to an old French fort in the wilderness that was a welcoming center for captured VC. Interrogation officers would come on the ward and beat up wounded men in black pajamas without even recognizing Sarah. When the ward became crowded, they poisoned some of the men. It sickened her and she had to do something. She faced the officers and told them to get fucked.

The interrogations stopped for six hours. And then a man in a three-cornered hat came to Sarah's tent and she figured this was the end of her army life. But she couldn't understand the authority of that cocked hat. It was the kind of hat French generals must have worn two hundred years ago. He didn't reprimand her. He apologized for the poisonings on Sarah's ward. He was a young captain from military intelligence, Jonah Slyke, and he brought a parcel of food out of Danang and shared it

19

with Sarah. She had a baguette with the captain, blue cheese, and half a bottle of wine.

"Captain Jonah, if you're trying to soft-soap me, you've succeeded. But I won't have your poisoners around . . . and where'd you get the chapeau?"

"Took it off a French planter."

"In a game of cards?"

"No," he said, bowing to Sarah. "My game is paddleball."

That young captain was the paddleball champ of Vietnam. He'd been to Danang that morning, defending his championship against a light colonel from South Korea. She'd have considered it a blessing if Captain Jonah raped her in the tent. But he didn't paw her once. She couldn't get it on with a cultured man. Only the junkies pursued her.

A chopper came for the captain and ferried him to Saigon and Sarah allowed the interrogation teams back on the ward. Those bitches worked two to a bed, pummeling a captured VC from both sides of the blanket. The hospital was quiet for a day, and then a VC in one of the beds got hold of a gun and started shooting people on Sarah's ward. She could have shot back at him with her .45s, but Sarah wouldn't blow such a skinny man into the woods. She might have ruined his black pajamas. An interrogation officer crept behind the bed and slapped him with a rubber pipe. That VC was pulled off the ward, but the surgeons wouldn't look at the men who'd been shot until Sarah came crashing like a water buffalo into their tents. The wounded were all VC, and Sarah wondered for a moment if that nice young captain hadn't staged this little drama on the ward so the Bayonne belle would sympathize with his thugs.

The compound was getting her crazy. She went down to the landing zone and stood in line. The hospital had a taxi service to Saigon. She caught a chopper that was returning from its ice-cream run. The door gunner strapped her in without asking who she was. She sat near a pile of ice-cream cartons the crew hadn't been able to deliver. It was foggy on the ice-cream run.

The chopper rose up straight into another fog and Sarah had a black cloud with her on the seat, like an enormous ball of burnt cotton candy. The door gunner grabbed at her chest in the dark. She might have been flattered on a less foggy run.

"Soldier," she said into the black cloud.

"Yes, ma'am."

"Do you feel metal near your groin? That's a .45."

The cloud lifted over the roof and the hands went off her chest and the door gunner leaned out of the ship with his safety line and hurled ice cream at the trees like a bombardier.

Sarah wished she'd found another ferry, and then that mother rode the currents above the trees and she could have been on a gondola cradled by wind, because the chopper didn't seem to have any weight at all. She wasn't old Sarah from the boonies. She was Batwoman approaching Saigon. The Saigon Cathedral poked right out of the delta like a knitting needle in a yellow sky. The river was mustard that moved until Sarah swore it was a snake in the grass. The chopper dipped and that door gunner tried the stupidest thing. He blessed the city and dropped a tub of ice cream over Saigon.

Sarah shouted as hard as she could, but her voice had to carry under the slap of helicopter blades. "That's quite an act you have, slick. Dropping ice cream."

The door gunner grinned. "It's nothing but Saigon, lieutenant, ma'am. Whore City, USA."

They landed on the roof of Tonto One, a bachelor officers' compound in the middle of old Saigon. She wanted to park in this crappy hotel but you needed a billet stub to stay at the Tonto.

"We have no unassigned rooms," the billetmaster told her.

She went downstairs to a sidewalk café and had a dinner of green beans and croissants. She drank a glass of cold white wine

and forgot about her pockmarks. Sarah was back in civilization.
The boulevard that sheltered her café was the widest she'd ever
been on. Whore City? The door gunner was wrong. It was the
nearest thing to wonderland for a girl from Bengal High. Sarah
had been to Central Park with her softball team, but she couldn't
feel safe in New York City. She'd get lost on the subway and
land in some smelly street where the roofs were shedding bricks.
Manhattan had too many rivers. The street lamps were hard
on your eyes. The boulevards didn't have canopies where a girl
could sit and drink white wine.

She was finishing a croissant when she saw Captain Jonah
with a beauty from the Red Cross. Sarah imagined her own complexion and tried to sink into the table. She'd get on the ferry
to Hanoi and drown herself. Goddamn world didn't know what
it meant to be an ugly woman.

She paid her bill and tried to sneak out, but Jonah Slyke
trapped her at the door. "Come on over and meet some of my
people."

"Love to, captain, but I'm in a rush."

She wasn't going to chat with any pale beauty.

"Where are you staying, sis?"

She looked into Jonah's green eyes. "I never decide that until
I've had my second glass of wine."

"Take my room at the Tonto."

"They're kind of picky about their clientele."

"Nonsense. Tell the innkeeper you're my guest."

He went back to his beauty and Sarah got out the door. She
had to stop at the next café and tank up with two more glasses
of wine before she dared approach the billetmaster again. "Excuse
me but I'm Captain Jonah's guest." The billetmaster gave her
a bunch of hand towels.

She was put on a floor of bachelor men and she could hear
them sigh through the walls, but none of the bachelors visited
her during the night. She wore the captain's robe on her way

to the shower room. She was just another officer to these men.

She had croissants and café au lait at a milk bar in the morning and watched the fierce pull of pedicabs on the boulevard. The sidewalk was ringed with bicycles and motor scooters. A general passed in a jeep. Sarah was getting used to traffic in Saigon.

She ate scallops at a floating restaurant near the Club Nautique and slept a second night at the Tonto Inn. She could have gone naked and none of the officers would have noticed.

She had her croissants and stared at traffic for a week and was ferried home to the bush from the roof of Tonto One. The hospital chief didn't say a word about Sarah's absence from the ward. She fell into her old routines, avoiding the corpsmen's hands in her blouse and looking for poisoners among the interrogation teams. She had to threaten surgeons with her .45s, or they wouldn't have bothered to sew up the men on her ward.

"Fishman," the chief reminded her. "Most of this crop is VC . . . they'll die one way or the other."

"Could be, but we're a hospital, not a butcher station."

"Look again."

She looked and saw pajama men who didn't have a chance. The same pajama men were boobytrapping GIs. Soldiers would come out of the bush with only half their groins and that's when she'd feel like sneaking onto the ward and smothering the pajama men with their own blankets.

Didn't smother a single pajama man. She'd stuff her pockets with tampons and catch the ferry to Saigon. It turned into a joke among her corpsmen.

"What's Lieutenant Sarah doing in the big bad ville?"

"Eating candy."

"With officers or grunts?"

"With just about any old thing."

Surgeons, corpsmen, interrogators, and wounded grunts would speculate about Sarah. They wondered if she was sleeping with the ferryman who took her to Whore City. But Saigon Sarah didn't have a ferryman. She crept onto whatever gondola she could find and lived like a monk in Jonah's room. The captain was never there. She couldn't give up her virtue to an invisible man.

Other soldier nurses became the property of generals and civilian pilots, but the Bayonne belle had a stubbornness about her. She walked the boulevards, learned to abide without people or friends. She'd have her two nights in the ville and look for the nearest ferryman. It was always on the ride back to the boonies that a depression would seize her, as if she were being ferried to her daddy's house and she'd have to hide in her own loveless room with silk giraffes to console her.

And while she was on the ward one afternoon, a wounded soldier fell from the sky. He was choppered in from the stinking wilderness, but the medevac that carried him didn't bother to land. It dropped the soldier and disappeared. She couldn't tell if he was an ordinary grunt or a Green Beret, because he was bandaged from head to toe. She started to unravel him, getting at his ankles first. He was naked under the bandages and she wouldn't promise there was something familiar about his testicles, but she felt an odd sympathy for the dust on him and the moles. She pulled a leech off his back and hadn't found a wound so far. Then she unwrapped the soldier above his chin and she recognized him before she arrived at his brains.

"Howie Biedersbill, what the hell are you doing on my ward?"

He wasn't at all surprised about meeting Sarah ten thousand miles from New Jersey. They could have been roasting wieners under the Bayonne Bridge. She didn't know whether to kiss Howie or arrest him for impersonating a wounded man. She had to hold back from fiddling with the fur on his chest. Here was Howie Biedersbill, her heart's desire, and she couldn't consult her officer's manual, because there was nothing in the book about belated boyfriends dropping from the sky in a mummy's costume.

"Did you enjoy Egypt a lot?"

"Shh," he said. "I have a war name now. I'm the Teacher."

He was showing off his army education. "What is it you teach?"

"Henry James."

Sarah was a nurse and not a librarian. She couldn't keep up with reading lists. Was this Henry an expert on war and peace like Uncle Ho Chi Minh? She had to put the mummy boy in his place. "Who taught you to read Henry James?"

"A friend of Captain Jonah's."

"You work for him? Then you're just a goddamn interrogator. You take pajama men out of their hooches and call them VC. You slap the sons of bitches until they're dead. Teacher, I'm disappointed in you."

But the mummy wouldn't concede an inch. "Do I look like one of them pogues? I'm captain's demolition man."

"And a goddamn Green Beret."

He smirked at the mention of green. "The green beanie is for cowboys," he said. "I'm a Blue Beret."

She'd never seen a war with so many hats. Red berets, green berets, black berets, and blue. They were all their own little armies. They'd sit in the highlands six months and bake out a war. They didn't seem responsible to ordinary generals in Saigon. They were disciplined bandits on zombie patrols.

"I suppose the blue beanies are sentimental mothers. They saw you were getting thin and they sent you to your old sweetheart from Bengal High."

"Captain sent me," Teacher said.

"Howard Biedersbill, did you discuss my anatomy with Captain Jonah?"

"Not a word. And don't say Howard. Howard's dead. I'm your new corpsman. I've been assigned to you." He uncrumpled a piece of paper he was hiding in his fist. He'd come to Sarah through some civilian agency, and she didn't much care for this agency's handiwork. It said *Teacher* where Howie's name should have been.

She had to give the zombie some corpsman's clothes. Teacher didn't believe in underwear. He traveled in bare feet and a medic's gown. She was sorry to see him wrapped up again. She'd begun to admire the moles on his body. He slept in a hooch with nine other medics, and she worried about him because those junkie corpsmen might not cherish a soldier from the blue beanies. He fought the junkies on his first night and tamed them all.

They decided not to be on evil terms with any man who was so adept at fixing boobytraps. He began to license their junk, so they couldn't shoot up around the ward. He sat with the sons of bitches and read them Henry James and allowed them to eat from the opium ball in his pocket. Her heart's desire was a filthy opium eater.

He invited himself inside her tent and said to Sarah that eating opium was part of his reconnaissance work. "If it looks like Charlie Cong's gonna grab hold of your ass, well, you swallow the whole ball, and they can't interrogate you."

He offered her a lick and Sarah refused. She couldn't run a ward while she was wiped out. So she didn't feed on the ball, but talking led to kissing, and kissing got their clothes off, and this time that brilliant imbecile solved the strategy of her brassiere cups and took an interest in the rest of Saigon. She blushed at where his mouth went but she didn't deny him the least part of herself. She'd never have guessed that love could be such an acrobat.

The imbecile moved into her tent. She outranked that little zombie by a mile, but she ended up being his mama-san. Teach had a love of communal life. He shared his property with her, and she became part owner of his opium ball. He sold chunks of the ball to helicopter pilots who'd heard about his stash and landed at Fort Cayenne to taste what Teacher was carrying. She had thousands of dollars in her brassiere that the ball had earned.

But an opium ball couldn't cure the hospital's ills. Sarah had no penicillin and hardly any blood. The cupboards were bare at Fort Cayenne. The hospital had run out of food. She complained to the chief surgeon.

"Are you starving people?"

"It's not my fault if nothing comes to us. We get our supplies from Uncle Luc."

"That pirate," she said. "Can't you bargain with Uncle Luc?"

"What do we have to bargain with?"

An opium ball, she muttered to herself. Uncle Luc was the headman of the province, and he had his own little PX in the delta. Uncle sold to the Viet Cong, to restaurants in Saigon, to the nuns of Dalat, and the blue beanies.

She told Teacher about her plan to trade penicillin, blood, and fruit cocktail for a big piece of the ball.

"That jarhead won't trade with you."

"Why not?"

"Because the chiefs have different monopolies and Uncle Luc has to live by the laws. He does penicillin, but he can't do drugs."

"Then I'll offer him some of our cash."

Her zombie man retreated into his brown eyes. "Hon, he won't trade with you. He'd consider it prehistoric to put back the penicillin he stole. He'll circulate the stuff."

"Well, couldn't he rape another hospital and give us their supply?"

"Sarah, this is the only gig he's got."

"Then I'll put out for the son of a bitch."

She expected Teacher to argue her down, but he shrugged one shoulder. "Go ahead. Uncle won't do penicillin for tail."

"That's final. I'll go to the little uncle and woo him with some of your Henry James."

"You'll never find the PX. He moves it from ville to ville."

Teacher went into the bush without saying good-bye and re-

27

turned with two farmers in black pajamas who carried a month of fruit cocktail on their coolie poles. The blood and penicillin arrived in Uncle Luc's own jeep.

Sarah was content with her ward of VCs. No one starved. She fed her patients fruit cocktail and whatever vegetables she could scare up. But the hospital had other trouble. It couldn't hold on to its chaplains. The last two padres developed nervous symptoms in the bush and they couldn't administer to a handful of wounded soldiers. A new padre came on the ward. He carried a .45 and didn't twitch like the previous chaplains. She couldn't make out his denomination, because he wouldn't carry a chaplain's bag. The interrogators joked about the padre and called him Rabbi Collinswood. He wasn't mean or anything. He secured chocolate for Sarah and distributed it to soldiers, civilians, and VC, but he stood around and smoked with the interrogation teams a lot and he didn't have the slightest sign of tobacco on his tongue. He was a rabbi with white teeth who kept himself at a forty-degree angle to Sarah. He'd become a silky son of a bitch whenever she tried to pull him into a conversation.

"Padre, how many churches have you had in the Nam?"

He sniffed at her with one nostril. "Churches?"

"You know. Hospital gigs."

"I have my orders, lieutenant, same as you. I go where my colonel sends me."

"But you don't smell like a chaplain . . . I mean, you're not sanctimonious at all. And you don't bless everybody, like a damn fool."

The padre smiled with his perfect teeth. "Perhaps I ought to bless you then, Sister Sarah."

Sarah was a compromising sort and she'd have learned to live with Rabbi Collinswood, but he disappeared from the ward one day. It wouldn't have bothered her if Teach hadn't disappeared with that silky son of a bitch. She wasn't born in a tree. That was the first rabbi who'd graduated from intelligence school.

She heard a week later that Uncle Luc had been killed. VC

execution squad, the surgeons told her, but Sarah could smell the Blue Berets. Her man had been out on a zombie mission with Rabbi Collinswood. Rabbi returned to the hospital without the Teacher. And this time she didn't suck oranges at forty degrees with the son of a bitch.

"Where's my man?"

"Lower your voice," the rabbi said.

"Padre, we're both equipped with .45s. What would you say to a shoot-out on the lawn?"

"I'd say fine, but my colonel might not like the idea of Sarah Fish in a body bag."

"That's mostly birdshit. You're a Blue Beret and you don't depend on outside colonels."

Her tour was extended another nine months. It had nothing to do with being a nurse. She was cut off from the ordinary twists of command. Someone had requested she remain on the ward, and that someone was Captain Jonah.

She didn't care what kind of creature she'd become. She'd drink surgeon's blood to stay in the Nam. Where else did she have to go? She waited like a dumb bride for the Teacher to come back. She consumed candy and croissants and was celibate more than a year.

A few surgeons had fled the hospital and relocated in Saigon. People were telling her that Danang was about to fall, but she didn't consider Danang a part of her country. It was like saying that New Zealand had a hemorrhage, or Colorado was eaten by alligators.

Jonah arrived on the compound.

"Tell me, captain, will my man ever get to kill another province chief around here? I'd sure like to see him."

"He's given up plastique," the captain said. "Teacher's back in Long Binh jail."

"You're a genius," she said. "Couldn't you free your own commando?"

"And start a civil war?"

"It won't be the first time in Nam."

"You're right," he said. "But I can't hold up an entire brig."

"What about your Blue Berets?"

"The beanies have been dispersed. They're phantom fighters. They don't exist."

"And you?"

"I'm a captain at the end of his tour," he told her and ferried out of Cayenne.

No one dropped ice cream on the old fort. It ran out of toilet paper in a week. The supply sergeant disappeared in a jeep with cans of fruit cocktail. Sarah heard the sound of his engine. She shot at the mother and missed. He was a bandit and deserved to die.

She had much more freedom on the ward. The interrogation thugs were recalled to Saigon. Sarah prayed that her doctors wouldn't get pulled, but every surgeon she had was choppered to a medical base on the South China Sea. She was left with her corpsmen and one Marine. That Marine was her sheriff and her jailer. She was beginning to understand the logistics of her French hospital. It was some kind of secret op, a chicken coop for captured VC. And that's why she hadn't received orders once she'd arrived. She was on zombie patrol in the bush.

She baked croissants that broke in her hand. But she could still bribe the Marine. She performed a little striptease and fed him bits of her opium ball and he allowed her into the radio hut. They worked for half an hour and couldn't discover the frequency to Long Binh jail.

"Judy to LBJ, Judy to LBJ, do you read me, man?"

All they could get in that dumb shack was Radio North Vietnam. Hanoi Hannah was cooing at helicopter pilots.

Hello, you ferrymen from 33rd Supply. Are you missing a door gunner tonight? Charlie's learned how to do you. He's swatting your ass out of the sky. Ask the boys on Hill 662

what happened to the ice-cream run. Charlie loves vanilla.
He's going ape on your ice cream.

Sarah was delirious. That bitch could have gone to Bengal
High. It sucked on her spirit hearing Hannah coo like that. It
was as if the enemy were in your underpants, and Sarah had
to reply. She hollered into the call phone.

"This is Saigon Sarah in the old French hospital ville. I'm
talking to you Charlies in the bush. There's trouble in your
vanilla beans, Charles. The ice cream you've been biting on is
laced with buffalo shit. It was the very last op of the Blue Berets,
lending Charlie bitter ice cream."

"That was a beauty, sis," the Marine said. "You've stuck it
to Charles, but he'll never hear you. The station's dead."

The corpsmen entered the shack and discovered Sarah in her
panties and an open blouse. They didn't moo at that lone Marine.
They eyed Sarah's cleft and climbed on the radio. They weren't
troubled about frequencies and signs in a code book. They caressed the radio and tried to signal the White House.

"I don't want Henry Kissinger," Sarah had to shout. "I want
the Long Binh jail. Teacher's in that goddamn brig."

The corpsmen got Long Binh and raised the commandant out
of bed. They were worthless in a hospital situation, but they
knew how to sing orders on the radio. The commandant con-
fessed that no one named Teacher was in his brig.

"Damn," Sarah said. "He's probably at Long Binh under his
old name, Howie Biedersbill."

The corpsmen listened to the commandant on the subject of
Howie Biedersbill and then signed off. LBJ did have a Biedersbill
once, but that Biedersbill was registered with Graves. "A permanent registration," the commandant had told the corpsmen.

"It's a cover-up," Sarah muttered. "Making believe that my
Howie is dead."

The Marine tried to caress her in front of the corpsmen, but

31

Sarah got into her clothes. He wouldn't stop pawing her, and she had to pull on her .45s. "Hey, I'm not your personal cow."

"We have a bargain," the Marine said. "I got you on the radio, bitch."

The corpsmen rocked on bare feet. "Who's he calling a bitch?"

They threw the Marine down and tore at him until Sarah broke them apart. She unbuttoned her blouse and let each corpsman and the Marine feel one of her titties. That's how she kept the peace.

The Marine caught jungle fever and wouldn't take to bed. "Think I want to be nursed by a pack of junkies and a Jersey whore?"

Sarah and the corpsmen couldn't wrestle him into the ground. He'd acquired a lunatic strength. He wouldn't lay on a ward with captured VC.

"We'll defend you, Abraham," the corpsmen promised. But the Marine couldn't be soothed. He walked the compound in a ferocious sweat and died on his feet.

They didn't have a body bag for him and they couldn't get a chopper to cart him to Graves. No ferryman would come for the dead at Sarah's fort. They had to stick Abraham in the refrigerator.

The beanies must have sentenced the hospital to commando oblivion. There was no more fruit cocktail in the bin. Sarah had to send the corpsmen out foraging for food. She shouldn't have slighted those boys. They intercepted a Viet Cong patrol and returned with a mess of C-rations. No wonder the Charlies were terrific jungle fighters. Charlie had American food. It set Sarah to thinking about Nam. Charlie Cong had more access to fruit cocktail than her soldiers did.

She fed her VC before she'd open a can of cocktail for herself. They lived without medicine or proper drinking water. She remembered the ice-cream run as an event out of another war. She was Sarah Fish, the maid of an old French hospital in Vietnam.

She couldn't figure why her hospital had all the luck. Charles should have overrun the fort by now. She had junkie corpsmen to defend her, and she had her own .45s. The junkies foraged and she fed the VC. She asked God to protect each fruit-cocktail hour. She was turning religious in the bush. She wasn't sure if it was Jehovah she prayed to, or Howie's Jesus.

Just as she was trying to resolve the problem, she heard rotors whirling in the sky and that old padre stepped into her yard. She offered him a can of fruit cocktail. He sat with her, drinking yellow juice. He tasted her opium ball.

"The jarheads are coming. As of today this hospital is closed."

"Closed, Rabbi Collinswood? Since when do rabbis close a hospital?"

"I'm not Rabbi Collinswood. My name is Albert Peck."

"Are you the commander of the beanies?"

"I'm a civilian," he said.

And Sarah laughed. "Then I outrank you. You're under my orders, Civilian Peck."

He punched her in the face. She fell off her stool, and the junkies ran over with scalpels and grenades. "Are you hurt, little mother?"

"Not at all," she said. "I'm having a friendly argument with the rabbi here . . . go on out, children, and play."

She scratched a bit of tar from her opium ball and this crooked rabbi never even thanked her for saving his life.

"You'll be burnt out by tomorrow," he said. "The jarheads don't appreciate mama-sans with .45s. They're frightened to death of lady warriors. You could disrupt their climb to heaven. They'll confer with their ancestors and agree that the best way of zapping a white mama is shoving candles in her eye until all the juice is sucked from her head."

"Who told you so much about Charles' philosophy?"

"It's my business to interpret Buddha heaven . . . now will you saddle up, Sister Sarah?"

"Rabbi, I'm not leaving without my corpsmen."

"I know that. We'll get them on the second run."

"No. We leave together or we don't leave at all."

"It's not the Staten Island Ferry. I can't lug corpsmen everywhere."

"Then tootle on back to your boat. Because I'm staying here."

"Damn you, I'll take the junkies. Do you have any mascots you'd like to bring along?"

"Just my patients on the ward."

"I can't stuff the ship with VC. We'll never get off the ground."

"And I can't abandon my patients. It's not ethical, rabbi."

Albert's head began to rattle. "Anything else?"

"Well, there's a dead man in the fridge."

"Jesus Christ. I'm not trucking a corpse."

"Then I'll sit with him until Charlie comes. He's a Marine. I'm not letting him lie in the jungle with no Americans around."

"Should have waxed you a year ago. You're a mental case."

But he didn't stop the junkies from taking Abraham out of the refrigerator and wrapping him in a blanket while Sarah dressed the five VC on her ward and marched them to the ferry. The ferryman screamed.

"You promised me one referral, Al. A round-eyed bitch with pockmarks. And you give me a basketball team . . . with gooks in the backcourt and a dead man on the bench. I'm not moving without my fee."

"Damn you, Fred. I left my bankbook in Saigon."

"Then the mothers will have to wait here for your autograph, because it's cash-and-carry on my ship."

"That won't look good in your file, Fred. The Air Cav behaving like goddamn mercenaries."

"Tickle yourself," the ferryman said. "I'm sick of toting your garbage around."

Albert battled with the ferryman on the helicopter's lip. He might have won, but the crew chief dragged him through the door and he was swallowed up into the ferry.

Sarah cursed until Fred appeared. She tossed him all the money Teacher had made selling bits of the opium ball. The ferryman grinned and allowed Sarah's people on board. But he had trouble getting started. He'd rise off the ground and then the helicopter would fall. He tore the seats out of the cabin and hurled them through the belly hole. But the helicopter didn't rise more than another foot.

"It's that dead Marine," Albert rasped. "Get rid of him."

"No," the ferryman said. "That boy stays. He's a cash customer, dead or alive. The nurse paid for him."

The crew dumped boxes of ammunition until the helicopter held in the air. It rose up over the hospital like some womb bird and Sarah felt a sudden fondness for this Fred. She kissed him while the chopper loitered in a cloud.

"Hey," the ferryman said. "Is that a proposal?"

And he wouldn't let Albert or his own men say a bad word about Sarah. He was her protector now. He drove into strange air pockets and wobbled down low, trying to draw enemy fire, so he could do some dumb ballet between tracer bullets. But no one fired at him from the ground.

He brought the helicopter down on the roof of a hospital tub in the South China Sea and Sarah let him feel under her blouse. It was the one good-bye she could offer.

"Sorry I can't be kinder to you, Fred."

And he rode up into the sky with his men. Sarah searched for Albert until she realized the son of a bitch had gone off with Fred.

She slept in a room of nurses and couldn't find the corpsmen when she woke. She'd been tricked. The padre had landed her and then removed all traces of her hospital and himself. The corpsmen had to be on another tub. She'd been so busy with Fred, she'd forgotten to kiss the junkies who'd kept her alive.

She had a week in Okinawa where she was held in a kind of genteel quarantine. The army fed her steak and wouldn't allow her to visit with other nurses. She arrived in San Francisco with her combat pay and was flown to New Jersey. She could have been the lieutenant of Siberia or captain of the Saigon Zoo, because no one bothered to process her. She took off her uniform at the airport and went to her father's house. Her mom and dad didn't cry so much now that she was in civilian clothes.

She lounged in bed and ate bits of opium on the sly and her discharge arrived in the mail. She wasn't expecting a thank-you note from Henry Kissinger, but she thought the army could have said a few words about her days and nights in the Nam. It was nothing but a card with computer holes.

She wouldn't become a civilian nurse. She'd have thought of her own lost medics and begun to cry. Sarah stayed in bed. Her father didn't bitch at her. He brought her dinner up in a tray. While she swallowed asparagus, he offered her a job. She could help her daddy write greeting-card poems and she didn't have to get out of bed.

"But I'm rusty, dad. I can't turn a rhyme. I don't have the technique."

"Nonsense," he said. "You have my gifts and more."

And so she scribbled greeting-card verses from her bed and signed them Sarah Fish. Her verses had a morbid touch, but daddy didn't mind.

> *Dearest, I'll love you in Colorado,*
> *I'll love you in Danang.*
> *I'll love you when the leaves turn blue*
> *And the elephant grass begins to die.*
> *Wherever you are, my darling,*
> *I'll pay the ferryman and climb aboard.*

She was writing love songs to Howie Biedersbill, but daddy didn't have to know. He marketed all her poems. Sarah was satisfied. She had her opium ball and a career in bed. She'd have gone on like that, buried herself in Bayonne, lived and died, if her daddy hadn't interfered. He brought home a suitor for Sarah from his synagogue. There was nothing wrong with the suitor. He had all his hair. He sold greeting cards like her dad. It didn't bother her that he was twice her age and that his underwear stuck out of his pants. Sarah could overlook such details. She had a warm heart. But she couldn't pretend this dude was Howie Biedersbill.

She wouldn't go to the movies with him, and daddy wanted to know why.

"I'm engaged," she said.

"Engaged? I haven't seen you once with a man. Where did you meet him? In Vietnam? Is he a killer by any chance?" Daddy grabbed her shoulders. "What's his name?"

"The Teacher," she said.

"That's not a name. Tell me. I'm your father. Who's your fiancé?"

"Howie Biedersbill."

Daddy coughed and banged his fists until the blood went out of his knuckles. "The Biedersbill boy, the Biedersbill boy. That's how come you volunteered to be an army nurse. So you could continue your romance with Howie Biedersbill."

She couldn't decide whether to squeeze her own nipples or strangle her dad. "I didn't follow Howie to Vietnam. He just happened to be there."

"That's some coincidence, my darling daughter." He pulled harder and harder on her shoulders until Sarah's mom arrived.

"Herman, you'll do damage to yourself," she said while Sarah was in her father's grip.

"Daughter, promise me you'll end your engagement."

She was twenty-five and she'd been through the Nam and she still needed daddy to approve her fiancés. Herman Fish, the greeting-card man, was shaking her into the floor.

"I promise," she muttered. "I'll break it off."

"Good," her father said and released his daughter the poet. "Then you can start seeing Tucker Weiss." Weiss was the suitor her daddy had found. She laughed and cried, thinking of Tucker Weiss with underwear sailing out of his pants, and she hurled cups and saucers at her mom and dad. Hilma Fishman retreated to the downstairs toilet, but her daddy stood his ground. He was courageous in his madness over Sarah's men. A saucer broke against his hand.

"You're right to wound me," her daddy said. "I shouldn't bring husbands into the house. I'm a meddler. We'll forget Tucker Weiss."

She ran upstairs to her writing board and scribbled a poem to Howie.

> *Love is a cradle,*
> *Love is a dark brown ball.*
> *The world could blow a storm around you*
> *And I'd wrestle that storm.*
> *I'm stronger than the Navy,*
> *Stronger than the Marines.*
> *I'll bring you out of whatever storm you're in.*

Her daddy wasn't blind. Biedersbill was the source of everything she wrote. He still paid her three dollars a line. She was Sarah Fish, and she'd sentenced herself to bed, waiting for Howie Biedersbill.

Howie didn't come. She had this ache in her body that bespoke the absence of a man. She dreamt of Howie Biedersbill doing criminal things to her. Tucker Weiss would appear at the end of the dream in Howie's place and she'd get up in the middle of the night with a sob that nearly broke her collarbone and her daddy would be there in his pajamas. He'd take her in his arms without a word and sing her back to sleep, that man who sat downstairs in the synagogue, Herman Fish. Sarah could never sit with her dad. She remembered going up to the balcony with

38

with her mom, like some stepchild who wasn't good enough
to live near the scrolls. That was Sarah's synagogue.

Sarah put away her scribble board. Herman didn't badger her
for poems. He wasn't trying to live off his daughter's sweat.
He'd hoped that the verses would be a vacation from Vietnam.
He took his daughter to the movies. He fed her chocolate cones
and prayed she'd discover a life without the Biedersbill boy,
who was born bad and had been thrown out of New Jersey.

Sarah had her opium ball and she survived, waiting for the
monsoons on her bed. The first snow of winter had started her
crying. She wanted helicopters in wet air, and all she got was
the Bayonne Bridge.

Months went by. She endured three winters in bed. Sarah
was becoming an invalid in her own little ward. But something
shook her out of that sleep. Gooney birds were pecking at her
windowsill, or she was hearing glass rip in her head. That's what
happens when you've eaten up your tar ball. Sarah went to the
window. She couldn't find a bird. Someone was standing in the
yard and tossing pieces of snow at the window. He had a ring
of fur around his neck.

Sarah shivered once and went down to meet him. Jonah stood
in the yard with a moustache and a curl behind his ears. He
looked funny without his captain's suit. Some folks just weren't
meant to be civilians.

"Aren't you going to hug me, sis?"

"Where's my man? Tell me and I'll hug you."

"He's in the psycho ward at Dix."

It didn't surprise her. She hugged the captain with one arm,
but he wouldn't let Sarah have her distance. He grabbed her
around and raised her off the snow.

"You're going to walk your man right out of Dix."

"With my .45s?" she asked.

"Don't be dumb. You'll put on your uniform, visit a while,
and lead him out the door."

He handed her a tag that said PSYCH STATION I and a card

that identified her as the army's own little psychiatric nurse. Sarah didn't need a fiancé. She was the last bride of the blue beanies, going out on a commando op against the United States.

"Don't come home with the Teach. They'll be looking for you and him. Your father will have a fit."

He knew more about her dad than Sarah did. He scribbled out an address in New York. Then he kissed her hand like a cavalier and gave Sarah a fresh tar ball, wrapped in silver foil. "That's a present from King George."

"Who the hell is George and how did he get so familiar?"

"Ah," the captain said. "George is just another beanie."

He stepped out into the snow and she realized he didn't have galoshes. He'd come to her in dress shoes. He stopped near her daddy's gate. "Don't forget to bring some clothes for Biedersbill."

Jonah's scheme troubled her during the night. It wasn't a simple operation sandwiched between endless times in bed. She'd have to saddle up for good. Suddenly she missed her father. You couldn't buy another daddy in the street.

Sarah raided her daddy's closet. She acquired shoes, hat, pants, shirt, and elephant-sized underwear for the Teach and stuffed them in a shopping bag. She didn't want to advertise to the army that she was stealing the Biedersbill boy. Then Sarah got down on her knees in the master bedroom where her mom and dad had slept for thirty years under an ancient blanket. They were both in winter pajamas, like sleeping seagulls with their tails wrapped in wool. She stooped and picked at her father's hair. A kiss might have woken him, and she'd have to explain why she'd gotten her uniform out of the camphor chest in the attic and put it on. Daddy would figure she was returning to the Nam.

She took the early bus to Trenton and Fort Dix with camphor in her pockets. It was a sorry string of visitors on board, undernourished girls going to their sweethearts in the army. Sarah wore her camphored cloak, but she wasn't that different from the girls. She had her own sweetheart to capture.

The girls stood in line at the gate and Sarah waltzed right in with a pair of .45s at the bottom of her shopping bag. A jeep chauffeured her to the psychiatric section. It didn't matter that no one recognized her face. Her uniform got her to the sergeant of the ward, a tough old bird who couldn't stop looking at her blouse.

"Biedersbill," she said.

"Ah, the man without a name. You have to shout, 'Teacher, Teacher,' and sock him in the ear, else he won't answer you."

She had to set this old bird straight. "He is the Teacher, son. He went clandestine over in the Nam, and Teacher was his code name. He had some of the hairiest ops of the war. Probably saved your life. The slopes would be in New Jersey without that magic man."

The old bird apologized and sent for the Teach. Sarah clutched the bits of camphor in her pockets to keep from crying, because this wasn't the Howie she'd gone to high school with. It wasn't even Howie's ghost. It was a rumpled, graying child in hospital fatigues, holding a metal box. He had runty eyes that couldn't search the ward and seek out Sarah. The Teach had stayed in Nam, and she had to deal with some carcass of his. But she concentrated hard and could hear a scream behind that wall of flesh. He was asking for Sarah, but he couldn't remember with his eyes.

Sarah took Teach by the hand, strolled with him down a corridor until she discovered a broom closet. She stepped into the closet with Teach, pulled off his clothes under a twenty-watt bulb, saw the welts and puckers of Vietnam, and got him into her daddy's things, which were elephantine on the Teach.

Corporals saluted Sarah and winked at her companion, who looked like someone's uncle lost in an army camp. She had no trouble at the gate. Jonah Slyke was a genius.

Teach never let go of his metal box. Wouldn't say a word on the bus. They stopped in New Brunswick and ate a whole banana pie. Sarah put the opium ball in his lap. He wasn't even curious about the silver wrapper. It lay there while he licked the pie off his fingers.

They got on the bus to New York. He looked out the window at the goddamn turnpike as if he were Aladdin stuck in a frame of glass. He could pull perfect geometry from a road sign. Teach had given his soul to highways and trees. Sarah didn't interrupt that Aladdin's look. She couldn't have trapped him into a conversation if she'd tried.

The terminal in Manhattan had so many hills, she thought she'd come to another Vietnam. It was the Teacher who led her down the stairs. Terrain like this could comfort him.

They hiked across town, men staring at a female officer and a guy swimming in his clothes. She found the captain's address. He'd sent her to a paddleball club.

Jonah came downstairs to greet them in a headband and little white sneakers. Teacher smiled at the captain and his eyes caught a pinch of fire. It bothered Sarah, because the zombie hadn't smiled at her once. Then she realized what Howie was smiling at. He'd remembered the captain's paddleball clothes from the Nam.

"How are you, Teach?" the captain asked.

"Diddley well."

Sarah poked that runt in her father's pants. "You were a wonderful conversationalist on the bus, Teach. You talk to the captain like you discovered him yesterday. Why can't you talk to me?"

But his eyes retreated to the back of his skull and he was Aladdin again, looking at walls and glass doors, and she decided not to provoke the Biedersbill boy.

Jonah handed her the key to a deserted Hebrew school at the end of the borough. "It's a rathole. But it's yours. No one will find you down there."

He stuffed an envelope in her pocket and called it honeymoon bread and he told Sarah not to pester him at the paddleball club. "When I need you, sis, I'll come to Indian country."

"And what if I should need you, captain?"

"You'll have to wait for my next visit."

So she walked Howie to Avenue C and they locked themselves inside the talmud torah. It was a rat's paradise and she had to announce her tenure to the rats. She ran after them with a broom, but they simply changed corners on her. And then the Teacher, who'd been standing like a catatonic in the talmud torah, lit the broom and set fire to the rats' tails.

Sarah didn't fall into a peaceful coma without the rats. She kicked dust out the windows and turned that old talmud torah into a giant ward. Teach sat in the middle of the ward with his metal box. He opened the box and started to bawl, took out a stethoscope, clapped it to his neck like a love charm, and the crying stopped. Sarah saw a baby fiddle in Teacher's box. It had one lousy string and a bow that was all bent. He hung the fiddle on his shoulder and scraped with the bow. It was the saddest music Sarah had ever heard. Like the squeal of a pig. But the scraping soothed her little man. He put gold plugs in his ear, painted his cheeks dark blue, and sucked on a black bottle until his eyes went green, but he wouldn't tell Sarah about that bottle.

She had to open his treasure box while he was asleep. Sarah drank from the bottle and gulped black salt. Her head rushed all over the place. Sarah swooned.

She woke with a rag on her face. Her teeth were chattering. The ground under her felt like New Jersey. She noticed Biedersbill and remembered where she was.

"What day is it?"

"Dunno," her little darling said.

"How long have I been dozing?"

He twitched and said a week.

"What's in your bottle?"

"Candy," he said and went to his fiddle.

She had to wait for the captain's first visit to find out who this Biedersbill was. Teach's bottle-sucking didn't bother Jonah.

"Hell, sis, all the montagnards chew a little poison. It's great for the blood."

"I took a lick and was out for a week."

"That's natural," he said. "It softens your memory if you drink too much."

Teach scraped on his fiddle and Jonah enjoyed that sound of a wounded pig. "It's nothing, sis. He's remembering George, the dumb montagnard who thought he was king. Teacher lived with him a while."

"Is that how he turned gray? Living with George?"

"It's the highlands, sis. Wet mountains aren't so hot for the skin."

"I'd say it's more than skin that's bugging Biedersbill."

Jonah smiled. "You're right. The little mother misses his wife."

The captain meant to dig at her heart, but Sarah wouldn't give him the satisfaction of seeing her cry. "Didn't know Teach got married in the Nam."

"Sure, sis. It was a mountain marriage. George was best man."

"Did the bride have a name?"

"Hélène. She had the sweetest little body and a hundred suitors until Biedersbill came around. Hélène has royal blood. She's the king's sister."

"That's quite a family," Sarah said. "What happened to her?"

"Hélène's in a relocation camp. George never learned how to negotiate with Hanoi."

"And Biedersbill mourns her by keeping away from me."

"It's nothing personal, sis. Teach is a magician. The king's tribe taught him their tricks. And magicians aren't high on romance. Hélène had to divorce the little mother. He was into poisoning people . . . with the candy in his supply box."

The captain swiped an apple from her larder and whistled his way out of the Hebrew school. And she wanted to scratch the Teacher's eyes and get him to swallow his fiddle, but she couldn't be violent with a ghost. He'd loved her at Cayenne

44

and had his wife in the hills. Sarah swore she wouldn't discuss Hélène. But her heart was all mottled from that little man.

Teacher put his fiddle back and twitched in the corner without his gold plugs and Sarah gathered a little gang around herself. That gang was a gift. Jonah presented her with a Russian named Vladimir who was built like a garbage truck, thick around the shoulders and chest. Vladimir was a runaway from Brighton Beach. He'd been the strongman to a family of Jewish bakers, but the bakers had turned on him for some imbecilic reason, and he was forced to hide in Alphabetville. Sarah welcomed that fact. The bakers were dumb to let go of Vladimir. He was the best enforcer an unmarried girl could have. Vladimir never spoke. He frightened you with the lines of his shoulders and chest.

Sarah started a pacification program around Vladi and that twitching Biedersbill. She hurled marauders out of Indian country, settled disputes between warring tribes, and made sure the dental mills didn't charge too much. Locals called her the Hebrew godmother and presented her with broiled chickens and pounds of dollar bills.

But she was a godmother on borrowed land. The Hebrew school didn't belong to her. She was only the captain's man. He'd arrive with chunks of tar to fatten her opium ball. Never kissed her or monkeyed with her blouse. He'd beg little favors off Saigon.

"Remember that old padre from Vietnam . . ."

"Albert Peck?"

"Well, Albert's niece is running wild. Little Lulu Peck. Banging everybody in sight at the sailors' mission, and she's just about seventeen. Could you hold her here . . . until she calms down?"

Lulu wasn't at any sailors' mission. Sarah found her next to the talmud torah, licking stones for nourishment, and carried her through the door. The girl was wearing enough paint to outfit a department store. She had blue stripes on her forehead, green lip gloss, brown mascara behind her ears. Saigon dug Lulu's face into the sink. The girl wiggled and screamed and slapped at the water, but she came up human. Lulu was a pretty thing without her war paint.

"What are you staring at, big tits? Are you sorry I'm not old and fat like you? I could lend you my brush. I'll patch up the holes in your face if you'll tell my dad to disappear from my life."

Sarah smiled. She was back in the country of dads and daughters. "I don't do business with your dad. I bank with Jonah Slyke."

"It's the same thing," Lulu said. "Jonah is dad's lawyer and he's my lawyer too."

It was a generation where children had lawyers. Sarah didn't belong. She was the girl who sat upstairs in the synagogue. And she'd never get downstairs to that place of business near the ark. She didn't even know the captain was a lawyer. She figured he went around the world playing paddleball.

But she tamed the little daughter, combed her hair, and invented paella in the Hebrew school stove. Sarah had to bake something, and she loved the idea of yellow rice. She carried a tube of saffron inside her blouse.

Her heart was still mottled from Biedersbill. She couldn't forgive that little man for marrying a montagnard. She'd unwrap the tar ball, nibble on a piece, and run to Biedersbill, promise to tear him open with her .45s.

"Howie, are you laughing at me behind your closet eyes?"

He began to mewl with a dry mouth and Sarah was ashamed, threatening a refugee from the maniac ward at Dix. She fell in love with Harrison Ford's blue eyes. He was in some dumb film called *Blade Runner*. Sarah saw that film every week at the St. Marks. She had to have someone to love. And why shouldn't it have been Harrison Ford? But in her dreams that Blade Runner clutched a metal box with a fiddle inside and a stethoscope.

She sat on her .45s until Jonah appeared.

"Captain, I think Biedersbill ought to find another Hebrew school for himself."

"Calm down," the captain said. "He can't go two steps without falling . . . I need a favor, sis. A man will stop at the talmud torah. He'll be looking for Lulu. I want you to hold him for a little while. He's my college roommate. Marvin de la Mare. The truth of it is I'm in love with his wife."

Well, she had to declare herself on the side of love. "Stuck on the wife, huh?"

"Don't think I could survive without her, sis."

"It's that bad?"

"Worse than you could imagine."

"And Marvin is in your way?"

"That's about it."

"What's her name?" Sarah asked, interested all of a sudden.

"Lliana."

"She blonde or a dark bitch like me?"

"Blonde."

"Aw," Sarah said. "I'll capture old Marve for you."

She'd heard that name before. Lulu had talked about Marvin de la Mare. Sounded like someone who belonged on a greeting card. She expected him to have pockmarks like herself, pockmarks and a big fat ass.

She cursed Jonah Slyke the minute she discovered this Marvin at her door. His ass was thin as a bullet. His face was smooth and dark. He was handsomer than Harrison Ford. He had brown eyes with amber darts in them and a perfect build. She had this idiotic impulse to see his naked shoulder.

She gave him some celery soda imported from Second Avenue. Her heart wasn't mottled any more. It pumped like an engine that could carry a talmud torah. He had a slow and gentle voice.

"Is Lulu around, Miss Saigon?"

"She's my houseguest, and you can call me Sarah."

She wished she could go on like that, talking nonsense with

47

Marvin de la Mare. Suppose he grew angry after she held him prisoner? The amber would go out of his eyes and his voice would get harsh and she'd have to fight to see his shoulder. But she'd made a bargain with Captain Jonah.

Vladimir came up behind Marvin while he was drinking celery soda and struck him once on the head with his open hand.

The celery soda spilled out of Marvin's fist. He didn't topple right away. A bubble of spit appeared along the side of his mouth. He started to say something and then he fell into Sarah's arms. It was the falling, gentle and sweet, that maddened her with desire. She would have bitten his face if Vladi hadn't been around. It was as if she had a burning in her bladder that wouldn't leave. Loving Marvin de la Mare was like having to sit on the sink and wait for a wicked pee.

Vladimir carried him into her room and left her alone with Marve. She was too excited to undress him, excited and scared. What if Vladi misjudged that blow on the head and she lost her Harrison Ford? She promised to sit upstairs in the synagogue for a month if Marvin woke up after tomorrow.

She didn't take off his clothes. She fed him soup with a pinch of poison she'd borrowed from Biedersbill. He was able to swallow in his sleep. He yawned once. She lay next to Marve like some virgin princess with pockmarks on her face. Marve was her prince, sentenced to sleep. She touched his mouth with a finger and the prince stirred, moaned in his gentle voice, and Saigon got her courage back. She kissed old Marvin and took off her clothes. She must have been stupid or something, because the prince's groin was waking up, and she didn't consider it illegal to shuck off his pants, long as he was aroused.

She had her honeymoon with the sleeping beauty, loved him into the mattress day and night. But Saigon began to doubt her own good luck. She wondered what montagnard candy and a knock on the head had to do with Marvin's appetite. His swelling wouldn't go down. She was the only aphrodisiac a prince could ever want.

He'd wake up for a moment, pull on his lip, and seemed lucid enough to Sarah. He wasn't her prisoner now. He was Harrison Ford of the dark eyes, who needed twenty-two hours of sleep to devote himself to Saigon Sarah.

She locked her door and neglected the talmud torah. She'd fight her wars the minute sleeping beauty got out of bed. But she was godmother to a whole district, and her obligations nagged at Sarah. So she left Marvin for an hour and strolled Avenue C with her .45s.

But Saigon soon regretted that stroll. She found the little daughter in bed with Marve on her return to the talmud torah. The bitch had no shame. Lulu took advantage of a sleeping beauty.

"Get out of my bed, baby-san."

"No."

"I could make you disappear for a long time. You'll wish you'd never left your father's crib. That's my man you're fooling with."

"Your man, big tits? You lassoed him like you lassoed me. We're getting married after he dumps his wife."

"And when did he propose?"

"He didn't have to. I proposed to him."

"Well, I don't give a damn about his wife. He's my husband now."

"That's some marriage when you have to knock a man out."

'It's not your business," Sarah said.

"Marve is my business. He's been my business twelve or thirteen years. He's the one who raised me."

"Then what are you doing in bed with your dad?"

"He's not my dad. We're lovers, and you can ask him."

"How can I ask him when his eyes are closed?"

"You have to tickle him in the right spot."

"Don't you talk indecent in front of my man."

"Then wake him, tits, and we'll find out if he's fonder of you or me. . . . I want my lawyer. You can't trap us in an old Hebrew school."

"It's your lawyer who put you here, baby-san."

And she wondered if Jonah had planned the little op on her bed, if she and Marve and Lulu girl were just another piece of the Nam, unconscious commandos on Jonah's ward. She couldn't step outside a commando operation.

"Share him," Lulu said.

"No."

"Share him with me. Big tits, I'm not giving him up."

She'd been outmaneuvered by a child. But she couldn't let go of Marve. It was hard to become a maiden again after she'd been with Harrison Ford.

She unbuttoned her blouse, thinking of Marvin's chest, that tree of hair above his groin, when she discovered a face in the door. The eyes had that look of pain she remembered from her ward, eyes that begged for morphine when she had no morphine to give . . . until Teacher arrived at Cayenne with his tar ball and she went up and down the ward spooning that dark tea into everybody's mouth.

But she had no tea for the man at the door. Teacher looked at Marve and her with his morphine eyes, and she knew she'd have to give up Harrison Ford.

ALPHABET-VILLE

2

SARAH saw.

Her mistress hadn't lost his rainbow. The colors moved on Marvin's chest. Teach had covered Marve with crayons and mud. He was always doing that and feeding him black candy until Marve stared at the wall with the dull fix of the dead. He was awful pretty, even with the paralysis Teach had laid on him. Marve could dance and that's it. He was Sarah's sleeping beauty.

Wasn't right to call him mistress. He'd been her concubine for a month. And she had to give him up or Teach would have withered into an absolute ghost. She'd been engaged to the Teacher sixteen years, the longest courtship in New Jersey. But she'd stopped being a Jersey girl. She was an outlaw in a Hebrew school, with two .45s near her tits.

The rainbow moved again. Teach must have crawled up to Marve last night and painted him fresh. It was the stupidest rainbow. Started at the side of Marvin's mouth and descended to his nipple. Teach had copied it from the montagnards. Her little man had once been a mountain fighter for the CIA. He'd come home from the Nam with a nervous twitch. Couldn't make love to Sarah but he knew how to paralyze and poison people.

The beauty moaned in his sleep. Must have been dreaming of the wife he left behind. Sarah had kidnapped him almost a year ago and she wasn't sorry. She'd have kidnapped him again. Even if she'd made a vow not to fondle Marve or lick the colors off his chest. Her own little man wouldn't give her the satisfaction of a squeeze or a kiss.

Sarah was close to temptation. God had fiddled with her face, lent her pockmarks, nasty little holes of desire. She wanted to straddle Marve in the middle of his dream. All she had to do was raise her skirt a bit, and pockmarks would have done the rest.

She hiked up her skirt and stood over Marve and then she discovered her face in Marvin's mirror. It wasn't Meryl Streep. It was Snow White's mother-in-law, the ugliest bitch in town.

Sarah let the skirt fall below her knees. She climbed onto the mattress and balanced herself with the .45s on her hips and Marve between her legs.

"Marvey . . . wake up."

But he was in a goddamn coma, a poisonous sleep, and she could feel that little man behind her, her fiancé, Howard Biedersbill, the Teach. He'd come upon you like a Vietnamese wind, with silent puffs of air. Sarah had served in the boonies. She knew all about particular winds, watching men rot without morphine, blood, or candy bars.

"Sarah," Teach said, "he won't wake up until you call him majesty."

"He's not my majesty, Teach. He's only Marve."

"He's K-k-k-king George."

She'd started him going, and now he'd stutter and twitch and pull shrapnel out of his hair. He was always pulling shrapnel. Teach was a human junkyard. He still wore his stethoscope from the Nam. He had to search behind every wall for some stinking bomb. He went nowhere without that pair of rubber tits.

"Marve," she said, like an incantation. But the beauty never blinked. And old Sarah was getting angry. "Will you get up, Mr. Marvin de la Mare?"

Teach twitched and grinned at her. "He won't move, Sarah. He's not programmed to stir to that name."

"Then how come he'll only answer to King George?" But she shouldn't have bothered asking. Teach had lived with a gang of magicians in the highlands. He'd run with a mountain king, and her little man had nothing better to do, so he made Marve over into that idiot, King George. It was pure spite. Teach only did it because Marve had been her mistress for a month.

"Damn you," she said, "and damn him . . . majesty, will you wake up?"

Marve lifted his head off the pillow at the first mention of majesty, and everybody knew he wasn't a king. He was only an exotic dancer labeled King George. It was Teach who taught him all those mountain tricks, trying to get him to behave like George. Why shouldn't she have capitalized on all that technique? She had to feed a talmud torah. Marve was her prisoner and didn't have to work at all. But it was nothing special to have one cabaret night a week. The best damn churches and synagogues had bingo games and bazaars. Sarah was entitled to her cabaret.

"Majesty," she said, bowing to Marve. "It's not healthy to sleep more than twenty hours in a row. It ruins your bodily functions. Did you forget? We're having our cabaret tonight."

"Didn't forget," he said, yawning at her, and the rainbow wiggled like some Technicolor sleeve. "Where's Lulu?"

And Sarah had to lie. "Baby-san is out shopping."

"Shopping, Sarah? For seven days?"

Damn if old Marve didn't wake up quick. "Well, she's a fastidious creature."

"So fastidious she forgot to come back?"

That little creature was hanging out at the sailors' mission on Avenue B. And Sarah hoped she'd never return. But Lulu was the reason Marve had come to Alphabetville. Lulu was almost his niece. And Marve had been commissioned by her dad to look for the little creature.

"Aw," Sarah said. "You know baby-san. She's voluptuous. She got sidetracked somewhere." *At the sailors' mission, your majesty.*

Marve got dressed. He put on an Afghan shirt and a canary-colored coat. It was the Teacher's doing. Teach loved to dress him like that crazy magician from the highlands, that deposed king who was rotting in a concentration camp. Marve had gold plugs in his ear and blue under his eye: the mark of a magician. He wore gypsy dancing shoes and tied a silk scarf over his brains. He was handsomer than history, a parrot-king decked in different colors. It tickled Sarah, because he always danced in the raw.

"Would his majesty like some Cheerios or bacon and eggs?"

"It's too late for breakfast," Marve said. "Have to find Lulu."

And he abandoned Sarah without a kiss or a welcoming sign.

Sarah cornered the Teach. "Marve's not the same."

"How's that? He's always looking for Lulu."

"He's different, I'm telling you. He goes from twenty hours of dreaming to jumping out of bed. You've taken him off his diet, Howard Beidersbill."

Teach fed him doses of poison. It made Marve docile and less interested in his wife. He'd once been an editor for Lulu's dad. Now he was a dancing fool.

"Follow him, for God's sake," Sarah said to the Teach. "He could fall down and forget he has a home with us. He has no I.D. The cops will drag him into some shelter."

"I have chores to do."

"The hell with your chores. Marvin comes first."

"F-f-f-first to you," Teach said. And she clasped his hand.

"He's like a child, Teacher. All doped up."

Teach wiggled his hand free. "I'll get you King George."

"He has to dance by midnight."

"He'll dance," Teach said, pulling shrapnel from his hair. And then he was gone.

That left Vladimir to fix up the cabaret. But she didn't have to hunt him down. Her Russian was looping the canopy together in Sarah's main hall. He stood on a chair and pulled a canvas sheet over the metal supports, and now the platform he'd built for Sarah had a legitimate roof. It was Sarah's design. She'd copied it from the wedding canopy at her father's synagogue. A bride always had to get married under a roof. That was Hebrew law. And Sarah had brought her own bride's roof into the talmud torah. Wasn't Marve something of a bride? He danced in honor of holy and unholy ghosts, Vietnamese, American, and montagnard. But she dreamt of another wedding under the canopy. Her own. Might as well marry a ghost. One without a twitch, if you please. But Sarah wasn't a lucky girl. Whatever ghost she picked would pull shrapnel and wear a stethoscope.

Vladi stretched the canvas over the last metal bar, and Sarah had her roof. The chair shivered under his bulk. She was frightened for him and the talmud torah. His bulk could break a floor. He wasn't an open-air prince like Marve, with beautiful calves and a long curving back. Vladimir was broad as a whale. He had to sidle through most doors. Sarah gave him asylum at the talmud torah. He was custodian of her cabaret. He was also her ablest soldier. Gypsies and confidence men ran from Vladimir. But he couldn't shake the Davidoffs of Brighton Beach.

The Davidoffs had once owned Vladimir. Now they hunted him. They patrolled Sarah's territories in a rotten truck. Who the hell were the Davidoffs? A family of two fat aunts, Zoya and Adelina, and their darling nephew, Samuil, a virtuoso on the violin. He'd become an armory expert in the United States. Rigged together a beebee gun with enough barrels to blind a moose. He was a menace to Alphabetville. Shot Sarah in the ass a week ago. And Sarah couldn't fight back. Vladimir was tied to those bakers.

It had something to do with the KGB. The Russians were getting even for the commando work she'd done in the Nam.

Vladi came down off his chair. He had such a Russian look around his eye—like some bordertown Raskolnikov—that Sarah didn't have the heart to ask him if Zoya and Adelina were humping for the KGB. Vladi wouldn't sing a word to her. He was the quietest man east of Avenue A. All the walking wounded arrived at Sarah's doorstep, all the refugees. Lulu, Vladimir, Marve, and old Biedersbill. She'd take them into the canopy, under God's little roof, and marry herself to man, woman, or child, and she didn't care if Zoya and the KGB showed up at the wedding. Sarah had her .45s.

The Teacher, alias Howard Biedersbill, didn't have to travel far to notice Marvin's schedule. Twenty minutes of clarity in the morning and then a fall into the gloom. Marve was stuck on Avenue C. Couldn't even tell what mission he was on. Might have stood there all day if the Teacher hadn't come along.

"Morning, majesty."

Marve looked at him with a certain scorn. "Can't fool me. We're into the afternoon."

Teach could have sauntered over to the sailors' mission and

rescued Lulu Peck, but he had other things on his mind. Like money. He had to collect from the cocaine supermarkets before sundown. And he couldn't leave Marve in the middle of the road. Some infant might steal his pants. But suppose the poison wasn't a hundred percent? Teach could have a prick of clarity now and then. He'd tattle to Sarah about the supermarkets. Teach couldn't take a chance. So he pressed his fingers over Marve's eyes until his majesty screamed. It was the montagnard way. All that pressure acted like a temporary stroke. Now Teach could bring him anywhere.

He went with Marve into a gutted building on Ninth, between C and D. He wouldn't go down into the cellar where all the coca was stored. He walked up to the executive suite, a room at the end of a broken staircase. Teach had to test for booby traps, because there was a war going on inside the Bolivian maf. Cousins were killing cousins. It was hard times in the coca trade. A new government had come to Boliv, and it was too early to tell if the younger generals, who helped distribute the coca leaves, were in or out. So there was all sorts of sabotage. Half of Boliv might sink into coca leaves. It was a country with a single crop. Cocaine.

Teach pulled on his stethoscope and put the silver disk against the wall. Nothing breathed. Nothing crawled. Two baby bandits nickered at him from the stairwell. They didn't have a hair on their chins. The Bolivs wouldn't hire bar-mitzvah boys. These two bandits were under twelve. Teach would have had to slap them down the stairs if a man hadn't come out of the executive suite with five pounds of money. The money was in a garbage sack.

"Hey, Teacher," the man said, "who's your friend?"

"King George."

The baby bandits nickered again. Even in the dark they could see the bald white of Marvin's eyes. The man had to quiet them. He was Capablanca, a cousin to the former chief of the Bolivian air force. He was rootless now. His cousins in La Paz wouldn't

bring him home. He wandered from building to building in Alphabetville, dismantling his supermarket every other week.
Teach guessed Capablanca would die within the year.

But Capa was good to him. Teach was the local voodoo man.
He could bring the federales down on your head.

Capablanca smiled. "The other king is in a concentration camp.
How come I never heard of this George?"

"That's because he keeps a low profile."

And Teach took off with the money. He let Marve carry the
garbage bag to the next drop, a roof on East Ninth. They waltzed
from drop to drop. Teach acquired two more bags. The man at
the fourth drop had no money for him. His name was Nibio,
and he had six generals in his family. Teach slapped him in
front of his bodyguards, sour men in T-shirts who looked the
other way. They didn't have enough enthusiasm to trouble the
Teach.

"On my mother's life, Teacher, they ripped us off this afternoon."

"Don't mention your mother," Teach said. "Who ripped you
off?"

"Capablanca's people."

"Impossible," Teach said. "I was with him half an hour
ago."

"That's how you got paid. He stole from us."

"You can't stay here. The rent is due."

"I'll double it next week," Nibio said. "I promise."

"The padre doesn't like promises."

"He knows we're good. We wouldn't mess with our uptown
Uncle."

Teach grabbed Nibio and tied his collars into a knot. "Should
I lend you to my man?"

"What man?" Nibio asked, looking at Marve.

"King George. His specialty is throwing Bolivians off the roof."

"Listen," Nibio said. "He's got crazy eyes."

"That's because I haven't lent him a Bolivian today."

Nibio started to cry. It disturbed the Teach to watch a grown man blubber like that. He untied Nibio's collars.

"Give me what you got."

Nibio had to borrow from his bodyguards. It came to a thousand. Teach tucked the money into Marve's shirt.

"That's some cash register you have," Nibio muttered under his teeth.

"George is no register. He's our king."

They returned to Capablanca's roost. Teach had Marve wait outside the building. "Majesty . . . don't move."

Marve stood with the money bags, sniffing east and west. There had to be a coffee plantation hidden somewhere in the ruins. Coffee and green peas. The green peas were from far away. He had a swirling in his head, a bundle of black holes. He couldn't have even pronounced his name. He liked the funny little man who took him on trips to the roof. The little man had a doctor's nipples around his neck.

While Marve contemplated, Teach crept upstairs. He found no pleasure in stalking little boys. But he had to disarm the baby bandits. He hunkered under the stairwell and grabbed their feet. Pistols flew out of their pants. Teach counted five or six. He rolled the infants into a bundle, manacled them with the sleeves of their own shirts, like a pair of murderous twins, and entered the executive suite. He wasn't carrying the boys' pistols, South American Colts that weren't so reliable in the dark. He couldn't have shot his way into Capablanca, who had Howitzers behind him, sleek cannons with gorgeous blue muzzles. Teach was only declaring his presence to Capablanca. He'd gotten beyond the baby bandits who'd been taught to kill. They were the best protection a supermarket could have, because twelve-year-olds were candidates for children's court. They could shoot your eyes out and sit in some infants' farm in the Bronx for the next seventeen years.

"Capa," Teacher said. "Should have told me you have money problems. You took from Nibio to give to me."

"It was a personal matter. Nothing to do with my debts."

"Agreed. But you gave me Nibio's share. Now I want yours."

The left side of Capablanca's mouth began to curl. His nostrils shivered like a wolf's. "Teacher, it wasn't Uncle who sent you back. He's not that greedy. Why'd you come?"

"Because I'm a collector," Teacher said. "And a collector collects."

Capablanca wasn't wrong. Albert Peck would have warned Teach away from a second visit. Uncle Albert would have organized a war party, borrowed a couple of federal agents and locked Capablanca out of Alphabetville. But Teach didn't want to disturb Uncle Al. Albert was his hero. Albert had taught him Henry James when Teach was a convict at Long Binh jail. He wouldn't have survived Vietnam without Uncle Al.

"Are you hurting, Capa?" Teach said without malice.

"Yes. I have cousin problems. And the gringos are making it worse. They're closing the trade routes and bribing whoever they can."

"That's Uncle Sam," Teach said.

"It's tight. Very tight."

"Then give me one small bundle and I'll tell Uncle Al what the situation is on your street. He understands the narcos have gone ape in Bolivia. Uncle Al can't control that."

Capablanca stuffed money into a garbage bag. He didn't bother to weigh it.

"Thanks," Teach said, and slid the bag under his shirt. He bowed to Capablanca, climbed over the baby bandits on the stairs, and went down to Marve, who hadn't even blinked.

"Old Reliable," Teacher said and accompanied Marve to an art gallery between A and B. The art gallery sat in the middle of a blitz. It was the storefront of a building that had no other occupants. There was rubble all around it and a sign that said, WELCOME TO SUNNYSIDE: ART OBJECTS, INC. It was Uncle Albert's personal post office. But the art objects did exist. Sunnyside's walls were cluttered with paintings of Alphabetville. Bricks and blades of grass. Faces with eyes in their mouths. School chimneys that belched angelic smoke. Customers came from as far as Queens to look at the art.

The gallery was run by a woman called Renata. Teach guessed she was a Russian agent, because of the pen she carried, a fat mother of a Mont Blanc, which the KGB sometimes used as a sword pen. But Renata's pen had ink. She wrote sales slips with her Mont Blanc. And she disliked the Teach. She had beautiful legs, but she wouldn't wash in her art gallery. Renata was always there. She accepted Teach's garbage bags, hid half of them behind her desk, and put the other half into a vinyl suitcase for Teach. Was Renata holding Moscow's share? It bothered the Teach. He didn't like being half a Russian agent. He knew Uncle Al had unconventional habits. Albert hunted scalps wherever he could. Henry Kissinger had hounded him from Vietnam. But Teach wished Uncle wouldn't go on hunting trips with Moscow men and women.

Renata never acknowledged Marve. She growled at the Teach. "You were supposed to come at six."

"I got held up," Teach said. "Had to hit the same supermarket twice."

"Six is your time slot. I'm not interested in the maneuvers you make."

"Ah, but I came to see your art."

"Shut your mouth," she said, and Teach wondered if her pen really did have a sword. She was Moscow's paymaster, no matter what her gallery was all about.

"Renata, I'd like to learn. I did a course in Henry James. I studied the master, but he wouldn't put eyes inside a mouth."

"Darling," she said with a dirty stinking smile. "Don't lecture me on graybeards. You haven't the least idea what New Wave is about."

There was plenty of New Wave in *The Princess Casamassima*.
"How much for the school chimneys?"

"Stick to coca dollars. Collecting art is outside your hemisphere."

"How much?"

He reached into Marve's shirt and pulled out Nibio's money.
Then he removed the painting from the wall. "Don't cry, Renata.
I'm keeping you in business."

Teach carried the painting under his arm and Renata summoned a cab for him. He knew it was no ordinary cab. It was
a KGB car that danced out of some garage according to Renata's
telephone signals. None of these Russkis had Russian accents.
Renata could have been an heiress out of Henry James if she'd
wash once in a while. And her taxi driver was much more fluent
than the Teacher or Marve, who clutched the vinyl suitcase
and looked out the window of the cab until they arrived at
Gramercy Park. Teach didn't have to tip the driver. He and
Marve were Russian freight.

He brought the painting and Marve into the Gramercy Park
Hotel and up to the padre, Uncle Al. Uncle lived in a dark
suite on the ninth floor. His rooms faced a brick wall. Darkness
was appropriate for a commando chief. But Teach couldn't talk
about the commandos any more. It wasn't Nam. It wasn't even
Nicaragua. It was Twenty-second Street. At the heel of Lexington
Avenue. Uncle hardly stepped outside. His command center was
a dusty living room. He rang down for sandwiches when he
had the urge to eat. He was in his sixties now. He looked like
a misfit who needed a shave.

"Padre," Teach said. "I'm an art collector now."

"Congratulations." But Albert didn't look at Renata's masterpiece. He was watching Marve.

"Ah," Teach said. "He can't recognize you. Marve's in a
coma."

"The coma might not last. You shouldn't have brought him,

Howard. He could recognize me somewhere in his rotting brain. I was his tutor at Dartmouth, or did you forget?"

How could Teach forget good old Dartmouth, where Marve had studied with Jonah Slyke? Jonah was Marve's lawyer, and he was living with Marve's wife. It was Captain Jonah who'd sentenced Marve to Alphabetville, so he could have that blonde cow to himself, Lliana de la Mare. It was Jonah who mingled with federal agents, Jonah who could call upon the FBIs. It seemed incredible to the Teach, because Uncle himself was such a pariah.

"Marve doesn't remember tutorials. He's King George."

"Howard, spare me the details of his identity crisis. He can be a montagnard all he wants, but the dancing has to stop. He's calling attention to us every time he wiggles his ass on Sarah's hard floor."

"Uncle, his dancing brings us bucks. I didn't ask for Marve. It was Jonah's idea. He dropped Marve on us. And I'm going to return the gift.

"It's too late," the padre said. "Lliana's divorcing Marve. She intends to marry Jonah."

"Ah, how could she resist a rainbow man? Look at him. He's beautiful."

Uncle smiled. "Jonah wouldn't stand for it. He'll send the army after you . . . take Marve to Sarah. And shut the cabaret. Howard, is that clear?"

"Clear as a C-c-c-cambodian bell . . . majesty, give Uncle his suitcase."

Marve handed the suitcase to Uncle Al, but Albert didn't count the money.

"We're short," Teach said. "Capablanca's a highwayman. He's diddling the other supermarkets."

"That's dangerous. We could have civil war."

"It's Bolivia's fault. Nobody can say what general's going to get goosed next. Can't have stability without the generals."

65

"Why not? Five Hueys, Howard, and we could annex Boliv to New Jersey."

That's what Teacher liked. A goddamn military op. But he felt sad. Because it wouldn't have been much of an op without King George and his magicians. And George was in a concentration camp. The magicians couldn't get along with Hanoi.

"Uncle, what should I do about Capablanca?"

"Jonah will quiet him."

"Ah, I thought he was getting married to Marve's wife."

Albert scraped his teeth. "Only with my blessing," he said. "Lliana listens to me." Albert could have been a janitor who'd entered some hard times. He wasn't like his older brother, Carlo Peck, who wore linen suits at seventy-five. Carlo had been Marvey's boss until Marve fell away from publishing and landed in Alphabetville. Teach had to nudge Marve. "Tell the padre good-bye."

Uncle Albert had posed as a chaplain in Vietnam. He'd deliver sermons on Henry James and wear a .45 under his chaplain's cloak. He'd captured the Teacher that way, brought him into his commando unit from the brig at Long Binh. He'd saved Teacher's life. Teach would have shriveled inside Long Binh jail without Henry James. Mother of God. He'd have to go along with Albert's Russian game. But Teach didn't like it. He wasn't a goddamn mercenary, even if he read *Soldier of Fortune* every month. He had to keep up with the latest revolution. How could he remember what the Russkis were doing in Afghanistan without *SOF?* The newspapers didn't tell you shit. He couldn't trust *The New York Times* to list all the ingredients in a Kabul cocktail. Teach had to depend on *SOF.*

He rode down to the lobby with Marve. He'd promised Sarah to return him in time for the cabaret. Teach had been a sorcerer in Vietnam. He knew how to change personalities, like a bionic engineer. He stood Marve at the corner and blew into his nose. He couldn't fathom all of montagnard science. An explosion of air in the nostrils served as an antidote to poison in the blood.

Teacher blew again. He rubbed Marvin's shoulders and wiped spittle under his neck. Marve moaned once and little points of green came into his eyes.

Teach worked on him for half an hour. And when he was satisfied, he pinched Marvin's cheek. "Who are you?"

"M-m-marve," Marvin said.

"And who am I?"

Marve scrutinized the Teach. "You're my little man with the stethoscope."

Ah, the dancer was still under his spell. Teach twisted Marve's shoulders, turned him uptown, and took off with the painting. He was guilty as hell. He hadn't grown up with the montagnards. He'd borrowed their trade, and he wasn't sure how long Marve's clarity would last . . . long enough to get him home to Lliana girl? Teach blamed Captain Jonah. Jonah shouldn't have interfered with a magician's fiancée. It didn't matter that Teach had lost his dinglebell. Swallowed too much poison to have a dick . . . ah, the Teach was jealous. Sarah preferred Marve and Harrison Ford. She liked long guys with green or blue blinkers. And he was only Howard Biedersbill, a stick of a man.

Lana Turner.

Lana, Lana, Lana Turner was clapped to Marvin's tongue. He was thirsty. His brains were baked. Couldn't remember leaving his office at Gallatin & Peck. Had he gone to Doris Quinn? Doris was his author. She lived near Beth Israel. Kept having love affairs with psychiatrists and milkmen. Marve had to nurse her books along. Doris would break down every six months. It was Marve who finished her entries in *Manhattan Spy* and brewed coffee for Doris most afternoons.

Yes, he'd gone to Doris. And Doris had bitched to him about

Lliana's name. Lliana couldn't help it if Mama York had named her after Lana Turner in *The Postman Always Rings Twice*. It meant trouble. A Park Avenue matron identifying with a vamp in white shorts. So Mama York added a curlicue to disguise her devotion to Lana Turner. That's how *Lliana* got born. But Doris laughed at Marve. Said Lliana wasn't worth Lana Turner's white shorts. Marve remembered now.

Lliana had rung him up. Wanted him to come home and make love in the middle of the afternoon. Marve said no. Lulu had run away again, disappeared into Alphabet City, and Marve was going down to look. Lliana started accusing him, said he'd been romancing Carlo's little girl, and Marve had to defend himself.

Lliana, she's practically my goddaughter.

Don't give me that Uncle Marvin junk. You've seen the inside of her underpants.

Thousands of times. I dressed her for kindergarten.

That's some kindergarten. The bitch is seventeen.

Kids grow up, Lliana. You can't expect her to stay five and a half.

Come home, she said. *It's your last chance. Lliana or Lulu.*

Baby, I can't . . . I promised the old man. He's been a zombie without his daughter.

Go on, Lancelot. Look for the bitch.

But Lancelot couldn't find his horse. Marve had stumbled toward Avenue B and stopped at Doris' place. That's when they'd talked about Lana Turner. And then he'd gone down to Alphabetville, thinking of Lana Turner's legs. But he couldn't have reached Avenue A or B. He was climbing Murray Hill to his wife. He'd met a stethoscope man in the street. The man had kissed him on the nose without a reason. Marve could have called a cop. Or visited his old professor, Albert Peck. Albert had introduced him to Carlo, gotten him his job at Gallatin & Peck. Marve didn't have any real credentials for a publishing house. His dad had been a green-pea farmer and died on him.

Marve was raised by an aunt in Coeur d'Alene. He'd gone from Idaho to Dartmouth on an orphan's scholarship. Carlo had given him his own suits to wear and took him out of the back closets at Gallatin & Peck, let him play with Lulu.

That kiss on the nose bothered Marve and he didn't visit his old prof. The view from Albert's windows depressed him. An endless ribbon of bricks. Albert had gone to Vietnam and become a military preacher, a preacher without a particular church. He didn't return to Dartmouth. He haunted his hotel and tutored Lliana in literature. Her current craze was Rimbaud. She studied Rimbaud with Albert two nights a week, while Marve played paddleball with his old roommate, Jonah Slyke. Jonah was the family lawyer. They'd all sat at Albert's feet. But Marve wouldn't go upstairs to Albert. He wasn't in the mood for Rimbaud and bricks.

The bricks clung to Marve. Bricks and Lana Turner's legs. His nose itched from the little stethoscope man. He arrived at Thirty-sixth and Park. Lived like an exalted guest in Lliana's apartment, a gift from Mama York, who had her own small bedroom at Lliana's until she died. The bedroom had been promised to Lliana and Marve's future child, but Lliana claimed it for her literary materials: the baby in the bedroom was Rimbaud.

Marve was no alien on Murray Hill. He recognized the markings on Fred the doorman's cap, that old familiar blue braid. He'd come from a farm where his mother and father never talked, dead or alive. He'd been just as silent to his younger brother, Niles, who'd never gotten out of Idaho. The kid was an itinerant farmer, without an address, condemned to the silences that had been visited upon him. But Marve could depend on the good graces of a doorman to pull him out of his own silence. Marve tipped Fred on Christmas for the quality of Fred's hellos.

"How are you, Fred?"

"Fine, sir."

"Did your girl get into medical school?"

The doorman's eyes burrowed out from under the cap. "Sissie didn't have the marks, sir. She picked marriage for her career. But thanks for asking."

How could his daughter have gotten married over the weekend? The doorman must have misunderstood. He was talking about another Sissie, some niece he'd forgotten to mention.

"That's a pity, Fred."

"How, sir? We're not all the elite. Marriage is as holy as medical school . . . should I ring the missus? She's bashful about surprises."

Marve could have carried Fred across the lobby and stripped him of his uniform on the back stairs, but he had an evil headache. He wanted his brother Niles. He'd give up editing, go back to Coeur d'Alene.

"Lliana," he said. Had to reassure himself on the elevator. I'm Marvin de la Mare and my shoes come from Rome. I visited Keats' house. I made love to my wife in a hotel near the Spanish Steps. I've been to Sartre's grave. I know the Prado by heart. I edit Doris Quinn.

The litany calmed him on his ride up. He searched for his housekey in the hall. Had to search again. His key ring was in the wrong pocket. Lliana hadn't collected the mail. It stood on the little English cabinet Mama York had donated to the hall. She'd had the porter hand-deliver Lliana's mail.

Marve let himself in. He put down the mail and called for his wife.

A door opened in the apartment's winding inner hall. Lliana jumped out at him. She hadn't bothered with her housecoat. She'd come to him raw from reading Rimbaud. He could sense a fury build in the wings of her back. Had he interrupted her? She's the one who'd called him home.

She started to slap. He wasn't alarmed. He figured the slaps were some exaggerated love play. He could hardly tell with Lliana, who'd once opened her skirts for him on the Spanish Steps, in front of pilgrims, tourists, monks. He'd had to tie her hands to the bedpost on that same trip, enter her like the roughest knave. So it took him a while to discover that her slaps held no anticipation for him. He didn't cover up or grab her hands. He noticed the beautiful line her hair made with the movement of her arm. Lliana had the faintest moustache. He'd first fallen in love with Lliana over the curl of her elbow. Her body was like a series of soft, resilient pipes. He'd met her at a party given by his other boss, the dead one, Robert Gallatin. She was a college chum to one of the Gallatin girls. Marve discovered her elbows and then her knees. He wanted to marry her the minute he looked into her eyes. She'd held off his embraces for a month, and Marve remembered the illness she provoked. He couldn't breathe. Desire was like a rag in his throat. So why should these slaps be any different from the other days of his devotion?

He worried when the slapping stopped. "Get out of here," she said.

He heard a noise in the deepest bend of the hall. A man trundled out of Rimbaud's room in Marve's silk robe. It was Jonah Slyke. Marve didn't feel angry at Jonah in the silk. It was as if the silences of his childhood had tumbled down on him. And then his attack of muteness was over.

"Lliana, did you have to give him my robe?"

Neither of them bothered to explain. They looked as surly as Fred downstairs.

"Marve," Jonah said. "You're not supposed to come here . . . we have a restraining order."

"You're fucking my wife and you tell me about restraining orders? Lliana, how long has this been going on?"

"Marve . . ."

"Stay out of this," Marve said to his lawyer. "I'm talking to my wife."

"What's the use?" Lliana asked, getting dressed in the hall. "I want him out of here."

71

It was like a striptease in reverse, with Lliana abandoning herself to a body stocking. Marve was fascinated by the pull of material over Lliana's legs. She wore a shirt without a bra and daubed her cheekbones, oblivious to Marvin de la Mare.

"Are you listening, Jonah? I don't have time for his shit."

If only he could unravel the secret of that stethoscope man. Then things might have fallen into place. He'd have ravished Lliana on the floor, and Jonah would be at his gym with a sleek silver paddle.

"Baby, can't we try again?"

Lliana grabbed him by the hair and shoved his head into her mother's hall mirror. Marve screamed. He had a crescent of blue paint under his eye and bars of color at the side of his mouth. Pieces of gold in his ear, a canary-colored jacket. He sucked at his image in the glass. His heels were higher than a flamenco dancer. A scarf sat on his head like a highwayman's hat.

"Lliana, I'll be all right. Just let me change."

He tried to touch his wife.

"Keep that degenerate away from me. Jonah, you're responsible for him."

She searched for the right button on the intercom. "Fred, will you come up for this bastard? . . . and bring Benito."

Jonah put his arm around Marve. "You'd better get your ass out the door. Those monkeys mean business."

They arrived, the doorman and the porter Benito. They wouldn't suffer any protests from Marve. Fred had a sniper's glance at Lliana in her shirt and Marve knocked the doorman's cap over Benito's ears. Jonah had been some sort of commando in Vietnam. Marve elbowed the commando halfway down the hall. It was like a lacrosse match in a narrow space. He'd have won if Lliana hadn't fallen upon him too. He wasn't ruthless enough to punch his wife.

Jonah recovered himself, and the four of them landed on Marve. They spirited him out the rear door and into the service car, got him down to the basement, trucked him past the laundry room, Lliana delivering evil blows to his chest. Marve desired her more now than he ever did. He lost a heel and had to hobble on his flamenco shoes. They shoved him into the alley at the side of the house and up the tradesmen's entrance. Benito unlocked the gate, and the four of them pitched Marve into the street. Fred threw the missing heel into Marvin's shoulder. Benito shut the gate. Marve watched his wife disappear through the wires. He slumped onto a garbage can in his canary-colored coat, still dreaming of Lana Turner's legs.

3

TEACH returned home to Sarah with a painting squirreled
under his arm. A portrait of Alphabetville, he said. Sarah
saw chimneys with tongues on fire, in back of Teach's elbow.
She wouldn't tolerate such stupid shit at the talmud torah. She
wanted to know where Marvin was.

"Lost him in the street," her little man said. Biedersbill, who
was the deerslayer of Avenue C.

"So you picked up a painting on your search for Marve."

"Yeah," Teach said. "It's New Wave."

All Sarah could see were those ratty tongues of fire. "You're
not hanging that in my house."

"I have a room," Teach said. "I have rights."

"Not where that painting is concerned."

She sounded like the judge advocate who'd sent him to Long Binh jail. He'd wear the painting under his arm.

"M-m-marve will be back," he said, and it wasn't an absolute lie. Even if the blonde cow loved Marve's rainbow, the poison could still draw him to the talmud torah.

Teach carried the painting into a corner and sat down with the current *Soldier of Fortune*. He hunted through the table of contents and turned to an article on the drug war in Bolivia. SOF DROPS IN ON THE BOLIVIAN LEOPARDS. The Leopards were a strike force that had been sent into Chaparé, where the coca leaves were. They'd been ordered to flush out the dealers and destroy the coca crops. Teach had seen Leopards like that. They wore the boonie hats and jungle fatigues of any strike force. The article didn't interest him much. Dialogues with some captain who didn't know beans about fighting in the bush. It was the photographs that appealed to Teach, shots of the Leopards and their American advisers. Teach recognized Lubbock and Kroll. They'd come out of the same jail with Teach. They'd been commandos with him. And they were supposed to guard Uncle's farm in New Jersey. What were they doing in Boliv, with boonie hats? Were they freelancers now? Lubbock and Kroll didn't have the brains. Or the ambition. They beat up old men at Uncle's farm. They couldn't have gone to Chaparé without Albert's blessing. And why would Uncle train Leopards to cut the heart out of the Bolivian maf, when he had an investment in coca dollars?

Teach brooded about the photographs. It couldn't have been a mistake. That was Lubbock under the boonie hat, and wherever Lubbock went was Kroll.

Teach chewed a bit of poison from his pocket. The walls began to swim. His insights were always better after a chew. That dance between Capa and Nibio bothered Teach. Nibio had all the powerful cousins. Not Capablanca. Nibio should have been the high-wayman.

Teach took the painting with him down to Nibio's territories near Avenue D. The supermarket was unattended. He couldn't find one of Nibio's soldiers on the way to the roof. Nothing stirred around the stairwells. Even the rats had fled. Teach discovered Nibio next to an abandoned pigeon coop. His neck wasn't broken. His face and hands were blue, poison blue. He'd drunk a lethal dose of black candy. But who had shoved the candy into Nibio's mouth? Teach was the only poisoner on the block.

He had to stop playing detective. If the wrong cousins found Nibio, there would be civil war. Worse. A war against the talmud torah. Because the cousins would assume that Nibio drank from Teacher's hand.

He left Nibio outside the coop and wandered over to Renata's art gallery. She sat with her dirty legs and smiled at the painting under Teach's arm. "So. You've come to return it. Didn't I tell you you're not the right man for New Wave?"

"Eat your heart out, dear. I'm devoted to your work. I need a transport job. Quick. A coca prince is lying on the roof. His sunburn is going fast."

Teach could have gone to Uncle himself, but Renata was his conduit in emergencies, and he didn't like to monkey with Albert's chain of command. Renata got on the line with Uncle's farm, the Chanticleer, which sat on a hill outside Passaic. She told the chief nurse that an ambulance was required. The farm had no ambulance. But it did have a bus.

The bus arrived with a couple of ambulance drivers. They weren't wearing boonie hats today. Lubbock and Kroll had come to Alphabetville in white coats. They'd scratched off Boliv. There wasn't a sign of the Chaparé on them. No dust. No combat boots. No mashed coca leaves. Could have been a pair of stupid angels.

Kroll chortled to the Teach. "How's Saigon Sarah? Does she still wear tampons around her neck?"

"Ah," Lubbock said. "She left the jungle years ago." Lubbock was the brighter one. He could piece a couple of sentences together without picking his nose.

Renata wouldn't let them spar with the Teach. She told them their business.

"Yes, ma'am," they said, frightened of a Moscow paymistress.

"Who's the deceased?"

"A coca prince called Nibio," Teach said.

"One of the Bogota bad boys?"

"He's Bolivian . . . you must have chased a few of his cousins out of Cochabamba."

Lubbock turned to the paymistress. "What's that little man talking about?"

"Did the Leopards feed you well?" Teach asked.

"Leopards? Leopards bore me, little man."

Teach got into the bus and drove to Nibio's former territories, wondering how many cousins Lubbock had tortured in the Leopards' behalf. Kroll carried blankets and a hospital stretcher up to the roof. Teach stood near the ledge and looked down upon the Alphabet Blocks. He couldn't see much devastation from the sky. A church, red bricks, gardens cut between the buildings, like a vicar's paradise. Only Teach wasn't sure who the vicar was.

Lubbock trussed up Nibio, and they carried him down like a papoose. No one questioned them on the street. Not even the dogs would bark. Nibio sat with Kroll in the rear of the bus. They'd bury him out at the farm. Albert was good at finding graveyards. Nibio wouldn't be the first corpse lying beneath the Chanticleer. Uncle housed all kinds of corpses. The live ones were upstairs. The Chanticleer had become a mansion for old men. Albert ran a kidnapping service. He stored other people's pests at the mansion, and Teach doped them up, fed them black candy in the right proportion, so the old men would have memory lapses and couldn't complain about their robbed evenings. Teach was a commando, and commandos had to exist at Uncle's edge.

77

That edge began to worry him, because Albert had dispatched his own spooks to Boliv and was becoming a goddamn leopard man. Teach had entered a fire zone and couldn't even tell who was wounded and who was whole. He loped back towards the talmud torah and ran into a brigade from Brighton Beach. The Davidoff people, dressed as if they'd come from Mars. Would normal humans wear leather in July? The Davidoffs had shot at him in the past and tried to run him down with their bakery truck, but Teach enjoyed their company. They never seemed serious about wasting him. They'd bump Teach at ten miles an hour or sting him with the family beebee gun, their own version of the Kalashnikov rifle. They looked sad, like strangers in a storm. The leather on their bodies was almost a scream. They reminded him of montagnard magicians, whose women had all the property rights and sometimes wore platform shoes in the jungle. The Davidoff women were short and fat, and they had painted mouths and the highest heels in Manhattan.

Vladimir, his own silent kin, had told Teach all about the Davidoffs. They collected around a redheaded boy, Samuil, their fiddler-king, who was the great white hope of the Soviet Union until he applied for a visa to Israel. Samuil was taken off the concert lists. The Russkis wouldn't even give Samuil a synagogue to play in. Called him a parasite and threw him out of Moscow with his uncle and his aunts, bakers in some old factory. The Davidoffs landed in Vienna and started to pillage a city that had so many wares. Weren't used to products in front of their eyes. The police had to hustle them back onto the plane to Tel Aviv. But the Davidoffs couldn't adjust to their adopted country. They'd been living four to a room so long, without closets, without a proper sink, they camped out like Bedouins in the rooms Tel Aviv had given them and didn't feel like baking chocolate and bread. They left for America after nine months. Settled in Brighton Beach, resumed their careers as bakers, and also turned to banditry. Hired a collection agent in their Little Odessa by the Sea.

That was Vladi himself, a refusenik out of Leningrad. He was ignorant of Hebrew, like the Davidoffs. He didn't prattle about synagogues. He broke people's heads. The Davidoffs adopted him instantly as Samuil's bodyguard, but the fiddler-king was safe around the boardwalk. Muscovites remembered his violin, a Stradivarius the color of cherrystones. Samuil was a saint with red hair. The worst goons wouldn't have harmed a violinist. So Vladi was more like a friend to the little pasha. The pasha's aunts, Zoya and Adelina, were interested in matrimony. They lusted after Vladimir in their leather suits, offered him a lifetime membership in the family club. He could become Samuil's "aunt" with Zoya or Adelina on his arm. But Vladimir wasn't into marriage. He wouldn't have Adelina. He wouldn't have Zoya. Is that when the aunts grew suspicious of him? Called him a Leningradnik and stopped drowning themselves in perfume. A normal man would have desired at least one of the Davidoff women.

Vladi had to take a fall. Zoya bribed some thug who'd been a guest at the Lubyanka. The thug swore that Vladimir had a Moscow manager and wasn't a refusenik at all. Had Vladi been Zoya's husband, it might not have mattered, because who the hell wasn't a spy in Brighton Beach? *Him*, someone might say about a thug eating salmon at the next table. *That's my KGB man.* But Vladimir was already compromised. The Davidoffs discovered that he did have a Moscow manager, and the manager was picking off émigrés who organized against the Soviet Union. That's when the Davidoffs abandoned some of their other business to catch this Moscow manager through Vladimir, but Vladi escaped into Alphabetville. And now the Davidoffs were here.

Samuil sat in the cab of the truck without his Kalashnikov. Teacher wouldn't have to suffer beebees along his spine.

"Where to buy the cocaine, please?" Samuil asked, like any tourist stuck in Alphabetville.

"Davidoff," Teach said. "I'll put in your bid."

And the little pasha laughed. He'd sensed the scarcity of Bolivian princes along C and D. "Is finished, your coca connection . . . how is KGBnik?"

That little mother meant Vladimir. "He's singing lullabies," Teach said, with a suck of his teeth.

"But lullabies is not so good. We have to talk with Volodnishka."

Ah, the Russkis had a million diminutives for every man. Like a candy jar of names. Vladi, Volodya, Volodnishka.

"Davidoff, he might not want to meet you. He's in retirement at the talmud torah."

"Is not happy away from his people. He loves the water."

Teach felt like a spy among the Davidoffs. Vladi's Moscow manager worked for Uncle Al. That was the way with Uncle's commandos. Mix and mingle. Mingle and mix. Leopards in Boliv and spy-handlers in Brighton Beach. He would have liked to turn all of Albert's Russian machinery over to the Davidoffs, but he couldn't.

Zoya and Adelina stared at him from the back of the truck. They were sizing him up as a husband. But he'd never pass the test. He twitched too much and he had no Russian blood. The pasha's aunts weren't unpretty in their fatness. But even if they'd wanted him, he was sworn to Sarah.

"Comrade Biedersbill, we are worried about King George. Is he uptown with the coca leaves?"

"He's not into coca," Teach said. "Majesty's visiting with his wife."

"Maybe he needs a nurse, yes? You, for example. You are a good nurse."

Observant little mothers, the Teacher thought. He was Marvin's nurse. It's a pity he couldn't give them their Moscow manager. He'd have hurt Vladimir. That Moscow man was really a pimp from Leningrad on loan to Uncle Al. A stinking double agent who was flipped around so many times, you couldn't tell if his hump was in Moscow, Hanoi, or Massachusetts. He had dealings all over the world. Bartered fountain pens in Ho Chi Minh City. Collected scarves in Kowloon. Ran agents in Brighton Beach until the Davidoffs unmasked his little enterprise. And now he was on the run. His residence in Manhattan was Uncle's rooms and Renata's art gallery. But he couldn't go near Renata any more. The Davidoffs had shot him in the face with the Kalashnikov, marred his fair complexion. He was blond, very blond. Called himself Kostya, or Konstantin. Teach knew him in the Nam. Even then that Moscow mother had soldiered for Uncle Al. He had more lives than a commissar's cat. His teeth were sharp for a fat man, but the fat man didn't bite. Konstantin favored blackmail. He was holding Vladimir's three sisters in Leningrad.

"Comrade," Samuil said. "Is maybe George a Moscow courier?"

"Do couriers dance without their clothes?"

"Then why so far uptown?"

"Told you," Teach said. "He's getting familiar with his wife."

"And is wife a musician for KGB?"

"She's a blonde cow. Lliana de la Mare."

"Sometimes Moscow have cows on the payroll."

"Then I'm a cow," Teach said, and he walked away from the pasha's truck with Marve on his mind. That old majesty would have to make it home to Alphabetville without a nurse.

Marve hobbled down off Murray Hill on his one high heel. He'd become a drifter, like his brother Niles. He visited the men's room at the Gramercy Park Hotel, tore open his shirt to follow the path of colors on him. Mother of Coeur d'Alene, he was wearing a rainbow on his chest and he was angry. No one had the right to decorate Marve without his knowledge.

Buttoned his shirt and took the elevator up to his old Dartmouth prof, Albert Peck. Albert never shopped or considered the usual amenities. He was an elegant gypsy, even at Dartmouth. He wouldn't keep a house, like Marvin's other profs. He entertained his students in a furnished closet.

He'd been fatter then. Albert had become a thin man since the Big Green. He wore tube socks and a tattered robe. He didn't ask about the colors under Marve's eye. Was he communing with Rimbaud and Henry James? Albert was a bit of a flake. He'd introduced soft ice cream to Phnom Penh, but he couldn't get his ass off the ground in America.

Marve clutched the moth-bitten sleeve of Albert's robe. "I come home and Lliana's like a wild lady. Lashes at me. I find Jonah in her bed . . ."

"She just called. Lliana figured you'd come to the Gramercy."

"I was talking to Doris about Lana Turner. And then . . . I lose a year."

"Eleven months," Albert said, like a wise man in a magic, moth-bitten coat.

"Lliana knew where I was?"

"We all did. You wouldn't come back to Lliana. You had your nest in Alphabetville."

"But I was looking for Lulu? Where was she?"

"In the same nest."

Marve clutched more of Albert's sleeve. He'd been chief aquisitions editor for Carlo Peck. Carlo couldn't have survived without him. The old man was losing authors right and left. "How did Carlo put together his winter list?"

"My brother always manages," Albert said. "Sit down. I'll order something to eat. You can bunk with me until you find another place."

Marve felt twice as obscure with Albert around. He needed that stethoscope man who twitched and pulled on his scalp. The stethoscope man knew more about Marve than Albert did. He clutched his own shirt and revealed the depths of his rainbow. "What's that?"

Albert must have retreated into Henry James. He wouldn't consider the rainbow. And then he said, "Looks like a montagnard insignia. To placate certain devils."

"And what's a devil doing on me?"

Albert shrugged. He was still in the jungle somewhere, selling soft ice cream. Marve left Albert's living room.

People shunned him on the elevator, the man from Indian country with a rainbow on cheek and chest. Marve hiked down to King Street with his broken heel. Had to find out what happened to Carlo's winter list. Marve couldn't stop thinking like an editor. Carlo's wife opened the door. Corinne had to be thirty-nine, but she stood near the door with Lulu's brazen eyes. Carlo had captured her out of Sarah Lawrence and she lived inside his cove. It was a narrow place. She was delighted with Marve's canary clothes. Kissed him on the mouth, like an obedient girl with the promise of sex.

"Marve, you should have rung up. Carlo doesn't like to have his dinner disturbed."

"It's all right," Marve said, squeezing past Corinne. He climbed down to the lower floor where Carlo took his meals. The windows were just below the sidewalk, and that allowed Carlo to view King Street from the hip down. He didn't want faces near the window.

Carlo was the last of the great publishing pirates. He specialized in folklore and travel books. Gallatin had been the money man, but Gallatin was dead. The firm had prospered because Carlo never allowed Gallatin near a book. He'd married a young wife when he was fifty-six. Corinne went from creative writing to Carlo's townhouse on King Street. The old pirate had lectured up at Bronxville and captured Corinne with his bandit's eyes. He'd never been married before. He discarded all his mistresses for Corinne, gave up long hunting trips, eating tours of Italy and France, monastic retreats with his sales force, to nourish the young wife. She gave birth after a winter with the pirate, and Carlo found himself with another woman to nourish. But Lulu kept escaping from King Street. The crisis with his daughter had diminished him, eaten into his natural bounty. Marve stroked the sales manager, commissioned books, kept authors loyal to the house. It was Marve who saw Doris Quinn through her breakdowns, encouraged her to add more chapters to the *Spy*. No one but Doris would have ventured into Indian country, anatomized Avenue D, opened Alphabetville to tourists.

The old man was eating flounder in his favorite chair. He wouldn't look up at Marve. He shouted for Corinne. "Bring our boy a spritz."

Corinne scratched around at the sideboard and brought Marve a spritzer with white wine and lemon peel.

"Had a funny day, Carlo. Lliana threw me out. And I visited with your brother."

Carlo was suddenly less interested in his flounder. "How is Albert? Still sleepwalking at his hotel?"

"Albert's fit. But Lliana's temperamental. She summoned the porter. He put his hands on me. And our beloved lawyer was there. Jonah helped."

"Of course he helped. He's going to marry Lliana. Why didn't you grumble when you still had a chance? You signed the settlement papers."

"Carlo, I was a married man this morning."

"In your dreams," the pirate said.

"But you can't prepare a catalogue. I've been carrying the house. Your authors would have flown the coop if I hadn't romanced them with lunch."

"Carried the house? We've been thriving without you."

"Who's your editor?"

"I don't need one."

"You've been signing up authors yourself?"

"Indeed."

"What about Doris Quinn?"

"We had to drop her from the list."

"Doris went to another house?"

"She doesn't have a house. No publisher wants a crazy bitch . . . oh, I might bring her back if she promises to limit her breakdowns to one a year."

"What does she live on?"

"Doris gets some royalties from us."

"And you never see her?"

"Who has the time? I'm swimming in manuscripts."

"And I have a slight case of amnesia."

"You didn't have much amnesia when you signed the settlement papers."

"Carlo, help me. What happened? I was supposed to look for Lulu. And . . ."

"You disappeared into Doris' Indian country."

"No one thought to bring me out?"

"We tried, damn you. Jonah hired detectives. You didn't want to come out. We talked on the phone."

"You and I?"

"We had several conversations."

"What about?"

"I don't remember word for word. You were adamant."

Marve cried into the soda water. "I was looking for Lulu, and you just let me float . . ."

"Do you call it floating when you beat up two detectives we hired?"

"Couldn't they tell I was sick?"

"You didn't sound sick on the phone. You were pretty damned sure of yourself."

"And Lulu? Didn't you care about Lulu?"

"Of course I cared. But she had you. You were together in Indian country."

"Carlo, what day is it?"

"It's Tuesday. You ought to be quick enough to tell that."

Marve said good-bye and the pirate hurled up his dinner napkin. He was a celebrity. He'd hunted with Dash Hammett and been on the radio with Groucho Marx.

"Wait a minute. You barge in, ruin my appetite, and then you run off . . . without a forwarding address. Where can I reach you?"

"Alphabetville."

"That's not good enough. Suppose I want to get in touch with Lulu. I'm her dad. She might come into a small inheritance. Corinne's people are rich."

"You have your detectives, Carlo. Send them out on the case."

He hobbled up the stairs with Corinne behind him. She grabbed his yellow coat to stop Marve from springing out the door. He wasn't eager to look into her face. She might have dragged him to some dark cupboard under the eaves. Fondling her would have been a form of child abuse.

But she hadn't followed him upstairs to hug the colors on his chest. "Take me to my daughter. You live with Lulu in that awful place."

"I don't live anywhere, Corinne."

And he stepped out onto King Street. He had an appointment with Jonah Slyke, but Jonah wasn't aware of it. Tuesday and Thursday were Jonah's nights at the paddleball club unless the lawyer had changed his habits.

Marve showed up at the club's Eighteenth Street address. He didn't have much trouble at the door. The girl in the membership office recognized him. He'd fallen behind in his dues, but the girl let him in.

He went up one flight and pulled Jonah out of his glass cage.

Jonah swore at him with the old silver paddle in his hand. Jonah brought it back from Vietnam, where he'd been paddleball champ.

"Come to my office, but don't shadow my game."

"Jonah, we have to talk."

"I'm serious. I don't do business at the club."

The lawyer started to go back into his cage when Marvin seized him by his gym shorts. He was always a little jealous of Jonah. Marve had scraped at manuscripts with a green pencil while Jonah wrestled crocodiles in the Nam.

"Don't handle me. I'll sit you down in the nearest precinct."

"Then you tell me what this is all about."

"I'll tell you," Jonah said, waving the silver paddle in Marve's eye. "You left an old man to run a publishing house all by himself, and didn't even have the decency to give him a day's notice. You're nothing but an animal now."

"And you sleep with the animal's wife. When did you start with her?"

"I don't owe you an explanation. If you bother her again, you'll get yourself a seat on Rikers Island."

"Jonah, just explain to me what happened."

"You're with the Avenue C mob. You dance, you sing, you steal."

"Is Doris at her old address?"

"Doris tried to drown herself. She has a twenty-four-hour keeper. Can't you remember the simplest thing?"

"Just give me Doris' address."

"Belleville Apartments. It's on Thirteenth, near Second. A home for rich alcoholics and madwomen. You can't miss it. A brownstone with a blue awning."

"Thanks, Jonah. And I didn't mean to hurt your game," Marve said, leaving that field of glass cages. He crept down from Eighteenth Street, wondering if they had a midnight mass at Belleville.

A panel truck was behind him. The truck had a placard on its roof that advertised a bakery in Brighton Beach. Two fat women were in the cockpit. They crooned at him from their window.

"Zdrastvitye, King George. Did you meet with Moscow today?"

Marve saw a gun with barrels taped together. It was like staring into a skull of eyes. A boy with red hair leaned out the cockpit and aimed the gun at Marve. The boy had as many worry lines as Marve himself. "Majesty, regards from the Davidoffs."

Marve dove into an alley. He got as far as the alley's garbage cans when the gun went off over his head. It was like a little storm of fists had socked the cans. Marve knew the sound of beebees. That wizened boy with red hair had assembled an armada of beebee guns around a central barrel.

He heard the truck drive away, but he wasn't free of the Davidoffs. The two fat women were waiting for him in leather pants as he crawled out from behind the garbage cans. He darted between the women on his one good heel, got to the corner, and hopped to Thirteenth. His heart beat Idaho blood and green peas and he arrived at the blue awning of Doris' nursing home. Marve didn't see a bloody light in the windows. He rang the bell. Nothing stirred in the house. Jonah had sent him to the wrong address.

He was about to go when the intercom squawked. "Give us a name."

"King George," he blurted, remembering what the Davidoffs had called him.

The door buzzed and Marve went in. Belleville was dark. Marve groped around in the hallway until he banged into some stairs. He sniffed the walls of this rotten place. The walls smelled of glue. He could feel a man at the top of the stairs. "Who is it?"

"It's Neck, your majesty. Who'd you think?"

Marve appealed to Neck. "Where's the light?"

"You told me to put on the blinkers."

"But I could stumble, Neck, going up the stairs."

"That's different, your majesty. You got logic on your side."

Neck switched on a light and Marve understood the poetry of that name. The man's large head rose directly out of his chest. He carried a .45 under his belt. The gun was enormous. Marve climbed the stairs.

"Where's Doris?"

"Sleeping, your majesty."

A woman scuttled between them. She had a crumpled nurse's bonnet. He'd come to the land of the strange on Thirteenth Street. Neck and a nurse's hat.

This nurse was carrying a tray. She had a mouth of missing teeth. "Sorry, sir," she said to Marve. "But Madame won't eat by herself."

"Then take me to Doris."

While Neck stood at the top of the stairs, the nurse led Marve through a filthy corridor and into a room speckled with candle-light. Doris was on the bed. She wore a man's robe, and Marve was frightened for her, because she had a gray streak in her scalp, over the left eye, like a surgeon's mark. "Lana Turner," he muttered, but Doris couldn't remember the talk they'd had about Lliana's name.

He fed her carrots and cooked prunes. Marve wasn't sure whether Doris was his prisoner, and he couldn't ask Neck. The thug might grow suspicious, and Marve would end up as Doris' roommate, two children trapped in candlelight.

He had to whisper, so the nurse wouldn't hear. She might have gone to Neck, and Marve would have to dance around a .45.

"Doris, where do I live?"

"Saigon," she said. "Saigon Sarah. You belong to her Hebrew school."

"And I dance for Sarah?"

"Only when you're in the mood."

"Doris, can I trust that goon on the stairs?"

"Neck's a sweetheart. He prays for me."

"But can I trust him?"

"Like your own dad," she said.

"I'll get you out of here. Give me a little time . . . what's the nurse's name?"

"Gwen," she said. "Gwendolyn."

"Is Gwen a stool pigeon?"

"I'm the pigeon," Doris said, reaching up to touch Marve's hair. "Lie down with me for a minute, Marve."

He climbed onto the bed while the nurse stood sentry at the door. They were the Avenue C mob, Neck, the nurse, and him. Their enemy was a truck of fat women and a boy with red hair.

"Kiss me," Doris said, but he was embarrassed to kiss her in front of Gwen.

"Kiss me."

He pecked her mouth. "Doris, I'll come for you . . . soon as I can."

He went out the door and the nurse tracked him with her own candle. "Sir, your leg is bleeding."

He looked down. His shoe was sailing in blood. The nurse caught him smiling like an imbecile.

"Sir, I ought to look at the leg."

He followed her inside her little station. She sat him on a bench, rolled up his cuff, took off his shoe and bloody stocking, and examined him under the candle. His leg was all brown near the ankle, with blood welling up from two small holes.

"A souvenir," he said. "From the Davidoffs. But how come I couldn't feel it?"

Gwen bathed his leg, dug two beebees out of him with a pair of surgical pliers, heated a blue ointment on a tiny burner, daubed his ankle with that evil-smelling stuff, and wrapped the leg until he looked like a soldier with one puttee.

"You'd best stay off it, sir, and sleep with us."

"Gwen, help me on with the shoe."

"She'll bleed, sir, and you'll provide a target for the Davidoffs."
He appealed to her. "Gwen . . ."

She smiled, left her station, and returned with a man's sock, stretched the sock over his foot, laced up the shoe, and pulled down the cuff.

"Thank you, Gwen. You're my battle nurse."

His bandage rubbed a little. He kissed Gwen on her cheek and limped towards the stairs with his one puttee.

Neck appeared from behind a wall. Marve was frightened of that head without a stalk. It had nothing to swivel on. One day Neck's chin would pierce his own heart.

"Majesty, should I ride you home to the Hebrew school?"

That gentleness coming from the creases of a huge head disturbed Marve. He had to get away from the purring beast. "Thank you, Neck. I'll walk." Marve climbed down the stairs and took his puttee out the door.

The moon hung over Second Avenue like a graying ball. It put no light in the sky, simply declared itself. And it was under such a moon that Marve entered Indian country. He saw a garden in the burnt shell of a building and he wasn't sure if he should laugh or cry, because he'd stumbled upon a small pea farm. He couldn't mistake the flowers, the sticks that held the vines. He'd traveled over the border into Idaho. He resisted the urge to climb this garden gate and tend the flowers. He'd live and die a green-pea man.

He limped away from the garden, got to Avenue C. He found bottle clubs where men sat in chairs and sucked on pints of whiskey out of paper bags, as if the world had been reduced to a whiskey bottle and a wall. He found minimarkets with palm trees painted in the windows, whole landscapes of vegetables and fruits that seemed to belie the ratty nature of this street where old men lived in abandoned refrigerators and children had to turn water bectles into toys. But he couldn't find that Hebrew school of Saigon's.

No one attacked, or hissed at him from the windows. He had

free play under a fat moon. He crossed the street and discovered a picture of himself on a signboard. He was naked in the sign, his groin shadowed with ink. He had words on his shoulder.

KING GEORGE

BEST MALE DANCER

MEMBERS ONLY

He noticed a legend on the wall: FREE TALMUD TORAH OF BER- LIN, 1899. He was in front of a red brick building with broken windowsills and a roof with crooked black teeth.

A woman called to him from the door, which was wrapped in an iron grille. "Majesty, you're late."

Didn't have to guess who the woman was. "I'm coming, Sarah." He carried the signboard into the talmud torah with him and Saigon didn't say a word.

He'd entered a huge vault with a platform in the middle, surrounded by chairs. People lunged at him as he searched for a path between the chairs. He'd lost Saigon Sarah.

Someone grabbed his arm and led him to a closet at the rear of the vault. Marve laid down his signboard and undressed in the closet. He heard clapping from the chairs.

Saigon walked into the closet. "Damn," she said. "Are you dicking around again? . . . Teacher, come in and help."

A narrow man with twitching eyes came up to Marve and touched him with a crayon. It all seemed clear. Marve had found his stethoscope man. But he couldn't get him alone. Saigon stared at Marve's leg.

"Who bandaged you like that?'

"Gwen."

"That bitch couldn't bundle a dead dog."

"Wouldn't have known I was bleeding without Gwen."

Saigon never asked him what the bleeding was about. She collected Teacher and shoved Marve out of the closet. Marve picked up his signboard and banged into a wall. The wall wore blue.

"Jesus, Vladimir, will you get out of his majesty's way? He's got a show to do."

Marve tried apologizing to the wall. It was only a man in a blue serge suit that Marve could imagine on some Czechoslovakian waiter a hundred years ago. The cuffs ended at the forearm on this primitive suit, which could barely drape the man. His chest occupied most of the corridor.

It was Teacher who got him to move. "Vladi, don't be selfish. The king has to perform."

Vladimir let him through and Marve had to face the shouting from the chairs. Women had come to watch him dance. They weren't women who lived in abandoned refrigerators. They didn't taste of Avenue C. They'd arrived at the talmud torah in chinchilla wraps. Their limousines probably let them off and parked around Confucius Square. Marve began to notice more and more men. The women had brought their husbands to the talmud torah.

He felt like shouting to Vladi. "Clear the deck." But he might have caused a revolution. He'd have to suffer men's eyes on his groin.

He mounted the platform and was immediately joined by Teach, the stethoscope man, who tucked himself into the corner with a tin fiddle as the women screamed for Marve.

"Majesty, majesty, do your mountain roll."

Teacher scraped the fiddle with a crooked bow and Marve hugged the signboard and hobbled in his puttee like a sour bear. Women giggled at him, showed their husbands that King George wasn't dangerous, but they hadn't gone into a dungeon land of cocaine dealers, risked having their tires slashed, their bodies assaulted by derelicts, their purses stolen, their eyes gouged, to be entertained by a bear. A bear couldn't get them to purr under the chinchilla. They expected exotic dancing under the

93

roof of a talmud torah in the worst part of Indian country.

Marve didn't know how to deliver. He tried to follow Teach's fiddle and bow, but he'd become that dancing bear with a puttee. He shuffled with the sign in his arms.

A face peered at him out of the bitter, porous lights that were strung on a wire canopy over the platform. It was Saigon with a golden complexion.

"Marvey," she said. "Drop your blanket."

He listened to the golden face and put his signboard down and danced to Sarah's eyes. He raised his arms. His belly rolled. He didn't have to follow the wheedling noise of a fiddle. He took Teach's stethoscope into the dance.

His body had a special physics. It was as if the rainbow could lift a talmud torah, cause women and men to float above a camp of chairs. His dancing tore at the notion of gravity inside Alphabetville.

He was a man from Coeur d'Alene doing the mountain roll. He'd broken out of a tightness that sat on him thirty years. He danced to escape the territory of alfalfa and peas. His confusion began to drop like a crust of feathers someone had layered on his back. He shook the feathers off and discovered his own fall into the talmud torah. He was a lodger here. And he could sneeze out the names of the other lodgers at this boarding house. All he had to do was dance. He lived with Saigon, Teacher, and Vladimir.

He danced to the edge of the platform, where women grabbed at his feet. He laughed and hopped over a swarm of arms. The women hurled their affection for him in hard cash. His ankles caught in a heap of twenty-dollar bills. He tripped and landed in the money, lay there for a minute, his old confusion coming back. He couldn't understand what pink mouths were doing near his knees. Hands opened and closed like crazy flowers.

He saw Saigon between the canopy wires. Her mouth wasn't pink. But the golden lights had turned on Saigon, clawed at her face.

"Don't drag your ass, majesty. Get up."

But he couldn't. All the clarity he'd accomplished in his dance' had gone out of him. He rocked in the money and couldn't remember where he was. He wanted his wife and the guarantee of more closet space. He'd kick Rimbaud out of the apartment, assert himself as king. He was frightened without his clothes.

He pitied the marks on Sarah's face. Climbed on one knee to touch Saigon and comfort her. But he never reached far enough. He grabbed one of the canopy struts, twenty-dollar bills clinging to his back.

"Majesty, will you dance before these mamas wreck the place?"

He began his bear shuffle, with the fiddle behind him, and then his belly undulated, just like that. Money fell from Marve and scattered around the cabaret. Women stood on chairs to clutch the bills Marve had worn on his back.

Sarah clapped her hands and the fiddling stopped. Vladi made a path for Marve from the twenty-dollar bills to his dressing closet and Marve got into his clothes and then he peeked out of his closet. The Hebrew school had emptied, and the rings of vacant chairs surrounding the platform made him feel he'd landed in some desolate garden where even his father's alfalfa wouldn't grow.

Alphabetville.

4

TEACH rose at six in the morning and had a suck of black candy. The poison slapped through his skull like a whole tin of Maxwell House. It was Teacher's coffee. He'd never have been able to manage Uncle's estates on a different diet. The candy kept him near the edge of doom, and Teach functioned better with a long hard pull of hopelessness. He'd been to hell once, but the Holy Ghost dragged him out just when Teach was getting acquainted with Old Nick.

Nick wouldn't take you twice. The devil wore a rainbow on him like Marve, and the devil was a dancer. But that was Marve snoring in the talmud torah, and Teach was tired of mixing candy for Marvin de la Mare, tired of painting him up like George. Teach could wish until his eyes went blue, but the magicians would never come out of their concentration camp. Hanoi had sentenced them to extinction. There was no room for sorcerers in commie heaven.

Didn't have time to dream of concentration camps. Teach had chores to do. He dressed in the dark of the talmud torah and took some blasting caps with him and six ounces of jelly. He wasn't concerned about the Davidoffs. It was that war among the coca princes. Sooner or later Teach would be sucked in. And he wasn't going to pull against baby bandits with nothing but wire tits around his neck. A stethoscope couldn't soothe a South American Colt.

A cab was waiting for him outside the talmud torah, one of Renata's Russian drivers. Teach didn't have to shout instructions into the driver's ear. The cab took him to King Street. Teach got out and knocked on Carlo's door. It was a quarter to seven, and the old publisher greeted him in a velvet robe. "Will you have some coffee until Corinne comes down?"

"A pleasure," Teach mumbled, with candy on his brain. Carlo brought him into the breakfast nook, and Teach had to fight all his commando instincts not to feel sorry for the old man. Carlo was foolish enough to think that Corinne was going up to Albert for lessons in Tolstoy and Proust. He wouldn't let Corinne ride away from King Street without an escort. But Teach was more like a pimp. Corinne would get her Tolstoy from a Russian teacher.

"Is she making progress?" Carlo asked, pouring espresso into some kind of children's cup. That cup never got Teach beyond one sip.

"Yes, sir," Teacher said. "They're battling it out with *War and Peace.*"

"I never admired Tolstoy. It's shameful, but I wouldn't have published him. All that talk about farms and furniture in Leningrad."

"Agreed," said the Teach, who hadn't read a word of Tolstoy. "Couldn't hold a candle to *The Princess Casamassima*."

"That's my sentiment, to be sure," the old man said. "I forget now. Were you one of Albert's pupils? Not a Dartmouth boy by any chance?"

"Nah," Teach said. "I never got to the Old Green. I met Albert in Vietnam."

The publisher couldn't have known much about Uncle's enterprises, or he wouldn't have delivered Corinne into Teacher's hands.

"More coffee?"

Teach burnt his tongue on a second children's cup, and Corinne came down into the breakfast nook. Ah, she was Lulu's mother all right, crazy about the worst sort of men. Lulu loved her sailors, and Corinne had her Russian hood in Albert's bedroom. She was wearing a dress that Teach remembered from certain sweet sixteen parties in Hoboken a billion years ago. Her mouth was puckered like a child's, but there was nothing kittenish about her legs. Corinne had a woman's graces under her party dress. But Teach could have been imagining things, because he knew the dress would come off in half an hour.

She drank her coffee in silence.

"So tell us," Carlo said. "Tell us something about Proust."

"He despised fountain pens."

Carlo winced at his wife. "Is that why I send you off at seven in the morning? To lecture me on fountain pens?"

Corinne started to cry. "I get so confused every time you start your inquisition."

"It is not an inquisition. Ask Mr. Biedersbill. I'm a concerned husband, that's all."

"We're reading Proust in French," she told him. "It's difficult, because Proust didn't believe in paragraphs. And sometimes we have to stop in the middle of a sentence."

"Are you already in love with Swann?"

"No," she said. "He reminds me of an aristocrat from Dutchess County. He's a terrible snob. Doesn't deserve Odette."

"I see," the old man said, dismissing Corinne with a twirl of his coffee cup. "Take her, Mr. Biedersbill."

Corinne twisted out of the breakfast nook and followed Teach into the cab. Held his hand during the ride like a naughty girl. Teach could feel the hot pulse of her body. She never spoke to him on the ride up to Uncle Al. She was thinking of her Russian friend, but she wouldn't let go of his hand. Teach couldn't get away from minding people. He was everybody's nurse.

The cab parked across from Albert's hotel, and Teach went up with Corinne. He didn't like to consider Carlo as the cuckold of King Street. It bothered Teach that Albert would make his own brother wear horns. Uncle had to whore a lot to keep his army going, but he didn't have to whore behind his brother's back.

Teach sat on the sofa with Albert and Corinne until a naked Russian with fat blue eyes marched out of the bedroom with vodka in a Pepsi Cola bottle. The Russian bowed to Teach without bothering to cover his balls.

"Lo, Henry James."

It was Vladi's Moscow manager, and he still had pits on that side of his face where Samuil had shot him. Teach wished the Davidoffs had done a little more. But he was pleased that Konstantin couldn't prowl. He was a prisoner in Albert's rooms every time he got to Manhattan. His chest had gone soft, but Konstantin had a runner's legs and nicks on his back from his days in Vietnam.

He smiled and led Corinne into the bedroom and started to sing behind the closed door. Not a Russian song. It was "Lucy in the Sky with Diamonds." Konstantin was a Beatles freak. He'd made a fortune smuggling "Sergeant Pepper" into Leningrad with the help of the KGB.

Teach figured he'd go insane if he had to hear Beatles songs under the tyranny of a Russian baritone. But Albert winked at him and the two of them sneaked downstairs to Gramercy Park. Albert had his own key to that private little garden. They entered through the north gate. It was the only exercise Albert could abide, a stroll in the garden, near the central statue and the garden shed. Where was the Albert who'd walked through Cambodia and Laos? He huffed after one tiny parade through the park and had to find a bench.

"Uncle, did Henry James ever have a key to this park?"

Albert laughed. "I doubt it. Henry lived down the road on Washington Square. Does that disappoint you, Howard? Why such a gloomy face?"

"Ah," Teach said. "It's the old man."

"What old man?"

"Carlo. Thinks Corinne is studying Proust."

"She is studying . . . with Konstantin. And don't you pity the son of a bitch. Carlo likes to bust my ass. Says it hurts his image to have a brother who lives like a hobo in a hotel. He's a darling man. Taunts his little girl until she runs away and holds his wife in a closet on King Street. Howard, what could I ever teach Corinne? She's a real retarded beauty. Should have married you."

Teach started to twitch. "I'm engaged," he said.

"But you ought to encourage her," Albert said. "She'd fall head over heels. Howard, you're hard to resist."

Teach picked shrapnel from his hair. "C-c-couldn't marry."

"Then we'll will her to Marve, because Konstantin isn't that reliable. He can hardly romance her from Ho Chi Minh ville. You promised me Marve wouldn't dance last night. I thought you had him doped up."

"I d-d-did."

"Howard, you're losing your touch. And you're my main magician."

It was the Teach who kept Colombia out of Alphabetville and lent Uncle's territories to the Bolivian maf. He kidnapped old Colombian chiefs and carried them to Uncle's farm in New Jersey. But that didn't explain Nibio's death or Lubbock's stint with the Leopards in Chaparé.

"Uncle, did Renata tell you about the accident on the roof?"

"Of course. Nibio must have strangled on his own gin."

"Uncle, he doesn't drink gin. He was poisoned."

"Thank you, Howard. Are you the coroner now?"

"He was poisoned," Teach said. "His hands were blue."

"And blue hands make it an official verdict? I don't care. His cousins got to him."

"They would have cut off his neck. That's how it's done in the Chaparé."

"But the Bolivians adjust their style to Avenue D."

"Then who taught Capablanca how to mix black candy?"

"Stop it," Uncle said. "Capa could buy his poison in any store."

"That's true. But you haven't asked me to wind Capa's clock."

"I'll handle him," Uncle said. "You patrol the supermarkets."

"There aren't any supermarkets," Teach said. "The coca shops are closed."

"They'll open again . . . in good time."

"Uncle, if it's getting hot in Boliv, why didn't you send me? Lubbock's a butcher. He can't even light a fuse. I could have taught the Leopards how to lay a mine."

"Has Lub been bragging to you?" the padre asked.

"No. I caught his picture in one of the mercenary mags."

"It's unfortunate, because I'm not at liberty to discuss that particular op. Let's just say some of our friends are betting that the civilian government is about to fall."

"So we fuck with the coca crop and there's goddamn chaos and the generals take over again."

"That's the scenario, Howard."

"But aren't you off the CIA?"

"I am," the padre said. "Swear to Christ. I'm on the Company's shit list. You know that. But we're an army for hire . . . have to end the conversation, Howard. The good wife has come downstairs."

Teach noticed Corinne through the spears of the north wall. She looked like an abandoned child in front of the Gramercy, even with her hips showing through the party dress. Konstantin had wooed her with his baritone's body, but she hadn't succumbed to "Sergeant Pepper." Russian magic was slow. Teach said good-bye to Uncle on his bench, strolled out of the garden, and returned Corinne to the Russian cab that had waited during her literature lesson. She was much more talkative on the ride downtown. But Corinne's talk saddened the Teach. It was like the unwinding of a doll. He'd have to wax Konstantin, but he couldn't say when. Vladi's three sisters were in Leningrad, under that Russki's dominion.

"Howard," she said, clutching his hand. "If Carlo quizzes me, what should I say?"

"Tell him you had a change of heart."

Corinne ruffled her nose. "I don't understand."

Ah, she was damn desirable for a closet wife. "Say Albert led you from Proust to Henry James."

"But I haven't touched Henry James in years."

"Ah," Teach said, "just fling titles at your old man."

"What titles?" she asked, pulling Teach's hand onto her lap, so he couldn't stray from her.

"*Beast in the Jungle. Bostonians. Wings on the Dove.*"

"You can't fool Carlo with titles. He's read those bloody books."

"All the better," Teach said. "Tell him John Marcher is a dope."

"Who's John Marcher?" she asked, with a desperate sawing of his hand against her chest.

102

"The beast in the jungle. Henry James himself."

Corinne sawed further and further into her chest. "I'll never convince Carlo of that."

"It's not your problem," Teach said. "Blame it on Uncle Al."

The sawing stopped. But she didn't confide in him about Konstantin. He was only Corinne's collector. He delivered her to King Street. Carlo was outside the door in a white linen suit. Wouldn't go off to work without Corinne. And Teach had an anger in him that went deeper than Henry James. The Russki must have told her that Teach was Uncle's man at the talmud torah, and she'd never even asked him about Lulu. He'd have lied to old Corinne and wouldn't have brought up Lulu's fondness for sailors, but she still should have asked . . . unless the Russki romanced her with nothing but Beatles songs.

Corinne stepped out of the cab, kissed Carlo, and went into that King Street jail. The old man curtsied in his linen suit. He was off to his publishing house with a dark leather satchel, discovering the new Henry James. But Carlo was deceiving himself. There'd never be another *Princess Casamassima.*

Teach was safe as pudding. Safe as pie. Sarah wouldn't suspect his morning liberty. The cab would get him to her door by nine. That was enough. The talmud torah never rose before noon.

Marve woke in a corner, wearing pants and shirt. Someone must have dressed him during the night. Vladimir slept on the other side of the room with both his fists in a ball. That sleep was so full of tension, it built furrows into Vladimir's skull.

Marve brought a name with him out of the blanket. He'd forgotten Lulu while he danced. He rinsed his mouth in Saigon's sink and descended upon the garden patch he'd discovered last

103

night. Vaulted a chicken-wire gate, but he didn't land clear. His foot got trapped, bringing down the gate. He crawled out from under the wires and sat on the pocked earth, among tendrils and sticks. He'd crushed a swatch of blue flowers in his clumsy fall.

He noticed a gray lump near the sticks. The lump had dirty blonde hair caught in the tendrils. He'd come upon Lulu, face down in the earth. Carlo's girl was lying in a poor man's garden on Twelfth Street.

Marve freed her hair and gathered Lulu up into his arms. A pink mouth and one eye broke from the mud on her face.

"Did I ask for you, King George?"

He carried her out of the garden and over the felled gate. Lulu hissed into his chest.

"I'll sue your pants off, you son of a bitch. I'll hire Jonah Slyke. It's a criminal offense to steal girls from the Twelfth Street Block Association."

"Sure," he said. "Saigon is princess of that association."

"Jonah will defend me."

"Jonah's busy with my wife. Tell me, little daughter, what are you doing here?"

"I'm on vacation from big tits."

"Sarah, you mean?" Marve had to be cautious with the girl. She could have lived on the moon over Avenue D. He'd been uncle, brother, and playmate to her since she'd come out of the crib. She was like his own combative child, but with a woman's body now. She was all hips and bosom in her rotting dress, Corinne without the fractured eyes, more of an adult than her ma. Suddenly his own spill into the talmud torah made sense. He guarded Lulu and danced on the side.

"Little daughter, when was the last time we spoke?"

"Are you a nut? I had a fight with big tits a week ago. You were there. She said I was putting out for sailors and it's a lie. I never slept with a sailor in my life."

She dug her head into Marvin's shoulder and was quiet all the way to the talmud torah.

Saigon met them at the door. She raged at Marve, swearing she wouldn't accept the girl.

"Fine," Marve said. "I'll register her at the Hotel Bowery, and you'll have that on your conscience."

"Don't you vex me, Marve."

"I wouldn't dream of it. Just get yourself another dancer. Because I go where Lulu goes."

Saigon clutched her bosoms. "I'm swooning, son."

They might have continued for an hour, with Marve cradling Lulu and Saigon circling around them in her blackest mood, if Teacher hadn't appeared with his stethoscope and bloodshot eyes.

"The girl's a slut," Sarah said.

"Slut yourself," Lulu told her. "Mama-san, you're just an old witch with sores on your face. You've never had a man in your life."

Saigon went to scratch Lulu's eyes, but Marve hid her behind his shoulder, and it was he who got scratched. Marve had a long tear down the back of his shirt. He carried Lulu away from Saigon and around the platform, which was still littered with money. No one had bothered to sweep up the twenty-dollar bills.

He deposited Lulu into the talmud torah's ground-floor tub, scrubbing Lulu and her things. He wasn't embarrassed about the feel of her breasts, or the sight of pubic hair in filthy water. He'd bathed Lulu the first time when she was six. She'd been desirable even then, and she was almost as desirable now.

She closed her eyes when Marve scrubbed under her arms, but he wasn't giving Lulu a pleasure bath. He got most of the mud off, and then he stood her up in the tub like a scarecrow and began to dry her with Saigon's towel.

Lulu's wardrobe was gone. Sarah must have used the girl's

blouses and underpants to wrap wet pipes. Marve had to dress her out of his own bin. She wore his rolled-up trousers and a shirt from Afghanistan that was as brown as a clot on the moon. She was better-tempered after her bath. Lulu followed Marve around the talmud torah, standing behind his sleeve.

"Looks like you got yourself a creature," Saigon said, but Lulu was beyond any argument. She peeked at nothing outside Marvin's sleeve. She was becoming that child of three who clung to Marve and cried for hours when he left, furious at Carlo and Corinne. She was the grand seductress at four, who coerced Marve into spending the night with her big brown eyes and the lipstick her daddy allowed her to wear. He was a bachelor then and Carlo gave him the attic room. Marve was always the glorified guest. A guest in his father's house, a guest with Lliana, and now a guest with Saigon, who offered champagne to her soldiers at four in the afternoon. She sat them down under the canopy and drank with her soldiers while Lulu sulked and polished her toenails. Saigon wouldn't feed her champagne.

"Missed you, baby-san. Ask the Teacher. We were in mourning without your face for a month."

"I was only gone a week."

"It felt like a month," Sarah said. "Did you find a good hotel? Or did you put out for the Salvation Army?"

"I'll put out for whoever I want."

"I know. Takes a laundry list to keep track of your men."

"Give her a cup," Teacher said from under the canopy.

"No sir. I'm responsible for the little bitch."

But Sarah relented and let Lulu drink out of her own cup. And Lulu followed her into the kitchen. The Teacher put placemats and silverware on the floor, preparing for some kind of holy meal. Saigon and Lulu squabbled for an hour and then the two of them came out of the kitchen with wooden bowls and a big pot of paella.

Vladi took his place mat into the corner. He liked to eat alone.

But he didn't chew with his eyes on the wall. He wouldn't break that knot of community with the gang.

The rice was deep yellow, the sausages dark brown, and the long red stripes of pimientos reminded Marve of salamanders sunning themselves on pieces of chicken in a pot. He gobbled yellow rice until Sarah groaned, "What time is it? We'll miss the midnight show. Where's that Neck?"

Saigon abandoned her pot and grabbed at Lulu. "Saddle up. Come on."

Marve was caught with a salamander on his tongue. It couldn't have been midnight. The sun hadn't gone down. He swallowed the salamander with champagne and heard Neck's horn. The gang shuffled out of the talmud torah and into Sarah's white limo with Doris and Gwen, who were sitting in the back. Doris' eyes seemed without blood. She didn't respond when Marve shoved into the cushions between her and Gwen.

"Sarah, why couldn't Doris live with us?"

Sarah growled from her front seat. "I already have one infant on my hands."

"I'm not an infant," Lulu said.

"No matter, baby-san. When I marry you to Samuil, our troubles will end."

"I'm not putting out for a Russian fiddler."

"Don't curse Vladi's people," Sarah said.

Teacher sat in the long middle crib of the car and pulled on the stethoscope. "Lulu doesn't have to get married."

"Are you our judge or something?" Saigon asked, but the Teacher had plugged his ears.

Neck drove out of Alphabetville and dropped the gang on Second Avenue, outside the St. Marks Cinema, which was showing *Blade Runner* at midnight. Marve had seen the film with his wife. He loved Los Angeles of 2019, a vast dying Chinatown filled with poisoned dust. Cowboys rode the landscape in hovercars, practicing for a life on Jupiter, while Deckard, a bounty hunter played by Harrison Ford, sets out to kill a small band of human replicants, "skin jobs" who started a revolt in space and have returned illegally to Los Angeles. Deckard was Philip Marlowe stuck in *Paradise Lost*, where Satan was an android and God was the head of the Tyrell Corporation, which produced all the best "skin jobs."

Saigon saw the film each Wednesday night at the St. Marks. Her devotion had nothing to do with androids. She was in love with Harrison Ford. And she arrived each Wednesday before sundown to make sure she didn't miss her Blade Runner. The St. Marks sold her tickets in advance. She went through the turnstile with her gang and waited in the lobby, near the popcorn machine. The gang had hours to kill, but Saigon wasn't bored. She dreamt of the Blade Runner while Teacher and Vladi covered the exits, watching for the Davidoffs.

Doris ate popcorn and licked the butter off her hands.

Lulu looked at herself.

Marve was going mad in the lobby. And then his eyeballs started to pull at him. He was following Harrison Ford through Los Angeles. What the hell had Saigon put in her paella? He was up in a hovercar with Deckard, around the roofs. Huge neon signs flashed on and off, advertising Coca-Cola. But the legend was in Chinese.

Saigon clutched his arm. "Wake up, majesty. You can't nod off on us. We're going in."

He'd dreamt his way to midnight, noticed how dark the street had become. He entered the auditorium, followed Sarah down to the front row, and sat between her and Doris. He couldn't understand why Sarah had worried so much about seats. The gang had the front of the theatre to itself. Sarah unwrapped a lump of silverfoil. Under the foil was a tarry, evil-smelling ball. She chewed a piece while the lights went out and passed the ball to Marve. He ate a bit of the opium ball. It was like having cooked tar in his mouth. He passed the stinky ball to Doris.

Blade Runner fell onto the screen and Sarah sat back in the dark with Harrison Ford. The Blade Runner had blue eyes and cropped hair. Marve blinked, because the Blade Runner looked like his brother Niles. The neon lights could have been Coeur d'Alene. Marve was riding home in his seat at the St. Marks. He started to cry. He wouldn't have believed he'd ever miss Idaho. "Niles," he muttered. "Where's Niles?"

"Shhh," Saigon said. "Majesty, you're spoiling the show."

Marve watched Harrison Ford destroy "skin jobs" with a blunderbuss from the twenty-first century. The Blade Runner falls in love with Rachel of the Tyrell Corporation. Rachel wears a dress with boxed shoulders, like a 1940s vamp. But her long, dollish eyelashes give her away. She's a complex "skin job," with all sorts of memory implants. Rachel's never been touched, but a history of sexual intercourse has been built into her body. The Blade Runner introduces her to human love with a violent kiss. Her hair uncoils. She's the most beautiful "skin job" Marve has ever seen. Suddenly the lashes get smaller and Marve is looking at his wife. It's Lliana who's with the Blade Runner, Lliana who was Tyrell's doll, and Marve began crying again. He was the "skin job." The talmud torah had programmed him to dance like King George. He had George's gold in his ear. He had a blue crescent under one eye. But the talmud torah had screwed up. He was neither Marvin nor George, but a skin job sentenced to Avenue C. That's why Los Angeles, 2019 was so familiar. It was one more Alphabetville.

Teach was faithful to Sarah. Wouldn't fall asleep in the middle of the movie, although he knew the scenes by heart. He was alert to old Deckard. Could have used the Blade Runner in Nam.

Deckard might have made a good run with the montagnards. But Teach had radar in back of his head. It was a system he'd developed in the boonies. No demolition rat could have survived without it. The twitch in his neck warned the Teach that baby hitmen were behind him. He absconded from his seat without a lick of Sarah's tar ball. He had different candy in his mouth. The candy came from jungle bark and the teeth of certain spiders and snakes. Snakes were perfect food for a movie house.

He'd been to other movie houses, like the Richelieu in old Saigon, where Teach had watched gangster films with King George. Ah, he missed *Shoot the Piano Player*. All that bang-bang in the snow. He kind of wished the Blade Runner spoke French. Then he might have warmed to old Deck. But Deckard couldn't help him now. Teach crawled up the aisle like a god-damn commando without nightfighter paint. He didn't have to camouflage himself for Capablanca's children.

He'd battled children before. Ten-year-old sappers who'd broken through the concertina wire at some base camp. They'd have killed the Teach if they could, blown him into the land of Abraham Lincoln. He'd admired those brats while he dug them out of the wire. And he could have spoiled Capa's children too, looped the rubber strings of his stethoscope around their necks, but he wasn't in the mood to strangle baby bandits. He crouched behind them and banged their heads together once, twice. They'd sleep through the rest of Harrison Ford. Teach gathered up all their guns and tossed them into the trash can near the popcorn machine.

He was stuck with a time problem. Had to find Capablanca before Harrison Ford disappeared from the screen. Sarah would bitch like hell if her whole gang wasn't there at the end of the film.

Teach didn't have to scour Indian country. He knew Capa would keep away from his store. Uncle had closed C and D to drugs. The commandos were waiting for a new regime in Bolivia.

But where would Capablanca go? Capa wasn't an ordinary thug. His people had been kings somewhere, although Teach couldn't remember the country. Spain, Portugal, or early Arizona? Capa had studied marketing at an American university, and marketing prepared him for the life of a coca prince.

Teach tried the Ukrainian coffee shop across the street, because it would have been an ideal canteen and listening post if Capablanca meant to unglue Sarah at the St. Marks and wipe out all the talent her talmud torah had. Capa sat at the window with his Bolivian maf. Generals, diplomats, and thugs of the old military junta. Capa himself wore a Monte Cristo cape. Teach couldn't tell how many millions Capa had made off his supermarket. *Forbes* magazine wouldn't list the holdings of a coca prince. But why did Capa stare so hard when the Teacher walked in? He had tiny spots of terror in his eyes.

No one made room for Teach at Capablanca's table. The fallen generals picked their teeth. Capa seemed to withdraw into his cape. Left a dish of potato dumplings to cool under his nose. It was Teach who had to start the interview.

"Capa, I didn't know your children were fans of Harrison Ford."

"We all love gringos with blue eyes," Capablanca said. "It's the dark ones who frighten us. You shouldn't have come here, twitch."

"Why should a prince be so impolite?" Teach asked. "The twitching is my own business. It's an honorable flaw. I picked it up in Vietnam . . ."

"Together with your pockmarked lady."

"It's not nice to insult Saigon Sarah."

"Pardon me," Capablanca said, playing to his generals. "She's the Hebrew godmother. Outlaws gypsies and all the Medicaid mills."

"She owns Alphabetville."

"In her sleep. Mi amor, does she know that the gypsies pay

111

you a percentage of whatever they steal from the housing projects? She must think you're her Robin Hood. Does your lady do business with the FBI? Or trade recipes with the Puerto Rican nationalists on the next block? Do the narcs come for lunch?"

"Sarah wouldn't invite them," Teach said.

"But did she invite you to poison Nibio?"

"I didn't poison him."

"Teacher, it has your trademark. Nibio wasn't dumb. He wouldn't toast his enemies with a poisoned cup. He thought he was drinking with a friend."

"Ah," Teach muttered. "Now I get the picture. The baby bandits weren't interested in Saigon."

Capablanca snarled into his potato dumplings. "I don't scare Hebrew godmothers. I sent them to give you a kiss, the Judas kiss you gave my cousin . . ."

"Wasn't my kiss."

"You could be right," Capablanca said. "But we can't continue." He thrust one arm out of the cape, pointed to the ceiling, and mouthed the word *wire*. Teach didn't need an education from Capablanca on the art of bugging devices. He knew the federales would wire Capa's favorite coffee shop. Capa loved to sing an aria or two into their microphones. He was fond of the federales.

"Come to my finca, little magic man."

Capa's finca was a fortified loft on Lafayette Street. Teach had never been invited there. He wouldn't turn Capablanca down.

One of the generals paid the bill. A hundred dollars for Capablanca's coffee and potato dumplings. That was the largesse of a prince. Teach was disappointed Capa hadn't brought his money scale to weigh the coffee shop's tip. Ah, Teach was a street kid. He couldn't get used to millionaires.

Capa's limousine wasn't white like Sarah's. And it wasn't secondhand. It was a long black mother that could have carried

112

the Bolivian infantry to any war zone in Manhattan. Teach sat between the generals who politely felt him up for hardware. They didn't notice the blasting caps and Teach's supply of jelly. He whistled "Sergeant Pepper" to the Bolivian maf. Capa shrugged. Teach was just a crazy assassin who'd been blown up in the Nam and turned into a walking bag of shrapnel. A charity case who poisoned people.

They arrived at Capa's finca on Lafayette. Capa diddled with a code of numbers near the front door and a voice summoned him into the finca. That voice had a familiar scratch to the Teach. Everybody climbed a set of stairs. A door opened and Teach recognized Renata of the art gallery, but she'd lost her dirty legs. She wore a silk robe at the finca, and Teach began to dream of a Moscow-Bolivian axis. The loft was wide as a soccer field. The coca wasn't there. It had Renata's paintings and a wonderland of books. Renata wouldn't even shake Teach's hand. She talked literature with old Capablanca. It was like a seminar in Uncle's living room. They mentioned some mother called El Nobel. They were going to visit El Nobel in a Caribbean port and pay homage at his feet. Capa didn't care if El Nobel was from Colombia. El Nobel had a Bolivian sensibility.

Fuck El Nobel, Teacher thought. But he was curious and jealous at the same time. "Capa, who's this El Nobel guy?"

"Gabito," Capa said with a mean little laugh. "Maestro García Márquez. Haven't you read *A Hundred Years of Solitude?*"

"Had my own hundred years," Teach muttered.

"You don't have writers in your country. Not like El Nobel."

"What about Henry James?"

"Nothing but a painter of the rich."

"It's not his fault, Capa, if he didn't have the benefit of poor parents."

"Muy bien! A critic," Capablanca said. "Did you speak of Henry James when you poisoned Nibio?"

"I wasn't on such intimate terms."

Renata crawled under Capablanca's cape, leaving only her head for Teach to see. "He's lying. He's one of Jonah's people. He's a narc."

"Sister, I don't get along with Jonah Slyke."

"He was your captain in Vietnam. You listen to Jonah."

It was hard for Teach to talk to a head floating out of Capablanca's cape. "Ask Uncle about it."

"We already asked," Renata said, emerging from the cape. "Capa, I think we should throw him to the dogs."

Teach cursed himself and all his shrapnel for having bought one of her paintings.

"Admit it," she said. "You're a narc." She touched herself under the robe and Capa's fallen generals surrounded the Teach. "I'll bet he's wearing a wire."

Teach had to smile. "I am wired," he said. "I have enough plastic on me to send you all into the clouds."

"He's bluffing," Renata said.

Teach dangled a plasting cap from his stethoscope. "It's an old trick I learned from the Cong. You use your own body as the detonator. All I have to do is fall down."

"What kind of magic is that?" Capa said. "You'd kill yourself."

"I've been dead before . . ."

Capablanca snapped his fingers at the generals. "He likes to play Jesus. Get him out of here."

"I'm not finished yet," Teacher said. "Capa, someone's been copying my M.O."

"Sure," Capablanca said. "King George ran out of his concentration camp to murder Nibio . . . have you noticed any montagnards in the street?"

"I'm not the only one who served with the Yards."

"But you were George's sidekick, his little magician."

"I didn't kill Nibio."

"Then find me who did. I'll lend you a couple of days . . . in honor of El Nobel. And then I'll burn your talmud torah to the ground."

"Capa, are you forgetting so soon? I'm the demolition rat. And you have a finca with lots of books."

"Two days, magic man. That's it."

Teach scrambled down the stairs. He wasn't thinking of the talmud torah's fate. Sarah was in his skull. He couldn't miss the last five minutes of Harrison Ford. He leapt into a gypsy cab, clawing bunches of money. The driver got him to Second Avenue and Teach pushed through the turnstile and into the heart of the movie house.

5

TOOK Saigon half the night to recover from Harrison Ford. She'd sit in the cabaret with her legs crossed, wishing the Blade Runner would come down from old Los Angeles to be with her gang. There was a knock on the door.

"Christ," she said.

The knocking continued until the canopy shook. "Who is it?" Sarah growled. "If you're selling religious articles, I'm not interested. We're atheists after eleven o'clock."

"Open the door, mama-san. It's me, Neck. I have a gift for you."

"Go away."

"Mama-san, the gift can't wait."

Neck wasn't alone. He stood with a redheaded boy. She dragged them inside and bolted the door and then she started to laugh. Neck had brought her Samuil Davidoff in a green slipover and tight leather pants.

"Saigon, I found the little mother snooping all by himself. He's jealous of your cabaret. I didn't want to carve him up. He's too valuable for carving. We could ransom him off. The Davidoffs would pay a gold brick for Samuil."

Lulu had come out of some forlorn closet when she heard the commotion. She waltzed around Samuil like a critic at a fashion show. She admired the green slipover and buttocks wrapped in leather. "He's cute."

"Romeo and Juliet," Saigon said with a sneer. "This is a dangerous man. He likes to shoot at our people. And he's not your type, baby-san. He used to walk around with a Stradivarius. But he started eating his fiddle, strings and all, and his aunt Zoya had to bring him to the United States, because swallowing a Stradivarius is a crime in the Soviet Union."

"I say he's cute."

"Cute?" Sarah said. "He's not even a sailor."

"Shut up about sailors."

"Mama," Neck said. "Maybe we ought to marry them. It would bring up the ransom price. We could ask majesty to officiate. A king's as good as any preacher."

"Let him go," Teacher said with a twitch.

"Ah, Teach, don't be so generous with my property. I'll give him to Vladimir. Vladimir knows what to do with a Davidoff. The Davidoffs have been chopping his tail. Should I tell you how many hits the limo has taken from Samuil's beebee gun? He's a menace."

"Let him go."

Neck clapped his hands with a sound that thundered over the canopy and went into the roof. "I catch the little mother and now I have to release him. Can't I snap his trigger finger?"

Neck stalked the talmud torah, traveled from face to face, but he found no sympathy, not even from Vladimir.

"Samuil, why'd you come sneaking around on cabaret night?"

"Not interested in cabaret," Samuil said. "We have to talk with KGBnik."

"What KGBnik?"

"Volodnishka."

"Mama-san, give me the signal. I'll punch him dead."

Teacher's twitch grew worse. "Let him go."

Vladimir took Samuil away from Neck and marched him to the front of the talmud torah. Samuil twisted out of Vladimir's reach long enough to kiss Lulu's hand. The girl was astonished. No one had ever kissed her hand before.

Samuil bowed. "Come to Brighton Beach. We go boardwalking together."

"Hear that?" Neck said. "He's making filthy proposals to our girl."

"Wouldn't mind proposals like that," Sarah muttered. "Sam's a Jewish gentleman. He belongs in the Moscow Art Theatre."

Samuil returned to Vladimir and they marched into the street without shutting the door.

All Marve could remember was that Samuil had shot at him from a truck. He couldn't make sense of warfare that included beebees and hand-kissing. He went to the door. Davidoffs materialized across the street, women tottering in high heels, the same women who'd menaced Marve outside Jonah's paddleball club. They all shouted at Vladimir: Samuil, the two women, and an old, old man. The Davidoffs knocked him down. It was like a house falling with the concentration of a ballerina.

"Majesty, shut the door," Teacher screamed from the depths of the talmud torah.

"Teach, they're stepping on him."

"It's a family quarrel," the Teacher said.

Belly dancing hadn't prepared Marve for the intrigues of a

talmud torah. Gulp champagne, go to midnight movies, and watch a clan of Russians walk on Vladimir.

Vladi returned with his collar destroyed and blood under his eye, like Marve's blue crescent. He sat down under the canopy as if nothing had happened. He yawned. Neck returned to Belleville. Sarah bolted the door.

Lulu went upstairs with Vladimir. Marve followed them to the talmud torah's mattress rooms.

"Goodnight," Sarah said.

Teacher started up the stairs, but Saigon beckoned to him. "We have to talk."

He clutched his face and tried to stifle the twitching. But his hands failed. He sat down next to Sarah with his stethoscope.

"You explain to me, Howard Biedersbill, why Samuil thinks he can come into my talmud torah and not get punished?"

"He didn't come," Teacher said. "Neck trapped him."

"You can't trap a fiddler like that. Neck's too dumb. Samuil wanted to get caught."

" 'S nothing, Sarah. If Vladi didn't quarrel with the Davidoffs, he couldn't have come to us."

"Swear on your mother's life and the life of King George that Vladi isn't KGB."

"How can I swear? If Vladi's a KGBnik, he never told me."

"Have you noticed that Marvey's different?"

"Na," the Teacher said.

"He's different. Did you let up on the black candy?"

She would have dug the truth out of him, but his twitching was so severe, he might have fainted and strangled to death on the cords of his stethoscope.

"Go on to bed," she told him.

Teacher took his twitching up the stairs.

War Cries Over Avenue C

'Twas under an apple tree
I saw her white eyes.
Was it cowgirl or demon lady?
Dedushka, I didn't even care.

Samuil hummed an old circus song on his way to the truck.
Was he thinking of Vladimir or Lulu Peck? He'd learnt about
that demon lady in his Uncle Izak's lap long before he'd ever
started to fiddle. Izak had once been Stalin's favorite clown.
In his youth old Uncle Izak would dance and guzzle vodka
with a team of polar bears. He'd taught the bears to play ice
hockey and swoon to "Dark Eyes" and demon ladies. Stalin
laughed and laughed. But all that laughter couldn't save old
Uncle Izak. He was sent right from the Moscow Circus to a
labor camp after one of Stalin's attacks against intellectual Jewish
clowns. Izak was eighty-three. He lived in the truck with Samuil's
aunts. That truck was their dacha on wheels.

The Davidoffs had a seven-room apartment over the boardwalk
at Brighton Beach. It was an apartment house that satisfied
Samuil's sense of culture. It had minarets and a cracked tower.
But there were too many Odessans in the neighborhood. You
could always tell them by their steel teeth. The Odessans were
uncivilized. They belched and farted at their tables without a
thought to Samuil's aunts. Their tongues were green from Odessa
borscht. They had little respect for Samuil's former status as
a fiddler. Some of them recalled Izak's bears. They could admire a clown from a labor camp. But a Stradivarius was only
wood.

Not all the Odessans were bad. Two of the worst families
had tried to extort money from the Davidoffs. They'd broken
the windows of the Davidoff bakery on Brighton Sixth Street.
And so the Davidoffs had hired an enforcer, a lonely bear of a
man who drank weak tea at the Café Tashkent. The Davidoffs
liked his strong arms. And they forgave him for having been

born in Peterburg. Their Volodnishka knocked a bit of peace into the Odessans' skulls. And Samuil turned the Tashkent's tables around and began to extort from the extorters.

Vladimir lived in the seven rooms with them. He had his own corner of a minaret. Zoya and Adelina fell in love with his silent ways. And then the Davidoffs discovered through an old KGB informer that Vladimir had come to spy on them. He was nothing but a *shpik*. Oh, they weren't ignorant. Brighton Beach was stuffed with KGB men. The KGB slurped borcht at the Odessa, the Zodiac, and the Tashkent. It was all a picnic to Samuil, who sold them dark bread at his bakery until the picnic stopped. Because suddenly the most active refuseniks of Brighton Beach, women and men who paraded on Fifth Avenue outside Aeroflot or disturbed the little Soviet colony on Long Island, would suffer heart attacks or drown. And just as the Davidoffs started to question Volodnishka, to shake answers out of him, he disappeared, like dust under the boardwalk.

And that's when they realized the Soviets had a master plan, a Jewish Department for Brighton Beach. Stories began to circulate. Another Oprichnina, people said, a ministry of murderers and thieves. The original Oprichniks belonged to Ivan the Terrible. Ivan's boys traveled across Muscovy murdering for the tsar. Plundered whenever they wished and wore whatever uniforms pleased them. They could be generals, grocers, monks. The idea was to build a ring of terror around their beloved Ivan.

But the modern Oprichniks went too far. They embarrassed Moscow during détente. The KGB had to haul them in. A few of the Oprichniks managed to remain alive. One of them was a fat playboy called Konstantin who trafficked in currencies, trinkets, and cocaine. Konstantin had sent their Volodnishka to spy school. Samuil remembered him from Moscow. A fat man had interrogated him inside the Lubyanka after Samuil applied for an exit visa. This fat man told Samuil that he was used to strangling fiddlers, that he was prepared to shit on any boy who wore the title of "people's artist." The fat man never touched him, but Samuil was sure it was an old Oprichnina trick.

What to do? The Davidoffs were left with their cracked tower. Samuil loved the beat of the ocean. He could have lived on frankfurters at the Gastronom Moscow. But strange things happened. Their apartment was ransacked twice and they discovered they were selling poisoned honey cake. Who had gone into their flour barrels? It didn't feel like the KGB. And Samuil began to wonder if there were American Oprichniks, thugs who paddled somewhere between the FBI and the CIA.

And then a man appeared on the boardwalk, outside the Davidoffs' windows. It wasn't Konstantin. It was a captain in civilian clothes, some Yankee Doodle with the name of Jonah Slyke. An Oprichnik, Samuil swore to himself. And he was clever with Yankee Doodle.

"Comrade captain, if you're not a regular counterspy, what could happen if we killed you?"

It was a bluff. Even with their poisoned barrels, the Davidoffs were bakers. They hadn't killed a man or woman they could remember. But the captain considered their proposal. "If you kill me, how will you ever find Vladimir . . . or Konstantin?"

"You know where our Volodnishka is?"

"Hiding in a Hebrew school on Avenue C."

"Avenue C Rockaway?" Samuil asked, because he only understood beaches in America.

"No," the captain said. "Alphabetville."

"Is a second boardwalk?"

"Kiddo, you have to cross the bridge. Vladimir is in Manhattan."

"Konstantin also?"

"Yes, the Russki goes there sometimes."

"But why you telling us?"

"Because we have a mutual friend. I'd like you to keep Vladimir pinned where he is. Patrol Alphabetville and report to me."

"What is to report?"

"All the shit that's going down. Take your truck and scan the place. And then I'll give you Konstantin."

"Captain, what is your agency? Are you American Marines?"

"Yeah," Jonah said. "I'm with the Marines."

"And why Marines interested in Volodnishka?"

"That's the way it is."

An American Oprichnik. Samuil was convinced. He built a beebee gun with the help of Uncle Izak, who remembered all the odd ballistics of a circus cannon. And they toured this Alphabetville. Samuil had an instant nostalgia for Brighton Beach. He'd never seen such a city of broken windows. There wasn't a cup of borscht to be had on Avenue B. Faces of gloom. Priests without a flock. Gardens where grass wouldn't grow. But Samuil's education was quick. He discovered crops of cocaine. Crops that moved from building to building like a circus. But this circus had no clowns, only a little twitching man with a doctor's earplugs who collected tribute from the coca people. He didn't return the tribute to his talmud torah. He brought it to a little store in the woods of Alphabetville.

Samuil wasn't a hijacknik. He let the circus operate, because he knew Konstantin was growing somewhere in the cocaine. All he had to do was watch. And then, in the magic husk of winter, with snow on the ground, he saw the Oprichnik walking on Avenue A. Samuil meant to scoop him up. But Konstantin must have smelled the truck. He ran. Samuil loaded his circus gun. Splattered the Oprichnik with a mess of beebees. But Konstantin got away.

The Davidoffs entered a fallow period. They could tease this gang of Hebrew school children, frustrate their plans, shoot at Saigon Sarah, but it couldn't bring them closer to Konstantin. And that's when Samuil allowed himself to be captured by Sarah's henchman, because he had to meet Volodnishka one more time. The Davidoffs' old enforcer didn't bark. Vladimir came out into the street. Samuil had to hold himself from hugging that KGBnik who'd been like a brother to the Davidoffs on Brighton Beach. Couldn't have tamed the Odessans without Volodnishka. But he wouldn't tell them where Konstantin was. It took the strength of the whole family to toss him to the ground. And Volodnishka wouldn't even fight back. Old Uncle Izak cried. Because he loved Volodnishka like one of his polar bears.

And that's when Samuil hummed his song, scouting the terrain before he returned to the truck. The talmud torah's little demon lady upset Samuil Davidoff. She suffers, he thought. Like me. And to Samuil suffering was the most important thing. Also Lulu's legs. And the cup of her behind. Not like the skinny freckled girls at Moscow's Central Music School, with their chins discolored from the hummocks of their fiddles and fingers full of horns. He didn't require a fiddler girl to compete with him and worry over Mozart. It was Lulu he desired.

He climbed aboard the truck. His aunts were in a somber mood. They'd turned Vladimir into their own mountain, tramped all over him. But they weren't satisfied. Adelina would have taken him back, locked him in the toilet at Brighton Beach so he couldn't spy. But Zoya had a stiffer heart. She would walk on Vladimir, but that's as deep as her relationship would go.

"Darlings," he said. "We will find the Oprichnik by ourself." He wouldn't talk Russian any more, not to his aunts, not to Uncle Izak, who only understood the dialect of clowns. Izak could make his circus anywhere. Inside a truck, or on the sand. Sure, they missed Moscow. Who wouldn't? They were Russians, like Vladimir and that miserable Oprichnik, even though Moscow considered them nothing but Yids with contaminated passports. *Jewish nationals.* Jesus, what if Samuel had wanted to become a KGB man? He couldn't with a "Jewish" passport. But Moscow trusted him with a Stradivarius. The son of bakers and clowns had been a prodigy at six, a national hero at nine. He took second place at the Tchaikovsky when he was fourteen. Second place! A pisshead like him. Had to let Samuil take special classes at the Moscow Conservatory. Finland asked to borrow little Davidoff. The Ministry of Culture said no. Wouldn't let the pisser out of their sight. He toured the provinces. He was pampered. Given an apartment with his aunts near Red Army Street. No more communal toilets for little Davidoff. He could piss in peace. Shop at special stores, with cosmonauts and generals. Zoya and Adelina shared his allowance of rubles. Uncle Izak was resurrected as a "hero clown." But Samuil enjoyed his fiddling less and less. He was favored to win the next Tchaikovsky. And then there would be tours in Poland, Finland, France.

Samuil thought of his uncle, Stalin's clown. Izak was restless. He wanted to see the world. So Samuil trotted to the office of visas and registration and stood in line. The clerks laughed at him. What could little Davidoff want with an exit visa? Him, without a sponsor in Israel or his parents' permission. He didn't need parents. He had his uncle and his aunts, and he could produce some Davidoffs in the Sinai to sponsor him.

The clerks wouldn't accept his signature. A house Jew from the Ministry of Culture visited him and slapped his own fists on the Davidoff kitchen table. "Suicide," he said. "A golden career. Is that something to piss away?" But Samuil showed up at the office of visas with Izak and his aunts. He had documents from Israel. The clerks couldn't ignore him now. Samuil Davidoff, *second* in the Tchaikovsky competition, had applied for a visa. All his tours were canceled. A commissar arrived to collect his Stradivarius and return it to the State. He lost his private toilet. The Davidoffs were shoved into a communal apartment on the Warsaw Road. Not one neighbor said hello. The family could only piss at a certain hour. They stopped taking baths. The Ministry of Culture sent him a student violin. He was ordered to play at hospitals and workers' cafeterias and assigned to the restaurant at the House of Writers, where he scraped gypsy songs in the lull between caviar and whitefish. He sat in the Lubyanka and listened to the fat man, Konstantin, who looked terribly unorthodox, wearing a sweater under the blue shoulder boards of the KGB.

"Samuil Mikhailovich, we could send your old uncle into an asylum."

"He would welcome it," Samuil said. "Asylums can always use a clown."

"And your aunts? Will they prosper in a labor camp?"

"Why not? They'll find husbands while they're mixing cement."

"And where shall we put you?"

"How should I know, comrade colonel?" Samuil had no idea if the fat man was a colonel or not. He'd never introduced himself. But that's how Samuil read the shoulder boards.

The KGB never harmed his uncle. Were they a little bit in awe of Stalin's favorite clown? And there was nothing in the Soviet Constitution that said a refusenik's aunts had to suffer in a labor camp. Samuil fiddled at the House of Writers for three years. The Tchaikovsky went to an imbecile from Tashkent. The imbecile appeared on Soviet television. Another wonder child. Then, one night, Samuil was pulled out of bed and put on a plane with his uncle and his aunts.

And now he had Brighton Beach. It was Adelina who drove the truck. She took them across the Manhattan Bridge while Zoya rocked herself to sleep. Skylines couldn't appeal to Zoya. Samuil stared at the Brooklyn waterfront through the pipes of the bridge. Manhattan was a city of scars. But Brooklyn was his Moscow. And he was always pleased when his aunt drove into the heart of the borough. She took the back streets. Adelina hated highways.

They got to Brooklyn's southern lip, that spike of land between Coney Island point and the back fields of Oriental Boulevard. The fiddler didn't feel right. He was the first to taste the smoke rising over Brightwater Court. Adelina parked the truck and the Davidoffs tried to walk to their apartment house. The street was cluttered with fire trucks. Odessans stood on the boardwalk and watched the Davidoffs' minaret dissolve into smoke. The family apartment was on fire. Samuil couldn't even get upstairs to save whatever heirlooms the Davidoffs had. Policeniks stood in the way. He retreated to the boardwalk and that's when he saw Captain Jonah eating an ice-cream pop.

"Comrade," Samuil said. "Who set us on fire?"

"I did."

Samuil's jaws shivered as Jonah licked the pop.

"Had to," Jonah said. "Or your people would have been zippered up."

"Please. What is to zipper up?"

"Some mothers were inside your apartment. It was a trap. They would have totaled each of you as you walked into the living room."

"Is KGB?"

"Kiddo, I saw their faces in the window. That was enough. So I dropped a little kerosene flag from the roof. Two of them. The mothers didn't have a chance."

"How you know they came to kill?"

"I know," the captain said. "Knowing is a big part of my business. They would have totaled your family. Take it from me."

Four men were carried down. Samuil recognized them under their burnt scalps. Four *shpiks*. Spies from the Tashkent. He couldn't believe they would have murdered his aunts. But what were they doing in the Davidoff apartment?

"It was Konstantin," Samuil said. "He hired them."

"Konstantin doesn't have the balls."

"He is assassin for KGB."

"That's the whole point," the captain said. "Would the KGB let him goose a family right near a public beach?"

"Then who is paying them?"

"Someone who wants you out of Alphabetville."

"Is Saigon Sarah?"

"Hell, no. She's a pockmarked bitch. But you keep an eye on her. Because she could have a rotten apple in her talmud torah . . . like that dancer, King George. You stop him if he tries to stroll uptown."

"But what does dancer have to do with the Tashkent?"

"I'll figure that out," the captain said, swallowing his ice-cream pop. "Gotta go." And he drifted away from the boardwalk.

Diaghilev, Samuil sang under his throat. This captain was another Diaghilev. He liked to stage productions. But Samuil wasn't Jonah's Nijinsky. Samuil wouldn't jump.

6

SARAH couldn't sleep. She sat downstairs under that bridal canopy, thinking of her fate. She was just another war widow, only she'd been widowed without ever making a marriage knot. Biedersbill had come back home to her like a Halloween character that was meant to scare.

Sarah looked up and found she had some company. That old captain of hers from the Nam was sitting in one of the chairs. Jonah Slyke. Captain had his own key to the talmud torah.

"Marve's been uptown, sis. He walked right in on Lliana and me. I can't afford to have that happen again. Lliana's jumpy. If I lose her, sis, the talmud torah will have to pay."

She hadn't been wrong about the Teach. Old Biedersbill must have taken Marve off the black candy.

"I'll make it up to you, captain. Marve won't go waltzing again."

"Uncle Albert doesn't want Marvin dancing at all. The Hebrew school was supposed to be quiet."

"What if it isn't? Uncle can raise our rent."

"He doesn't charge you rent. He allows you to sit with your shellshocked soldiers. But in ten years, when Wall Street travels to Indian country, you'll have a new Stock Exchange where the talmud torah is."

"You're crazy."

"So crazy that real estate has been climbing at a three-hundred-percent clip."

"Damn speculators," Saigon said. "Buying all the Alphabet Blocks. Teacher will blow up your Stock Exchange the minute it moves in."

"I wouldn't bet on that, sis."

"Well, why doesn't Uncle throw us out?"

"He's not antisocial. But he's recommending you shut the cabaret."

Jonah began to sniff at the stairs. His eyes grew thin in his head.

"Captain, how come you're so interested in my stairs?"

"I'm watching for Marve. He was my roommate, remember? Marve likes to walk in his sleep."

Jonah got up and Saigon accompanied him to the door. He kissed her on the mouth. Sarah got chagrined. Why hadn't he kissed her in the Nam when it might have mattered?

"Good-bye, sis."

Sarah marched upstairs to her squatters' den. She saw a light on in the little bitch's room. Lulu was painting her legs. Did a lady giant with long green hair down into the hollow of her anklebone.

"Don't you believe in knocking, mama-san?"

It was as if she'd been caught peeing on somebody's floor.

Saigon stepped forward half a foot. She was only trying to protect the bitch.

"Sarah, you're not welcome in my room."

The little bitch had peculiar ideas about property.

"I suppose you've been paying a whole lot of rent, baby-san."

"I'm a squatter," the girl said. "A squatter like you."

"Well, there's all kinds of squatters in this world, ones that work and ones that paint up their legs."

"I could move out if you're unhappy."

"Wouldn't dream of it. Your Uncle Marve would eat me alive."

"He's not my uncle, and leave him out of it."

Saigon couldn't win an argument with that little bitch. She walked into her own room, which was smaller than Lulu's and looked out onto a shaft. She preferred spider webs and dark spaces. Had a household of wrecks to support. It was like the Nam, only these wrecks were worse.

She was bitter about Biedersbill. He took a bride in the Nam, some mountain girl named Hélène, and he'd never told her. She could have gone to a marriage lawyer and sued the pants off Biedersbill. Fiancés weren't supposed to have jungle wives. But she couldn't hurl Teach onto the public record. He was an outlaw, same as Sarah. And the goddamn Pentagon would have come down on their tail.

Was he a collector or not? Teach hid Renata's painting inside the ratholes in his wall. He'd lost interest in her rendering of smoke over Alphabetville. She could stuff her New Wave into Capablanca's hat. Teach was returning to Vincent Van Gogh.

He loved the trees Van Gogh drew from his insane asylum. Sometimes, when he licked his black candy, Teach could understand why Vincent cut off an ear. It was that merciless pressure of being alive.

He felt forlorn without the supermarkets. He enjoyed collecting from coca princes. But there wasn't a prince to be found. He wished the government of Bolivia would start to fall, so the generals could come back, and there'd be enough coca leaves to go around. Alphabetville had become a tomb.

Teach bought a Hershey bar to swallow with the poison he ate, because chocolate was good with black candy. But he didn't have a chance to swallow. Capa's baby bandits rushed out of an alley with their Brazilian Colts. They'd grown tiny hairs on their chins since he'd last seen them. Mierda, he didn't have his blasting caps. It was high noon in Alphabetville and the infants were aiming at his ass. Doors shut around him. The bottle clubs and bodegas didn't want an interview with Capa's hitmen. But it still seemed crazy to the Teach. Capa must have talked to Uncle, and Uncle knew. Teach wouldn't poison Capa's cousin. So why were the banditos behaving like Buffalo Bill? The little mothers almost nicked his ear. He was lucky Brazil couldn't make much of a Colt. Teach did his zigzag run, hopped along the dead bricks, hearing guns burp against building walls, and thinking, oh my God, it was choppers and Charlie Cong, and war over Avenue C. But Teach had the best evade in the business. Duck and run.

He hauled his ass out of Alphabetville. He visited Capa's Ukrainian coffee shop, but the Bolivians weren't there. Went to the finca on Lafayette. He didn't have the code that would open Capa's door. He pressed random numbers on the code box. It was like choosing Chiclets. The door opened without the slightest electrical sweep. Teach hadn't found the code. The door was open all the time.

He was cautious on the stairs. Capablanca was capable of all kinds of shit. But Teach had no trouble with the upstairs door. He turned the knob and entered the finca. The landscape was calm. No one had molested Capablanca's books, but his generals were lying on the floor. Their bodies formed a ragged circle. Renata was with them. Her legs weren't so clean. They were turning blue. Ah, the whole goddamn corporation had eaten poison. Teach knew that crumpled mark around the eye, the first bewilderment of poison in the blood. Their hands were bunched into a fist. It was the old desire to fight. But they must have fallen after a step or two. Some magician had been up these stairs. The generals wouldn't have been taken by surprise. They'd never drink with a stranger. Teach couldn't recall another magician, unless it was George. And how did George collect a two-day pass from his concentration camp?

That was riddle number one. And where the hell was Capablanca? Teach had corpses to consider. He couldn't use Renata's disposal service. Renata wasn't alive. And he didn't know how to dial a Russian taxicab. He left the corpses and returned to the street and reached Uncle from a pay phone. He didn't chat much. It was all commando gobbledygook.

"Sunshine," he said into the telephone.

Uncle Albert arrived in fifteen minutes. *Sunshine* was their word for a crash dive in command. It meant Teach couldn't make do on his own.

Uncle whistled at the bodies on Capablanca's floor.

"Albert," Teacher said. "Is there some superagency in on this? I want to know. Did they smuggle King George onto the Concorde to do this job?"

"It wasn't George," Uncle said. "George is rotting with his tribe."

"Was it Henry Kissinger? I know he threw us out of Nam. But could he reach this far?"

"Kissinger has no time for corpses. He's writing books."

"Then tell me about the mothers who are stealing my M.O?"

"I'd say someone's been dogging our tracks."

"The Russkis?"

"I doubt it. We're freelancers, Howard. It could be anybody. A special branch within the FBI. Some section in the air force intelligence arm. It's catch-as-catch-can in this sort of game."

"What should we do?"

"Bury Capa's people and wait."

"But the Colombians will come in and establish their own supermarkets."

"Don't worry. We'll tell Jonah to put the narcs on Colombia's tail."

"Jonah's not that reliable now . . . he's flipped over Marvey's wife."

"But he still plays paddleball with the FBI. That's what counts. We're only renegades, Howard. A private army can't do that much."

Teach began to pick at his scalp. "Uncle, who's been buying up your army? Somebody asked you to send Lubbock and Kroll into the Bolivian veldt."

"Told you before. It's a secret."

"Well, I can't soldier with secrets like that."

Uncle looked at him. "I was doing a special favor for the Drug Enforcement boys. But we were also helping ourselves. Couldn't have prospered much longer without the generals."

"Uncle, the generals are dead."

"These were Capa's cousins. We have plenty more."

"And where's Capablanca?"

"Howard, he'll surface again. Capa's indestructable. He could be leading a coup."

"Against Bolivia . . . or our boys?"

"Both," the padre said with a smile. Ah, his face warmed, and Teach had his old Uncle back.

"Should I help you carry the generals into the hall?"

"Thank you, Howard, but Lubbock's my undertaker. We'll

leave the sorry work to him. I have something else. A fool's errand . . . for Carlo. He has to hunt down an author, and I'd like you to go along. He's too old to chase authors by himself. The man's a prick, but he's still my brother."

"Who's he chasing?"

"Some Yid poet from Brighton Beach. The poet used to free-lance for the KGB. Swears he has stories to sell. About the Lu-byanka. Carlo's a sucker for Lubyanka stories. I think the poet is trying to scratch him for a bundle of bread. A swindler, but I don't want Carlo to ride the subways alone."

"Uncle, I could borrow Sarah's limousine and deliver your brother in style."

"He's stubborn, Howard. Been riding subways for sixty years. Humor him, that's all. And if the poet tries something funny, well, you know what to do. Make sure Carlo comes home with his wallet. I'm not so fond of Brighton Beach. The Russians aren't into charity. They send their Jewish hoodlums to us, dis-guised as poets."

"But the Davidoff kid is a violinist."

"That's what I mean. The hoodlums all have an artistic cover."

"And Konstantin? What about him?"

"He's not from Brighton Beach. Concentrate on Carlo's poet. I don't want my brother victimized just because he's desperate for books."

Albert scribbled Carlo's business address, and Teacher walked to Union Square. He had to stand in a vestibule while a secretary announced him to Carlo. Teach looked at the walls of Gallatin & Peck. There were about thirty photographs, all of them signed to Carlo himself, but Teach could only recognize Dashiell Ham-mett. Ah, it was like being in the same room with the Thin Man. But Teach couldn't find a photograph of Henry James. The master must have died before Carlo started his publishing house.

The old man came out to greet him in a white suit.

135

"I'm embarrassed," Carlo said. "Albert thinks I ought to have a nurse."

"It's routine, sir. Brighton Beach is a bad place."

"What's so bad about a bunch of Jewish émigrés?"

"Nothing, sir. But the Russkis have been borrowing it as a playground for their spies."

"That's exactly what we have to find out, Mr. Biedersbill."

They took a cab to the D train. Carlo had a little purse of subway tokens. They sat on the train and rode to the end of the line, while the 'D' crept out of doors in Brooklyn and Teach could swear he'd gone to the country. The stations had trees on their roofs. Teach was troubled about something. He liked Dashiell Hammett. Hammett was next in line, after Henry James.

"Can you tell me, sir, why Mr. Hammett stopped writing? Wasn't even forty when he finished *The Thin Man.*"

"But the compulsion was gone. He was tired of stories and words. You can feel that in Nick and Nora Charles. They're loafers, really. Crime just happens to fall into their lap."

"That's not so unusual," the Teacher said, and Carlo started to laugh. They climbed down off the elevated station to Brighton Beach Avenue, a bazaar of stores under the tracks, with signs in Russian and English announcing denture clinics and different rye breads. Teach followed the old man and peeked from store to store. It was fish in the window, black muffins, breads rolled into a thousand braids, like the hair of some Russki goddess. Carlo and Teach were the tallest men around. Russkis were a shorter race. Might have suffered without homogenized milk.

The old man entered some nightclub-café called the Brown Bear, which had its own Rasputin, a singer with a beard and peasant shirt. The Brown Bear was packed with little men and women who wore leather and high heels, like the Davidoffs. The tables at the Brown Bear were concentrated in two long rows. Russians liked to eat on top of each other. Wasn't an inch between the tables. Rasputin scowled at the two tall men.

No waitress arrived to seat them, so they sat themselves opposite a man who seemed drained of blood. It was Carlo's poet, Nika Nikolayevich Troubnoy. Had he gone through Nam? His twitch was worse than the Teach's. His fingers were brown. He liked to roll tobacco in his hand. He'd light a cigarette, puff at it once, and then tear at the paper, as if he were skinning a live animal. That was Nika Nikolayevich Troubnoy. He had all the dark devices of a poet, the twitch, the brown fingers, bloodless eyes, but Teach could have sworn that this Troubnoy had never scribbled a line. He was too much the poet to bother about poetry.

Teach wanted to warn the old man. Watch this mother. But he was in a bind, because a publisher needed books. Why shouldn't Carlo have come to meet Troubnoy and listen to his tale?

But Troubnoy didn't talk much. He was into eating. Rasputin himself brought the poet chopped herring, red caviar in a sandwich, a stuffed chicken neck, magic borscht that was blue one minute and green the next. Troubnoy washed his food with gulps of vodka, which he drank with radishes and cucumbers on the side. He offered nothing to Carlo and the Teach. He burped at the end of the meal and nibbled on the tobacco in his hand.

"I will expect meaningful advance," he said to Carlo. "Seven thousand on signing, seven on delivery of manuscript, and seven on publication. I can't consult Solzhenitsyn, because Nobelniks don't talk with Brighton Beach, but my terms are fair. And no option clause. I am interested in only one book."

"Mr. Troubnoy," Carlo said, "why did you come to me?"

"Gallatin & Peck is distinguished publisher, no? And I am my own business agent. I start at the top."

"It's premature," Carlo said. "You talk dollars without a word of your book. What ever have you written, Mr. Troubnoy?"

"Twenty-five articles on symbolist movement. But that was only a rehearsal for my book on KGB."

"And your poetry?" Carlo asked.

"Sits unpublished. I was an outcast at Writers' Union."

"But do you have a sample I can show to some Russian expert? None of my people has ever heard of a Nikolayevich Troubnoy, not even in samizdat."

"Good reason to remain obscure in Soviet Union, Mr. Gallatin."

"I'm Peck," Carlo said. "Gallatin died ten years ago."

"I am sorry to hear. But KGB has gone into samizdat business. They distribute their own manuscripts and then arrest all the readers. I keep my poetry in my head."

"Fine, fine," Carlo said. "But how does that help us?"

"Is your editor?" Troubnoy said, looking at the Teach.

"No. He's my escort, Mr. Biedersbill. But you're safe around him. Now will you give us some facts, man? I didn't come to Brooklyn to dicker over the size of an advance. You'll have your first seven thousand if I feel there's a book."

Troubnoy ordered another round of appetizers and asked Carlo to join him, but not the Teach.

"Mr. Troubnoy," Carlo said. "I am in a rush. And it's hard to operate in the middle of your sandwiches."

Troubnoy abandoned the red caviar. But he seemed at such a loss, Carlo allowed him to finish eating again. His head wobbled from the vodka he drank.

"Banditov," he muttered.

"What? Mr. Troubnoy, I don't understand."

"KGB. We call them Banditov."

"We're not compiling a glossary," Carlo said. "I need some facts."

"The Banditov assigned an overlord to Brighton Beach, not one of their regular case workers, but a lone wolf. Dmitri Konstantinovich Rudin. He goes by twenty, thirty names. He had his own assassination bureau, but now is much more diversified. Konstantinovich has evolved into a higher type. He travels, he buys and sells for the Banditov, and he has informers on a leash."

"Come to the point," Carlo said. "Your Konstantinovich sounds like a minuscule James Bond."

"But is a difference. Moscow is not Her Majesty's Secret Service. And Konstantinovich is also America's man."

"Did you lure me out here just to tell me that the dictator of Brighton Beach is a double agent?"

"But not an ordinary double. He sells cocaine for Moscow and the CIA. Is curious, no? An agent who is his own entrepreneur. Moscow feeds him. America feeds him. Why, Mr. Peck, why?"

Ah, Teach said to himself. Nika Nikolayevich Troubnoy was a candidate for Uncle's farm in New Jersey. Sooner or later Teach would have to kidnap him. The poet knew a little too much about Konstantin's affairs. What if Carlo discovered that Konstantin was married to Uncle Al? Now it made sense. Albert wasn't protecting his brother. He was covering his ass. He'd sent Teach on the D train to sniff this canary.

Carlo scratched his nose. "What is it you're telling me, Mr. Troubnoy?"

"Konstantinovich is oversubscribed. Has too many sponsors." Troubnoy closed one eye. "Gentlemen, I think the White House is protecting him."

Carlo grabbed Teach's arm. "Mr. Biedersbill, am I growing dim? This man is suggesting that a grubby little Moscow spy-handler is Ronald Reagan's pal. And I'm supposed to offer him a book contract. Come on. We're wasting our time."

Teach would have liked to ask the poet a couple more questions. Troubnoy was onto something. Because how the hell did Konstantin become such a cavalier? But Carlo was finished with Troubnoy.

"Please, Mr. Peck. If you say a document on Konstantinovich is no good, what about a novel?"

But Carlo had already stood up. "Novels about moles in America wouldn't sell."

Troubnoy had a fever in his eye. He'd lost his fat advance. "But is not a mole, Mr. Peck. Konstantinovich is out in the open."

"Good-bye," Carlo said. And Teach went out the door with him, past Rasputin, past the red caviar and the magic borscht, while Troubnoy consoled himself with vodka. He'd dreamt so hard of his fat advance. He'd have to find another book baron like Gallatin & Peck. Troubnoy was Konstantin's *shpik*. He spied on Brighton Beach, but he'd become a known quantity. So he had to sell information back to the Beachniks, or he couldn't have kept himself in vodka. But how long would Konstantin tolerate Troubnoy's splintered loyalties? He had to make a killing fast. A book contract. And then the Johnny Carson show. He ordered radishes with sour cream and then choked on a radish. Troubnoy had another guest. Little Davidoff.

"Eat, eat," Samuil said.

But Davidoff depressed him. Should have made a fortune on the child. Hadn't he offered to become Samuil's agent in America? Troubnoy could have booked Carnegie Hall. A refusenik violinist was always in demand. But Samuil wouldn't even consider him as an agent. Troubnoy tried to threaten him with a gun. He was almost a KGB man, no? But Samuil's aunts started pulling out his hair under the boardwalk, and Troubnoy buried his gun in the sand.

Samuil took a radish and dug it into Troubnoy's sour cream. He'd been sitting at the far end of the Brown Bear, which was as close to a Moscow café as he could have in a village of Odessans. He was thinking of his family's seven rooms. The Davidoffs had found a temporary flat behind the bakery, on Brighton Sixth, but Samuil didn't intend to lose his minaret. He'd come to the Brown Bear for pickled eggplant and had noticed Biedersbill and another man talking to Nika, the prize *shpik*. It was Nika who'd denounced Vladimir to the Davidoffs for a hundred dollars cash.

"Nika, who was that old man?" Samuil said, biting into the radish.

"The commandant of Gallatin & Peck."

"Does Gallatin & Peck manufacture machine guns?"

"Samuil Mikhailovich—"

"Nika, we don't need patronymic. We are Brighton Beach."

"Pardon, Samuil," Troubnoy said, bowing so that his head scraped the radishes and kissed the sour cream. "Pardon, but Gallatin & Peck is distinguished publisher."

"That old man looks like a colonel from KGB."

"He is publisher of American history books. Is laughable what you say."

"And why does such important personage stop at your table?"

"Because I am writing a book," Troubnoy said, beating on the tablecloth with his fist. "Yes, Nika Nikolayevich is writing a book."

"A book," Samuil said. "And tell me subject? Your life as a *shpik*?"

"No," Troubnoy said. "Dmitri Konstantinovich Rudin and the White House."

Samuil reached across the radishes to take Troubnoy by the throat. "I pity you, Nika, if you advertise such a fable and Konstantin runs away. I pity your health. I pity your hair. I pity the radishes in your mouth."

"But I have right to earn my living," Troubnoy said, red fingermarks appearing on his throat. He started to cough. Rasputin arrived.

"Go away," Samuil said, and the bearded man left. Troubnoy was worse than a *shpik*. He was a failed financier. Tried to exploit the Moscow housing market. Russia's only real estate broker. He'd bribe clerks at the housing office and smuggle people into communal apartments until the KGB got hold of Troubnoy and tossed him into the Lubyanka and he became Konstantin's pet spy.

Samuil relinquished Troubnoy's throat. "Nika, give up literary ambition."

"I can't," Troubnoy said. "I have wife. Two sons."

"Better they should mourn you while you still alive. You will work for us."

"Nika Nikolayevich in a bakery? Never."

"Tomorrow at six in the morning. Nika, don't be late."

And Samuil returned to his platter of pickled eggplant. He was opening a charity clinic for Nika. But it was easier to have him in the bakery where he could watch Nika's moves than let him peddle his wares to American publishers like dirty Russian laundry.

Rasputin started to sing and Samuil couldn't digest his eggplant. He removed the Brown Bear's mandolin from the wall and scratched on it to drown that voice of a bullfrog. Rasputin croaked louder and louder, but he couldn't compete with a music box in little Davidoff's hands. He had to give up, and then with a sudden turn, Samuil twisted a melody out of the mandolin. It was Schubert, and he hadn't even planned to play.

"Little Davidoff," patrons cried.

Even Nika Nikolayevich Troubnoy was happy until he remembered the fortune he might have made on little Davidoff. And then he groaned into his empty plate, and his voice was sadder than Schubert, sadder than the Kremlin walls, almost as sad as the Lubyanka itself, that fortress of infinite rooms and guests, where Nika had lived nine months, not like a criminal, because no one had charged him of anything, but like an honored guest of the KGB. Nika understood the criminal codes. To profiteer in housing was punishable by death. But not one State prosecutor visited him inside the Lubyanka. Here, Nika realized, he was immune to Moscow. He had zakuski in his cell: caviar and jellied chicken. His cell wasn't even locked. He could roam the corridors, kibitz like a bird, play chess with some "nephew" of Boris Spassky. He met Hungarian revoltniks who hadn't seen sunshine or a cow in twenty years. He was free to hold dialogues with them. He danced with troubleniks from Stalin's time, poets who should have been dead. They had soup together, and Nika winked at his friends. The Lubyanka wasn't so bad. It's true, we're never near a window. And the *Pravda* they give us to wipe our ass is six months old. But it's a life, no? And then Nika Nikolayevich blubbered in his cell. It was suddenly important for him to see a cow again. He didn't want to chat with revoltniks, or poets who'd already disappeared. Zakuski wasn't enough. And that's when Konstantinovich appeared, walked into Nika's cell, whistled a song from the Beatles. And Nika knew in his groin that he'd always been this man's *shpik*. Why couldn't he have told this to the book baron? Was it fear that the Banditov would snatch him up and hurl him into the Lubyanka for keeps? To hell with advances and the Johnny Carson Show. Nika Nikolayevich would hold his scriptures inside his head.

LOOKING FOR HENRY JAMES

BECAUSE there's nothing in space, no other humans around. Black holes, stars in a sea of gas. Not a hint of Flash Gordon in the sky. The Blade Runner will never get to Mars.

We're all we've got. Children fighting an endless cannibal war. Should have remained rock apes. Apes can't do Shakespeare. They're good for eating berries.

Been wounding people since I was nineteen. Nam was our junior college. And all the mothers think it was a tennis match between gooks and grunts. Gooks were the least of it. Uncle could have taken his gig to Guatemala. He brought

Guatemala to Alphabetville. We dance around with old Konstantin, but we're not the Kremlin's people. We were part of Saigon Station once upon a time, had a seat in the Chancery until Kissinger threw us out. The padre had to develop on his own. And when Jimmy Connors plays Andrei Gromyko at Wimbledon, we'll be there, sitting in the queen's box.

Gromyko will have to drink oxygen after each set. When he arrives at match point, we'll jump out of the queen's box and declare ourselves champions of the field. Padre will wear the crown at Wimbledon. We'll kidnap the queen and hold her in some lost cricket ground. She can eat to her heart's desire. Padre will put Lady Di on the throne. We'll want a glamorous mama to head up our agency.

Why not bring Di to Alphabetville? Because the padre is loyal to Henry James. And London is where Henry established himself. For love of Henry we'll learn to be Brits. I'll seize a home in Belgravia and capture a girl to my liking, plant my dinglebell in her thighs and prove I'm not as impotent as Henry James. But I'll miss Saigon while I'm rutting the little lady. And I'll wonder who's kissing her now.

Snippens, I'll tell the little lady. You're my dove. But a lad like me can only give his dingle once. I've retired from all that love business. I'm keeper of the padre's seal. I deliver his justice. I'm the lord executioner of his little realm. I've smothered people for his sake, poisoned them, planted bombs under their feet. We're desperadoes, and we've always been, even when we rode for the CIA.

Our hearts belong to Lady Di, but Lord knows where we'll ride tomorrow. The Kremlin, or downtown Hanoi. You can't rest much when you're Uncle Albert's little man.

—Biedersbill

7

HE could hear them arguing. It was about Marve and his blonde wife. Teach stood behind the door. It was his fault. He'd reduced Marve's dosage of black candy. And now Jonah was angry, because Marve had come back to haunt Murray Hill.

"Uncle," Jonah said. "If I lose Lliana, I'll throw some trouble into your paradise. Lliana will discover things about her guru."

"Lliana wouldn't believe you. And it's not very brilliant to threaten your old college prof."

"Don't confuse me with the Teach. I'm not a hairbrain. I have enough documents in my closet to send a heap of governments down on your tail. Some folks might call you a treasonable prick."

"And what would they call you?"

"A lawyer who's done a little fancy bargaining for himself."

"Yes, with all the government boys. You're quite the free-lancer. But you've been straying from your regular course. Brighton Beach isn't your kingdom, Jonah. Why did you interfere with the Davidoffs and burn their castle?"

"I run the Davidoffs, dad. They do little favors for me. Didn't want them totaled by some dummies from Odessa who happen to work for the KGB."

"So you got the feds to tap all the lines in Brighton Beach, and now you're Samuil's magician . . . fancy work." There was a pause and then Uncle said, "What documents would you have in your closet, fancy man?"

"Notes I've taken. About you and your Russian friend."

"Ah, Konstantin. But you've forgotten something, little son. Kostya was given to us by the Company. Not much of a Russian spy if he's monitored by our own children."

"Monitored, padre? He fucks both sides."

"That's the rewards of a double agent. You always get more than you give. Kostya's a businessman. And if you should chase him out of the country, he'll open shop somewhere else."

"Somewhere like Saigon?"

"Ho Chi Minh City. You ought to keep abreast of world affairs."

"Why? Ho town could be Stalingrad by tomorrow. The point is that your fat friend is flooding Saigon's black market with his fountain pens."

"What of it? He handles goods for the KGB."

"It's a lark," Jonah said. "You and the KGB in one corporation . . . Lliana, Uncle. That's all I want."

"It's not so easy. Can't keep Marve in Alphabetville all his life."

"Why not? He has a perfect little harem."

"You shouldn't have gone to Sarah without us. We'd have found a better way to mugger Marve. He's too visible with his dancing."

"I told you the dancing will stop. It's the Teacher. He gets it off, painting Marve in George's colors."

"I'll deal with Howard on my own. Now what will make you happy?"

"If Marve becomes a permanent settler in Alphabetville."

"Done," the padre said. "You should be less greedy and kiss your old prof."

Teacher giggled in the hall, imagining that kiss. He grew jealous. The padre had never asked him for a kiss. He was the scarecrow of this organization. Unkissable. He ducked into a linen closet and waited for Jonah to leave. Then he marched into the padre's living room at the hotel. Padre wore a pullover, like the Davidoffs. He had pinched cheeks. He was disappearing under his clothes.

"Ah, you just missed your captain," the padre said. But there was no embrace.

"Didn't miss him. I avoided the mother."

"He's cross with you. Thinks you've been stingy with your chemicals where Marvin is concerned."

"It's my privilege, Uncle."

"But he can't live without Lliana."

"That's his problem," Teacher said. He was beginning to twitch. Why couldn't he return Marve to the blonde cow? Marve had mucked long enough in the talmud torah.

"I suppose you're right," the padre said. "We'll have to send Jonah to the farm. He's becoming a bloody nuisance. Howard, did you hear him threaten me?"

"Uncle, that's not the only threat. You ought to worry about the poet of Brighton Beach."

Uncle's nostrils filled with air. "What poet?"

"Troubnoy, that author you sent me to meet."

"I'm not following you, Howard. I asked you to babysit with my brother."

"I did. But Carlo's author had a little romance with the KGB."

"Wonderful," the padre said. "Your poet is like half the people on the boardwalk."

"Ah, but he had a special romance with Konstantin. And if we're not careful, Uncle, this Troubnoy will lead your brother back to us."

"Carlo's not that clever. And if Troubnoy's stuff is incriminating, we'll rifle his book out of Carlo's office. My brother will never miss it. He's gone a little senile."

"Like Marvin de la Mare . . . Carlo wasn't interested in Troubnoy's book. But what if that caviar boy goes to another publisher?"

"We'll deal with him, Howard. But Jonah comes first. He can touch us more than any Yid poet."

Old fat eyes came out of the bedroom in apricot-colored pants. Konstantin, the Russian CIA man. Went around the world looking for clothes. Fat eyes made his fortune in coca leaves and fountain pens. But Bolivia had gone dry, and now pens were his particular gold. He was fond of that black beauty called Mont Blanc, the most expensive little mother in the world. Always had one in his breast pocket, with a white star on its skull. Teach had first met fat eyes in the Nam. But that was in the days before fountain pens. Renata had a Mont Blanc before she died. But Teach hadn't noticed it on her corpse. He wondered who had picked her pen.

Konstantin smiled. "Troubnoy's a worm. If he ever writes a book, it will be the memoirs of the bullfrog he had as a boy. But we shouldn't be rash about Jonah. Jonah's valuable to us."

"He'll be more valuable on the farm," Uncle said.

"And what should we do with this Lliana lady? Two men disappearing on her. She'll run to the police."

"No," Albert said. "She'll run to me. Lliana depends on her old padre. We'll find an excuse. We'll say Jonah skipped with some of our funds. She won't cry with Marve in her bed . . . Kostya, we can't have Jonah making threats. He'll start dictating terms to us. Howard will handle him."

"Howard and Vladimir," fat eyes said.

"Why bring Vladi into it? Howard is more than enough."

"Vladimir's my insurance," Konstantin said with a grin. But Teach didn't know what fat eyes had to grin about. He couldn't go into the street. Even a fountain pen with a white star couldn't save him. He had pocks in his head from that beebee gun of Samuil's. He'd have as many pits as Sarah if he didn't watch out. And Teach might fall in love with Konstantin's complexion.

"Howard, you'll go with Vladimir," the padre said. "You'll burn all the material in Jonah's office and then you'll escort him to the farm. Nothing rough. I want him with both his cheeks. And you're not to grab him while Lliana is around."

"Uncle, would I let a blonde cow catch me with a man?"

"She's not a cow," the padre said.

"Uncle, it's just an expression."

Teach couldn't take his eyes away from the white skull of Konstantin's pen. Konstantin smiled. "How are you, Henry James?"

"Fat as a Mont Blanc pen," Teach said. "Ever look at the beebees in your face?"

"Stop that," the padre said.

"Uncle, let him talk. Teacher always amuses me."

"What's the weather like in Ho Chi Minh?"

"You've been there, Henry James."

"Ah, I thought the monsoons might shift with Russians around. Do you sell a lot of pens outside the old cathedral?"

Konstantin laughed. "I sell mostly to bush mamas, like Hélène. You remember Hélène, don't you, little man?"

"That's enough," the padre said.

153

Teacher leaned across Konstantin's chest. "I'll kill you one of these days."

"No you won't. You'd worry about Vladi's sisters. You're the perfect soldier."

"Stop it, I said," the padre growled and Teach began to pull shrapnel out of his hair. He always pulled shrapnel around Konstantin.

His twitch got worse. He left the padre's rooms and pulled shrapnel in the elevator. He started remembering Hélène, the montagnard princess who'd once been his mountain wife. Teach had slept a hammock away from her in the hills . . . . Took his twitching body into the street. He thought of Henry James in Manhattan a hundred years ago and the twitching stopped.

He stole Sarah's white limousine from Neck and borrowed Vladimir. Vladi was his best friend in Manhattan, but they hardly ever spoke. Vladi had three sisters in Leningrad and he shoveled dirt for the KGB on account of them. Might as well have been a dead man. He didn't have a passion for ice cream like everyone else in the talmud torah. He wouldn't take a mistress off the street. He never counted his money. Sarah could have cheated him blind. Vladimir existed in some frozen land where money and ice cream didn't matter.

They broke into the captain's law office with one of Vladimir's tricks. He ripped the door out of the wall and carried it into the office. Teach couldn't take a chance. He listened for bombs with the tits of his stethoscope. Teach uncovered nothing with his tits and Vladi stuffed Jonah's files into several trash bags. There were letters from Lliana, but Teach wouldn't read them.

They left Jonah's door near the windowsill, took the trash bags, and shoved them into the incinerator. Then they drove down to Murray Hill, got out of the white limousine, and waited for Jonah under an awning. He arrived with the blonde cow, and the Teach had to alter his appraisal of her. She was too long and skinny for a cow. Her ankles would have broken under

154

a cow's bulk. But she had the hair of a princess in one of Henry's novels. His face hurt from staring so hard. The corners of her mouth curled under. She had eyes like a hornet's sting. Now he understood Jonah. A man would have killed for the love of that slender cow.

She pressed into Jonah's ribs and laughed. "Darling," she said, "one little drink."

The captain hunched his shoulders. "I have work to do."

"At this hour? Darling, admit it. You're hiding a chippy in the paddleball club."

Teacher shivered when the cow said darling. He watched her pull Jonah into the lobby. He blew on his hands. He thought of kidnapping all the cow's men and leaving her inside an empty circle.

"Vladi, want an ice-cream soda? I think she'll keep him for the night."

The Teach had forgotten that Vladimir wasn't into ice cream. And it was lucky they hadn't abandoned their perch. Jonah came down in fifteen minutes.

Teach called out to him. "Lo, cap."

Jonah's ears tightened. He searched into the dark of the awning and smiled, recognizing the Teacher, but he couldn't see Vladimir.

"Did the padre send you, Teach?"

"Sort of."

"Are you going to cut my eyes out the montagnard way? I'd like to pick my own execution."

"Ah," the Teacher said. "Murray Hill isn't Vietnam."

Vladimir reached from under the awning and rapped Jonah once on the neck. Jonah's face crumpled like a sleeping child. Vladi saved him from falling until Teacher got the car. They folded him into the front and the captain slept in Vladimir's arms.

It was as neat an abduction as Howard could remember. They

155

whisked Jonah off Murray Hill without being discovered by a
soul, shepherded him into New Jersey and out to the padre's
farm, a manor-house with a hundred little porches, the Chanticleer, run by the Baroness de Roth, whose husband had been
a tea planter in Vietnam. The Chanticleer was a nursing home
with a few involuntary guests. Uncle didn't have to drown his
enemies. He had them doped up at the Chanticleer, a citadel
of quiet men. It was Howard who did the doping and prepared
dishes of montagnard candy. Each of the Chanticleer's nurses
was a graduate of the Nam who'd been attached to one of the
padre's experimental stations. The guards were former beanies.

It was like a regular homecoming for Teach at the Chanticleer.
But the nurses and the guards had never been his mates. He'd
been adopted by the Elephanters, montagnard magicians who
shrank from other people and wouldn't construct a village for
themselves. None of the Elephanters would have tolerated a room
at the Chanticleer.

Lubbock and Kroll, who'd been corporals together under the
padre, greeted him at the front gate.

"Hullo, Teach," Lubbock said. "How's life in Sarah's barn?"

"Not as dreary as laying eggs for the Baroness de Roth."

"You shouldn't badmouth the Baroness," said Kroll, who had
eyebrows that came together in a kiss of hair. "The old bird
will be eighty-five on Monday. Have a little respect . . . who's
that in the car?"

"The captain," Teacher said.

"I can see that," said Lubbock, rolling his eyes. "It's the other
fellow we're interested in."

"That's Vladimir," Teacher said.

And the two beanies started to chortle. "Lubbock," Kroll said.
"It's the Russian saint. He's been spying on the little Hebrews
of Brighton Beach. But the Hebes got rough and padre had to
rescue him."

"Ask the sucker if he'll dance for us," Lubbock said. "Dance
like a saint."

"Vladimir isn't into dancing," Teacher said. "Now go on. We've got work to do for Uncle Albert."

"I'll process the captain for you," said Lubbock, who'd served under Jonah in the Nam and didn't have the slightest pity for his old captain. The beanies couldn't forgive Jonah for having been a Dartmouth man. Lubbock and Kroll had come out of obscure circumstances, like the Teacher himself, and Jonah was nothing but a paddleball champ. He'd gone through the Nam in short pants.

"Aw," Kroll said with a kiss of his eyebrows. "Leave the captain with us. We won't stomp him more than once."

"Touch him, Kroll," the Teacher said, "and you'll make Uncle Albert cry. The captain was his very own student. They did Dartmouth together. Now go on."

Teacher drove up to the front porch and deposited Jonah with the head nurse, Simonson, who'd operated Uncle's nursing pool in the Nam. She'd gone from Danang to the Chanticleer without a glitch. She was a burly woman with a kind face and a few of Sarah's pockmarks. Teach had been her boyfriend once, before Sarah arrived in the Nam. She had a residual fondness for him. He'd make love to her while reciting Henry James. Teach knew she wouldn't harm the captain.

"Teacher, does he get the total cure, or just a bed rest?"

"Albert didn't say."

Teach was about to go with Vladimir when he saw a balding man with a gray beard strut in the parlor. He started to pull shrapnel out of his scalp until his hands were flecked with blood. "Who is that guy?"

"Don't bother with him," Simonson said. "He's not the padre's. He's a regular guest."

"Regular my ass," the Teacher said. "That's Henry James."

"Get out of here. He's Boris Spitalnick from North Bergen."

"It's Henry James."

That same man with the bald head had been dogging him for years.

"Hey grandpa, when did you finish *The Golden Bowl?*"

The man caressed his beard and looked more and more like Henry James.

"Why did you spend all those years on the New York Edition? Couldn't you have done a war novel?"

The man began to cry, and Teacher wondered if it was Henry James or some impostor who liked to pose as Henry and follow the Teacher from place to place.

"You shouldn't persecute me so much," the man said, doing a narrow dance on his toes, and the Teacher felt ashamed. He pulled a twenty-dollar bill from his wallet.

"Candy money," he said, but Simonson grabbed the bill away.

"We don't allow loose cash," she said, tucking the bill inside her uniform. "We'll put it toward Mr. Spitalnick's account."

Simonson always had good manners, even in Vietnam. He might have loved her a little if it hadn't been for old Saigon. He'd die loving Sarah.

Teach had a sudden wish to circumnavigate the Chanticleer's porches. Couldn't say why. Did he want to meet all the men he'd kidnapped? No, he had some weird intuition that he'd stumble onto a former friend. So he went around the porches until he discovered Capablanca sleeping in a deck chair without his Monte Cristo cape. He could tell by the even snores that Capa wasn't on a candy diet. It was just an ordinary vacation on the porch. Capa lay in one of the Chanticleer's long shirts. Teach took out a crayon from his pocket and scribbled *El Nobel* on Capa's forehead.

Capa woke up, saw the words on his forehead in the Chanticleer's window, and started to shake while Teach stood over the deck chair.

"Capa, do you still love your Gabito and his hundred years of solitude? Tell me, who's the greatest writer in the world?"

"Henry James."

The Teacher wiped Capa's forehead with his sleeve.

"Capa, how the fuck did you get to the farm?"

"I swear to Christ, it's Jonah's fault. He's the one who started the war. He's been stuffing us with narcs."

"So you ran to Uncle?"

"I had to beg. I kissed his heels. *Albert, I need a rest.*"

"But I work for Albert, remember? And you and your generals swore I poisoned Nibio. Weren't you afraid Uncle would feed you some of my candy?"

Capa rose out of his deck chair. "It wasn't you. That skunk Jonah hired the magician, King George."

"How could he do that? George is in a camp for montagnards."

"It doesn't matter. Jonah has his ways. He can reach right into Hanoi . . . I came home to the finca. I found my generales on the floor with Renata. What could I do?"

"Mourn. Wasn't Renata your own special lady?"

"Sometimes," Capablanca said. "I shared her with Uncle Albert. And I was running too hard to mourn."

"And now you're here in the comfort of Uncle's nest. But you have a neighbor."

"Who's that?" Capa asked, clutching the handles of his chair.

"Jonah Slyke."

Capa sank down, his buttocks forming a pear in the fabric.

"You don't have to fret," Teach told Capablanca. "He's unconscious. And Uncle's nurses will keep him like that. But you could be nice to Jonah and read him Henry James."

Teach returned to the limousine and drove off with Vladimir. He wasn't thinking of Capablanca or the padre's hundred porches. He couldn't get old Henry out of his head.

He'd gone through the first nineteen years of his life without Henry James. Celebrated his twentieth birthday in the brig at Long Binh. He was Howie Biedersbill and he wore his stethoscope at LBJ. He'd been a demolitions rat, removing gook mines from buildings, toilets, and roads. But he'd fought with his sergeant on the Rat Patrol, got into a booby-trap war with him, and the sergeant was killed while going into a toilet.

Howard didn't congregate with the normal flow of prisoners. He lived with undesirables like Neck, who'd been a turnscrew at LBJ until he strangled a soldier.

The undesirables were forgotten men who feasted on wormy rice and an occasional candy bar. Howard couldn't understand why this army chaplain, Albert Peck, would come to visit. It was the chaplain who brought the candy bars. A thin man with hollowed eyes. He lectured to the undesirables, sat in a narrow room with them, surrounded by chicken wire. The chaplain wore a gun and his boots were covered with jungle rot. He smelled like a grunt. He didn't bring them nudie calendars of Marilyn Monroe. He talked of Henry James.

No one fell asleep on Chaplain Peck. He told them of a man who remained a bachelor all his life, walking, bicycling, and scribbling notes to himself.

Howard needed Henry James. But the librarian was no help. LBJ hadn't discovered *The Princess Casamassima*. The chaplain had to smuggle in books for his pupils. Howard plagued him with questions on all the booby traps in *The Beast in the Jungle*.

"Where's the beast? The whole story is a tiger hunt that never happens."

"I don't get it," said Lubbock, who'd become a bank robber in Vietnam. "That's beyond my powers."

"What powers?"

Lubbock took a razor from his shoe and tried to slash at Biedersbill. But the chaplain kicked Lubbock into the wire mesh. "Howard's right. Henry James is the perfect commando. He practices evasion with purity of line."

Lubbock got interested all of a sudden. He smelled that Henry had something to do with war. *The Beast in the Jungle* was a textbook on counterinsurgency, Lubbock decided.

But Howard wasn't looking for military clues. When that chaplain couldn't come for a month, he began giving classes in Henry James. The undesirables flocked to Howard and called him Teach.

Lubbock kept his distance. "Teacher, that chaplain's a spy. He didn't come to educate us. He needs recruits."

"You're infantile," Teacher said. "The padre adores us."

"Do padres wear grenades in their belts? He's a spook."

"I'll kill you," Teacher said. "He wouldn't peddle his ass for the CIA and visit us with books."

"He's forming a special op to cancel the meanest cadre Charlie has."

"He's got nothing to do with Charles," said the Teach. But he couldn't understand why the undesirables were falling away from him. Neck, whom everyone despised because he'd been their own turnkey before he strangled some soldier in a jealous fit, Neck who sat with them in the deepest corners of the brig, had disappeared. Then Lubbock smiled and was gone. Then Percy, the millionaire's boy who couldn't stay out of trouble. Then Kroll. The Teach had an entire gallery to himself. But he missed having other murderers around.

Then a new man arrived, with gold studs in his ear and a dark streak under his eye. They'd sent him a montagnard, and it was like a monstrous joke to the Teach, because this montagnard was a practicing illiterate. He called himself King George and had delusions about his grandeur in Vietnam.

"Bow to me, motherfucker," he said to the Teach.

Teach could have bitten the studs off this montagnard's ear, but the little man might bleed to death, and Teach preferred having a companion at LBJ, even if it was a lunatic. So he bowed.

"Everything up to snuff, your majesty? Would you like a bit of straw in your quilt?"

"Shut up."

He tried reciting Henry James, but the montagnard leapt on him, and Teach had to apologize for breaking the silence.

George shivered and moaned at night, and Teach couldn't tell if it was malaria or mountain clap. No doctor would come for King George and it discouraged the Teach to hear all this moaning. He took that little man into his arms and rocked him. It felt peculiar, since the montagnard was taller than Teach.

"Stop that moaning, majesty. Teacher is here."

George never said thank you. He allowed the Teacher to rock him and then he'd fall asleep in the Teacher's arms.

"That's what I call friendship," Teacher muttered. "I'm nursey to this son of a bitch."

But the king left him soon and Teach shuddered against the wire walls until the screws came, beat him on the shoulders, stripped off his I.D., and tossed him out of LBJ. He was wearing prison fatigues. He had a few piastres in his pocket, enough for bubble gum. He might have wandered for a week, but a corporal from his old company found him, and he rode with the Rat Patrol into Saigon. Teach got off outside the American Mission.

Marines at the gate mocked his prison clothes. "Where'd you borrow those hand-me-downs?"

"From Chaplain Peck. He's with the spooks upstairs."

"Sorry, handsome. There's no Chaplain Peck on our roster."

"That's because the CIA stuck him in the fridge."

Teach crossed Thong Nhut Boulevard and entered Le Milk-bar Contretemps, where all the Long Noses used to take their coffee and croissants. But there weren't many Long Noses around. Saigon had been Nam's own little Paris during the reign of the Long Noses. Now the Long Noses themselves had gone out of style.

The chaplain entered the Contretemps in a blue cord suit and aviator glasses.

"Blue becomes you, padre . . . is that your preaching clothes?"

"Not at all. I'm the tutor to dependent children and embassy wives. I teach arithmetic, Spanish, French, and classics of the western world."

"Could I be in your class?"

"You've been to school with me, Howard. I gave you the best I have."

"But you stole all the other pupils, padre."

"Steal? I took over their contracts. The army leased them to me."

"What about King George?"

"He's my ablest pupil, Howard, after yourself."

"Then you've been growing morons, because I never heard of a king with the montagnards. I had to majesty that little mother, or he would have torn out my throat."

"But Howard, he is a king and a sorcerer. He's hoping to unite all the hill people under one flag."

"Then he's doomed to folly. The Yards can't agree on what to call red and blue. How's George going to tame them?"

"With my help," the padre said.

And Teach was suspicious. "Are you ever a chaplain?"

"Now and then."

"And the rest of the time you're a spook with Saigon Station. You have a wonderful cover, padre. Doing arithmetic in dark glasses."

"I'm not a CIA man, Howard. I'm on loan to the Company. Developing a nodule for Saigon Station."

"Is that old nodule something from Henry James?"

"You could call it that," said the padre. "It's a clump of ideas, too far out for the regular boys. I have my own war room at the Station, a closet really, but it's big enough for us. We're a different kind of commando, Howard. We conduct a war that runs counter to the war that's going on. We embrace whoever wins . . . and loses. We don't stop at any border. If we can

163

use the Cong, we'll fight on their side for a week, help them wax a band of Korean Rangers. We go anywhere to get what we want."

"And what is it you want, an army that's read *The Princess Casamassima?*"

"No," said the padre. "I'd like to score a win in the Nam that has nothing to do with picking up real estate. You have to absorb the whole fucking war, make the enemy part of your op, work him into the battle screen, hamburgers and all. That's what we do. We're not allowed official status. The Company's scared of Kissinger and his peace negotiations. We get our soup and supplies from the contingency fund. We don't have shoulder patches or bracelets. Some of us wear a blue beanie."

"Why blue?"

"Because the army wears green and the frogmen wear black. Blue is the color that was left to us."

"Now I understand. You put on your chaplain's coat and wander into all the little jails in Nam. You visit Murderers' Row and test your candidates on their ability to handle Henry James. How come I'm not good enough to wear that beanie of yours?"

"You haven't been indoctrinated yet. You've still got all your maidenhair."

"What maidenhair?" said the Teach, who considered wrecking the Contretemps and the padre from Saigon Station. "I was blown up twice, unwiring booby traps. There's no maidenhairs in them wires. Send me back to the Rat Patrol if you're not satisfied."

The padre laughed behind his aviator glasses. "You haven't seen our headquarters at the Richelieu."

"You mean the crazy movie house on Le Loi that never heard of Jack Nicholson? It's strictly for the Long Noses. They watch foreign films and pick up ten-year-old whores in back of the No Smoking sign."

The padre took his glasses off and Teach realized what was disturbing about that face. It had once belonged to a fat man.

The skin was pulled back at the cheeks to provide little pockets where flesh had been.

"You're filled with Yankee prejudices," the padre said. "Go to the Richelieu."

Teach traveled down to Rainbow Road, a strip of massage parlors, taco stands, and bottle clubs, where Nam ceased to exist, and it was Texas with neon signs, milk bars with Kissinger in the window, supply sergeants selling Carvel ice cream, baby-sans in Harvard sweatshirts, Korean Rangers in ten-gallon hats, until Teach could have sworn America itself was only merchandise, and he was glad to arrive at the Richelieu on Le Loi. He paid his last bits of orange money to get inside and couldn't even afford the price of a candy bar. Little girls kept grabbing his ankles from the aisles.

"Slugger, want a heavy date?"

He cursed the padre for sending him here and then a hand reached around him, stronger and thicker than a child's, and shoved him into a seat. "Hey," he said. "I'll booby-trap the first ten rows. Lea' me alone."

He recognized the glint of gold in the dark. It was George's ear furniture. He'd been shoved next to the king. Old George wasn't in prison rags this afternoon. Under the projector's ratty light Teach saw a blue beret on the king's head.

George dug something into his hand. A fistful of paper money. Teach couldn't tell if it was orange or green. He wouldn't read money at the Richelieu.

"Uncle Albert says you must be short."

"I was just with the old man," Teacher said. "Why didn't I get my beanie allowance from him?"

"Not an allowance," the king said. "It's a loan. Uncle couldn't lay greenbacks on you near the embassy walls."

Teach would never understand how a montagnard could talk like a grunt. "You come here often, majesty?"

"Day and night. I get language practice."

"Ah," the Teacher said. "You're learning French."

The king was silent and then he said, "I studied with the nuns in Dalat. My tribe was always loyal to the French. It's American English I'm worried about."

"But these films are French."

"I read the subtitles," his majesty said.

The little mother was beginning to make sense. "Majesty, what about the child prostitutes working the Richelieu? Do we have to tolerate that?"

"They're not prostitutes. They're beanie scouts."

"Ah," the Teacher said. "An early warning system at the Richelieu. Is that why they grabbed my ankles? To see if I had some blasting jelly in my socks?"

"Or knives," the king said. "Or a neat ankle holster . . . come on. We're going, little Howard."

The girls pleaded with George as he went up the aisle. "Majesty man, majesty man."

"Later," he said, stuffing their heads down into the seats. Ah, mousy girls in a movie theatre.

There was a jeep outside the Richelieu, waiting for his majesty. The driver was a kid from the shore patrol.

They drove down Le Loi into the Chinese city of Cholon. The driver dropped them at a smelly canal. They'd come to the hindquarters of Saigon, a system of canals that resembled a floating garbage truck. They passed little towns of refrigerator cartons where entire families lived along the canals. They passed a hotel for enlisted men, children camping at the bottom of the hotel wall. They passed Chinese restaurants where old men sat with cans of Coca-Cola.

The king led him off the narrow road they were on and they kept moving from canal to canal. He saw boatmen ply a stream that would have been too shallow to bathe a rat. They arrived at a street of hovels and the king took him through a door, into Albert's little country. The soldiers behind the door had their beanies on. They tilted their heads to the king. "How's it going, majesty?"

"Tolerable," the king said to fists of people.

Teach could have been at a class reunion, because he recognized Lubbock and Percy, the millionaire's boy, among the beanies. Percival Wentworth McShane IV, who'd snuck into the army at sixteen, after going AWOL from some prison called Andover. He had a scar that ran from his eye to the edge of his lip. He'd scalp Viet Cong and then donate his army allowance to an orphan's home in the hills. Perce was in love with Henry Kissinger. He'd fight whoever said an unkind word about "Dr. Henry." He'd come from a clan that dueled a lot. He was always dueling. He'd killed a pair of Australian businessmen with a shard of glass. He couldn't have been much older than seventeen, and except for the scar, he looked like he belonged in a crib.

Percy hugged the Teacher around the Neck. "Glad to see you, little man."

Teach was content until he discovered the girl behind the bar. She was no mama-san who went into the back room with beanies. Perce explained the girl's career. She was an aristocratic halfbreed, a métisse with a Chinese mother and a French dad. Myriam Foucault. The French dad had returned to the Long Noses without Myriam and her mother and now the mother was dead and Myriam had inherited this bar, the Four Hundred Blows. She was as tall as a beanie, and she had powerful caves under her eyes, the cheekbones of a Chinese-Paris princess.

The beanies were devoted to Myriam. They bought her slippers and scarves in the shopping palaces of French Saigon. Myriam had gone to school at the Convent des Oiseaux in Dalat, but Teach wasn't interested in Myriam's dossier. Her sunken eyes got him to think of his lost high-school sweetheart, Sarah Fish. Sarah was heftier than the métisse, but both of them were skinny around the eyes. Teach hadn't seen his little mama in five years. He'd never told her he was in the Nam. He wondered if she'd married the football team at Bengal High.

Perce nudged him out of his dream and pointed to Myriam. "She's not for you, little man."

"I suppose the beanies would wrestle me off if I tried. I wouldn't take her to a boomboom house. I'd like to marry your princess."

"She's not up for marriage or any other kind of sale . . . she's already spoken for."

"Ah, she must be Lubbock's mama-san."

"I doubt if it's Lubbock. We all took an oath not to mess with the little mama."

Teacher stole a beer and sidled up to George. "That little mama with the cheekbones. Majesty, who's her man?"

But the king wouldn't answer him, and Teach began to suspect that the beanies were all faithful knights to Myriam Foucault. He had to endure the mystery of Myriam's man . . .

He shared a villa with Percy and George on old Pasteur Street in French Saigon. He was a beanie now, but no one had given him a hat to wear. He couldn't even tell about the padre's commando missions, because he never left Saigon. He had his stethoscope and the clothes he'd worn in prison. He'd become an aide to the king. He sat with George at the Richelieu and discovered how Uncle Albert financed his operations. George was the biggest opium dealer in the Nam. The king's source was his own tribe of poisoners and magicians, who collected black balls of opium that were bartered to Saigon generals, PX sergeants, drivers for the shore patrol, Chinese bankers, innkeepers, and whorehouse matrons.

But the king had to compete with Corsican milk-bar men. The milk-bar men kept trying to murder George, and Teach had to blow up their milk bars in the middle of the night when customers weren't around.

It wasn't Uncle Al who supplied Teach with maps and blueprints of Little Corsica. It was the beanie captain, Jonah Slyke. He had a perfect cover. Paddleball champ. He hopped from tournament to tournament, providing information to beanies in the field. He'd fly out of Quang Tri to sit with Howard inside some milk bar they intended to blow. Teach liked the simple justice of it. Jonah wouldn't do a milk bar he never sat in.

Teach must have caught him at a bad time. They sat in a milk bar behind the cathedral and Jonah had forgotten to bring his blueprints. He drank whiskey out of a bag, mooning over the wife of some college friend. He had a photo of her, but she looked like a cow as far as Teach could tell.

"Lliana," the captain mumbled.

Teach tried to console him. "Couldn't you kidnap her the beanie way?"

"I'm not sure she likes me."

"Crazy about her and you haven't kissed her yet? Where'd you meet the girl?"

"At her wedding. Flew ten thousand miles to get there."

"Only saw her once? What did you like about her?"

"Ears," the captain said. "Lliana's ears wiggled when she ate. My dad was a country lawyer. Never had a dime. I wasn't bred to wiggle my ears to a dish of smoked salmon."

Teach couldn't understand what wiggling ears had to do with love. He brought the captain home to his bachelors' club and fragged the milk bar without a blueprint.

He was sick of fighting Corsicans and Uncle sent him on a holiday to Cayenne. Uncle was the real magician of Saigon. Uncle had produced Howard's sweetheart, delivered Sarah Fish to an old French fort. And Howard parachuted in. She pretended to be angry at him and his absence of five years, but he wormed his way into her tent, carrying a bit of sadness around on his back. He couldn't help thinking about the infants he'd have raised in New Jersey if her dad had been fonder of him. He wouldn't have had to booby-trap milk bars and men.

Lying next to her round body, his hand on her breast, he wasn't so interested in blue berets. But he couldn't get permanent with Sarah. Promised Uncle he'd finish up his chores in Saigon. He returned to the big bad ville without telling Sarah. There wasn't a beanie at the Four Hundred Blows. It was filled with Korean Rangers. Myriam Foucault wouldn't talk to him in French. He traveled to the Richelieu, but the king wasn't about, and the baby-sans wouldn't bother to undress his ankles. They were holding hands with foreign businessmen, and he got the feeling that these little daughters hadn't stayed loyal to George. Teach went to the villa, but he couldn't find Perce or the king on Pasteur Street. They hadn't even left their skivvies in the shelves. Teach had returned to a colony of ghosts.

He began hearing voices behind his wall. He wondered if squatters had come to Pasteur Street, hiding from Henry Kissinger.

He crossed from his garden into the outlands behind his wall. A woman stood with a two-year-old child in her arms. This squatter wore designer jeans. It was Myriam of the Four Hundred Blows, with an unexpected baby boy in her arms.

Myriam kept rocking the baby and sucking her teeth.

"Papa-san, would you like to come to bed with me?"

What happened to that mystery cavalier she had?

Myriam clutched his arm. "I can make you happy, papa-san."

"Let's forget the love business. What is it you want?"

"An exit visa."

"I'll talk to Uncle Albert. He can get you a visa."

But he didn't like that little turmoil in her face. Her cheek only twitched once, but he wasn't Myriam's fool. Albert was her cavalier.

"Myriam, is that his son? . . . answer me. Is that Albert's son you're holding?"

"Yes."

It was the Teacher who was twitching now. "Well, why can't Albert help?"

"Please, papa-san. Don't tell him we talked."

"Mama, I won't breathe a word."

His teeth were gnashing all night. Woke up and found Uncle Albert in his living room, eating little sandwiches out of the fridge.

"Howard, has Myriam been bothering you?"

"You're a dad, goddammit. Are you planning to donate her and the little boy to General Giap?"

"Howard, we're not sitting in Hanoi."

"Hanoi's around the corner. Kissinger's going to sell Saigon . . . what about Myriam?"

"I'll take care of her, I said. And you're leaving the delta for good. Pack your bags."

"I don't need to pack for Cayenne."

Uncle stuffed the little sandwiches into his mouth. "Forget Cayenne. You're going invisible for a while."

"Invisible? Where's that?"

"With the king. George has gone home to his people. I'm sending you there."

"A little R&R in the mountains, Uncle? What if I get restless?"

"You'll shoot yourself. Or live with one of the king's wives. He's got nine or ten near Pleiku. Take the fattest wife you find. You'll sleep better."

"And you?"

"I'm closing shop. Kissinger is on my tail."

Teach packed his underwear, stood on the lawn, and a chopper swam down from the sky. The guns were light and the crew was small, an Air America pilot and Neck, with his curious, twisted body, brains like a cannonball, and a menace in his eyes. Must have been thinking of the soldier he'd murdered for tampering with his Vietnamese wife. He'd started out as Teacher's jailer and then sat in the brig.

"Neck, what happened to your mama-san?"

"She died of shame."

"And you're a widower now . . . all alone?"

That crumpled head began to cry and Teach wasn't sure how to console him. "Neck, are you going to live with me and the king?"

"No, little man. I've got other chores to do."

The chopper landed on a mountain shelf and Teach climbed down into an orange mist that felt like live candy floating off the mountain. He wanted to say good-bye to Neck, but he lost sight of the chopper in all that orange candy.

And then the candy cleared and he realized the mist wasn't orange at all. The rocks were orange, a deep burnt orange that was like the rust of the world. King George stepped out of the rust. He had his old commando hat and a tiger suit that melded with the rocks. Behind him were six montagnards, all the grown men of his tribe. George simplified their names for the Teach. The six of them were Hatchet, Swamp, Blood, Fever, Peppermint, and Judith. George told the Teach not to mind a woman's name on a man. It was a means of fooling the village devils, who preferred women to men.

The strikers had crossbows slung on their backs and quivers in their belts, like captured lightning bolts. Teach followed them down off the shelf. They were back inside the timberline, and the rocks turned gradually from orange to green. They'd gone under the king's rust, and Teach was glad to smell a living tree. He stumbled upon a village that was one stinking house on stilts, with a pack of women outside, sucking on silver pipes with a long, narrow bowl and shaking a chicken claw to please some goddamn devil. The women had blouses open at the chest. They wouldn't cover themselves for the Teach. They went on smoking their pipes, with a brood of children entangled in their legs. They were fatter than their men and didn't seem half as gloomy.

George's sister was called Hélène. Her grass coils and chicken claw were as imperfect as the other women's, but Hélène was something of a matriarch.

She was younger than George. Thirty or so, with a round face and breasts that reminded him of Lieutenant Sarah and the loss he had to endure. He wouldn't get much respite in these hills. He was drawn to this mountain mama.

She spoke to the Teach in a sullen French. The Elephanters had a long history of sullenness. They were magicians who couldn't get along with other people. Couldn't even form a proper village. Families would poison one another's wells. A madman in some clan would kidnap a child and instigate a fifty-year feud. They'd started as herders of elephants. They groomed their elephants, babied them, fed them out of one communal bowl. But because the magicians had so many debts, they bartered their stock away. The tribe became too poor to support a household of elephants. They went deeper into the wilderness and would have been content if the Viet Minh hadn't tried to shove them into a work gang. They began an alliance with the French, had their own little army, but after the fall of Dienbienphu, the Viet Minh captured their best sorcerers and carted them to Hanoi. George's older brother, Frédéric, the tribe's most accomplished magician, cooperated with the Viet Minh. It mortified the Elephant People. They burrowed deeper into the hills, but clung to the language of the Long Noses.

Teach sat down to eat a meal of jungle mush and green rice. The women had first dig at the communal pot, then the six warriors, then the infants of the tribe, then Teacher and George. It was a curious business being king. Last one into the mush.

Teach wondered about the little table in front of the house that was cluttered with delicacies and doughy things. The table had its own little chair. Was it reserved for an infant sorcerer? But none of the children sat down at the table to eat.

It pained the Teach to stare at all this food while he had to settle for green rice. He smelled the dough and turned dizzy. He could hear voices in his head inviting him to the table. But Teach sensed he wouldn't survive the meal.

That dough was demon food, prepared by the women. The devils of George's tribe were greedy mothers. They wouldn't poke around in a pot. They demanded grub that the magicians couldn't afford. The women exhausted themselves baking for demons who never stopped multiplying. Wherever the magicians went, new devils gathered around them.

The six warriors went off to collect opium bricks from their cousins in Cambodia. While the warriors were away, the wives went to work brewing poison in great stinking tubs. George stayed behind to keep the children out of the women's hair. He was a goddamn royal babysitter. He whittled sticks and clubs for the brats, sang them songs, and danced for their amusement. He'd shuck off his tiger-striped suit, rinse his mouth with beer, paint his body until he was a dark blue man, hire a teenager to accompany him on a tin fiddle, and then he'd dance in back of the spirit table, the wives and teenage girls admiring his genitals as the poison cooked.

The king was light of foot on his mountain. The women laughed and licked their teeth and remarked how much they intended to pay for the king. The poor son of a bitch was a stud among his own people. But he had to give back the coins he collected, because he was so far into debt.

He danced for an hour, his muscles churning under the paint, pieces of sun spangling his blue back, and then he walked into the Elephanters' bungalow with three of the fattest wives.

The fat wives left the bungalow, one by one, and returned to the poison tubs. And then the king came out to sit on his porch. All the animation was gone from his body. He could have been a local devil smothered in blue paint. His eyes were dull as a white jar. It was the image of a king hopelessly in debt.

But there was an incredible industry around him. The women kept adding to the poison stew. Teach saw mushrooms and berries ground into pulp. Pieces of bark were chewed and spat into the tubs. Centipedes were chopped up in front of his eyes. Fangs were twisted out of a snake's head.

Hélène determined what went into each tub. The Elephanters had poisons to paralyze and kill or put their enemies into a long coma. They had brews to instill madness, endless vomiting, or amnesia. They had poisons that would only deaden one side of a man's face, others that would bring on silence or induce a constant chatter until the blood broke in an enemy's ear.

Nothing was left to whim. The poisons were tested on mountain rats and pigs, always with an arrowhead, dipped into a tub. The mamas would mark a rat's ear or chase down a pig and jab its belly with a poisoned arrow. The rats would scuttle in the grass as if they'd absorbed an egg cream in their blood and then they'd squeal and drop with gutters of foam in their mouths. None of them could travel the length of the bungalow, once they were pricked. But the pigs were less accountable. They wouldn't die on command. They'd linger under the bungalow. And the bellowing that went on at night, their death groans, threw the Teach into a turmoil. He wasn't sure whether he could last out his exile with the Elephanters. The pigs would scrape the underboards in their agony, and Teach felt a madness grab hold of him. But the pigs died, and the women stopped dipping arrowheads. They'd cooked enough.

The warriors came out of Cambodia with a sack of opium bricks. Within an hour of their homecoming, a pair of visitors arrived. Teach's mates from Long Binh, Lubbock and Kroll. They walked out of the rust with no montagnard to guide them. The two beanies had been to Elephant country before.

They didn't stop to pay homage to the king. They dumped the opium bricks into a mail bag and took the jars of poison Hélène had prepared for them. They reserved their deepest attention for the outline of her breasts. Hélène had shut her blouse to the beanies, but that couldn't discourage Lubbock and Kroll.

"Majesty," Lubbock said, "how much for your sister?"

"I don't handle her affairs."

"Try and convince her," Lubbock said, cradling an M–60 machine gun that could have knocked the village and all its people into dust. "I mean, you're the old majesty around here. You've got six braves. Don't they have pull with a fat sis?"

None of the warriors would respond, not Swamp, not Blood,

not Judith, who drank rice beer and kept out of the king's argument.

"You can't have her," Teach said.

The two beanies laughed.

"Lub, you smell something?"

"Yeah," Lubbock said. "Elephant piss."

"Well, the piss is talking to us . . . it looks like the Teach, Lub. You think the tribe's been doing its tricks? Majesty's a magician, aint he?"

"She's my little mama," Teach said, staring into the mouth of the machine gun.

"You're off your rocker, piss."

They grabbed their goods and skulked out of Elephant country. And Teach had to endure the silence around him. Hélène opened her blouse. He might have gotten used to her breasts if the tribe didn't have blouses. But that mix of material and chest was driving him crazy. His eyes kept going under where her blouse began. He was like a burrowing thing that followed stripes of skin.

Teach squinted at the spirit table to cure his eyes of Hélène, but nothing could satisfy George.

"You shouldn't have meddled in our business."

"Majesty, they were insulting Hélène."

"Then it's for me to repay the insult. You're a guest."

"But they might have started tickling her."

"She's been tickled by other men," the king said under his teeth. "She's our official hostess, little man. She sleeps with all the strangers who come here. She slept with Lubbock, but she didn't like him. That's what the quarrel was all about. Hélène wouldn't take his money, and he thought I should persuade her, because we'd been beanies together. But I have no power over Hélène."

Teach was disappointed. He'd been with the tribe a week and Hélène hadn't offered to play post office with him.

"Lubbock's still a whore," Teach said.

"I know that. But he's Uncle's courier."

"And we're desperadoes. We run from Henry Kissinger and work between the lines."

"You're wrong," the king said. "We're an army of liberation."

"And what are you going to liberate?"

"All the montagnards."

Six warriors to build a kingdom. Howard cupped his chin to keep from giggling and George produced a wormy banner with white stars wandering in a green field. "We'll make our own republic in the highlands."

"Uncle's been telling you lies."

"No," George said. "We had a revolution before Kissinger, in '65."

And the king told about that revolution. He was born a slave, like his brother Frédéric. His dad had married a tribal beauty and gone into debt. The wedding feast lasted a month, because the devils hated to give up a beauty to any man and George's dad had to sell his unborn sons to pay for the meals. Hélène escaped this misery, since the devils were partial to girls. But Frédéric and George were tribal toys. After Frédéric was kidnapped by the Viet Minh, the burden of his chores fell upon his brother. George was twice a slave. But he had long hair and a coltish look, in spite of his tribal sullenness, and the matriarchs smiled on George. They slept with him, painted his eyebrows blue, like a girl, so the demon gods would also favor George, and while they shook their chicken claws and drank rice beer sweetened with a bit of poison, they decided that George should be king, not of the Elephanters, whose slave he was, but of the whole mountain population, looked upon as savages by the lowlanders and exploited by the Viet Cong.

The Elephanters seduced, poisoned, and cajoled, with quivers of arrows and girls. Concubines went along on the trip. Warriors donated women to the enterprise, nieces, daughters, and teenage wives, hoping to convince the elders of some recalcitrant tribe. But the concubines started to fight among themselves. They walked out of camp and George was left with his sister Hélène. She whored for the Elephant nation, bedding down with highland chiefs until George's army swelled.

Villages that remained immune to Hélène were subject to sorcery. Spirit tables disappeared, wells turned sour, chiefs choked to death. And an epidemic of rainbows would poison the sky. There was nothing worse than a rainbow. A phantom lived behind its ribbon of colors, stealing the blood of mountain men and women.

Rainbows seemed to beset those villages the Elephanters left behind. Even the stubbornest chiefs sensed King George had arrows that could rip the sky and produce rainbows at will. No one wanted to court the wrath of a magician king. Warriors lay with the king's sister and fell into line.

But a general from North Vietnam, Nguyen Van Tuan, attacked the tail of George's caravan with a band of montagnard irregulars. The irregulars weren't vulnerable to magic. They murdered sorcerers and matriarchs. They could survive poisoned water. Rainbows meant nothing to them. A fancy patch in the sky. George grew more and more sullen about such disrespect until he realized who the general was. Only a sorcerer could reverse Elephant magic. The king was fighting his own brother. Nguyen Van Tuan had to be the name Frédéric took in Hanoi.

There were no more converts. The tribes in George's path abandoned their villages. He'd lost the power of the rainbow. The king was heartsore. He returned to the Elephanters without his revolution.

George landed on some perimeter between slave and king. He slept with older women, he danced, he whittled knives for the children. But the Elephanters couldn't forget that dream of war when George gathered an army with rainbows on his shoulder. He still had the lengthy shadow of a king.

And Teach considered the rainbow woman, Hélène, who'd slept with all the mountain chiefs and inspired a revolution on her rump. Ah, her history as a concubine hadn't ruined Hélène. Howard couldn't help desiring her skin.

He went to sleep in the hammock the tribe had given him. There must have been thirty Elephanters inside the bungalow at night, with no partitions, no doors. Just hammocks on a range of hooks and everybody snoring. It was like Long Binh, without the notion of a jail.

He tried to imagine the curl of her body in a hammock, but he couldn't remember where her hammock was, since so many hammocks looked the same. He had a little mama at Cayenne. But Hélène of the high cheeks plagued him in his hammock. He twisted around like a squirrel in a storm.

Didn't have to scout for Hélène in the morning. She'd moved her hammock next to his. She went through her rituals, unbundled herself, and sat naked in the hammock, with her back to Biedersbill, who couldn't miss the sweep of her shoulders and the little fingers of her spine. Ah, he was troubled by the rainbow woman's back. Each dent was like a love charm in Teach's blood.

She dressed in the hammock and turned around, revealing the fall of her breasts through an open blouse. She talked French to her girlfriends, ignoring the Teach. They mentioned the Baroness de Roth. The Elephanters had worked for the Baroness on her tea plantation, during the reign of the Long Noses. The Baroness had introduced them to pamplemousse and the tribe went ape. Pamplemousse was a bigger delicacy than ice cream. Teach couldn't understand why a village of magicians would hunger after grapefruit.

An evangelist wandered into the village, ate green rice with the tribe, smoked one of the silver pipes, and sang sad songs about Jesus. He accompanied himself on a banjo, while the children scraped along on their montagnard fiddles, but Hélène never went near the evangelist. Teach had a spooky feeling that she was saving herself for him. Some goddamn marriage had been consummated with Teach's hidden consent. She was his mountain bride who slept in a neighboring hammock.

The evangelist's nostrils widened when he looked at Hélène. Teach had a suspicion that this mother was laying on Christ for her. The evangelist hung around so long, eating mush, drinking rice beer, that Teach decided to ask the king about him.

"Who is that Billy Christian?"

"Helmholtz," the king said. "Sings for Saigon Station."

"A spook? What's he doing here?"

"He's in love with Hélène."

An anger rose up in the Teacher's neck. He was figuring how to booby-trap the banjo. "Is Billy Christian her goddamn steady?"

"Once upon a time he was."

"Well, if the mother goes near her, he's dead."

"Hélène knows that, little man. That's why she's on good behavior."

The whole tribe had married him off and Teach was stuck in the dark, with all sorts of suitors behind him. They'd cuckold him before he ever got close to Hélène.

"I'm engaged to Sarah Fish," he said.

The king laughed. "Your lowland mama doesn't count, little man."

Howard got into his hammock and stayed there. He was shivering when Hélène undressed with her back to him and curled into the hammock.

"Monsieur," she said, "bonne nuit!"

Ah, if she'd seduced every other mother in the mountains, why couldn't she cross the line to Teach's hammock and seduce him? He had black dreams. Phantoms crouching everywhere.

He was grateful when the king woke him. Hélène wasn't in her hammock. The whole damn bungalow had emptied. Teach couldn't say what spirits had driven them out. Something was peculiar about the king. It wasn't his sullenness. Teach had gotten used to that. The king had a rainbow rubbed on him, a rainbow with an insecure arc. The bow started at his mouth, traveled under the hollows of his cheek, where the arc spilled onto his collarbone, and ended at the nipple. Teach understood the reason for this art. The mamas had decided to mount one more revolution. And George was their rainbow king.

Nobody had to tell Teach to pack. The magicians were leaving this place. They took their hammocks, their chicken claws, their poison tubs, tobacco, salt pots, arrows, antidotes, jewels and silver pipes, opium balls they'd fashioned from their last Cambodian brick and ate like cotton candy, a mound of plastique that Judith kept in a rag, jungle knives, French cigarettes that the matriarchs liked to smoke when their mouths grew sore from silver pipes, cutlery to prepare food for the devils, children's toys, French panties from Saigon for the teenage girls, a medicine chest of roots, barks, and herbs, white cotton leggings that the women sometimes wore, a clutch of high-heeled shoes, the spirit table, and the spirit chair.

That caravan of sorcerers, trinkets, and cigarettes hiked above the timberline into all the rust. Teach was angry about giving up trees again. His mouth tasted bitter from being near so much orange rock. The caravan climbed like some living bug with a variety of legs. It could have formed its own highway to Danang and Teach wouldn't have been able to tell. He'd lost his bearing in the king's rust. He moved along with the magicians, avoiding Hélène. He didn't want to dream of breasts on this climb, but the mamas smiled at him in a suspicious way, and he knew he was coupled with Hélène no matter what part of the caravan he occupied. Judith was up front and George was in the rear, playing with the children That sign of revolution on his chest, a fallen rainbow, didn't excuse him from his ordinary burdens. He was still babysitter to the tribe.

And Teach was a little man with a stethoscope. All he could do was sniff out bombs under a flat road. Charlie Cong hadn't bothered to booby-trap a mountain full of rock slides and vertical caves hidden in the rust, into which a man might fall and fall and no one would ever hear him. It was Judith who tested the

ground for those terrible caves, gliding over the rust with the
corns on his feet. And Teach was paltry in a pair of army boots.
He had no magical corns. A stethoscope couldn't predict a rock
slide or where the ground went hollow. He felt like a hopeless
worm, a drudge among archers and magicians. He apprenticed
himself to the matriarchs on this trip, learned how to store poisons. He smoked a pipe with the mamas and swallowed bits of
poison, like they did, to build up his resistance to fumes in a
tub. The poison tasted good.

But he couldn't avoid Hélène, who was mistress of the tubs.
She laughed with her girlfriends while Teach went to cooking
school with all the wives.

And then his fucking life fell apart. Hélène had to go in and
seduce a chief. They'd come to a village that was as miserable
as their own had been. These were distant cousins to George.
A tribe without teeth. The spirit table had nothing but mush.
George's cousins were at the end of the world. Most of the devils
had abandoned them. Their chief was a crazed, half-starved man,
done up in blue. He insisted that all his own people and all
the Elephanters observe him as he copulated with Hélène. He
must have thought that so public a ceremony would lure the
demon gods back to his village. And Howard had to admit that
the chief wasn't crazy at all.

He'd seen Hélène rub an ointment into her fingernails, and
he knew what her seductions were about. She'd scratch the chief
while he rutted with her, and the poison would collect in his
back. He'd be out of commission whether he joined the caravan
or not.

Teach couldn't escape the ceremony. He'd arrived with the
Elephanters and he had to watch. He drank his rice beer, he
gobbled mush. The children of both tribes got up an orchestra
and played for the chief and Hélène.

She did a montagnard striptease, shucking blouse, skirt, and
high-heeled shoes with a simple twist. She lay down on her
hammock, which she'd brought into this stinking bungalow and

182

used like a tribal blanket. The chief drank more beer and unbuttoned his fly. It was his privilege of rank to enter her without taking off his jungle fatigues. He snorted a couple of times as Hélène drew a ribbon on his back and smiled up at Howard softly, with infinite peace, as if she were asking a husband to endure the hazards of her occupation.

Howard read the markings on that poor mother's back. The chief's blood would rot with every single caress.

George inherited the whole tribe of cousins, meager men and women who'd never handled a crossbow or mixed poison in a tub. Their chief landed in the rust. His people hardly missed him at all. They were part of the revolution now. His ears bled one morning and he sat down to die. The caravan left him with a few gourds of green rice.

There were other conversions, with Hélène stepping into a bungalow on high heels and George escaping with a village full of hungry women and old men.

The caravan had more and more mouths to feed and the same six bowmen, with Judith up front, where he always was. But Judith had an accident. Drank too much after lunch and lost the feeling in his corns. He missed a soft spot in the ground and vanished under the rust. No one could remember hearing him fall. The mountain had eaten him up.

George wailed, and everybody wailed with him, converts, children, and Hélène. The mamas kneeled in front of the spirit table. The devils had conspired to destroy Judith. It wouldn't have mattered how shrewd his corns were in nibbling orange earth. The demon gods had abandoned Judith and the magicians.

The king clawed the rainbow on him. Women ripped their breasts. Teach shivered at all the crying and tearing around him. But he wouldn't piss a revolution away on devils that didn't even come up to his knee. He jumped over that treacherous piece of rust and called to the king.

"Majesty, I'll be your point man."

The crying stopped. People gawked at him. He'd discovered

a way to beat the devils. George helped children scurry over the invisible hole and the caravan started to move.

Teach was scared. He didn't have boots with scanners in them that could bounce an echo off a cave's hidden wall. He was a runt from the Rat Patrol. He'd have to sniff for weaknesses in the rust. Soon as he suspected a cave, he'd tap the ground and listen for hollow spots with his stethoscope.

He survived that day, ordering the caravan around hollows and holes. Hélène seduced another chief. The king touched up his rainbow, restoring the outline of the arc. Teach ate more poison with the wives.

Children were frightened of him. Converts got out of his way. He was no longer the lovesick foreigner who hungered after Hélène. He was the phantom who'd come out of a rainbow to walk in front of George.

He didn't feel like a phantom. He was a man who had to test the ground for holes. He figured to survive a couple of days and no more. He wanted something from the rainbow woman before he inherited his hole. A bit of love? Assurance that he wasn't only one more man waiting to be seduced. He looked for her after the caravan had gone to bed. It was like waltzing on a minefield full of mamas. He found Hélène. She was folded in her hammock.

She stared up at him out of the folds with a cat's eyes.

He went under the hammock with her. Teach didn't have to fumble with Hélène's clothes. She was naked in her nighttime nest. She slid her hand down his body, touched him like a sorceress, and he was naked in a minute.

She wasn't under the hammock when he woke. He got dressed, washed his face in a shelf of rainwater, and marched the caravan through the orange mist.

They arrived in a valley that could have been Cambodia. He wasn't needed to tap the ground. There were no caves in this grass. Teach must have come to a rendezvous point. Percy, the millionaire's boy, was waiting for them with a tub of ammunition and a blue-eyed man. The blue-eyed man carried a grenade launcher. Perce called him Konstantin. He seemed fat for a soldier. The bowmen weren't shy around Konstantin. They picked up the rifles Perce had brought.

Ah, it was a different ballgame. The Elephanters hadn't come to practice conversion in this valley. They gathered slaves and prisoners of war. Hélène didn't have to put on high heels. With Perce as point man, the Elephanters would knock a tribe to pieces.

Howard stopped the king after a bloody rush into a village. "Majesty, why don't you ask the rock apes to join us. Damn you. One day you're into devils, and the next you're a beanie, doing Uncle's chores."

"Not true," the king said, but he'd covered up most of the rainbow. He wore a tiger shirt with Konstantin. "I'm collecting the Yards into a nation."

George's country of Elephanters, slaves, and beanies swooped down on a bunch of farmers and took all their opium bricks. Several of the farmers were dumb enough to fight. They died for their bricks.

George grew less attentive to the children. He'd only dance after dark, when the caravan was safe. The king wasn't in a rainbow war; he'd rubbed the bands of color off his cheek.

And while the king danced, Konstantin approached Howard with the mamas' deck of rummy cards. "I'd love to play you for Hélène." He was blonder than a man in a jungle ought to be. Konstantin didn't sweat. He controlled the world with his fat blue eyes.

"Didn't you hear me, Teach? A little rummy for Hélène. You haven't been attentive to her. I'll bet your little mama is starved."

Teach dove at fat eyes, clipped him in the groin, and the two of them wrestled on the ground in front of children and slaves. The king had to quit his dancing to hold them apart.

Konstantin returned to his grenade launcher, but Teach wasn't satisfied. He nibbled a deadly root. It wasn't out of spite. He had to expand his intake of poison to get some immunity going. His ears leaked for half an hour. He coughed and went to bed.

Majesty had a gift for him in the morning. It was the nation's flag, that wormy, twisted field of green with white stars in no apparent order. The flag was knotted to a bamboo pole.

"I want you to be our standard bearer."

"Is that flag for when we separate farmers from their dope?"

"We're not doing farmers any more. We're getting up a nation. We'll push Charles off our back."

Konstantin came running over with his breakfast of green rice. "What's this shit?"

"A flag," the Teacher said. "Our flag. The Elephanter republic."

Fat eyes wore a photographer's vest with a hundred pockets. He kept jabbing his fingers into zippered holes.

"Majesty, it doesn't pay to advertise your army. Not yet." Konstantin called Percy over to witness the flag. "Perce, King George is going crazy. He can't run his colors around here."

Perce was like a porcupine dressed in pistols and grenades. He'd become the Elephanters' armory, ribbed with bandoliers. But he wouldn't support Konstantin. "I go with George."

Fat eyes played gin with the mamas, beating them out of their cotton leggings and silver pipes. But the mamas overlooked his greed to swipe their treasure. They wouldn't poison him. They believed a devil lived in his blue eyes.

Teach didn't care about Konstantin's eyes. He was a soldier again, like the long range recon boys, who never wore skivvies in the field. He planted booby traps, shot tough customers in the tail, listened to walls with his stethoscope inside a village that might have gone VC. He took shrapnel in the head, was nearly blown to deviltown while listening to the walls of some ambiguous tribe. But he walked out of the debris, his hair singed, his face utterly black. The king had no surgeons to look after his skull, and Howard wouldn't take to bed. He was delirious for a week. Hélène had to guide him, or he would have gone over a cliff. She held him under her hammock at night, saving all the metal dandruff that surfaced on his skull. He chewed bits of poison and went back into the war.

Howard was too wheezy to lay traps. He carried the flag, tying his wrists to the bamboo pole. He seemed to improve, living under a green banner. He was shoving along one afternoon, when the ground split and he fell into a hole. He was going to die like Judith, in a well that didn't stop. But he'd landed in a shallow spot. His banner draped obscenely out of the hole, like a swathe of green hair.

He couldn't climb out of that well. A pair of men in army pants scrutinized him from the top of the hole. Teach understood who they were: North Vietnamese irregulars in captured clothes. Ah, it was Tuan's band. They must have been stalking the Ele-phanter republic.

The two men raised the Teacher with a rope. He couldn't have been wrong about their cheekbones. They were monta-gnards, but they didn't speak French. They cut the flag from Teach's wrists, jumped on that green field, mocked the stars, and pretended to wipe their butts within its borders. They were so occupied with the flag, Teach could have escaped if his skull hadn't been full of metal.

He was brought to the irregulars' camp, an outpost on the bitten lee of a hill. Twenty buggers with a field radio, smoking American cigarettes. They had goddamn C-rations for Howard. Applesauce and lima beans.

Five men arrived in brown pajama suits and soft caps, and Teach started to shiver. He'd heard of the "brown soldiers," proselytizers from Hanoi. He'd fallen into the hands of education cadre. They proselytized him with bamboo sticks while they sang about the North. Their songs echoed off the shrapnel and his ears began to ring.

Four of the brownies smiled and beat him on the shoulders. The fifth brownie had Hélène's eyes. It was Tuan in brown pajamas to throw enemies off his scent.

Tuan squatted near Teach, who was lying in the Elephanter flag, and slapped his face. "Can you guess who I am?"

"Frédéric of the Elephant People."

"King Frédéric," Tuan muttered. "Chéri, you look surprised. That flag you're wearing was sewn by the French. The Long Noses wanted to help us break from Vietnam. I was appointed king and encouraged to revolt. But after a month the Long Noses began to steal my revolution. I abdicated and went to live in Hanoi."

Teach was twenty-one, a grand old man for Vietnam, but he still preferred to stay alive. "General, what's going to happen to me?"

"What happens to any pirate. You'll be put on trial."

He'd get fifty years in the Hanoi Hilton. And Henry Kissinger wouldn't trade for old Biedersbill.

Tuan disappeared and the other four brownies kicked him to sleep. He had applesauce in the morning and started to sweat. It wasn't because of yesterday's kicks. Teach had become addicted to the poison he ate. He had to have his bitter root.

He didn't suffer any more kicks. He'd gone into a long dream. He woke with fat eyes bearing down on him. Konstantin had come into camp.

"Hello, Henry James."

Teach felt a bitterness in his blood that wasn't from the poison he'd swallowed. He had this deep suspicion that George, Tuan, and Konstantin belonged to one war party. The goddamn nation had two kings. Frédéric and George. Hélène was their poison princess. Teacher was the knave, that dummy who did their service. And Konstantin was the nation's Henry Kissinger, shuttling everywhere.

Teach looked up at the fat blue eyes. "You taking me to Washington or Hanoi?"

"Don't be silly. You're going back to the republic with our flag. The king's been grieving for you."

"How'd you get here?" Teacher asked.

"That's simple, little man. I started negotiations with General Tuan. Put my ass on the line for you."

"Why should Tuan give me up? I'm terrific capital for Radio Hanoi. The American in the middle of a montagnard revolt."

"No one believes Hanoi Hannah and her rotten little radio show. They'll think you're one of the white ghosts that love to run with a renegade tribe."

"Always wanted to meet Hanoi Hannah."

"Well, you'll have to disappoint the bitch. Majesty needs his flag."

"You'll have to be his bearer. I like it with Tuan. I get apple-sauce. I'm not leaving."

Fat eyes stomped on Teach. "You have a choice, little man. You can waltz out with the flag, or I can kick your ass up into Buddha heaven."

Teach got up and wobbled around with the flag hanging from his shoulders. Konstantin pointed him down the hill. Teach walked a crooked line from Tuan's camp to the Elephant nation.

The whole damn tribe rejoiced. The king hugged him and Hélène put his hand inside her blouse.

Mamas and children crowded near him to touch his knee. It was as if the phantom had come back from devilville without the usual scars of the dead. He could have inherited the spirit chair and the mamas would have fed him cake. All he had to do was pretend. But Teach was too sad to play a demon.

It was on his return to the Elephanters that he started to twitch. The mamas had committed themselves to revolution. They couldn't have known about that package deal with Tuan. George was the rainbow king, some kind of dupe. The man behind the rainbow was Uncle Al.

Teach gobbled poison until his hands turned black. He wept most of the time. The Elephanters used the flag as an ambulance to carry him into war zones. They poisoned wells and bathed him lovingly. They'd come to admire their phantom.

He slept in Hélène's arms, whispered that he loved her, and woke in the psycho ward at Dix. Surgeons picked at his scalp. The hospital mothers were amazed that he could breathe. They couldn't get the poison out of his blood. He missed his family, the montagnards. He dreamt of carrying the flag from battle to battle and fell into sweet bliss.

And then Sarah came to Dix and all the fury of being alive started again. He twitched. He pulled shrapnel from his hair, policed the Alphabet Blocks. But all his activities were only inter-sections of a dream. He was somebody's soldier, Sarah's fiancé, disciple of Uncle Albert and Henry James.

INSIDE THE CHANTI-CLEER

8

October 11, 1983
Dear Diary,

SARAH figured she'd play with a word book, do out all her affairs, morning and night, but she couldn't scratch a line. Some hidden hand was holding her, but whose hand? The Hebrew school was a house of cards . . . worse than that. It was a field mine that sucked customers in and let them explode off the fuses in their blood. She felt chagrined. Biedersbill soldiered for her, but he was in love with Hélène of the hills, and he wouldn't talk to Sarah. He'd dig into his scalp the minute she asked him a question. She'd have a floor full of shrapnel if she didn't leave Biedersbill alone. But she had to find out who was sabotaging the talmud torah.

She slid her diary into the shelf under her tar ball and brushed her teeth, because Sarah had to go abroad and she was nervous about the big bad world. She'd hardly budged in four years. Went as far as Second Avenue once a week to catch Harrison Ford. And Second Avenue was Arabia to her. Full of people with shopping bags and pizza pies. But she'd choke on dust if she didn't get off her ass.

Sarah wouldn't risk the far territories without her .45s. She carried them under her waistband as she walked. The dead lots between C and B comforted her. Sarah had her own Berlin. No one seemed to recognize the Hebrew godmother. An alley cat called and Sarah answered with a wail. It was Indian country and she was happy here. But she started to twitch like the Teacher once she got to A. Two groceries back to back terrified her. It was civilization again.

She shut her eyes on the boutiques that seemed to grow from every other ground floor. Sarah wasn't used to such industry. She arrived at Jonah's paddleball club in a shiver. The captain had told her never to come by, but she didn't care if he took her lieutenant's bars away. Lieutenants didn't hold much water in Alphabetville.

The captain wasn't at his club, and the members were snotty to her. Insisted that Jonah was out of town.

"When's he coming back?"

"We're not sure," said the membership girl. "You might ask his associates, Gallatin & Peck."

Sarah traveled deeper into straight country. Delicatessens all in a row. Bakeries and coffee shops. She found a little park in the middle of nowhere. But it had a locked gate and she couldn't get in. That's how it was with civilized folks. And then her heart nearly hurled her off her feet. The padre was inside the gate with Biedersbill, jabbering like nobody's business. She could have shot them in the pants with her .45s. She bit her knuckles and then Biedersbill left. Took his twitch to the north side of

194

the park and vanished through a gate Sarah couldn't see. Her little man. The padre's pet.

But she wasn't nervous now. She called into the park. "Sweetheart, darling, daddy dear," and Albert came running. Rubble sat in the hollows under his eyes. His nostrils quivered.

"You're making a spectacle of yourself, Sister Sarah."

"Only trying to be nice. Padre, let me in."

"Can't," he said. "This is a private park."

"But your worm got in. Twitching Biedersbill."

"He's no worm," the padre said. "We were reminiscing about the war."

"How come you won't reminisce with me?"

"You're an ungrateful girl. Gave you a home and you did floor shows on my property without asking permission."

"Well, that's what happens when you don't have a lease. Where's Jonah?"

"Out of town."

"That's what they told me at his club. Said he's associated with Gallatin & Peck."

"He's their lawyer."

"Seems he's everybody's lawyer . . . padre, aren't you interested in your niece? You never visit Lulu."

"Didn't know I was welcome on Avenue C."

"I could write you a ticket," she said, turning her back on that old gate. She couldn't get what she wanted from Uncle Albert. He was the hidden hand that squeezed her and the Hebrew school.

She traveled down from the padre's park, angry over Biedersbill. She'd gotten engaged to a goddamn snake in the grass.

A poem started to lick inside her head. She returned to the Hebrew school, locked her door, and scribbled a bit, the lines coming to her like the hull of a synagogue. It wasn't a religious poem. But she couldn't help thinking her poetry was some kind of church. Line upon line to build a synagogue of ink, while she sat further and further from the tabernacle. Right in the roof of her poem.

> *He washes your bra in his own invisible ink*
> *Cuts your hair while you snore*
> *Gives you licorice and toilet paper*
> *Like a devil dad*
> *Call him Citizen Peck*
> *He's the padre who ran out of the jungle*
> *To build alphabet blocks.*

The son of a bitch bought and sold jungles, towns, and talmud torahs. Every somersault she did in Alphabetville was supervised by Citizen Peck. If she'd been Lliana doll, she wouldn't have had to boss a talmud torah. Men would have come in long parades to sniff her underpants. She'd have no one but Harrison Ford and the Teach.

Hurt her to think of Biedersbill, because that Teach must have been born in the padre's coat. Beanies couldn't break away. Biedersbill was just another spy in her talmud torah. She caught him squatting over the brick where she kept the gang's money. The jungles had dampened his arithmetic. He was slow in counting bills. Sarah offered to help the little spying mother.

"Have you decided to bank with somebody else, Mr. Biedersbill?"

He started to twitch and he couldn't get all the money back under the brick. Sarah had to bundle it into that tiny grave.

She loved him even if he was a spy, adored his twitch and the shrapnel in his hair. She'd rather have him spying in the talmud torah than not have him at all. She was attached to Biedersbill. He was like a husband who'd given her grief.

"We have work to do. You're my escort this afternoon."

She packed the opium ball, because Sarah didn't think she could survive this trek without a couple of chews.

Passed baby-san's room. The little bitch was doing up her toe-nails in orange and black. Sarah had grown possessive of Lulu, wouldn't return her to Carlo and Corinne. The talmud torah with all its shouting wars was a better home than King Street. Lulu had her place here. She wasn't daddy's disobedient daughter. She was Lulu of the nail polish. She prepared the gang's yellow rice.

"Hon, should we get you some strawberry popcorn?"

"No," the girl said. "I'm on a diet."

What the hell was she dieting for? So she could shove it in Marve's face? "You love strawberry popcorn."

"Jesus, mama-san, are you telling me what I love? I hate popcorn," Lulu said. "I live on the juice of a lemon. And six glasses of water."

"Good," Sarah uttered between her teeth. A diet like that might clear her own face and she'd become neat as a pin, with boobs for basic symmetry.

Sarah went out the door with that blinking, twitching Biedersbill.

Starve herself.

She wasn't Little Lulu any more. There was a conspiracy going around to keep her a juvenile. And she couldn't always tell who the conspirators were. Carlo, of course. Uncle Albert. The two dozen shrinks she'd had and Saigon Sarah. She couldn't get big tits out of her life. Lulu wasn't looking for an adoption agency. She wanted her man, and her man had his nose in the attic, dreaming of his lost wife.

She didn't care what the shrinks said, all that razzle-dazzle about Marve being a substitute for her dad, the father figure she wanted to fuck. Dr. Hoyt had called her the young Lady Don Juan searching for that ultimate dad who'd lick her and give her an allowance. Well, all she had to do was undress on the doctor's couch and Hoyt would have joined the daddy list.

"Primary attachment problems," the doctor had said. Corinne hadn't stroked her enough. And Carlo didn't know how to touch. He was looking for literary geniuses. Gabriel García Garp. Dickens DiMaggio. Well, she didn't have any problems with secondary attachments, because Marve started stroking her at six. Oh, he didn't stick his hand under her dress and all that. But Corinne was too loaded down with anxiety attacks to dress her and take Little Lulu to the park. It was Marve who buttoned her up, Marve who bought her mocha fudge, Marve who carried her around on his shoulders. Altitude can make a difference, no matter what the shrinks said. You grow up fast, living on a man's shoulders. She was the tallest little person in the district.

Marve was always the man in her life. Her daddy was a ghost, and Corinne would retreat into bed with an ice pack over her ears. That's the kind of mother she had. Going into and coming out of swoons. Being married to Carlo was worse than Vietnam.

It was Marve who raised her like an outside older cousin, or a faraway prince who'd come to work for her dad. She'd loved him the second she'd looked into his brown eyes. Big tits was deaf, dumb, and blind over Harrison Ford, a nurd without Marve's mouth. Blue eyes up on a screen, chasing androids all the time.

She drank a glass of lemon water and went to her man, who was sitting down to a poker game with Vladimir. She had to sashay a little to get Marve's attention from the cards. His head was stuck in aces somewhere, and she'd starved herself for him. She sat down in his lap. He was tied up with aces, jacks, and kings. Vladimir collected his money and walked out of the game, leaving Marve with a plantation of hearts and clubs and two-headed kings and queens.

198

"Lulu, why'd you scare him away?"

"I didn't scare. I took a seat is all."

"That's some seat. He must have thought you were reading his cards."

"I wouldn't do that," she said. "And why bother about winning or losing? You can't spend money in this rathole."

His mouth crinkled, and she remembered that look from eleven years ago, the smile of a wicked boy who didn't know how to be wicked enough.

"When will you marry me, Marve? . . . I'm serious."

"Christ, I was your babysitter once upon a time."

"You had your fun with Lulu a couple of months ago. You wouldn't let me out of your bed."

The smile was gone, and his eyes inherited the Teacher's dull look. He threw her off his lap.

"It was a mistake. I had amnesia. But I'm all right now."

"You were better off as my babysitter. You had more fun. Now you babysit for a talmud torah without students. You dance for housewives from uptown and you wear a rainbow on your nipple . . . marry me and take me out of here."

"Don't love you, sugar, in a marrying kind of way."

"You loved me enough when you had to."

"Told you. It was a mistake."

"The only mistake was big tits. She ruined it for us. Otherwise you'd still be living with me."

"I was living with both of you. Wasn't that the picture?"

"You tolerated her because of her fat ass. But you loved me. I wouldn't lie about that."

"Didn't say you'd lie. All right, I loved you for a week. I don't know how it happened, but I loved you for a week . . ."

"It was five weeks. That's how long you were with me and big tits."

"Five weeks? You can't stay unconscious that long."

"Who says you were unconscious? You sang all the time. You

brought me flowers. You told me I had the sweetest pussy in the United States.''

''I wouldn't have said that. You were a child . . .''

She took him by the collar of his shirt and bent the wings back until he started to wince. ''I was seventeen and I loved you and you loved me.''

She released him and wanted to run away, but he trapped her in his arms. She was twitching worse than her mother, worse than the Teach. He sat her down and rocked her in his lap and she was Little Lulu again. Not much of a mistress or a wife.

Sarah had never gone out alone with the Teach. That little man had a powerful effect on Indian country. People made way for his blinking body. His twitch could empty a sidewalk. Doors closed. Window blinds went down. The whole Alphabetville seemed to withdraw into itself.

''You do a lot of walking around here?'' she asked the Teach.

He answered with a shiver down one shoulder, but she wouldn't let him escape into his old Vietnam blues.

''Asked you a question, Teach.''

''It's my job to walk. I'm one of your walkers.''

''But why is it everybody welcomes you with their back?''

''Because I'm part of your gang. It's you they're running from. You're the Hebrew godmother.''

''I'm the bitch with holes in her face.''

''G-g-g-godmother,'' the Teacher said, and she knew not to contradict him, or he'd be stuttering all the way to Belleville. But she didn't buy his song. It's true, she'd lost her connection with the streets. She'd sucked on her opium ball in the talmud torah's back rooms, but the little mamas and papas hadn't fled from her before now. Children would hand her paper flowers they'd twisted together in school. The lone farmacia on Avenue B always had some gift, like bubble bath or bicarbonate of soda, when she passed its windows. Now the farmacia was like a tomb.

They passed a ruined garden and rose up out of Alphabetville, into the land of croissants and grocery stores. It was rough to deal with civilization twice in one day. But she had to inspect her outposts, or the talmud torah would sink. She stopped in front of Belleville, the gang's own R&R center. Teach waited for her to press the intercom.

"Use your key," Sarah told him.

"They'll be upset, inviting ourselves like this. Doris needs time to adjust to strangers."

"Use your key."

Teach searched his pockets and produced the key to Belleville. He opened the door with a double turn of the key and Sarah pushed him aside. They stood in the dark, waiting for Neck.

"Sing," a voice said from the top of the stairs. "Sing if you want your life."

"I am singing," Sarah said. "It's only me. Now will you put on the light, Neck, before I land in the cellar and die."

Neck delivered her out of the dark. He stood in his skivvies, with a shotgun under his arm. She heard classical music, Mozart or something, behind Neck.

"Shouldn't you invite us to the party?" she said, climbing the stairs.

"Wouldn't do that, mama-san." But he didn't menace her with the shotgun.

"I'm coming up," she told him, thinking she'd have to go to her .45s, but she still might not make it to the top of the stairs. Neck could have switched off the light and given her a barrel or two. But Teach was behind her. She'd brought Biedersbill as her totem pole.

Neck looked at the Teacher and got out of her way. Sarah

went towards Mozart. It could have been Scarlatti or some other shit. All classical music was Mozart to her. She found Doris and Gwendolyn the nurse wearing bathrobes and kissing in bed, under the light of a candle. They had two enormous wine glasses on the bed with them. Goblets, Sarah would say. You'd piss a mile, drinking out of a goblet like that. Old Scarlatti was on the tape deck. Two hundred violins and Doris and Gwen flicking tongues into each other's mouth like a pair of lizards. It wasn't the kissing that bothered her. It was their reptile tongues.

"Is that what you call therapy, Gwen?"

The nurse nearly leapt out of her robe. The goblets spilled. And old Gwen, who'd lost all her teeth to a dentist in Saigon, recovered herself.

"What are you doing here?"

"Checking on the patient," Sarah said.

"Did Neck send you up?"

"I don't need his approval, honey. Neck works for me."

Gwendolyn laughed. "You silly cow. Go back where you belong."

Sarah slapped the nurse off the bed with the butt of a .45. Gwendolyn lay where she'd fallen, her shoulders rocking with a soft moan. Doris wasn't alarmed. She picked up her goblet and drank what was left.

Scarlatti was giving Sarah a headache. "Marve's been worrying about you, dear. How do you like our rest home? I had it laid out for you and captain hired Gwen. She's a bit of a whore, our Gwen. I don't mind the kissing and all, but how's your writing arm, little Doris?"

"Rusty," Doris said. "I'm retired . . . couldn't run down to the grocery without some leech looking for an autograph."

"It's the price of popularity," Sarah said. *Wouldn't mind a few autograph-hunters. But the population isn't into pockmarks.*

"Sarah, they would have eaten my blood. You've no idea. If

you and Marve hadn't helped me I'd have gone into a convent, or killed myself . . . thank you, Sarah."

"Oh, I'm bighearted. I'd rip open the world for one of Marvin's friends. Get into your clothes."

"I couldn't go out there again to all those leeches."

Sarah stepped around the bed, stood on Gwendolyn's back, and began hurling clothes out of Quinn's closet. She couldn't get away from violins.

Doris reached down and hugged her nurse and Sarah had to dress them both. Doris and Gwen gave their arms and legs to her like defeated dolls. Sarah wrapped them in cardigans and sashes and kerchiefs and kilts until they resembled Vietnamese river pirates, and then she threw them into the hall, where they continued to hug, and Sarah had to knock them into the bannisters and down the stairs while the nurse cried for help. "Somebody save us."

She looked to Teach and she looked to Neck, but they'd already abandoned her to Saigon Sarah.

"Neck, Neck," she moaned. "I'm with you."

Neck wouldn't allow her near his cuffs. He opened the door and flung the two women into the street. The nurse persisted, trying to crawl back into the house, and Neck closed the door on her.

"Trash," he said. "Were they kissing upstairs, mama-san? It's not my fault. I'm not Gwen's moral guardian. I'd better go and clean their mess."

He started up the stairs, but Sarah called to him over the drill of violins. "I'm not finished with you, Neck. You're driving us to Jersey."

"Jesus, I forgot to tell you. The car's not in shipshape. Have to take her in to the shop."

"You have three minutes to warm her up, Neck."

"But we can't escape out the front. The girls will be watching us. Gwen will make a stink."

"Then we'll use the back door, Neck."

Neck shrugged and went around to the back. Sarah chewed on the dark crust of her opium ball. It was pumpernickel with a wicked pull. Teach wouldn't share the ball with her. He watched a crack in the ceiling. Then he followed Sarah out to the side of Belleville. They walked along a row of alleys and entered the street from the garden of an abandoned house.

Neck was waiting in the gang's white limousine. Sarah climbed onto the cushions with Teach. It was an old corporation car Sarah had retrieved from a downtown garage that specialized in kidnapped sedans. There was a bar sculpted into the leather seats, but Sarah had no use for alcohol, and she'd left all the paraphernalia of mixing drinks to rot against the leather. But she loved the car's tinted glass. Not a soul could see inside. And this gave her an advantage over the enemies the gang might have. She'd paid sixteen thousand dollars for the white limousine in one of her expansive moods. But Sarah's ambition was gone. She couldn't plot more than a day at a time. She'd light a candle to Jehovah if the son of a bitch could guarantee that Lulu and Marve would get to tomorrow.

And don't forget her dad. He'd been delivered to a nursing home with Alzheimer's disease. Her dad had gone senile in the years since she'd arrived in Alphabetville. He'd given up his job with the greeting-card companies when he discovered he could no longer do a poem. It wasn't simply that words had gone out of his head. He'd begun to forget details of his past and present life. Struggling with his disease, he'd deny he ever had a wife. He'd go on a trip to Camden and end up in Dutch country. The wife he couldn't remember had to take his car away. He'd sit upstairs in his room, squeeze out two words of a poem, and start to cry. Old Hilma offered to lend him the words, to scratch at her own vocabulary for him. But he was lucid enough to reject her offer. "Strange lady," he said. "You can't write a two-headed poem." He cried for six months and Hilma put him in the home.

Sarah planned to send Teach after Hilma with a bomb, but she couldn't wipe out her own mom. It would have been like incest. And so she was riding to Jersey to see her dad.

Howie slept in the cushions like a goddamn child. He was still her totem pole, even with his eyes shut. Neck wouldn't get funny with Teach in the car. But she had to wonder how long that totem would last. He'd desert Sarah in the end and jump to the padre's side. But before that happened she'd introduce her old fiancé to Herman Fish.

The home where her daddy was stood on a hill behind Passaic. It was policed by little sisters. They had more security at the Chanticleer than at the American Mission in old Saigon. Neck couldn't park on the little sisters' lawn. He had to sit in the limo, near the front gate. The little nuns seemed suspicious of Biedersbill. They kept watching him blink.

"We're veterans, for Christ's sake. We kept New Jersey safe from the gooks."

But nothing seemed to satisfy them. Sarah had to leave a hundred-dollar deposit at the front desk.

"We wouldn't steal your fixtures. We're not cat thieves."

"Lower your voice," said the sister-in-chief, a certain Mrs. Simonson.

Sarah took Teach by the hand and led him toward a fistful of rooms on the second floor. She found her mother drifting outside the rooms. Hilma seemed like the one with Alzheimer's disease. Her eyes scarcely focused. She muttered to herself.

Sarah turned spiteful. All she could think was that Hilma would inherit the next room to dad's. She couldn't summon the slightest pity. Sarah's mom had treated her like a stepsister. Her dad had barked at her, barked his love, but old Hilma sat in the distance.

Sarah sneaked past her mother with Biedersbill and went into her father's room. She couldn't understand it at all. She must have come to a king's manor, because her dad lay in a room with eleven windows and three different views. He had a river

205

on one side, trees on the other, and the front gate in the window near his bed. And what a bed he'd been given by the little nuns. Sarah imagined a full tribe of people floating on the headboard. The frame was wide as a small sea. The nuns must have roped two mattresses together. Her dad lay on a coverlet stitched with golden thread. He wore special pajamas, blue as God's beard. He didn't look like Alzheimer's. Her dad was the king of this place.

She approached the bed with Biedersbill. "Dad, I brought you a guest."

His eyes traveled past her face. Her dad wasn't recognizing his subjects today. He chewed on something, but Sarah couldn't determine what was in his mouth.

"Dad, do you remember Howie from Bayonne? It's the Biedersbill boy."

The chewing stopped.

"He's good to me, dad. We'll get married one of these days." She knew it was a lie, but she didn't want her dad to think that she had a trivial relationship with the Biedersbill boy. Her dad understood marriage and divorce. He was a love poet, and he must have asked himself how come Howie had been her fiancé since Bengal High. Herman wouldn't approve of extended courtships. He'd never have allowed that kind of frozen love in his greeting cards.

"Howie, say a few words to my father?"

But the situation must have reminded Howie of a fire zone. He twitched and blinked, and she had to dig at him with an elbow.

"Say something. He's sick."

"Glad to meet you, Mr. Fish."

The chewing started up again. The turmoil went from cheek to cheek. Sarah lowered her head and took a lick off the opium ball. She wanted the moon to come down and sit on her father's bed. She wondered if Teach could work a little of his montagnard magic for her dad. She took another lick. And that's when the chief nun entered the room.

Sarah was getting suspicious about the lay of the land. Who the hell had hired the little sisters and outfitted her dad in God's pajamas?

"Is this a charity op, Mrs. Simonson? Because my father isn't exactly rich."

"It's run by the Baroness de Roth."

"Well, how come the Baroness hasn't asked me for a contribution? I have the cash."

"No one pays here," Simonson said. "The Baroness has her own foundation."

"That doesn't dazzle me . . . I was a nurse once. In the Nam. I don't see signs of degeneration in my dad. He looks like he did ten years ago. He's on the quiet side, that's all. Dad's not speaking today."

"My dear, he can't remember who he is."

"That's no tragedy," Sarah said. "Why should he be sandbagged with sixty years of rotten dreams?"

"He can't go to the toilet without a nurse."

"Well, what are nurses for? I'm not convinced this is the place for my dad."

"Where else would he have absolute devotion and a lovely room?"

Sarah was about to say Belleville, but she'd just fired Gwen, and she was in the middle of a war with Uncle Albert. Her dad was better off at the Chanticleer, she had to admit. But she wasn't crazy about the little sisters.

"Ma'am," she said. "Has my father ever talked to you?"

"Not exactly," Simonson said.

"What does that mean? Has he engaged you in a dialogue or not?"

"No. But I did hear him repeat one sentence and I marked it down."

Good dog, Sarah had the urge to say, but she might not have gotten her father's sentence out of the bitch.

"Who the hell was my father talking to?"

Simonson frowned. "We don't curse at the Chanticleer. Nor do we adopt such a truculent tone. It might upset your father. If you must know, he was talking to no one in particular."

Sarah had a sudden pull of joy. She almost hugged that little nun. The hell with Alzheimer's! Her dad was writing a poem. He always sounded the first line to himself.

"Can you read me my father's sentence, Mrs. Simonson?"

The nurse stuck on her spectacles and fiddled with a piece of paper. "The trees are black where she is."

Sarah brooded over the line. Didn't seem like a love poem. Love couldn't grow on a black tree.

"Mrs. Simonson, was there something else?"

"Come, my dear, you mustn't disturb your poor father. Faces excite him. He starts to chew on his tongue."

"Well, give him a candy, for Christ's sake."

The nun was pissed off again. "That would be criminal. Your father could choke on candy. You ought to know that much if you ever were a nurse."

Simonson shouldn't have knocked down Sarah's credentials. "Had my tour extended twice at Cayenne. I was in the boonies next to three years. There wasn't a whole lot of Alzheimer's among the Viet Cong. I still think my father can chew a candy."

She kissed her dad on his one fat cheek. He didn't respond to the kiss. His eyes wouldn't light on Sarah. He'd removed himself from all his subjects. Sarah took the Teach's hand and waltzed out of the room with Mrs. Simonson.

Thank God Hilma wasn't in the hall, or that nurse would have scolded Sarah for neglecting her mom.

"So glad you could come, my dear. The Baroness always likes to have the loved ones of her guests on the grounds."

"Thank the Baroness for me," Sarah said. "She's awful kind to take my dad."

Sarah left with Biedersbill, but she didn't go far. She began to feel his pockets and found a lick of money. She returned to the Chanticleer and slapped eight hundred dollars down on Simonson's desk. "Service," she said.

Simonson refused to look at the money. "We're not a hotel. I thought I made that clear. The Baroness doesn't screen her guests to learn who can pay. It would be against the rules of her foundation."

"Well, I won't have my dad accepting charity."

"My dear, I'll have to call the police if you don't remove yourselves and the money."

"The money stays."

A door opened behind Simonson's desk and a little woman with stooped shoulders and a parrot's beak stepped out of her office. "Quel est ce bruit?"

"It's nothing, Baroness. Nothing at all. A slight misunderstanding with Fish's daughter and her fiancé."

"Bring them inside, Simonson."

And the three of them followed the Baroness into her office. The Baroness de Roth only had one window, with a view of the Chanticleer's kitchen barrels.

"Speak up," said the Baroness, who seemed more interested in Howie's twitch than in Sarah herself.

"Baroness, I'm grateful you've given dad the chance to live on your estate. I know he doesn't eat much, but it costs a lot to have nurses around the clock, and . . ."

"And, and, and," said the Baroness, her parrot's beak twitching with a fury. She seemed like a companion to Biedersbill.

It was Howie who calmed the Baroness by speaking in French.

"Mademoiselle est agité, madame la baronne. Elle—"

"Keep it in English," Sarah said. She felt betrayed. Biedersbill stuttered in English and sang like a bird to the Baroness. Where did that little man study French? With the montagnards, or in the brig at Long Binh?

But the Baroness seemed satisfied. "Ah, you'd like to leave your father some spending money, is that it?"

"Sort of," Sarah said.

"How much?"

"Eight hundred . . . for a start."

"I'm sure he'll appreciate it. I'm fond of Mr. Fish. I sit with him as much as I can . . . Simonson, give the young lady a receipt."

"Yes, Baroness."

Simonson collected the money and wrote a voucher for it in a yellow pad. She tore the voucher from the pad and handed it to Sarah.

"Do come again."

Sarah walked out of the Chanticleer a second time. But this exit was a triumph for Howie and herself. She'd obliged the Baroness to accept the gang's money. There ought to be a plaque over her father's bed: Furnished by the Avenue C Foundation, in honor of Herman Fish and his love poems.

The trees are black where she is.

She wondered now if it was a poem on the Nam. She couldn't remember black trees at Fort Cayenne. And then she realized how stupid she was. Herman hadn't been to Cayenne. He'd have had to imagine what the Nam was about. But she was still brooding over Howie's betrayal of her in the Baroness's office.

"Why'd you talk French?"

"The Frenchies like to hear their own language," Howie said. "It th-throws them off guard."

"Couldn't you have warned me first?"

"I had to lay it on or we'd have gotten nowhere with the Baroness."

"Forgive you," Sarah said. "But don't do it again."

210

9

SARAH licked her opium ball and Neck drove her away from
the Chanticleer's walls. There were black trees on the Passaic
River, black trees on the turnpike, black trees growing from
Neck's ear. Ah, her dad's first line had been on the subject of
Sarah, in and out of Vietnam. Alzheimer's had toughened his
brain, got rid of the ordinary muck and debris, so Herman could
fall into dreams and not go out of there. He didn't have any
use for recognizing wives and daughters in the flesh. He was
deep inside a song. And Sarah ran a nursery for misfits. She
had Lulu and Marve and Vladimir to feed. You couldn't dream

near a bowl of yellow rice. So she licked her opium ball and discovered black trees.

She couldn't remember getting out of the car. But she was on her mattress at the talmud torah. She'd gone back to Cayenne. She was a nurse for Charlie now. Charlie's own helicopters were making an ice-cream run. But the damn ice cream wouldn't hit the ground. It developed roots as it rolled in the sky. And all she'd wanted was cherry vanilla from Charles.

Black trees were banging in her head. The sons of bitches had learned to talk. They banged and said, little mama, little mama. Sarah climbed off the mattress. It was Tuesday, and on Tuesday Marve danced. She began knocking about the talmud torah, screaming for her gang. Only a couple of bitches came out of their rooms. Baby-san was drying her nails and sleeping beauty was in his underpants. Old Marve had lovely knees. She'd rather look at him than any Bo Derek on the wall.

"Where's that Biedersbill?"

"Saw him go out with Vladimir," Lulu said.

"They're always going somewhere together," Sarah said between her teeth. "Was it talmud torah business, you think?"

"How would I know, mama-san?"

That figures. Baby was into toenails. And now they had to work on Marve. They stripped him of his underpants and he stood naked before the two of them. They didn't have Teach to mix the right colors and get him to look like a mountain king. Sarah dabbed the beauty's back with blood from a can. She didn't like the way Lulu was hovering near his balls. "Baby-san, you don't have to lay stripes on the inside of his thighs. Color his abdominal board."

"You do your stuff and I'll do mine," baby-san said. Sarah felt a stripe of pity for her. Baby suffered from that college girl's disease, anorexia. She was dying for Marve, starving herself. And what could Sarah do? If she allowed baby-san in Marve's room, she'd become anorexic herself. But she had to get baby-san to eat.

"Honey, wouldn't you like a cup of yellow rice?"

"I'm happy with lemon water."

Sarah ground her teeth. She'd have forced food into Lulu's mouth, but Marve wouldn't let her. What the hell did she know of mountain tribes? She'd served in the lowlands. The Elephanters could have been a piece of fiction prepared by Biedersbill. She'd murder that little man when she found him.

It was just another morning run to get Corinne. But Teach had borrowed Sarah's white limousine and brought Vladimir along. He left old Vladi in the van and sat in Carlo's breakfast nook having a heart-to-heart with the old publisher while Corinne was in the bedroom combing her hair.

"You don't think I was mistaken, do you, Mr. Biedersbill?"

"About Troubnoy? Sounds like an operator to me, sir."

"But there might have been some merit to his proposal."

"Not a chance," said the Teach. "The Russkis are always doing proposals. And their proposals stink."

Carlo laughed and sucked on his coffee. It was the same espresso Teach drank with him on the mornings he took Corinne. Dark stuff in a children's cup that could break against your teeth.

"This nonsense about a Dmitri Konstantinovich and the White House," Carlo said. "I wasn't going to fall for that. He was supposed to tell us about the Lubyanka."

"Ah, those lightweight spies love to invent prison stories."

The cup twitched in Teacher's hand. He'd grown fond of Carlo during these little chats and he didn't enjoy lying to the old man.

Corinne came down in a blue sweater. The sweater was for Konstantin, and she was like a raw purring cat. Her nostrils quivered with nervousness. Teach could imagine her in bed.

She'd bite Konstantin to pieces while she sat over him. He'd have to disappoint the little lady. Konstantin was hawking his pens on the other side of the world.

"What is it today, dear heart?" the old man asked. "Turgenev?" He still fell under the dream that Corinne was studying with Uncle Al.

"I think it's our morning for Rimbaud."

"I see. My brother is getting into the obscure."

"Rimbaud is not obscure," Corinne said, under her mascara. She looked like one of the brilliant human dolls in *Blade Runner*. Teach had to wonder if she didn't belong in the twenty-first century somewhere. She took him by the hand and pulled him out of the breakfast nook. Teach could barely say good-bye to Carlo. Corinne was laughing to herself. Her body shook under the blue sweater. Ah, the Blade Runner's sweet moll. Teach didn't dare utter a word until they were outside.

"Corinne, I'm sorry, but Konstantin's not at the hotel. He had to travel."

"Connie's not waiting for me?"

Connie, she called that mother Connie. Must have been his code name with all the American girls.

"It's business," Teach said.

"I know his business. Connie's a thief and a spy."

Lord, Teach moaned to himself. Will I have to kidnap her too? "What spy? Konstantin sells fountain pens."

"To the politburo in Hanoi . . . oh," she said. "Poor Teacher, I won't tell. What shall we do now that we have a free morning? . . . take me to Lulu."

"Can't."

"Why not?"

"Because it could upset the talmud torah. Sarah doesn't like other women in the house."

"Tough," Corinne said. "I'll rape you in the street if I can't say hello to my daughter. I'm not kidding, Teach. I'll start undressing you."

Teach had to signal to Vladimir, who grabbed Corinne from behind and hoisted her into the limousine. "Fuckers," she said. But the windows were rolled up, and King Street couldn't hear her.

Teach drove aimlessly, down to Battery Park. They looked at the Statue of Liberty from the limousine. The statue was all trussed up.

"I sent in a hundred dollars," Teach said. "To save the old girl. Liberty's coming apart at the seams."

"That's gallant of you, Teacher, but why didn't you cancel my morning class?"

"Carlo might have got suspicious."

"Couldn't you have said Albert had a cold?"

Teach offered her a commando's frown. "Albert can still give lessons with a cold."

Vladimir brought a breakfast of hot dogs into the limousine, and they all gobbled together. Teach had to wipe the mustard from Corinne's lip. Then he returned her to King Street. Carlo met them on the stoop.

"Mr. Biedersbill, I do think we ought to give Troubnoy another chance . . . perhaps in a couple of weeks."

Corinne walked past her husband and into the house.

Nika Nikolayevich Troubnoy was sick of Russian bakeries. He had to take orders from lunatic aunts and Stalin's ex-clown, Izak, who was the chief baker. His only possible companion at the bakery was Samuil himself. The aunts had fallen in love with some minstrel called Michael Jackson. They blasted his songs on the radio, and Troubnoy believed that the devil had something to do with it. The devil had entered Michael Jackson and twisted his sex around from girl to boy and girl again, like a whole melody of people. And then Samuil ruined Nika's life. It was bad enough that Troubnoy rolled chocolate six, seven hours with Michael Jackson on the radio. But did Samuil have to install a movie machine, a gift from the devil? Fed a little box into the machine, and Michael Jackson appeared in a five-minute movie. Zoya and Adelina played that movie over and over, and it was like thumbs in Nika's heart, because Michael Jackson's movie was all about the devil coming up from under the ground. *Thriller*, they called it. But Troubnoy wasn't fooled. It was a film about the Lubyanka and the dead who wouldn't stay dead. Zoya shivered to the music. And Adelina threw kisses in the air.

"Nika, darling Nika, come dance with me."

"I have a wife in Moscow," Troubnoy uttered in his own defense.

"That whore, she sold you to the KGB."

"Still a wife," Troubnoy said, rolling chocolate with a savage eye.

But he didn't have to bother about Michael Jackson this morning. It was Nika's day off. And he strolled to the chess tables in Manhattan Beach Park. His mind went to Reykjavik, 1971, and he grieved over Spassky's fall to Bobby Fischer, twelve years ago. Nika wasn't a chauvinist. He recognized the erratic genius of the American boy. But Spassky should have won. Boris was the Mozart of chess. Made pizzicato on the board. But they wouldn't let Boris play alone at Reykjavik. The KGB sat behind him, monitored his moves, and Mozart couldn't perform against a crazy American genius.

Now the KGB had installed its own champion, Anatoly Karpov, and Nika refused to follow Soviet chess. Karpov learned to play sitting at the Lubyanka's feet. The Banditov controlled all his tournaments. How could Nika take an interest in such a man?

Troubnoy sat with the patzers near the beach. He wouldn't

trade rooks with some Odessa champ. He might have a heart attack over the board. But there was a shadow in the corner of his left eye. Two shadows. Nika looked up. He'd have his heart attack without trading rooks. It was Vladimir and the publisher's assistant, Mr. Biedersbill. Nika could have yelled his lungs out, but it was useless to fight. America had its own KGB. This Biedersbill was part of the Banditov. Nika cursed his Jewish luck. He'd gone to the wrong publisher.

"Troubnoy," Teach said. "Will you please come with us?"

Nika got up from the table and started to cry. "Vladi, I didn't mean to sell you down river. I was desperate for cash."

Vladimir had been one of the walking dead inside the Lubyanka. Troubnoy sold this news to those rotten bakers. And now Vladimir had come with the American KGB to skin him alive.

"Vladi won't hurt you, Mr. Troubnoy. We're taking you to a convalescent home. You'll like it there. I can promise you a river under your window."

Absolutely. A river where the dead can row. But he took the Teacher's arm and accompanied him to Sarah's stretch limousine, parked on Oriental Boulevard. He whispered into Teach's ear. "Will Vladi leave marks on my neck?"

"Mr. Troubnoy, I thought you trusted me. Don't talk about marks."

Teach could smell the nearness of the ocean, but Vladi wouldn't breathe it in. Vladi had one thing on the brain. Sisters in Leningrad. And the world's aromas couldn't reach his head.

Nika panicked soon as they got to the Jersey marshes. He didn't believe that talk of a convalescent home. He was convinced they'd bury him in the muck. But Teach drove off the marshland and Nika found himself whistling Michael Jackson songs until they arrived at the Chanticleer.

Simonson had come out to greet Nika Nikolayevich. She wore a blue cape. "How nice of you to visit us, Mr. Troubnoy."

Nika stared at the sliver of neck under Simonson's cape front and followed her inside the Chanticleer. Teach looked at the balconies that ringed the Baroness's mansion like the slanting decks of a ship and wondered when the mansion would float away. He knew from Simonson's smile that a fresh batch of Elephant candy was in the kitchen. As he climbed the Baroness's stairs, he couldn't help thinking of Sarah's dad. Old Herman Fish on the second floor.

Teach walked into the kitchen where the Elephant candy stood in a gang of jars. He worked without spoons or measuring cups, cutting the poison in the jars with crystals of brown sugar. The poison stayed black, and Teacher's candy shone like diamond dust. He couldn't tell where the poison came from. The Elephanters no longer existed as a tribe. Hanoi had dispersed the republic, thrown its magicians into a concentration camp. George languished in the swamps somewhere, a king without resources. And Hélène was probably mistress of the camp commandant. So who was attending the poison tubs, gathering roots in the mountains, labeling jars, and smuggling them out of the harbor at Ho Chi Minh? A whole industry that stank of montagnards and Teach couldn't find one free magician.

He'd tried writing to George. But how do you address a lost republic? George's concentration camp wasn't listed in any handbook the Teacher had. Six or seven years without the rainbow king. All that candy had ruined the Teacher's arithmetic. But he had enough stuff in his head to recall a few things. Uncle shouldn't have sentenced Herman Fish to the Chanticleer, not without telling the Teach. It wasn't kind to play with Sarah's family.

He was returning to the limousine when Simonson shouted at him from the porch. "Teacher, you have a guest."

He left Vladi in the limo and strolled across the lawn. Some mother in a felt hat materialized on the porch. It was the padre, old Uncle Al.

Teach sat next to the padre in a porch chair. "How come Sarah's dad is sitting upstairs?"

"Why not? He's convalescing with us."

"Who brought him here?"

"Don't niggle, Howard. I learnt he was sick and I offered our services."

"You almost sank us. Didn't you suspect Sarah might come for a visit?"

"Why shouldn't she visit the Chanticleer? She's entitled to see her dad."

"What if a nurse said hello to me by accident while I was with Sarah? She has a temper, padre. She'll declare war on the Baroness and shoot us all to shit."

"But she discovered nothing, little son. And you were admirable, I'm told. Went into the Baroness's office as if you were an absolute stranger. So it's a dead issue. Our Sarah is in the dark."

Teacher sat under the porch's swollen roof, balconies creaking over his head. Could have sworn the mansion had moved. Ah, that's how it was. Miracles in a rotting place. He'd never recover from having been born in New Jersey. "Where the hell is Captain Jonah?"

"In heaven," the padre said. "Jonah died last week. We had to bury him in the old chicken yard."

"What happened?"

"Swallowed too much Elephant sauce."

"My candy wouldn't have killed him, padre. It was the same prescription I had for Marve."

"But Konstantin changed the prescription."

"That mother isn't your pharmacist. I am. Did Jonah die without a prayer?"

"Of course I prayed for him. Don't forget. I was a preacher in the Nam."

"How much praying did Konstantin do?"

"None," the padre said. "He's gone to Ho Chi Minh ville. He's an errant fellow, that Konstantin. Does what he wants. Got it into his head to kill Jonah out of spite. Kostya lost his grip. Banged too many nurses.

"Nurses aint all of it. Uncle, he's the one who's been copying my style. He poisoned Nibio and Capa's generals and old Renata. Why?"

"I told you. He's perverse. Wanted Boliv out of the way. He was doing a dance with the Colombian maf. But his dancing failed. Howard, Capablanca is back on the street. I've given him the Alphabet Blocks."

"Uncle, I read the *Times* every other day. I can't remember a coup in Boliv."

"Wasn't necessary, Howard, Coca is moving again."

"What about those government strikers in the Chaparé? Aren't the Leopards eating up your coca margin?"

"The Leopards have gone to sleep," Uncle said.

"So it was like a fucking war game. Whatever way it turns, you win. And Renata, wasn't she your lady?"

"Not at all," Uncle said. "I think it's time we finished our Russian friend. He might cause us some embarrassment. I'm sending you to Ho Chi Minh."

"What about Vladi's sisters? If I wind his clock, they'll go to an orphanage, padre. Or worse."

"I wouldn't compromise Vladimir. We'll get his sisters out of Leningrad. It's being arranged right now."

"Can they live with us at the talmud torah?"

"First we'll get them to Norway and then we'll see."

"Is it a promise? I couldn't do Konstantin, knowing the girls might be blitzed."

"Norway, Howard. I can't promise more than that . . . you'll leave for Ho this afternoon."

"Afternoon?" the Teacher said, hearing the balconies creak. "It's cabaret night and I have to paint up Marve."

"Too bad," the padre said. "It's not a goddamn picnic. We have to sneak you in from France. And there's only one flight a week. If you miss that, Konstantin might decide to dispose of the girls. He's crazy enough."

"Will you send Vladi home to Sarah?"

"Vladi stays here."

"What if the Davidoffs storm the talmud torah? Sarah's left with Lulu and Marve."

"Samuil isn't bloodthirsty. When he sees that Vladi's gone, he'll scrape a song on the walls and then you'll have some dancing out of Marve."

Teacher laughed, but a bitter squall came out of his throat, like the wind that drove the balconies. It was the sound a magician might make.

She was the only policeman she had tonight, Sarah and her .45s, which she kept in the folds of her gypsy gown. The cabaret was packed. There was no more place to sit and Sarah had to send customers away. She was about to shut the door when a woman alighted from a cab. She could tell this tall blonde bitch was Marvey's wife. Sarah hesitated for a moment. And in that moment she was lost.

"Wait," Lliana said, and Sarah surrendered to the voice, sniffed her own doom. She couldn't compete with a blonde like that. Lliana had the ankles of a racing horse.

"Thank you," the bitch said.

Sarah shoved a customer out of his chair and gave it to Lliana. Just another pirouette in her own little doom dance.

The uptown ladies in their mink stoles were clapping for his majesty of the talmud torah. Marve came out of his closet with blood from a can and the uptown ladies were already wild. He climbed the platform to the creak of a mountain fiddle. Baby-san was the musician tonight. She didn't copy the Teacher's style. She played according to the weather under her skirt. Lulu couldn't have told one highland from another. But she had Marve hopping like a mountain man.

Marve danced and danced. Was he a king tonight? He was always descending into someone else's skin. Had this dumb notion of himself as Orpheus in a talmud torah. But where was Eurydice? And as he rolled with the music he saw Eurydice's eye. Eurydice was blonde in that dark cavern where he danced, caged in by the wire struts of a canopy. Jews of New Jersey were married under a mounted shawl like that.

He followed Eurydice from strut to strut and pulled himself out of the fiddle's call. He wasn't Orpheus. He was a man looking for his wife. Lliana had come to see him dance.

Women were crowding the platform. The canopy began to quiver as they grabbed at the struts. They clapped money to Marve's thighs. It was like a sign of purchase. But he'd have to disappoint the mamas. He couldn't go away with them all.

He escaped between two struts, money falling from him like lizard skin. He didn't have Vladi to lead him to the dressing closet. So he sprinted from under the canopy, arrived at the closet, got dressed, and ran out for Lliana with his war paint on. Shoved politely as he could, but he kept landing into walls.

It was Lliana who found him. She kidnapped Marve from the talmud torah. They walked on Avenue C, away from all the women's limousines. Marve cursed Alphabetville. He didn't have a decent bar where he could take his wife. They wandered into a lot on East Eleventh Street. It was part of some abandoned garden that had continued to grow carrots and peas. The street-lights couldn't penetrate much of the garden. Lliana's shadow crept up a brick wall. It seemed to bend over the garden and eat at the sky. Marve hadn't met a shadow with such an appetite. And then his shadow started sucking sky and he wondered if the Teach had provided this garden with an optical nerve. There was nothing the Teacher couldn't do. Teach mixed blood in a can and made people into montagnards.

Marve was so busy counting shadows, he hadn't realized Lliana was holding his hand.

"It's dangerous down here. You'd better move uptown. Jonah is missing."

"I couldn't leave Sarah."

"Why not? Her friend the twitch is a war criminal and she's a racketeer nurse."

"She's no racketeer. She took Lulu in and saved her from the street."

"Then go with Lulu, because that gun moll doesn't have long to live."

"Who told you that?"

"Albert."

"I thought he's your Rimbaud connection."

"Stop it, Marve. The CIA wooed him out of Dartmouth years ago. He didn't go to Vietnam as a bloody scholar."

"Albert's supposed to be in retirement. He went back to scholarship after the fall of Saigon."

"But he knows what's going on in the street."

Marve clutched his wife in that dark garden, his shadow like a puppet show on the wall of a ruined apartment house. "Lliana, I'm the one who's been out on the street. Albert's strictly an uptown man." He kissed Lliana and couldn't tell if it was out of anger or the tunnelings of love. "We had a good time in Rome, didn't we, Lliana?"

He could see that old forked look, the split that grew down her forehead when she was exasperated with him. "What does Rome have to do with it? You think you understand the street, but you're a taxi dancer to the rich. Housewives come slumming to catch you dance. You're locked up all day in a brick vault you call a talmud torah. That gun moll keeps you blind."

"But Lliana, she fights the gypsies and the thieves. Dentists and doctors can't come here to skunk the poor. She was a nurse in Vietnam. She brought Howie Biedersbill home from the dead."

"My dumb little darling, that twitch is her paid killer."

"Teach doesn't kill. He carries a bomb kit to scare the gypsies away."

Another shadow crept up the wall. It was much longer and sleeker than his own. He looked towards Eleventh Street and noticed a limousine was keeping pace with his stroll in the garden. It wasn't one of those pick-up trucks waiting for customers to come out of the talmud torah. This limo had six doors. It was the talmud torah's private wagon, and Lliana was leading him towards that car. "Come," she said, holding his hand after he'd kissed her. He was beginning to feel like a husband again, as if his time at the talmud torah had been nothing but a long vacation from his wife.

The front door opened and old Neck came out. "How are you, majesty?"

It had to be all right if Neck was around. Neck opened one of the middle doors. The limo had deep cushions and Marve only saw a collection of feet. Lliana stooped to get inside, and Marve was next, but he heard a shout behind him.

"Don't you move, Marvin de la Mare."

He turned in the dark and discovered old Saigon with her .45s. But Lliana was calling to him from inside the car.

"Darling, save yourself."

All Marve could do was cry. He'd have followed that voice to the ruins of Phnom Penh, but he was registered with the talmud torah. He was part of the Avenue C mob. It was as if he had a tattoo on his ass, and the tattoo said *Sarah*. Lliana held out her arm to him. It was a lovely arm. It curled at the elbow like a snake about to wind.

And then there was Sarah.

"Neck, I'm telling you. If Marvey gets in, your little firm will be short a driver. I'll blow you into Chinatown."

Neck's mouth broke into an ugly smile. "You wouldn't dare, mama-san. All that noise would bring the fuzz."

He laughed at the certainty of his argument: the bitch couldn't splatter him without waking the police.

Sarah shot the car.

Neck stared at the wound in his fender and shoved Marve out of the way. "Go on home to your fat tit." He shut Lliana's door, climbed into the car, and drove out of Sarah's territories.

Sarah hugged her crying dancer. Teach had poisoned him with his montagnard magic, fed him mountain candy and Marve lost his mind. It had nothing to do with Sarah's powers as a temptress. She'd lured an unlucky man into her bed. She'd have returned Marve to the blonde wife, but it was too late. Lliana had gone to work for the padre. Why else would Lliana be traveling with Neck?

She wondered if Teach had an antidote for Marve's sleeping sickness, some chopped-up flower in a jar that would bring him back to the land of books. She'd take her money from under the brick and help him start a publishing house. He wouldn't have to work for Carlo Peck. Once Marve was on his feet, she'd worm a contract out of him for a book on the Nam. Not a war novel, with platoons and flags and helicopter fleets, but an account of her years as a nurse at Cayenne. *The Autobiography of a Vietnam War Nurse* by Sarah Fish. She'd include Captain Jonah, Rabbi Collinswood, and his interrogators from Saigon, and how the Teacher came down to her from the sky. She wouldn't forget the corpsmen who began their relationship with Sarah trying to feel her titties and ended up saving her life. But then she started thinking how the corpsmen disappeared in the South China Sea and Sarah didn't have the heart to write her autobiography. She'd have to disappoint old Marve and keep his new company off the best-seller lists.

10

The trees are black where she is
The water is brown with frog heads
And she is pale with a pale color . . .

SARAH was working on her daddy's poem. She took a lick
of her opium ball, stuck after the third line. It didn't sound
like a greeting card to Sarah unless Herman had a funeral in
mind. She woke from a nightmare, blue sweat on her lip like
a moustache of bad signs. She dreamt about the Chanticleer.
But her daddy wasn't in the dream. The bird woman had come
to her, old Baroness de Roth, and pecked at Sarah, started eating
off her face. Sarah didn't call out to her daddy. Herman was
upstairs in that king's room and he wouldn't have bothered with
the destruction of his daughter's face. She screamed for Hilma
instead.

"Mama, mama."

And Sarah knew where she had to go next. She rose up at six in the morning and showered in her tiny stall. She put on Teacher's underpants for good luck, packed her .45s and the opium ball, took a couple of thousand from under her money brick, and tried not to wake baby-san.

She tiptoed into Marve's room and kissed her crazy dancer. Marve woke up and watched her without blinking his eyes.

"Mama-san's got to go on an errand, but you stay inside. Look after Lulu and don't let her out of your sight."

"When will you be back?" he asked, barely wrinkling his lips.

"Soon as I can." She stepped out of the talmud torah and saw her limousine parked across the street. Was the padre slick enough to think he could trap Saigon Sarah with such a familiar toy? She smiled to herself. Why shouldn't old Neck chauffeur her across the Bayonne Bridge? She had her .45s.

Got into the limousine without asking Neck. She was the only passenger. Saigon had all the cushions to herself. She broke into the quiet of the car. "How are you, Neck?"

"Sweet as a fiddler in Saigon."

"You like your new employer?"

He seemed to chafe in his black driving coat. "I've always been your chauffeur, mama-san."

"That's good to hear. Take me to my mother in Bayonne."

"Bayonne it is," said Neck, and Saigon sank into the cushions, pointing a .45 at Neck from under the polka dots of her skirt, because he could shimmy and cry his allegiance to Sarah, but he was still the padre's man.

She arrived at her mama's house before seven, and she wouldn't permit Neck to wait in the car. He might signal to the padre on his CB, and she'd find herself surrounded by commandos. Neck had to accompany Sarah to the door. She didn't ring the bell or call upstairs to Hilma's room. The door was unlocked. Sarah went inside and made the chauffeur wipe his feet on the mat.

Old Hilma met them in the hall. She wasn't in her nightgown. She was dressed for business at seven o'clock. Mama was taking the shuttle to Mars. She greeted Neck like an old acquaintance, and it bothered Sarah.

"Neck, have you seen my mother before now?"

"Ah," the chauffeur said. "Once or twice."

Saigon had to wonder if Hilma Fish was on the padre's payroll.

"Mama, why are you up so early?"

"Can't sleep without your father," she said.

"But you're all dressed. Were you planning an excursion to the roof?"

"She's lonely," Neck answered for Hilma. "It aint so demoralizing when you wear clothes in the house."

"Didn't ask you, Neck." She sat her chauffeur down in the living room where he wouldn't be such a nuisance and she went into the kitchen with Hilma, but she was still tied to the padre's man. Her mother began to worry about old Neck.

"Sarah, he has a large frame. He'll get hungry sitting there. Should I feed him something?"

"No. I pay him to be hungry. Starving is good for the solar plexus."

But Sarah herself couldn't get a cup of coffee or a raisin bun and she had to settle into the same old story of Hilma's stinginess toward her. She'd come to make peace and was entering another war zone. She dropped a thousand dollars on the table.

"Mama, it's for you. . . . dad can't do greeting cards at the Chanticleer. It's not the right milieu. And I thought . . ."

Hilma stared at the money on the table. "Your father has his insurance policy. I won't need this."

"But mama, you could buy a hat or go on a trip."

"Without Herman? Never."

Her look had become so harsh, Sarah put the money away. She was an intruder in her mother's house, the girl who'd come between Herman and Hilma. She began to cry in some borderland near the back of her heart. She was that little girl again, upstairs in the synagogue with a haremful of women, a worthless creature in the eyes of God. And her daddy couldn't save her. He was downstairs with the velvet scrolls.

"Don't I mean something to you, mama?"

Hilma hardened like that bird woman, the Baroness de Roth. "That's not a question to ask. You're my daughter. You come from my blood."

"But do you like me, mama?"

"I don't have to like you," Hilma said. "I love you. That's enough. You always preferred your dad. It was in your nature . . . you visited him at the Chanticleer and couldn't even say a word to me. I don't exist."

"I'm sorry, mama. I . . ." Saigon tried to hug her, but Hilma pulled her body shut and it would have been like hugging someone in a wax museum.

"Strangers," Hilma said. "Strangers are more sympathetic to your mother than you are."

"What strangers?"

"The Baroness de Roth."

"Does she invite you into her room for sandwiches?"

"No. She comes here. She signed her name to your father's policies, put her mansion on the line for us. No one else would have done that."

Ah, the bird woman flies everywhere, Sarah muttered, and gives her signature away.

"How'd you meet the Baroness?"

"I can't remember," Hilma said. "She started coming . . . with Neck."

Hilma must have seen her daughter go dark. "Neck and the Baroness de Roth?"

"Of course. Neck moved Herman into the Chanticleer."

Sarah stood up with both .45s digging out of the polka dots and causing her skirt to mushroom above her knees.

"Where are you going, child?"

"To see the Baroness."

"But she's asleep. The Baroness doesn't have your hours."

"Then I'll have to wake the old bitch."

"But you've just arrived. Can't you stay with me?"

"I'll be back, mama. After I see the Baroness."

She pulled Neck from his chair and rushed into the street. She didn't say a word about the Baroness de Roth. She wasn't going to give Neck the chance to build a little story. It was the padre who'd put her father into the Chanticleer. But how did Uncle know Herman had Alzheimer's disease?

"Where we going now?" Neck asked.

"Uncle's roost."

"That's impossible, mama-san, because the last roost Uncle had was in the Nam."

"Then you go on and take me where you took my father, Neck."

Neck didn't argue her down or deny he'd ever driven her dad. He brought her to the Chanticleer. They had no trouble at the gate. The little sisters waved them in. Sarah had a certain bitterness towards the Chanticleer and its nuns, but she couldn't help admiring windows that were high as a horse.

Neck drove up to the mansion's front door. He climbed onto the porch with Sarah. Simonson didn't argue about Sarah's visit. "Some coffee, my dear? Or tea and cakes?"

"Never mind the continental breakfast. I've come to have it out with the Baroness."

"We're not barbarians," Simonson said. "The Baroness couldn't entertain you without her morning tea."

"Then I'll do tea with her," Sarah said. "Tell the Baroness I'm here."

"She knows about that. We heard you half a mile down the road. Come in, please."

And Simonson showed Sarah into the Baroness's private closet that had a view of garbage pails. High style in New Jersey, Sarah thought, living close to the kitchen like that.

Someone had already trundled in the tea dolly. It was filled with croissants and little cream cakes. The Baroness sat in a velvet robe. Sarah decided not to argue before she had a croissant.

The Baroness poured her a cup of tea. Sarah took a sip. She finished her croissant and went on drinking. The Baroness watched Sarah all the while and wouldn't eat. It made Sarah nervous to be the only gobbler in the room.

"Fess up, Baroness," she said. "You're in cahoots with the padre. He hired you to bring my father to your hotel . . ."

But the Baroness wouldn't confess a thing. And Sarah had to continue or look ridiculous in the Baroness's eyes, a spoiled brat who'd come at eight o'clock in the morning to argue and eat croissants. But her lips had gone dry and she discovered two Baronesses in place of one.

"You shouldn't have become my father's collateral. I'm rich enough . . . you didn't have to suck around after he got sick."

Ah, Sarah wasn't born in the zoo. She'd been tricked by this goddamn hotel. The Baroness had spiked her tea with some kind of candy. But they weren't going to put old Sarah to sleep. She stood up and warned both Baronesses de Roth.

"All I have to do is vomit and I'll be fit enough to cancel your hotel."

She was preparing to shoot the Baroness when Gwendolyn floated up to her and stuffed a needle into her side. Where the hell did Gwen come from? Sarah hadn't noticed her in the house.

Gwendolyn smiled and took the .45s out of Sarah's hands like some treasonable daughter.

"Didn't I fire you, Gwen?"

"You think you did, but you really fired your own tits."

It was much too difficult for her to comprehend. Sarah needed another croissant. But when she grabbed for it, her fingers didn't get far.

231

"I'll kill you," she said and tumbled into the dolly, bringing down the croissants and the little cream cakes.

It wasn't like a bloody coma. Saigon remembered everything. She was caught in some zone where time was touchable and thick. She wouldn't have needed her opium ball at the Baroness's hotel. People danced in and out of her eyes. She'd had a long talk with Vladimir but couldn't locate any of the words. Neck had come to her with chocolate pudding. Gwendolyn took her pulse.

And then she was pushed out of that lazy zone. People stopped being kind to her. It was like an ordinary day at the talmud torah, only her hands were tied, and she was sitting in a chair. She wouldn't have minded the rope gnawing her wrists, but her accommodations were imperfect. They'd put her in a room without a view, some kind of storage closet.

Gwendolyn came in without bothering to knock on the door. She carried a dish of applesauce and began feeding Sarah with a fat spoon. She stuck the spoon deep in Sarah's throat.

"How's my beauty?" she asked. But Sarah was stuffed with applesauce and couldn't answer Gwen.

"Mama-san, I've been thinking, you know. We might change your complexion while you're here. I could do it . . . scrape the fucking holes in your face. You'd be a different person."

Gwen dug the spoon out and Sarah said, "Even if I'm ugly, I'm not a toothless hag."

Gwen forgot about the applesauce and started beating Sarah's brains with the fat spoon. "Oh, look at the queen of Alphabetville, a cunt with a meager life-span."

The blows exhausted Gwen, who was breathing like a whale with bronchitis. Blood had trickled onto Sarah's nose, and Gwen began to trace its path with gobs of applesauce. She was proud of the dents she'd put in Sarah's skull.

Sarah could feel her memory slip with each blow of the spoon, but she was still shrewd enough to ask, "Where's Vladimir?"

"What would Vladi want with a tub of shit? He's not a tit freak. He likes his women svelte."

Gwen took the applesauce out with her and left Sarah with a bloody head. But Sarah didn't bleed for long. She'd gone back to that zone where blood was hard as a crayon and time was thick enough to hold in your hand. It could have been nightfall in Vietnam, but without the darkening elephant grass. Vladimir came to her again and wiped her forehead with a rag. Vladi was her nurse. He would only visit Sarah while she was stuck in that nightfall.

She woke with Neck's hands inside her blouse. He wasn't worse than other men, getting titty any way he can. She would have traded him titty for a bit of companionship, but old Neck was rude, even as he explored her chest.

"I've been wanting to squeeze you, little mama, for the longest time. You gave a lot to Marvey and the Teach, but you never give nothing to me."

"All you had to do was ask."

One of his hands came out and she noticed how black his nails were and Sarah wished she could have a bath, sitting right in the chair.

Old Neck was ingenious. He had a hundred ways of getting under her brassiere and he never seemed to tire of his little occupation. She was more frightened of Gwen and the Baroness than she was of old Neck. Neck wouldn't go deeper than her brassiere. He wasn't high enough in the padre's club to take more of a chance with her.

He was gone in half an hour and Sarah couldn't say if she was relieved or forlorn without his black fingernails. She got lonesome in her chair. The lord of the mansion arrived without croissants and chocolate pudding, that padre who was her Judas.

He saw what Neck had done to her brassiere, but he didn't offer to send in a nun with needle and thread. He was enjoying the sight of her tits, and she wondered if she could play Cleopatra with pockmarks for that cold man.

She could feel his eyes swallow up her skin. Go on, padre, ruin my bra with a kitchen knife. I'll be your Betty Grable and I won't tell. But Sarah couldn't sit on her tongue.

"Rotten skunk, you didn't have to drag my daddy to your farm."

"Sister, is that how you say hello? We're a registered shop. The Baroness is licensed in New Jersey."

"If she's a baroness, I'm the emperor's niece."

The padre looked at her with such scorn, she decided to shrink under her chair, bra and all.

"Sister Sarah," he said. "The first Baron de Roth outfitted half of Napoleon's army."

"Well, how did you get in line with such royal people?"

"Her late husband the Baron was a tea planter in Vietnam."

"It's all lovey-dovey, you and the Nam. How many baronesses did you recover from the South China Sea?"

"Only one," said the padre.

"And wasn't I a little bit of royalty at Cayenne? Your Baroness in the bush."

"You don't have the blood lines. Your dad is a penny poet."

"Then why did you bring him here?"

"Because you're still my favorite girl. Had to look after your old man, didn't I? Couldn't have him going to a state hospital."

"It's none of your business," Sarah said.

"Everything about you is my business . . . besides, you were becoming a pain in the ass, running your little ops, trying to frustrate the only real benefactor you ever had."

"Benefactor, my boots. I'd trust Hanoi Hannah over you. Take your talmud torah, padre. I don't need your assistance."

"Yes you do. You were always on my feeding line. You belonged to me the moment you got to the Nam. I invented your career as a nurse."

"How did you come to my dossier? I'll bet there's a thousand poet-nurses from New Jersey."

"But not all of them were engaged to the Teach . . . shouldn't have invested in you. You're a stupid little dreamer."

"Where the hell is Biedersbill?"

"In Saigon."

"You're suffering from some time disease, padre. Old Saigon is dead. Charlie's sitting in the presidential palace. It's his ville now."

"Teach is in Saigon."

Well, she wasn't going to argue with a lunatic. Let him swear Teach had gone to a ville that didn't exist. Teach couldn't find his way to Jersey without her.

"Nuns," she said. "The nurses at the Chanticleer, did you find them in the Nam?"

"Yes, most of them I did."

"Then you had other interrogation centers like Cayenne."

"Of course. Cayenne was nothing to us."

"And Gwendolyn had a ward of her own?"

"Not quite. Gwen didn't have a fixed location. She went to all the trouble spots. And Simonson was captain of the nurses."

"How come I never saw her at Cayenne?"

"She'd chopper in whenever you were off to Saigon. Simonson ran the hospital. You were my show nurse. I kept you on as a kindness to the Teach."

"And the talmud torah? Was that the Teacher's toy?"

"Almost," the padre said. "I needed a sheriff's band in the Alphabet Blocks. A touch of law and order. But you took it too seriously. Vladimir had to clean up your mess."

"Where the hell is Vladi?"

"Hiding from you. He's ashamed to meet his little mama while her hands are tied. But he dotes on you the minute you're asleep. I've raised a bunch of sentimental pirates."

"How soon will it be before the Baroness plucks out my eyes and feeds old Sarah to the chickens in the yard?"

"You think too much of yourself," the padre said. "If I'd wanted to maim you, I could have had it done a long time ago. Your father upstairs in his bedroom is all the insurance I need. You'll behave. I'm going to reunite you with your gang. We'll have a reunion party at the mansion. With their little mama out of the way, I can scoop up Marvin and my niece."

"Son of a bitch," Sarah said. "Lulu's your own family."

"Wouldn't dream of harming her. Lulu is happy as long as she has Marve around."

"You ought to wean her away from Marve," Sarah said, forgetting her own predicament. "You can't collect us all as prisoners."

"Why not? The Baroness has a big house."

And he left Sarah to sulk in her chair. It was the first time since she fled her daddy's house that she'd begun to pity herself. Padre was right. She'd had no other benefactor but him. She was never much of a nurse. She was a greeting-card writer, and not very good. Didn't even have the sense to bear a child. So she'd adopted dozens of children as she went from ward to ward. What hurt her most was Teacher's treachery. Pretending he'd never seen the Baroness when he was the mansion's darling boy. Sarah could understand old Vladimir. Padre had some hold on him. But she'd been engaged to Biedersbill before he and the padre ever met. He got interested in mummies as a boy and grew into a mummy himself. It was the bitterest thing that Howie should betray her. She didn't have the heart to finish her daddy's poem. The black trees Herman had written about wasn't Vietnam. All that blackness was Biedersbill.

SORCERERS IN SAIGON

11

PENS, pens. Fountain pens. Teach was chancellor of the Mont Blanc, that black beauty with a white star on its skull. He carried a sample in his pocket, just like Konstantin. The pen had been given to him in Paris. A bonbon from the Baroness's cousins, loaded with dark candy. There was enough poison in Teach's Mont Blanc to cripple a herd of elephants. All he had to do was scratch Konstantin's wrist. The cousins prepared him for Ho Chi Minh. They had scars over their eyes and broken mouths. Ah, the best royalty always looked like thieves.

Howard wasn't Howard any more. He was Rousseau, from

the Ministry of Education, and he didn't have to sneak around. He'd flown out of Paris with a fistful of cards and documents that could have been endorsed by all the different kings at Versailles. He was more French than any of the Long Noses at this dead airport. The Baroness's cousins had seen to that.

He wasn't followed or searched. Militiawomen met him at the gate. There was a border war going on between China and the new Nam, and ordinary soldiers had been pulled to the front. The Baroness's cousins warned him about this women's army that controlled the ville. *Vicious girls. They'll eat your head off.* They were led by some dragonlady, Colonel Mai-lan, who dressed in paratrooper's clothes and loved to shoot spies.

The women sat Rousseau in an American jeep. The driver wore an airman's white scarf. Mai-lan. All her adjuncts were squeezed into the back, with Rousseau's luggage. Mai-lan wasn't suspicious of his kindergarten French. She'd been a nursery-school teacher and had come to soldiering late. She intended to give Rousseau a tour of the ville's nursery schools.

The dragonlady had little whiskers, like an exotic cat, but she didn't pounce on Biedersbill. She drove him into a Saigon he'd never seen. It wasn't near the Richelieu, that French movie house where King George had once ruled with his child whores. It wasn't Pasteur Street and the old French boulevards, or the hidden canals of Cholon. It was a district beyond the Saigon Zoo. Just another shantytown, but it didn't have taco stands or a Mr. Softee truck. He heard a tiger bark.

They got down from the jeep and entered Nursery Number Seven. It wasn't a room where Teach would have deposited any children. It had no toys or curtains or candy bars. Mattresses on the floor, with infants lying six to a mattress, like puppies in a window. The puppies weren't too clean. The whole nursery had an unwashed smell. A babushka with a white beard guarded the children. She was doctor and watchman and captain of the nursery. Teach couldn't discover a tooth in her face. She bowed to Mai-lan and kissed her hand and muttered something.

"Soap," Mai-lan said to the Teacher in French. "She has no soap for the children."

They visited other nurseries. Militiawomen had to clutch the Teacher's hand. He grew pale by the fifth nursery.

Mai-lan let him off at the old bachelor officers' club, the Tonto, now a hotel for foreigners. Russian engineers sat in the lobby, eating tins of meat. Their stipends weren't big enough to support a restaurant. They all had their own silver spoons. He could tell they were Russians because their pants were too small. Moscow tailors wouldn't make allowances for men's shins.

He was given a second-floor suite, a monk's cell with a ceiling fan and a view of the old Presidential Gardens. There were huts now all over the grass and none of the flower designs that the mistresses of Saigon generals loved so much. Teach saw pregnant women lining up on the grass.

He played with the Mont Blanc's plunger, dreaming of fat eyes. Konstantin would drink the same kind of candy he'd fed to Nibio and Renata and Jonah Slyke.

Teach avoided the engineers, who suffered in wool suits, waiting for a Moscow winter. He crept down Hong Thap Tu in the direction of Cholon. The ville seemed forlorn without taco stands. Saigon had become a town of little girls and old men. Some of the girls were as blonde as Marve's wife, and they had blue eyes on Hong Thap Tu. They were Yankeegirls, the half-breed daughters of American soldiers. He tried to talk to them in English.

"How are you, honey bun?"

The Yankeegirls hissed. They were selling useless trinkets out on the boulevard, and they must have mistaken him for a Soviet engineer. He babbled to them in Vietnamese.

"Toi la ban," he said. "Toi la ban."

They hissed and mocked him with their blue eyes. And all the Teach could do was shiver. He'd zapped Corsicans in Saigon and hadn't lost much sleep. He'd cancel fat eyes and wouldn't think about him again. He'd poisoned, he'd bombed, he'd maimed, and nothing had bothered him, not the fire that sucked at Charles' skin, not the twisted bones of the unburied dead. That was outside his circuitry. But he had no formula for these girls. It didn't matter that his eyes weren't blue. He was stamped with their complexion.

The Yankeegirls offered Teach the trinkets in their wooden trays. "Bao nhieu?" he asked, but they wouldn't quote him a price. He wanted to buy all their goods. He had American dollars in his pants. The girls scorned his money. Their blue eyes were beyond simple greed.

He despaired of ever getting them to talk until one of them muttered "Charlie, Charlie Cong" in his face and then the girls scampered across the boulevard with their trinkets and left the Teacher without his brood.

He ventured into Cholon and found his way back to the Four Hundred Blows. A neon sign blinked as it had done under Henry Kissinger. The beautiful métisse, Myriam Foucault, was behind the bar. She wasn't glad to see him. Myriam pretended not to know Biedersbill.

She brought him a white-wine cassis and he sipped at it with more pleasure than he could have imagined. Cassis was meant for verandas and warm yellow skies. But he drank it inside a cave in Cholon.

He looked around the cave and discovered long-nosed aristocrats who'd been kicked out of France and had no other kingdom except this. But the bar wasn't filled with colons.

Teach recognized a different class of citizens. Europeans in yellow suits. They didn't have the look of colons. They sat with Chinese moneylenders at Myriam's bar. It took a while for the Teacher to catch that Konstantin was with them. And then Konstantin quit the moneylenders.

"Ah, my little man, Rousseau."

The padre had to tell Konstantin that Teach was coming, or the Russki would have gone ape, meeting Howard in Ho Chi Minh. Uncle invented a fable for Konstantin. The fable was that Teach had come to supervise a shipment of fountain pens and alarm clocks from France that was meant to flow into the black market. There was a shortage of fountain pens and clocks in Vietnam. Currencies fell and rose with the fountain pen.

"Why the precaution?" Konstantin said. "Uncle didn't need a babysitter until now. I was enough."

"The Long Noses tried to rip us off in Marseilles. They'll try again."

"You crazy? I own this port with General Tuan. You remember Tuan. He shook your hand once in Cambodia. Tuan's our big policeman, the montagnard sheriff of Ho Chi Minh. Myriam is his little mama."

"And what about Colonel Mai-lan?"

"The dragonlady? She's nothing. Hanoi's spy. When can I expect the shipment, Rousseau?"

"Four, five days."

There was no shipment. But Teach had to further the myth of fountain pens.

"Uncle still adore the *Blue Star of Marseilles?* That tub had better be on time. The unloaders are all women, and they have a sweet tooth. They'll wreck the harbor if your shipment doesn't arrive."

Konstantin's wrist moved like a fat little worm. Teach was dying to shove some black candy into that wrist. "Regards," he said.

Konstantin winked his fat eyes.

"Regards from Corinne. She misses her Connie."

The fat eyes turned thin. "Did you tell her where I am, Rousseau?"

"I'm not responsible for your pillow talk. She knew more about your plans than I did . . . how is she, Konstantin? A tiger under the pillows?"

Konstantin's eyes went fat again. "She's no better or worse than your Hélène."

"But Hélène didn't have an old harmless husband."

"Carlo's not all that harmless, Henry James."

"Yeah," Teach said. "He goes on a lot of wild goose runs for books."

Konstantin returned to his table of Chinese moneylenders and Teach finished his cassis. He left a castle of American quarters on the wooden rim of the bar and walked out of Myriam's. The métisse never turned to look at him. She'd been condemned to a ville where fountain pens were a form of gold.

Teach had to cross half a dozen canals. He couldn't buy an orange from the Chinese grocers. Their stalls were shut. Faces seemed to disappear at six o'clock. Nam was having a little old border war with China, and it wasn't too polite for citizens of Cholon to lay out on the street. Militiawomen in cardboard helmets patrolled the canals. They didn't discourage the Teacher's hike. He was only a foreigner to them, another white ghost.

Soon as he crossed the channel out of Cholon, two men in green pajama suits appeared. Tuan's own detectives. They invited him into a Russian sedan that stank of gasoline, passed the central police station, and delivered him to a broken schoolhouse near the docks.

Teach went into the schoolhouse. He didn't find other detectives in the hall. General Tuan sat in a schoolroom near the front door. He had red shoulder boards, like thickened wings. "How are you, Biedersbill? Still concerned about revolutions?"

"I'm a soldier of fortune these days."

"Yes, I've been following your career. You have your own prefecture in Manhattan. And you double as a sorcerer in New Jersey . . . poisoning old men's soup."

"It's not sorcery. Just an old Elephant trick. You ought to know, King Frédéric."

"We're a democratic country. We have no kings. You shouldn't have gone to Myriam. You might have compromised her."

"General, had to visit my old haunt in Cholon. Didn't know Myriam was still there. It could have been a snack bar for militiawomen."

"But I can't protect you if you rush into a bar that is crawling with every kind of agent."

"Like Konstantin."

"Is it wise to have the Russian think you're on a sentimental journey? You should be worrying about a cargo of clocks and pens. I've had to forge a manifest and bills of lading. Our harbor-master is a scrupulous man. He wouldn't appreciate ficticious fountain pens. If he gets jumpy, Konstantin is sure to pick it up."

"Then drown him in a canal."

"I can't be rude to our Russian brothers."

"Konstantin is a pimp, a KGB man who sleeps with the CIA."

"I've had to live with him, chéri. We can't survive without the Russian bear, and the bear is beginning to eat us up."

"Ah," the Teacher said. "That's where Rousseau comes along."

"Exactly. When Konstantin saddens our country with his death, we'll blame it on the Long Noses. It's much more convenient. The Russians will do some digging and discover that their apparatchik has been pocketing cash. I'll create a scenario that won't include myself. We'll scream at Paris for introducing assassins into our country, but we wouldn't want to lose our contacts with the West. Paris will fish around for this Rousseau, but the Long Noses will find nothing. How will they ever trace you to a Hebrew church in Manhattan?"

"General, I'll need a travel permit to George's camp. I wouldn't come to the Nam without visiting George."

Tuan's eyes pulled back like an Elephanter. He was King Frédéric again, the father betrayer to his own lost tribe. "I let George slip into Ho Chi Minh. He's a marginal thug right now. Lives out of the gutter. But he has a hundred policemen around him. We don't want him meddling in our affairs."

"I won't do Konstantin if I can't see George."

"Silly man, I could finish Konstantin myself and implicate you. I'll feed you to the Russians or put you in a hole."

"What makes you think Uncle would abandon a blue beanie?"

Tuan laughed and the desk rose off the ground like it was waltzing to a magician's will. "Are you counting on the Americans to come with their Hueys?"

"Hueys wouldn't be a bad idea. I mean, five gunships could take this ville . . . where's Hélène?"

"Where you can't find her," Tuan said.

"You let your own little sister rot in a camp."

"Don't lecture me. You're an assassin in a country that can't afford soap."

Teach walked away from Frédéric and landed in French Saigon. The villas had cracks in their walls and the creeping plants with purple vines were gone. He wondered if the Long Noses retrieved all their bougainvillaea. The boomboom parlors and taco stands had been shut, but not even Hanoi could kill the boulevards. Men under sixty might have been at the frontier, guarding against a Chinese invasion, but Saigon would never miss them.

A gang of girls riding Hondas nearly gunned him down. He didn't return to his hotel. He would have had to watch Russians scrape meat from tin cans. He went to old Pasteur Street, where he'd lived once upon a time, with Myriam Foucault tucked behind his garden. He had a feeling the villa wouldn't be unoccupied. He crawled under the gate and a mama-san came at him with a broom. Teach had to calm her. Told her in Vietnamese that he was Tuan's round-eyed chauffeur.

The mama-san brought him a bowl of tea. Teach wandered into a room where a boy was studying. Ah, another half-American brat. Without the blue eyes. The boy had Albert's peepers, brown, with little flaws of gold.

"Chaò cháu," he said to the boy, who wouldn't give up studying. Teacher asked him about his homework. The boy began to prattle in French. He was involved in the wars of Charlemagne, and Teach had to admit his own ignorance. History began with Henry James. They were getting along until Myriam arrived.

She slapped the mama-san for letting Teacher in. Then she told the boy to go into the garden and play. She called him Jeanick. She was growing a little Long Nose behind her walls.

"You have no business coming here," Myriam said. "I'll kill you, Teacher, if I lose my child."

She took a .44 Magnum out of Jeanick's toychest. The little mama had pistols all over the place.

"Didn't mean to invade your ville, but the padre sent me."

"The padre," she said, as if she were talking about some pelican across the street. "He's an opportunist. He collects people's lives."

"Maybe so, but he took me out of Long Binh. I was languishing, little mama. Albert taught me literature and wiped my tail."

"Not without a profit to himself."

"Don't blame him for being clever. He had to dance around Moscow and the CIA."

"He doesn't have to dance. Albert eats up agencies."

"You're still angry at him because he wouldn't bring you to America. He must have had his reasons."

Myriam returned the .44 Magnum to the toychest.

"You fool. He sentenced me to Saigon so I could rub the victorious colonels for him. He abandoned his own child."

"But you have the Blows, and Jeanick is learning French."

"And when Tuan dies, what will happen to me?"

"Mama, I'll put in your request to the padre if you want out. I'll ask him about Jeanick."

"Don't you dare. He'll steal my son and leave me to the winter monsoons."

"Then how can I help you?"

"By running as far as you can."

"I have to find George."

"You're worse than a fool. You're a madman. George is an enemy who's been allowed to live. The last of his people are in starvation centers. If you go near him, you'll ruin whatever

247

cover you have. And if you invite George to look for you, you'll get him killed."

"Can't tell me about that king. He'll consider it unkind if I leave without hugging him once. I'll offend his spirits."

He kissed the little mama on her forehead, the way he would have done in Cholon. She touched his neck with her fingernails and he walked on back to that hotel where the Russians were, devouring tin cans like trawlers on an empty ocean.

Rousseau killed two days with his fountain pen. Scratched notes to himself in poisoned ink. He felt useless without his stethoscope. Couldn't listen to walls and see if the mothers of Ho Chi Minh had bugged his room. He went to the Richelieu. The other movie houses were stuffed with Russian posters, and he wouldn't have gone in to watch some Anna Karenina on Dostoyevsky Street. Bought himself a ticket, blundered into the dark, and began to feel sorry for himself. He'd entered a cave in the middle of Saigon and didn't even have French characters to soothe him. There was nothing up on the ragged screen. The Richelieu forgot to hold regular hours. It was a refugee camp for school children. Teach discovered twelve-year-olds kissing in the aisles.

He'd fallen into a lovers' lane. But all that clutching wouldn't help Konstantin. Teach would lure him into the Richelieu, flood his wrist with black candy, and leave him there for the projectionist. Fat eyes could sit for a month. The Teacher searched for fire exits and walked in back of the screen. He found a little door that returned him to the street.

He would have fallen utterly into his dreams if the Yankeegirls hadn't intercepted him on the boulevards and grabbed at his heels. He pitied their blue eyes as much as he ever did, but he wouldn't accompany them into the alleys, where they seemed determined to sell him something.

"Charlie," they said. "Charlie Cong."

No one invited him to visit nursery schools again. He didn't have the gift of soap. Teach went back to the Richelieu, sat in the dark, without the least glimmer on the screen. It comforted him, hearing children grope in a special kind of puppy love. Old men began to walk the aisles. He could hear them barter with the children at the Richelieu. No wonder the projectionist left the house dark.

Teach felt a hand on his shoulder.

"Hey," he hissed. "I'm not for sale. Go on down the aisle and get yourself a piece of ass." It was stupid to bitch like that in a cave that couldn't have understood his English. He wasn't at the St. Marks Cinema. He resorted to Vietnamese.

The hand on his shoulder whispered to him. "Motherfucker, keep quiet."

Teach felt like a happy dog, ready to piss all over the place. He couldn't have confused that voice.

He reached for the hand and it slipped away.

"Stop that commotion. Look straight ahead."

"Majesty, you son of a bitch. There's nothing to look at. I'll bet the Richelieu's been dark since Uncle Sam went away. Jesus, how are you and who are you pulling for this year?"

"Tuan. I run Tuan's dope in from the mountains."

"Ah, my opium man." It had to be George who supplied bits of opium for Sarah, so she could have her tar ball.

"Scumbag," the king said. "I've been signaling to you for days."

"I didn't catch a sign. How did you signal?"

"With the blue-eyed ones."

George must have been waiting for him when the Yankeegirls tried to coax Teacher into the alleys. They weren't as hungry as Teacher thought. Did they move opium through the ville in their wooden trays?

"Teach, I've been reading my chicken paw."

"Claw, claw," Teach said. "It's monkeys and cats that keep a paw." But he knew what the king meant. The Elephanters liked to rip at the future with a blackened paw. "Well, what does the chicken foot say?"

"That you ought to skip America. You'll never survive the trip home."

"I'll survive," the Teacher said. "Your chicken foot is wrong. Majesty, I . . ."

George was no longer behind him. He'd been sloppy and stupid. Hadn't even told the king how glad he was to see him in Saigon. But the trick was he'd never seen George. He'd felt a hand on his shoulder and heard a voice, the king's voice.

Couldn't find a single blue-eyed brat on the boulevards. George must have captured them with his chicken paw.

Teach stumbled upon the Russian engineers, who were visiting an old-age home across from City Hall, where the local commissars and block chairmen had their offices. Block chairmen were as powerful as generals in Ho Chi Minh. They issued travel permits and checked each living soul in their precincts. The Baroness's cousins had warned him about them. They were leeches and spies. The block chairmen collected bribes for every little favor they did. And now they'd stepped out of City Hall to take a tribe of Russian engineers on a tour of a model old-age home.

The chairmen had put banners and pots of flowers in the front yard. They were celebrating the sixth anniversary of the home. Colonels and commissars drifted upon the grounds to greet the Russian engineers. A party of women arrived from two bicycle factories. No one challenged the Teach when he joined the crowd of celebrants. The engineers seemed less foolish away from their tin cans. They concerned themselves with the structure of the home, feeling for weak spots in the walls, testing the glass, climbing on ladders to authenticate the roof. They acquired a rhythm in their woollen suits, and it was the Teacher who felt foolish for having judged them in terms of the silver spoons they carried.

He entered the home along with the other guests and was appalled. Wheelchairs were made of sticks. Most of the beds were army cots inherited from the American regime in Saigon. The men who lay in them looked half-starved, though Teach saw oranges and lemons in little baskets at their feet.

A commissar announced that they were in the widowers' wing. The block chairmen themselves had painted the walls. They were proud of the widowers from their own precincts.

Teach wouldn't have minded it at all if these chairmen became the commissars of Alphabetville. They could have their lucre as long as they held a slot for him in some widowers' wing.

Blade Runner rumbled in his head. Sarah would have imposed her favorite film on the block chairmen. She knew how to argue with commissars and projectionists.

Teach returned to the Richelieu. Had to solve the riddle of the projection booth. He groped along the Richelieu's rear wall until he felt the handle of a door. The handle turned and Teach entered a narrow box with stairs. A man in green pajamas was asleep at the top of the stairs with a pistol in his lap. He was one of the detectives who'd brought him to Tuan's schoolhouse near the river. Teach climbed up to the mother and rapped him once on the back of the neck. That old pajama man slumped into the stairs and Teach stepped over him without disturbing the pistol. He landed in the projection booth with a bitter smile. The booth could barely hold him. Its floor was littered with grapefruit rinds. The projectionist sat on a small bench, ripping grapefruits with his teeth.

"Pamplemousse," the Teacher said. He was talking to a king with grapefruit slivers in his mouth. The king wore an Hawaiian shirt.

"You shouldn't have come up. My brother won't like it."

"This your goddamn republic, George? Headman of a children's whorehouse. Why didn't you stay on your mountain?"

"I had to come off. People were getting killed and my chicken paw didn't show me much of a kingdom."

"So Tuan promised you the Richelieu if you'd end the revolution."

"Something like that. A seat in Saigon."

"George, I've been wondering. How the hell does the padre keep getting his stash of poison?"

"From the same old source."

"You mean the Elephanters farm for Tuan in their prison camp? Son of a bitch."

"You're a Yank," the king said. "You have Henry James."

"And you have Hélène."

The king pushed deeper into his bench, like a dwarf on a spirit table. "Sister is in Tuan's care."

Teach grabbed at the pockets of George's Hawaiian shirt. "Can I give her some money?"

"Not a chance."

"George, does your sister remember me?"

"Only in her dreams."

"Ah," Teach said. "What about you?"

"I have Tuan."

"Don't count on it. When the time comes, he'll run to Texas or Hong Kong with all his demons and let you rot in the Richelieu."

George ripped at his pamplemousse. "I like it here. I show my films after all the children leave for the night. I have *Shoot the Piano Player.*"

"It's still a goddamn prison, watching Long Noses on a screen all by yourself. Come with me to New York. I'll buy you a movie house, George."

"But I have a movie house in Saigon."

"Would Hanoi put a montagnard general in charge of the

secret police if they cared about this ville? They've written it off. Look at you. A sorcerer in a town that has no future."

George took the chicken paw out of his pocket, but Teach wouldn't argue with a blackened foot. He stepped around the fallen policeman and quit the Richelieu.

He planned to kidnap George.

He'd have bribed the block chairmen, but it would take a week to find out who was corrupt. He'd have to do it all alone. Myriam wouldn't risk her bar for a couple of beanies.

He'd cancel fat eyes some other time. Couldn't allow the king to remain in Saigon as master of a dead movie house.

Teach began to pull shrapnel out of his hair. He'd been wounded in the head so many times, he felt like the Man in the Iron Mask. Booby-trapped twice, and once he was blown into a tree. He'd died up in that tree. Teach was sure of it. He soul had gone to shit, and the rest of him was preparing for purgatory. No bluff. Dying was like a big bellyache. You hollered and went to sleep. But it was a sleep where you dreamt without your goddamn body. His flesh was still in the tree. And Teach was floating, floating. He didn't have wings. It was the natural float of the dead. He encountered buddies who'd died like him. And that sergeant Teach had booby-trapped. It wasn't only Nam. Teach met uncles he barely could remember. Wasn't much time to say how do. His buddies barked for their wives and some infant son. Teach didn't have a son to bark about. He continued to float. But he suffered a wind of memory. He'd left a fiancée at Bengal High, *Sarah,* and now he could never float in her direction. He barked like the grunts around him. And his barking must have gotten to the Holy Ghost. Because God returned him to his body in the tree. That body had enough shrapnel in it to make a platoon of toy soldiers. But Teach was alive again. He was always having shrapnel problems. Bits of it would come loose like darkened balls of dandruff. And the moment he worried about something, he'd dig at the dandruff.

Some girl tried to pick him up outside a milk bar. She wore plastic rain boots and purple lip ice. Must have been a leftover from Uncle Sam, because she smiled at the Teach and understood he wasn't part of any Russian troupe. "Yankee boy," she said. He tossed the whore a ten-dollar bill, but that tenner didn't seem enough. "Yankee boy," she said.

"Malade," he muttered. "Incapacité, mamselle."

She only laughed at him, clutched his hand, and led Teach toward the harbor. Ah, a rendezvous in some old barrel. She wasn't a bad looker. He wouldn't have minded fumbling in her ao dai. He wasn't too feeble to sniff her underwear.

"Honey, what's your name?"

"Hélène," she said, still laughing, and Teach had a rotten feeling in the roots of his head that Ho town was conspiring against him. Was the bitch taking him to a gang of commissars down at the docks?

"Catch me next time, honey. I have to go."

But the little mama wouldn't release his hand.

They entered an alley and arrived at a whores' commune, hidden from the boulevards and Mai-lan's militiawomen. It was a series of hovels, sheet-metal shacks without the neon signatures of American Saigon, because whores weren't supposed to exist in commie heaven. Little Miss Rain Boots deposited him outside one of the shacks. Ah, not even a kiss for Biedersbill. "Hélène," she said and was on her way.

Teach stepped into the shack. He knew he'd have to endure some ceremony inside. The ceremony of his own life? It was a dark mother of a place. The Teacher was hit with a sweet smell that he couldn't mistake for perfume or river rot. There had to be an opium ball in the shack. He saw a woman in the corner

with the same purple lip ice and mascara thick as rubble. She
didn't have the other mama's ao dai. Her only garment was a
man's undershirt that she wore like a dress. She was either undernourished or unnaturally small. Teach could have clapped
both her ankles in his fist. He started to cry with a terror that
knotted his mouth and turned his cheeks to paper, as if he were
confronting the devils of his past, mother, father, uncles, aunts,
who'd left him to his own devices, forcing him to sense his
future isolation and seek out families as often as he could—
Long Binh, the talmud torah, George's hill—and watch the families corrode around him. Albert was his dad, George his big
and little brother, Sarah his mother-wife, Vladi his silent friend,
Hélène his mistress-child and devil daughter, here in this shack,
as corroded as a daughter could get. The rainbow princess had
stooped to purple lip ice. "Monsieur," she said in that royal
French she'd used on the mountain. "Mustn't cry."

He noticed her companion, a shrunken man with scorched
eyes. Ah, it was one of the white ghosts, the grunts who wouldn't
leave Nam, who tossed their dog tags in the Ben Nghe Canal
and grew into a shadow. The ghost smiled. "How are you, little
man?"

It was Perce, the millionaire's boy.

"Mother Mary," Teach said with a wet chin. "I'm home."

He nibbled on Perce's tar ball. It didn't stop him from shivering. He hadn't swallowed candy in a week. Should have borrowed
a drop from George. Or sucked on his own fountain pen.

"Is Tuan the ringmaster of this circus?" he asked.

"Mon pauvre," said Hélène. "My brother wouldn't protect a
white ghost."

"Then who's minding the circus? Some stringy lieutenant in
the women's militia?"

"King George," she said.

"That's kind of hard, considering he's locked up at the Richelieu."

"Majesty gets around," Perce said.

Ah, it was the old story. Saigon had always been a sleepy snake. Had enough venom on its tongue to start a firestorm. A flick of its tail could bring darkness over Cholon. But why should the snake rouse itself for Biedersbill?

"Can't I help?" the Teacher blubbered.

"Relax, little man. We just wanted to see you."

"But I can put you on Uncle's gravy list. You'd have provisions right off the black market. And Uncle could find you both an exit visa."

"Monsieur Howard," said Hélène. "There are no visas for a montagnard princess and her white ghost."

"But I could sneak you out of Nam. I'm sure I could."

That little starving couple smiled at him. Ah, Perce had found his mama. What's the difference where he had his bowl of rice? America was the land beyond the rainy season. It didn't mean much.

"Teacher," Perce said, "how's Konstantin?"

"That son of a bitch is dreaming of fountain pens."

"And your own little mama?"

Ah, it was silly to get on the subject of Harrison Ford if *Blade Runner* hadn't come to Ho Chi Minh. And what could he tell a millionaire's boy about Sarah Fish? That she ran a talmud torah and had a concubine named Marvin de la Mare?

"She's happy," Teach said.

"No baby children from her?" said Hélène, teasing him under all that eye dust. If Perce hadn't been his friend, he'd have carried her off on his back and demanded a suite at the Tonto. They'd have gone around Saigon with nothing more than Hélène's undershirt.

"Can't have babies," he said, and the rainbow princess didn't meddle. She kissed him on the mouth. The lip ice felt warm.

"We'll miss you," she said.

"But I can visit again."

"Not likely, monsieur. We move a lot."

"Can't I come to say good-bye?" Teach blubbered, bereft of one more family.

"You'll have to say it now."

Teach hugged those frail people and walked out of their little hooch. The alley he was on brought him to Quay Street. The canal boiled up the same foul green soup under the commies as it had under Kissinger. There were houses on stilts that looked like neckless cranes sleeping in the water. A barge floated past him with angry eyes painted on its belly to preserve it from the devils of the sea.

Teach arrived at the old port. He could see the brown lights of An Khanh Xa, that suburb across the Saigon River where beanies would go searching for pumpkin ice cream. He could taste the pumpkin in his mouth. Ah, there was nothing like gook ice cream.

A ship blocked part of Teach's view, the hull rising up from its harbor berth like the chest of a whale. Something about the tub bothered him. The dark stripe around her middle signaled the tub's name. *Blue Star of Marseilles*, a tub that shouldn't have been. The Baroness's cousins had coached him on the art of river pirates. No ship had sailed from Marseilles, and here was the *Blue Star* with her load of fountain pens. The pens weren't a fable at all. Teach was the fable.

Two men stood behind him. They looked like Brighton Beach-niks, not Russian engineers. They didn't menace the Teach. Simply took him by the arms and hurled him into a motor boat. Ah, Teach began to wish he'd stayed dead up in that old tree. The Russkis carted him around the bend in the river. Teach passed the dark box of the Majestic, now a commie hotel. Saw the top of the old cathedral. It was like a picnic through Saigon. He was going upriver with the Russkis. They delivered him to a barge above a ferry slip. The barge was looped with colored lights. The word *Viceroy* was painted along its castle. Ah, it was that floating restaurant where Saigon generals would have lunch with American diplomats. It was always tucked away in Kissinger's time, hidden somewhere in a secret canal. Teach had never seen it.

Konstantin welcomed him aboard. He couldn't find any of the dragonlady's people. It wasn't a house for the women's militia. And there were no detectives in green pajamas. Teach saw Chinese bankers from Cholon. Tall blondes with a Polish look. The blondes wore tight skirts and military boots. Opened vodka bottles with their teeth. He imagined them making love hour after hour, with the vodka sitting on their breasts. Ah, if God would only give him back his groin, he'd have swiped that vodka from the Polinkas' chests.

"Not so dreary as your hotel, eh Rousseau?"

"Didn't think Hanoi would sanction this kind of tub," Teach said.

"Why not? It's like any hard-currency shop. It brings in dollars to the regime. Twenty percent of the *Viceroy* is mine. But who else could manage it? I come at a bargain price."

"I don't see one Hanoi general," Teach said.

"It's off-limits to the Vietnamese. We're in international waters."

"Yeah," Teach said. "With the cathedral right down the block."

"Close your eyes, Rousseau, and the cathedral will be gone . . . you're the magician, not me."

"You've done all right holding up your end of the magic."

"Have to, little man. You have a poison pen in your pocket."

Teach picked at his scalp. "Did you bribe the Baroness's cousins?"

"Come, enjoy yourself. You're my guest, Rousseau."

"I'm Howie Biedersbill, and I intend to kill you."

"With what?" fat eyes said. "Give me your pen, please."

Teach took the Mont Blanc out of his pocket and thrust it

into Konstantin's fist. Fat eyes uncapped the pen and squirted ink into his mouth. "Terrible stuff," he announced with blackened teeth. "But harmless."

He had a lick of vodka and returned the pen to Teach, who tossed the Mont Blanc overboard. Then Konstantin took out his own pen. It became a knife with one twist of his hand. "Beautiful, eh? And I can still get it to write." He dug the knife-pen into his pants. "Shall I introduce you to some people? The girls are spectacular, Rousseau. Their specialty is shampooing men's armpits in vodka. Nice, don't you think?"

"Talk to me," Teach said.

"Ah, a little interrogation party. Then we should get away from the girls and go downstairs."

He brought Teach down one deck into the *Viceroy*'s bowels. They sat in a tiny cabin with bottles of vodka between them on a bench. Konstantin produced a pair of drinking glasses from his shirt. He spilled vodka into each glass and handed one to the Teach. "To your health, Henry James."

He drank with his black teeth biting into the glass. "I'm ready, Rousseau."

"Start with Renata of the dirty legs."

"She was a downtown painter with a pinch of talent. I offered her a job."

"But you made love to her first."

"Teacher, you amaze me. I'm a man, she's a woman, so what? You weren't blind. Her gallery was our drop."

"Why did you poison her?"

"Let's say it was necessary and leave it at that."

"You were freelancing with Colombia behind Albert's back. That's why you wasted Capa's generals."

"Teacher, Teacher," Konstantin said. "You mustn't believe everything Uncle tells you. Capa ordered the execution of his generals. He was cleaning house."

"And Uncle sent little Biedersbill here to be your next victim."

Konstantin began the second bottle. "Uncle's fond of you," he said.

"So why am I in this ville?"

"To flush out those two montagnard magicians. Uncle had to know if Frédéric and George are loyal to our regime."

"And I'm the golden goose. You're waiting to find out if the two kings would help you murder me."

"Teacher, you're getting good at this. Too bad you're in love with that pockmarked mama. She's a pain in the ass."

The glass splintered in Teach's mouth. He drank from the other side. "Sarah's my business. And I don't give a crap if George and General Tuan were supposed to write my ticket. Russki, I'm taking George out of Ho."

"That would be suicidal."

"I'm taking him, understand?"

"Don't return to the Richelieu," Konstantin said. "It could become a coffin."

A Polish blonde came into the cabin and whispered in Konstantin's ear. Konstantin giggled. "Henry James, this is Zdena. She fancies your tush. She's offered me a load of deutsche marks to borrow you for fifteen minutes. That's how it is with Polish beauties. They won't accept obstacles in love."

"Not now," Teach said.

"I'm telling you from the heart. Zdena has the finest calves in the universe. She'll adore you with a python's grip."

"Not now."

Zdena left the cabin in her soldier's boots.

"Lubyanka," Teach said, with bubbles in his mouth. "Carlo needs a book." Teach's head dropped below the necks of the vodka bottles. "I'm Carlo's pal."

"I can see that, but I don't have horror stories to tell. I fed my recruits caviar as often as I could."

"Connie," Teach said.

"Don't call me that."

"Connie, I'll have to duel you if you won't give up Carlo's wife . . . are Vladi's sisters safe?"

"Imbecile, I've kept them alive."

"Duel you," Teach said before he fell off the chair and rocked on the cabin floor. "Konstantin, who the fuck are you with your own private money boat in a country that doesn't have a dime? Don't sell me shit about hard and soft currencies. You're king of this river. And Saigon is your corral."

Konstantin picked Teach up and returned him to his chair. "Teacher, you flatter me too much. I'm not the first capitalist in the KGB. The ruble is nothing outside Russia. I have to trade with the West."

"You're a funny kind of trader. Coca leaves in one pocket and poison in the next. You run spies for the Russkis and you're also Albert's partner."

"The two don't conflict," Konstantin said.

"Troubnoy wasn't so wrong about you. You're CIA, or something else. You fought on our side in the Nam."

"I'm a beanie, Teacher. Just like you."

"Since when did Soviet bandits get to wear a blue hat?"

"I wore lots of hats," Konstantin said.

"I mean, you're a scary mother. Where the hell are you from? Do you have a mom and dad?"

"My father was a postman in Leningrad."

"Is that one more fable?"

Teacher climbed out of his chair. "Konstantin, you're into too many agencies. I can't keep count."

He wandered out of the tiny cabin and went upstairs. Saw the lights of some Vietnam suburb that could have been Bayonne itself. The vodka he'd had sank into his neck. And in his confusion, Teach expected a medevac chopper to land on the *Viceroy*'s main deck. He wanted gook ice cream. He began to cry, because no matter how long he lived, Charlie would keep coming through the concertina wire. And who knows if Charlie didn't have frogmen to raid the *Viceroy?* Charlie could wear a blonde wig and look like a Polinka. The Cong were the only magicians in Nam. George was just the king of an antisocial tribe.

Big blonde Zdena tried to dance with him.

"Charlie," he said, tumbling into her arms.

It wasn't purgatory where he woke, unless purgatory had a ceiling fan. It was his room at the Tonto. The blondinkas must have carried him in. Took him hours before he could feel his nose. And when he did, he could have sworn some guillotine had discovered his neck. Fat eyes should have warned him about the vodka's pull.

He wasn't able to walk until after dark. He showered in the Tonto's questionable water, pleased that the pressure was low. A strong shower might have broken him off at the neck. He dressed and ate nothing at all. Didn't care about Konstantin and his floating currency shop. He was still determined to kidnap George.

Crawled to the Richelieu. Took a seat and considered how he could steal George from the projection booth. He'd wait until the children were gone and go at George in the middle of *Shoot the Piano Player.*

Teach was still in a Russian coma, but he wasn't dreaming so hard that he couldn't feel the presence of a knife with a white star on its handle. The moment the knife moved, he heard a hiss. "Told you not to come, Henry James." The knife should have cut him from ear to ear, but it only slashed his cheek. He'd turned to meet the thrust, and whoever held the knife had overshot a little. He gave one long howl, because it felt like murder to have his face split, but even as he howled, he knocked the knife into the gutter between the rows of chairs.

Konstantin tried to grab his head and choke the Teacher. But Teach had fallen out of his vodka dream. He climbed into the next row, crashed against an old man who was fondling some child at the Richelieu. Fingers tried to claw at him. He lost most of his shirt before he arrived at the front row.

He was dizzy from the blood that welled in his cheek, but he didn't stop to wipe the blood. He remembered there wasn't a wall behind the screen, so he leapt into the screen and tore through it with his body, leaving gobs of blood around the hole he'd created.

He held his cheek together with one hand and slapped at the policeman who was stationed near the fire door. It was the merry land of Ho Chi Minh, and all the little mothers conspired to hurt the Teach. He stumbled out the back of the Richelieu. A police car was in the alley, a darling Volga sedan that blocked the Teacher's path. But there was no one in the car. He climbed over the engine like a wounded cobra, not thinking of fat eyes with a knife. He'd grown up within a universe of nuns, said his Hail Marys in the morning, sang to Jesus. Uncles had raised him, uncles and aunts. They'd either whipped him or left him alone. He began to steal cars at twelve. Fought with older boys, learned to take their beatings, went into the army and killed a man. He was expecting an endless sabbatical at Long Binh and then Uncle Albert arrived. Uncle did Dostoyevsky and Henry James like some book of Jesus . . .

He couldn't run from the mothers and hold his cheek. He felt like dying in back of the Richelieu. The Teacher turned delirious and danced on his feet. He started to swoon when a tiny corporation of hands clutched at him. It was the goddamn Yankeegirls. They threw the Teach onto the ground. Must have been thirty of them near the Teach. Had they come to trample him? They lifted Teach off the ground and carried him low, shielding his body with their ragged skirts. It was an act of camouflage, something General Giap might have dreamed of. Ah, tactical warfare in Ho Chi Minh.

War Cries Over Avenue C

Biedersbill blinked at the sky. Mumbled half a Hail Mary. He had the best little nuns in Indochina on his side. But it was a hopeless situation. He was dropping bits of his cheek on the floor. The blood had gone to his eyes. He began to hallucinate. Saw steeples before he sank into sleep.

DOSTOYEV-SKY STREET

12

SARAH hadn't come out of some ungovernable dream. She'd
returned to Bayonne with Howie Biedersbill. Kissing under
the bridge. No one had ever kissed like Howie kissed before
he disappeared to Egypt.

Sarah woke with the sound of her crying. She didn't have
Biedersbill. She was a prisoner at the old Baroness's estate. But
it was funny how her hands weren't tied. They hadn't put her
to sleep in a chair. Sarah had her own bed with the handsomest
eiderdown quilt. They were treating her like royalty at the Chanticleer. The whores had taken her out of the closet. She had a
room with windows, and the windows weren't barred.

Snow had fallen during the night, and Sarah looked out upon a snowy sea. The Chanticleer's gates were blunted with snow. It was like looking at drowned bits of metal. She could hear the little sisters chopping a path with their shovels. Neck was leading the brigade. Must have been trying to rescue her limousine. Sarah could see its hood, white on white. Simonson threw melting salts from a paper bag.

Sarah laughed, because the whores didn't have her now. She could have climbed down a window into the snow. She'd have crawled home to the talmud torah to be with Marve and Lulu. But her laughter didn't sound right. It was hoarse as a crow. She didn't have the strength to toy with windows. The whores had dropped candy into her orange juice, the same concoction Teach had given to Marve. She'd become useless if she suddenly forgot Biedersbill and her dad. A coffin with tits. She had to get to her dad, catch Herman's face for the last time.

Sarah struggled out of bed. She couldn't locate the simplest nightie in that room, so she wrapped the quilt around her and went into the hall with her own bare feet. She found that bitch, Doris Quinn, next door. Doris was sitting at her mirror, dolling herself.

"Come in, hon, and visit a while."

How could Sarah refuse? She'd have to fight every little sister at the Chanticleer. Sarah was tactful with the bitch. "Sorry I threw you out of Belleville."

"Oh, it's nothing," Doris said. "I'm better off here."

"You writing the padre's memoirs?"

"No, no. I wouldn't dare look at a line."

"You sure Carlo Peck doesn't squeeze pages out of you?"

"Carlo Peck?" she asked, painting her eyes. "Never met the man."

"Aren't you the Manhattan Spy? Interviewed me a couple of years ago, knocked on my door at the Hebrew school."

"I remember," Doris said. "You're the hairdresser from Avenue

A. But I'm retired from all that, hon. I've stopped interviewing people."

Sarah had the picture now. Old Doris suffered from the Chanticleer. They'd put her on a diet of zombie pills. That's why Doris couldn't write. Uncle Albert was erasing all the memories around him.

"Doris, what about Marve?"

"Beg your pardon."

The mothers had left old Doris with the history of a mouse. "Should I comb your hair?"

"That would be nice," Doris said, and Sarah took comb and brush off the mantelpiece, hovered over the Manhattan Spy, and started to groom her, working the comb into Quinn's thick gray hair. It was like being in a forest of steel.

Doris closed her eyes. "Lovely," she said, leaning back. "You were always my favorite hairdresser."

That's when the other nurse intruded upon them. Gwendolyn was wearing Sarah's .45s under her belt. She wasn't so aggressive today. "I'm glad you found your mettle, tits. Doris has to be going."

"Going where? The world is up to its ass in snow. You'll never make it out of this cottage."

"You're wrong, tits. The driveway is clean."

Sarah looked out the window. Son of a bitch. There was a fat line in the snow that traveled to the gates. The little sisters had rescued the Chanticleer in half an hour.

"Come, Doris, we have to ride to Marvey."

"But she doesn't even remember Marve," Sarah said.

"Of course she does. Don't you, puss?"

"I remember now."

Gwendolyn dressed her in snow boots and wrapped her in a cape. "Come, dear. Can't be late for Marve."

The padre intended to bring Marve out of the talmud torah with Doris's ghost. Once he had Lulu and Marve, he could shut the talmud torah and pretend Sarah didn't exist.

She strolled into the hall, passing rooms where old men lay. No one was curtained up or bothered by nuns with hammers in their hands. The Chanticleer could expect a white Christmas. It was a house where Santa Claus might have stopped on his way to New York City.

Little sisters curtsied to her in the hall. They didn't care with whom they mingled. They were bringing warmer blankets to the Baroness's guests. Sarah wandered into her father's room. Herman sat on his bed in royal-blue pajamas. He stared at nothing in particular. She'd come to finish that poem of her dad's before the poison bit too hard and she couldn't seize the words. But even if she solved the riddle of her daddy's poem, she couldn't get under the Alzheimer's and cure Herman Fish. They'd both been undone as greeting-card poets.

She walked up to the bed. "Dad, the mothers have poisoned me . . . oh, I'll survive it. But I'll forget you before it's dark. And if you see me tomorrow, dad, I didn't want you to think your daughter's abandoned you."

She took Herman's hand and squeezed it as hard as her strength would allow. Daddy didn't squeeze back.

"You weren't wrong about the Biedersbill boy. He's a scum-sucker. And don't you blame the Christian people. It's not their fault Howie betrayed us. He's the padre's man. Always was. Been leading me on for years. Our gang was nothing to him . . ."

"Don't say that."

She looked at her father's lips. Had he come out of his Alzheimer's to chat with her? But the lips hadn't moved. Herman could only talk inside his head. It wasn't a music he could share with his daughter.

"Show yourself, whoever you are. I'm Saigon Sarah and I don't take shit."

"It's me, little mama."

A goddamn engine shoved out from behind the curtains, a truck named Vladimir. He looked as sad as Vietnam.

"I ought to kill you, Vladi. I adopted you, rescued your ass from Brighton Beach. I fed you, gave you a home, and all the time you were laughing at old Sarah."

"Didn't laugh."

"But you still fucked me over."

"Have three sisters on Dostoyevsky Street."

"I knew the mothers had a hold on you, but I wouldn't have touched your sisters . . . what's their names?"

"Mashenka," he said. "Elena. Irina."

The sounding of the names wounded Sarah. She shouldn't have asked for names. Anonymous sisters didn't mean much. But *Mashenka, Elena, Irina,* that was a litany Sarah couldn't match. "Youngish girls?"

"Babies when I left. Irina was the oldest. Nine."

"Are you sure they're alive?"

"Yes. I get letters from them."

"Who's your post office?"

"The KGB."

"You mean, the padre put my father in a Russian nursing home?"

Vladimir rubbed himself with a curtain. "Your father's safe."

"Well, is Uncle a commie?"

"No. He plays with one KGB man, Konstantin."

"Then he is a red, goddammit. And I was a commie agent all along. I'll rot for that."

"You won't rot, little mama. The CIA is also handling Konstantin."

"That's vicious," Sarah said. "Putting out for both sides . . . Vladimir, did the nuns give me strong tea last night?"

"I think so, mama."

"And Uncle borrowed the Teacher's medicine bag?"

"Uncle has his own supply of pills from King George."

"How long has Doris been on that candy?"

"Months," Vladimir said.

"And after I've been zombied out, will they hurt my dad?"

"Mama, he has his room for life. But don't you worry. I wouldn't let you fall. When Uncle moves his op to France, he'll take you off the pill."

"Does the Baroness have a farm in Brittany?"

"I'm not sure."

"Is that where Teacher went?"

Vladi blew his nose in a hospital napkin. "Teacher's dead."

Sarah's knees shook under the gown she'd made of her quilt. She longed for the poison now. Memory was merciless. "Who told you about the Teach?"

"Konstantin."

"That mother's at the Chanticleer?"

"Arrived yesterday. Teacher's dying or dead. Kostya left him bleeding somewhere."

"Vladi, I want to meet your KGB man."

"Couldn't do that, mama. Konstantin would have a fit if he caught me with you."

"Then I'll find him myself."

Vladimir began to cry. "I'd have to stop you, mama."

His blubbering made her blubber too. "Vladi, you were all the muscle I ever had. A mountain couldn't get through you. And you're scared of one man."

"He trained me, mama, when he was running high. Konstantin was the only touch I had with my sisters. He brought a babushka to Dostoyevsky Street, called her auntie, or the girls would have been marched off to a home. Konstantin gives her a salary from his own pocket. He visits the girls, buys them toys, delivers my letters when he's around."

"Vladimir, you're nothing but a company man."

"Didn't have a choice, mama. I was promised ten years in a labor camp."

"What did you do that was so bad?"

Vladimir clutched the curtain. He was like a guy who could throw Finland into the Baltic Sea. "The mothers caught me selling a suitcase of salamis. Konstantin had to swear the salamis were mine. He took me into his little school. He was trying to make trouble for the zhids who'd landed at Brighton Beach. But Konstantin would never have trusted a Jew. So he turned me into one. I became Vladimir Israilovich. I studied torah with a rabbi from the KGB. I went to shul in Leningrad."

"Did you sit upstairs with the women or downstairs with the men?"

"Mama, I was nineteen . . ."

She couldn't imagine Vladimir at nineteen. She thought he'd be thirty for life.

"Damn you," she said. "I won't ruin your gig with Konstantin." She watched her father, impervious on the bed. A king in blue pajamas, protected from his subjects by senility. She could dance for him, undress, play Cleopatra or Salome, and he wouldn't have noticed Sarah. She said good-bye to her dad and shuffled back to her room, so Vladimir wouldn't be blamed for plotting with her against the KGB. Her memory didn't drop. But she had to lie down. The poison had a strange hold. Events shook in her like a beebee gun and exhausted Sarah. Hiding in the synagogue with a kerchief on her head. Kissing old Biedersbill under the bridge. Running away from home without ever getting fifty feet from her father's door.

"Zdrastvitye, Vladimir Israilovich."

Vladi had been skulking around like a bear on its toes, avoiding a whole panoply of nurses, allowing patients under his arms, but he couldn't avoid the KGB. Konstantin had a lemon-colored suit for the Jersey winter. His shoes would have been worthless in the snow.

Konstantin performed a jig on the stairs. "I almost forgot." He removed a thick packet of letters from his pants.

Vladi stared at the letters. His body shook with a need to have them. He nearly brought the staircase down.

Konstantin smiled. "Take, take," he said, stuffing the letters into Vladimir's paw. "I've been guarding them for you over a month."

Vladimir couldn't listen with letters in his hand. *Mashenka.* She was her sisters' scribe. He could smell her handwriting, drink the words.

"Go on," Konstantin said. "We'll talk later." He disappeared and Vladi ran behind the stairwell, his fingers shaking with such force, he wasn't able to read Mashenka's scrawl. He blubbered into his sleeve, feeling the roots of his powerlessness. He lived from moment to moment, waiting for the letters that Konstantin sometimes carried for months. Konstantin was his courier angel, his lord and letterbox.

Daragoy Volodnishka.

His grip had steadied, and he could mouth Mashenka's greeting. *Daragoy Volodnishka . . .*

We miss you so much. Uncle says you will be coming back from your service in America soon. Irina is ironing her blouse for that occasion. Elena has been admitted to technical school. She talks of moving to Moscow. She is foolish, dear brother, foolish and seventeen. She wants to marry a cosmonaut. She says your eyes are green. Is that true? I don't think her memory is so fortunate, even if she's the oldest. I suspect your eyes aren't green at all. Forgive me, brother darling, if that is not the case. I thank you for the bracelet. I wore it at the Pioneer Club. The other girls were so jealous. Not one of them has a brother in the United States. The girls are all like Elena. They want to marry cosmonauts and rich men. But I'll never marry, not until you come home
. . .

Vladimir didn't know what to do with himself. He was bawling like a baby. Should he kill that Uncle of theirs, Konstantin, and take his chances in Peterburg with the three girls? He had enough cash on him to bribe every concierge on Dostoyevsky Street. And what if he should steal his sisters out of Peter and bring them right to Jersey? It could be done. He'd rally the bargemen from the Moika district, pay them in gold. Bargemen could smuggle out three little girls. They weren't so little any more, and he wouldn't wish America on his sisters when they had the most beautiful city in the world. What was New York with its two pathetic rivers and an island without a proper lake? His Mashenka could eat on a river, sleep on a river, skate under a hundred bridges.

Vladimir had a crazy pull around his heart. He'd never have the chance to show his city to the Teach. Teach would have loved Peterburg. Vladimir wasn't thinking of statues and stones, the wealth of this canal or that. His city stank of writers. Vladimir wouldn't have taken Teach to Lev Tolstoy Square or the little museum at Dom Pushkina, where Teach could have introduced himself to Chekhov's inkpot and Gogol's chair. All they had to do was walk and they would have smelled where Gogol lived. But Peterburg couldn't produce Henry James.

Vladimir mourned the Teach with Mashenka's letters in his hand.

> . . . and we went to Mars Field, brother, and walked in the gardens, and Elena swore how much she remembered you, that you drank tea without jam. Irina said you couldn't have been so uncivilized. Elena had a fight with her. They asked me to arbitrate, and what could I answer? I wasn't even two when you were gone. I try to picture my brother with jam swirling in his tea. The picture doesn't come . . .

13

WASN'T Ho Chi Minh any more. Could have dropped into one of those wells on the king's highway. It felt like that. A floating, endless fall. It was where the king's bowman had gone, good old Judith. Worse than brimstone and all the hells he'd imagined as a boy, when the kind little nuns had assured him he was going to eternal ruin. Hot, stinking sulfur would have been better than such a deep fall. It was worse than when he'd died up in that damn tree. Didn't have the Holy Ghost behind him now. Teach had developed vertigo on this fall. His future seemed to spin out of his past while he floated in the earth's core. He'd spent his life seeking moms and dads.

Any wonder his dick had disappeared? You couldn't run around fucking your own family.

Teach was confused. He remembered lying in the belly of a ship. More than one ship. He wouldn't have forgotten the smell of water. The montagnards were landlocked people. They couldn't have taken their hell out to sea.

He looked up and screamed. Saw a rainbow crawl on a man's cheek. Saw gold studs and a sorcerer's blue crescent. "Son of a bitch," he said. "Majesty, I'm glad you got rid of your Hawaiian shirt."

But then he stared into the patch of eye above the crescent. The eye was slightly out of focus. It was Marvin de la Mare, and Teach had landed in the talmud torah. Lulu, the little cunt, was next to Marve, and they were monkeying with Howard's cheek.

"Who brought me here?" he grunted.

"Dunno," Lulu said. "We found you by the door."

He watched that wild-eyed Marve and his little cunt. They'd started a romance the second Lulu was born. She'd grow old with Marve in her dreams. And who knows what would happen to wild eyes himself? There'd always be a blur in Marve's head, like a long inkblot. Teach shouldn't have played sorcerer with another man's skull.

"Where's old Sarah?" he asked.

"Dunno," Lulu said. "She disappeared and I've had to do all the shopping. It's hard with the Davidoffs around. They tried to push me into their truck."

"They're interested in Vladimir. What would they want with you?"

"Ransom money. The Davidoffs must be short of cash."

"Why didn't Vladi speak with Zoya and Samuil?"

"Because he's been gone longer than big tits."

"It's not nice to call her that," Teacher said. "She took you in and taught you how to bake paella."

"Big tits stole my man. She went off with Neck one afternoon and forgot her obligations to us."

Ah, she'd gone back to the Chanticleer and this time they didn't let her out. Teach cursed his own arrogance. Traveled around the world without a thought to the danger she was in. Uncle had gotten sick of Sarah's Hebrew school. He wanted to close shop, but Lubbock and Kroll couldn't leap into Alphabet-ville with the Davidoffs around. The Teacher had to smile, because Samuil and Zoya were the twin angels of the talmud torah, stalking Avenue C. They'd brought some domestic tranquillity to the neighborhood.

He started to get up, but he had that old vertigo. He was falling into somebody's well.

"Kiddies, help me to my feet."

"You're hurt," Lulu said. "The whole side of your face has been bleeding a long time. Let me look for a new bandage."

"It'll have to wait . . . don't answer the door to anyone but me and the Davidoffs."

"You're delirious," Lulu said. "The Davidoffs aren't our friends."

"They will be. I'm going to recruit Samuil."

And Teach stumbled out of the talmud torah. His cheek was on fire. Ah, he owed Konstantin a scratch across the face. The winter monsoons must have come to Alphabetville. Wind and rain blew him down the block. His cheek twitched. He could have sworn that some mother was following him. It was the kind of tracking he remembered from George's mountain. He had an Elephanter behind him. But he couldn't see a soul in the street. It was too windy for drug salesmen. Teach dragged himself to the corner of Tenth and C. And then a bakery truck was upon him. The back door opened and he was scooped up into Davidoff country. He expected samovars, a balalaika or two, bits of Moscow in a panel truck. But he found a general store. Coca-Cola bottles, king-size bags of popcorn, chocolate bars, and a picture of Michael Jackson on the side wall. Ah, these mothers had gone the American way. The Davidoff clan had platform shoes and black leather pants. Samuil was in a lumber jacket. He sat like a pioneer with the different barrels of his beebee gun. The Davidoffs' hardware didn't frighten him. It was their terrible seriousness that was the family arsenal. High heels and leather pants weren't part of any decor. They were a declaration. The Davidoffs had come riding out of Moscow and Brighton Beach with their own vision of the New World. They wouldn't be trifled with.

It wasn't Zoya who addressed Teach, or the other fat aunt, Adelina. Samuil shook him with the beebee gun.

"Comrade, who hurt your cheek?"

"Konstantin."

"Mmm," Samuil said, like some high judge at a court of appeals. "The KGBnik is not such a whimsical fellow. What purpose would he have to mark your face?"

"He meant to finish me," the Teacher said.

"But you're alive, and Kostya is not careless."

"I had help."

"This explains it," Samuil said, nodding to Zoya and Adelina and his old uncle, Izak, who was dreaming of some extravagant chocolate cake that could have gone to GUM, Moscow's giant department store. But Samuil wasn't into cakes for GUM. He couldn't solve the mystery of Nika's disappearance from Brighton Beach. "Tell me, who has our baker?"

"What baker?" Teacher asked, thinking Samuil had begun to hallucinate in the truck.

"Nika Troubnoy."

"Oh," Teach said. "Took him to my Uncle Albert's farm. Had to. He was popping off about Konstantin and the White House. But Nika's all right. He gets his meals and a room with a porch."

"Hijacknik," Samuil said.

279

"Davidoff, I don't do those numbers any more."

"But why you come looking for us?"

"Because Konstantin has an army and I can't take him myself."

"How we know you're not working for Kostya? Kostya could paint blood on cheek. What is it that you proposing?"

"A partnership. We turn the KGBnik around, and instead of killing him, we oblige the mother to work for us. It's the only way out. And I don't want Vladimir touched."

"Partnership is impossible. Vladimir betrayed us. We will have to punish him and KGBnik."

"Vladimir's been punished enough. He's like a turtle that can't breathe. And what's a better punishment for Konstantin than to make him our pet? He'll have to hide us from the KGB. If we don't like his manners, we'll mail a letter to the Lubyanka."

Teacher looked around the truck. Where the hell were the skullcaps? He couldn't find a pinch of Jewry. It was a synagogue of popcorn.

"We will think your proposition," Samuil said.

"There isn't much thinking time. Sarah's been stolen and I have to save her."

"She's your generalka, not ours. We will think."

"Think about Lulu," Teach said. "She'll starve in the talmud torah without your help."

"I will feed her."

"Feed her for how long? She's devoted to Sarah . . . Samuil, you can't get to Konstantin without me. Konstantin has cannons and bombs and you have one beebee gun. He'll blow you to shit."

"I'll cure him with violin," Samuil said.

"I thought your fiddle was left behind."

"Will have to borrow," Samuil said, and the Davidoffs tittered in their leather clothes. The truck seemed to sway with their goddamn enthusiasm. All they had was a thirty-year-old fiddler without a fiddle. Samuil hadn't touched his Stradivarius in ten, eleven years. The whole clan was built around the absence of that fiddle.

Samuil helped Teach down off the truck. Ah, he'd get to the Chanticleer on his own. The Davidoffs must have held some sorcery in their truck. The rain had turned to snow. Teach wasn't dressed for winter. He still had the canvas shoes he'd worn in Ho Chi Minh.

Some mother was behind him, but he couldn't read complexions in falling snow. The flakes stuck to his eyebrows like common candy. Lampposts turned to coronets. Roofs bent to meet him. He swooned into silver tags of snow. Teach himself had gone to silver in a silver land.

Snow on Avenue C was nothing to a Davidoff, who swam every winter in Sokolniki Wood. Samuil had lived in snow until he was twelve, when his childhood was officially over. He had to vie with ferocious girls at Central Music School, girls with such technique that he practiced day and night just to stay alive. He could never forgive them for ruining his winters. He'd have gladly dropped behind in that contest of technique, but he would have disappointed his old uncle and his aunts, who crouched in a chocolate factory near the Ukraina Hotel, shaping marzipan animals with their fingers so Samuil could wear a proper suit at the conservatory. Da, da, his maestros said, little Davidoff, the nephew of Stalin's clown. Did they ever think about Izak's life in a labor camp? Samuil would sneak into the toilet at Moscow Central and watch the snow fall. But he fiddled until his elbow grew raw and annihilated the school's best little girls.

He saw the Teacher swoon in the snow and he was about to

pick him up when Neck arrived in the talmud torah's white car and a plan started to form in Samuil's head. He allowed Neck to steal the Teacher. The Davidoffs would have a man inside when they seized the Chanticleer. Samuil considered the Teacher his employee now.

Teach had visited the family truck with a broken face, talked of hideouts in New Jersey and a scheme to harness Konstantin, bend him to their will. The Davidoffs already knew about the Chanticleer. They'd followed Neck into New Jersey a couple of times. And Samuil himself had thought of pulling a profit out of Konstantin, turning him into a chocolate tit. But he couldn't make a deal with the Teacher. Had to confer with his aunts and Uncle Izak. And he did.

"A whole castle," Adelina said. "How will we steal a castle from the Banditov? I'm not liking this Teacher so much."

But Samuil meant to take the Chanticleer. Old Izak was on his side. Izak always loved a war. Stalin's labor camp hadn't ruined his spirit. Izak thrived among all the criminals, those *urkas* with dragons tattooed on their skin, men who should have eaten up a little clown, used him as their pony. But if Izak couldn't get the *urkas* to laugh, he could always bake them bread. And there were enough reversals in Russian life to let them think and think again about harming Stalin's clown. They tattooed his arm, considered him part of their brotherhood, and Izak did his ten years as an *urka*.

But God liked to complicate things for the Davidoffs. Samuil discovered another man in the snow, an idiot in a summer shirt and summer shoes. "Is Armenian?" Zoya asked, because the idiot had a dark face and it was always summer in Armenia. He was starving and the Davidoffs fed him soup. He swallowed two pounds of marble cake, his jaw deep in chocolate. Samuil was delicate with him. "Comrade, who are you?"

"King George."

Zoya and Adelina tittered behind their thumbs. One king to

a talmud torah was enough. Was this king also a dancer? But Samuil refused to laugh.

"A regular highness," he said. "From Vietnam?"

"I'm George of the Elephant republic."

"But why you come so far?"

"To save my friend the Teach. I lost him in the snow."

"Comrade king," Samuil said. "You're not a winter man."

"Also not a king," Adelina said. "The other George has rainbow."

The king blew air with his nose. "What other George?"

"The dancer," Adelina said, suddenly afraid. She'd never seen a man who could make his nostrils so wide.

The king turned to the rear wall of the Davidoff's truck, removed a crayon from his pocket, and a little dried mud, and started a rainbow under his lip, without the benefit of a mirror. He marked his cheek blue. The Davidoffs were astonished. "Is a king," they said.

George spoke English with a Russian accent. He had a crossbow and a bag of arrows under his shirt. Samuil wasn't fooled. He recognized a fellow fiddler, and he told George about Teach's abduction. "Your friend is at the Chanticleer." They plotted together, away from Samuil's aunts. Only Izak was allowed to listen.

"Your holiness, I'll mount my beebee gun on the roof and we will charge the big house in our truck."

"Uncle has killer commandos. They'll blow us away. We'll have to trick the mothers, take them by surprise. We'll need a diversion."

Samuil smiled, because he knew what that diversion would have to be. "Come," he said and descended into the snow with George. Samuil chewed on the flakes like a Moscow wolf, while the king hugged his own arms. George was blind in the snow, and Samuil had to lead him to the talmud torah. He knocked and knocked until he heard Lulu growl.

"Go away."

"Open," he said. "Is Samuil."

"Prove it. Anybody can pretend to be a Davidoff."

A cautious girl. This he admired. "Is only one Samuil," he said. "No pretenders. I invited you to boardwalk in our last conversation."

Lulu unbolted the door, and Samuil stepped inside with the king. Lulu was cross. "You didn't say you were bringing a guest."

"Is not a guest. Is Teacher's family, King George."

Nothing startled her. It was Marve who looked at George's rainbow and felt diminished. Here was Marve's own true model in an Hawaiian shirt. The king skulked around him, sniffing another rainbow man.

Marve held out his hand. "I'm Marvin. Teacher painted me to look like you. He was lonely for Vietnam."

But Samuil stepped between them. "Is no time for introductions. Where is fiddle, please?"

"What fiddle?" Lulu asked, even as she admired Samuil's pluck and his leather pants.

"Fiddle what belongs with cabaret."

"Oh, that old thing." Lulu strolled under the canopy and returned with Teach's mountain fiddle. Samuil held it under his chin and sawed at it with his hand. He could have been back at Moscow Central, competing with all those wizard girls. He hadn't lost his technique in eleven years. He did a little pizzicato for the king.

"Here is diversion."

But George was deep inside a winter daze. He'd never heard such sweet sounds from his own violin That little Russki with all the red hair was some kind of magician. He had fat aunts and an uncle with a beautiful face.

"Come," Samuil said. "We are already losing time." He had to shove his three new partners out the door.

Zoya and Adelina were waiting for him in the snow. Samuil

was eaten with guilt. His aunts had slaved for him. They wouldn't marry while Samuil studied technique with Moscow's "hero artists." And now they couldn't find husbands who were worthy of them. They'd both loved Vladimir, but he wouldn't dance with them or drink with them or come into their bed, even before they learnt Volodnishka was a *shpik*. Muscovites were scarce in America and Odessans were beneath his sisters' dignity. It pained him that they should live without love.

He kissed his aunts, Zoya and Adelina, who'd swallowed chocolate dust so many years, who'd come home with chocolate moustaches and chocolate masks, their faces buried under the dust, and ask him how his lessons were. And he'd never even cared about the violin.

Nu, pravilno. He'd never find husbands for them at a castle in New Jersey. But with all the sadness he felt, he'd still take that castle for the Davidoffs and rescue the Teach.

14

WINDOW white, window white.

Sarah wondered if her mind had leapt out to curtain her window with snow. She couldn't remember snow clinging to the window panes like that in her daddy's house. The whiteness cast a blue shine on the walls. That's how George's poison worked. Whiteness over everything. A warm, soft grave. She was Sarah Fish, the poetess, imprisoned at the Chanticleer hotel. Howie Biedersbill had been her lover.

She went naked to the window, opened it, and rattled the frame. But that whiteness held, and Sarah had to sweep off the snow from the sash with her hand. Now the planet was hers again. Another storm must have come while she was waiting for the poison to turn her insides into mud. The path the little sisters had cleared was completely covered over, but Sarah saw a bus come breaking through the cliffs of snow. It was her own white limo, with Neck at the wheel and Doris in the back with old Gwendolyn.

Neck jumped into the snow and called up to the Chanticleer. "Uncle, couldn't get to Marvey and the niece. But look what I found. An old acquaintance. He was lying like a dog in front of the talmud torah."

Neck dragged a body out of the limousine. She could recognize the way that body bent into the snow. Biedersbill. He was alive, and he had a big red gash on his cheek, and both his eyes were bloody. Old Neck was dragging him along.

"Uncle, he was playing hard to get. Had to convince him to come on this little trip . . . don't be bashful, Teach. Uncle wants to meet ya."

Damn the Chanticleer for taking her clothes. She had to wrap herself into the quilt again. She waltzed out of her room to meet Howie Biedersbill and tell him he was a turd for betraying her gang, but she wouldn't utter a syllable until she administered to his cheek. She clopped down the stairs and arrived at the front parlor as Neck rolled the Teacher through the door. Her fiancé landed on the carpet, gray as stone. Then he started to shiver. He had a smile on his broken face.

The padre called for Gwendolyn. Old Gwen appeared with Doris Quinn, like two Little Red Riding Hoods, one without her teeth.

"Gwendolyn, bandage him up, please."

Biedersbill grabbed for the padre's cuffs. "Didn't mean to survive, Uncle. It was an accident."

"Gwendolyn," the padre said.

And that's when Sarah bullied into that crowd of people. "Gwendolyn can get stuffed. I'll bandage Biedersbill."

Teacher searched with his swollen eyes. "Sweets, is that you?"

"Will somebody get her out of here?" the padre said.

Neck took Sarah by the scalp. "Glad to," he said. "I know what big tits needs." He let her ride the carpet, with his hand in her hair. Sarah screamed. Her savior, Vladimir, slapped Neck's hand and Neck retreated into the corner with a howl. Vladi had a pulse over his eye that could have destroyed the Chanticleer.

The struggle at the door had been pulled out of time, it seemed to Sarah. She felt like a person frozen into a play.

Wasn't Albert who smashed that little tableau. It was the Russian mother she'd never met. *Konstantin.* Konstantin smiled with his hands in lemon-colored pockets. "We wouldn't want your sisters to go barefoot in winter, eh Volodya?"

"Maybe we would," Vladimir said. "You shouldn't threaten so much."

"It's not a threat. I'm Mashenka's lifeline. You should be careful I'm not hurt."

"I am careful," Vladimir muttered. He picked up Sarah and carried her on his back. "I'll look after the little mother. She won't disturb you now."

He climbed up to the second floor without bending to Sarah's weight.

"Boss," Neck whispered to the padre. "Should I follow them? I could put out their lights."

"Shut up."

"Let him talk," Teacher spoke from the carpet. "It's good to know what you have planned for all of us."

Konstantin chided the Teach. "I liked you better when you were Rousseau. Didn't I tell you to keep away from the Richelieu? You would have been a corpse without that movie-house king and his brother."

"We'll settle with Tuan," the padre said. "And George was never reliable. He's consumed with ideas of royalty."

Sarah strained to listen from the second floor. She couldn't understand all the chatter about George. It was hard to concentrate from the heights of Vladimir's shoulder. She had to dodge the chandeliers. The little sisters looked at her from near the ground. Her brains were wobbly but she still felt glad. No matter what the mothers did to her, Teach was alive.

Gwen had Teach in her station. She was always fond of that thin little man. She couldn't understand how he preferred fat Sarah. She bathed his cheek and rubbed cream into the wound and then she bathed his eyes and bandaged old Biedersbill. "Teach," she whispered. "You're safe with me."

"I know that, Gwen. You're a living doll."

"We could run off together. Why don't you forget Sarah's fat behind?"

"Ah, Gwen, that's what love is. It makes you stick to one behind."

"But didn't she eat up Marve? She got down with him for months."

Gwen had to finish the conversation. The padre had come in. "Thanks, Gwendolyn. You can go now."

And Gwen took her ointments and her creams. She closed the door and left Teach and the padre in her station.

Teach was sitting in a chair. He could have leapt up and torn the padre's throat. But he might have missed. The blood from his cheek wouldn't stop welling into his eyes.

"Howard, you have a terrific flaw. Devotion to Saigon Sarah. I held on to her as long as I could. I gave her the talmud torah because of you."

"You gave her nothing without getting back. It was your house in the wilderness."

"But she abused it. In another month we would have had all kinds of police on our tail. I couldn't afford the luxury of keeping her. And I couldn't get rid of Sarah without sending you out of the country."

"Congratulations, Uncle. You can bury us in your deepest yard."

"What for? I like having you here. You're my brightest pupil. But be nice to Konstantin. He wants to kill you . . . sleep, Howard. You'll need your strength."

And the padre walked out of Gwen's station, whistling a tune he wasn't aware of. Prokofiev? Ah, *Peter and the Wolf.* But who was Peter? And who was the Wolf? He was fond of Howard, although he'd toyed with Howard's execution in Ho Chi Minh. The padre smiled, because he'd had a feeling those two montagnards would save Biedersbill. George was an antiquated king who gathered poisons and drugs, but was useless outside the Richelieu. Tuan was the important one. And the padre had discovered where Tuan's loyalties were, using Biedersbill as bait. The old general was still hooked into that tribe of magicians. Tuan had been among the padre's first pupils, a skinny boy magician known as Frédéric before his conversion in Hanoi. He'd arrived at the lycée in Dalat to perfect his French. The boy traveled across the highlands with his homeless tribe to start school. Frédéric had come to class in his warrior's paint, something of a king, but with ambiguous standing among the matriarchs. And the padre tutored him, taught him about that endless river where Rimbaud had traveled all his life.

The boy was shrewd. "Cher professeur," he said with the irony of a savage. "Am I on Rimbaud's river?"

"Of course."

And the boy returned to his tribe of mothers.

The padre stumbled onto a man. It was Lubbock banging a nurse. Lubbock crawled for his pants, his buttocks rising like hills in elephant country. The nurse was Simonson herself. The padre grew disappointed. He'd thought Simonson was too cultivated to lie with one of the padre's assassins. She covered her bosoms with a hand. But she couldn't have been trying very hard. The padre saw an open field of tits.

"Simonson, it's time to feed our pensioners some of the king's candy."

She ran off, never bothering with her blouse. Ah, he was raising amazons at the Chanticleer. The Baroness loved to have a crop of nubile women around. But the nurses were a bit bony and harsh. He preferred Lliana's looks. He'd invite her to Nice after he closed up the farm.

Lubbock climbed into his pants. "Uncle, you know how it is . . . Simonson has the hots for me."

"Where's Kroll? Out sporting with a nurse?"

Lubbock laughed, and the padre's other assassin appeared with his pants unzipped. Lubbock and Kroll, essential in New Jersey, but the padre wouldn't need them on the Promenade des Anglais.

"I'm worried about Vladimir," he said.

"We'll tame him," Lubbock said. "Should we visit Vladimir in his sleep?"

"No. He's liable to wake up all our pensioners with his screams. Catch him while he's taking a piss in the fields."

"Jesus," Lubbock said. "That Russki wouldn't piss in snow."

"Then invite him on a culture walk . . . soon. He's jumpy. And I don't like that."

"What about the fat bitch? Should we smother old Sarah?"

"She's harmless without Vladimir."

"And Biedersbill?" Kroll asked.

"He's lost enough blood to build a canal. Concentrate on Vladimir."

The padre stepped around his two assassins, sick of snow and New Jersey.

291

Saigon dreamt of balalaika music. Ah, she'd gone to Russia for the day. Leningrad. But this Leningrad didn't have rivers and churches and palaces with domes. It had a window and a dressing table. She wasn't dreaming at all. The music floated up from the window, which had lost its cover of snow. A wagon stood at the gates. She recognized the Davidoffs' bakery truck. Brighton Beach had come for Vladi. The Davidoff women wore high heels in the snow, and that genius, Samuil, had given up his violin to strum a balalaika for the Chanticleer.

Sarah heard a familiar twitch in the music. Wasn't a balalaika, no. It was Teach's tin fiddle that the little genius had acquired. He'd gotten rid of the bow and he pulled on the fiddle like a chicken plucker playing a Cossack melody. Deep snow was Samuil's microphone. The music had its own wires. Samuil's women danced near the truck. Sarah couldn't have imagined in all her life how glad she was to see the Davidoffs. She opened the window to holler at the truck.

"You Davidoffs, come on up to the house."

But her voice didn't carry. The wind returned it to Sarah, slapped it right back. It was like having a moat around her. She couldn't get to Samuil. She raced to the door in her bare feet. The mothers had locked her in.

"God damn you, open up."

She heard Vladi bray from the other side of the door. "Can't, little mama. Looks like there's trouble."

"But I'll tell the Davidoffs that Konstantin tricked you into spying on them."

"It's not the Davidoffs, mama. They wouldn't serenade us without a reason. They're tied to somebody else . . . mama, I have to go. Konstantin's calling."

"Don't go to him," Sarah said.

But Vladi had already gone to the stairs. Uncle's people were collecting in the big hall. Lubbock and Kroll picked their teeth as Simonson arrived in her blouse. The Baroness de Roth came out of her room. She traveled with a shawl, her birdlike face in a shiver. She wasn't prepared for balalaika music. Simonson wanted to reassure her. "It's nothing, Baroness. A mad tribe. They have some silly grievance against Vladimir. But they can't invade us."

"Course not," said Gwen. "They're an army of women and boys."

Neck assembled his Australian shotgun that *Soldier of Fortune* had been touting as an "all-weather gun." It could splatter birds or bush babies. "I'll give them a little music if they come close."

"That would be lovely for our reputation," the padre said. "Davidoffs dying in the snow."

"We could always lend them Vladimir," Konstantin laughed.

"They wouldn't come this far for Vladimir . . . children, I'm not so happy with their visit."

The Baroness kept smoking cigarettes. Gwen jumped against the window. "It's Marvey," she said. "He's naked."

Everyone stood near the Baroness's picture window and watched Marvin dance without clothes. He couldn't follow the balalaika. Half of him would disappear with every hop, while he struggled to stay on his feet.

Gwen laughed so hard the .45s dropped from her belt. "Uncle, should we invite him inside?"

The padre didn't enjoy the show. Marvin's moves disturbed him. There was a deliberate clumsiness. But he could sense this dancer wasn't a clumsy man. The dancer was decked in war paint. The blue on his body turned brilliant in the snow.

And then the painted bird abandoned his clumsy act. He swayed to the balalaika and contended with the hills of snow. Uncle Albert knew the dancing was for him.

"Cut the fucking lights."

"Why?" Neck asked.

"I want this place dark in half a minute."

Neck ran to find the circuit box. He threw every switch in

the mansion. He figured the padre's jungle fever was acting up. What harm could old Marvey do? The patients upstairs began to groan in a dark house. Bedlam had arrived. There wasn't even the simplest hall light to give comfort. All they had was a blue haze off the snow.

"Take your birdgun, Neck, and come with me."

Neck strolled out the door with the padre and stood on the Chanticleer's front porch. Old Marve was dancing like a dummy in the snow. Neck could see Marve's nipples and all that blue on him like the devil. Marve clapped to the Russian music while Neck stroked his gun. He didn't intend to shoot Marve. He was pointing at Samuil and the bakery truck. He wanted to explode the balalaika off Samuil's ribs and leave a tracery of pellets on the truck's side panel. But Uncle had no interest in the Davidoffs.

"Pull on the dancer," he said.

"Jesus, that's old Marve. He aint all there. Took the Teacher's potion and he just about lost his life."

"Pull, I said."

Neck swung the gun back to Marve and squeezed the trigger twice. Marve fell under the blast. Neck couldn't believe a man would race against birdshot and win. He split the gun open against his knee, emptied it, and reloaded the little mother. But old Marve had become a rubber man. Who the hell had taught him to duck a birdgun? Marve hadn't even been to the Nam. He danced away, clutching something in his hand. He'd inherited a bow and a bundle of arrows. Ran like a mountain deer. Snow didn't mean shit. The highlands had come to Jersey.

"That aint Marve. It's the king."

"Now you're getting clever."

"But he could have snuck up on us. Why'd he give his position away?"

"He's showing us what our birdshot can do. Back to the house, Neck."

"Will he charge us in the truck?"

"Not George. He'll do us alone."

Neck chortled into his fist. "With a children's bow? This aint the French and Indian War."

"I've seen that bow, Neck. Back to the house."

They bolted themselves inside the Chanticleer. All the nurses carried guns. Konstantin sat in the big hall playing solitaire. He wasn't frightened of a savage in blue paint. He hummed "Dark Eyes" to himself. Then "Sergeant Pepper." He was in Ho Chi Minh when John Lennon died. Lennon should have moved to the banks of the Neva. Konstantin would have found him a sweeter bride than Yoko, a girl from Finland, quiet, beautiful, with fire between her legs.

"Comrade," Uncle said. "You ought to worry more with a king in the house."

"Why, when I have Vladimir to protect me?"

"Who says he's in the house?" Neck muttered, morose. "He aint got wings. Can a montagnard fly?"

"He doesn't have to fly?" Konstantin said.

"Then who let him in?"

"He'll find a window. Our king loves to climb walls."

"I'll stop him," Neck insisted.

"You'll have to guard three hundred windows. Ask the Baroness."

But the Baroness de Roth left Uncle's ensemble and returned to her room. Had she sniffed the end of the Chanticleer, Neck began to wonder. He'd met George in the Nam and hadn't been impressed. A little guy who couldn't even grow a beard and wanted to become king of the Yards. Neck could stop the king's little arrows with an elbow. Konstantin was smart to play solitaire. And George? George could duck pellets in the snow, dance to Samuil's balalaika, but that montagnard was a duck without wings in this house.

Troubnoy hobbled down from the second floor. He had a red

robe at the farm. He felt lost without lights. The Chanticleer seemed like the Lubyanka to him. "I'm frightened," he said.

Simonson purred at him from the depths of her blouse. "Nika, mustn't be a bad boy. Mama will entertain you in a little while. Now go on back upstairs."

Troubnoy discovered Teach, who'd crept out of Gwen's station to lie on the floor. "Mr. Biedersbill, what happened to your face?"

"Get him out of here," the padre said, and Simonson took Nika by the hand and brought him up the stairs like a baby.

"Bye, Uncle Nick," Teach said with a mad smile, because America had just been explained to him. Teach hadn't crossed the South China Sea in a mythical boat, with blood under his chair. George had been his chaperone.

"Majesty?" Teach said, shouting at some ceiling he couldn't see with all the blood in his eye. He wiped the blood with his paw and found Lubbock and Kroll. "George, does Jersey suit you or not?"

"Shut him up," the padre said, and Kroll went to stifle Teach, but Vladimir stood in the way.

Lubbock jumped on Vladi with a length of wire he'd been sharpening all afternoon for Vladimir's throat. He'd wrapped the wire around two wooden handles and made his own garrote. The wire cut into Vladi's neck as Lubbock worked the handles. Vladi chewed blood and Kroll attacked from the front, with a hammer in his fist. The hammer landed once, leaving a pucker in Vladimir's skull, and then Vladi grabbed Kroll in his arms and broke Kroll's back, while the wire tore through his chin. His eyes closed. He couldn't get his hands under the garrote. Lubbock rose off the ground like some master bellringer and forced his weight onto the wire. Blood shot from Vladi's ears and he fell on top of Kroll.

Teacher cried. "Ah, Vladi. I'm hopeless. Couldn't even help . . ."

It took six nurses to roll Vladimir out of the way, while Lubbock stood with his bloody wire, celebrating himself. "Uncle, it was a piece of cake. Get me George and I'll give him a dose of wire." He was too excited to mourn Kroll, his partner and companion. He'd had breakfast and dinner every day with Kroll for the last sixteen years. Kroll mended his shirts and figured out his income tax. Kroll picked the movies they went to in Passaic and kept a strict account of the money they extorted from the old men at the farm. It was Kroll who decided which old men to bully. And Lubbock had already forgotten that Kroll was dead.

"Uncle, get me George . . ."

Uncle Albert had an arsenal around him, enough guns and garrotes to drop a staircase full of magicians, but he didn't feel safe. He'd jumped into the middle of North Viet patrols and never heard the sound of his own heart. But that dancing in the snow had been a touch too intimate. George was claiming Jersey for the magicians.

Uncle heard him on the stairs, discovered his feet in the snow-light. The king wore shoes in the mansion. Shoes and a shirt. One side of him was red. He'd caught a slap of birdshot. Uncle called out to him from the bottom of the stairs.

"It isn't fair, George, standing over us with your quiver. We only have our guns against your arrows."

Neck thought the padre had gone mad. He couldn't see a hair of the king. Patients groaned from the second floor. Then a voice shot down the stairs.

"Albert, no deals."

And Neck began to shake. It was like hearing a holy voice out of the hills. No half-pint magician could holler down from the roofs. God had come to the Chanticleer. Neck dropped his birdgun and hid under a windowseat.

Lubbock seized the birdgun and sighted up the stairs with that metal tit between the barrels. "Georgie boy, remember me? I made it with your sister every other Monday in the Nam."

"I remember."

Lubbock turned fierce. Suddenly reminded himself that his partner was dead and blamed it on the king's tricks. He'd have to endure the horror of breakfast without Kroll.

"I'm waiting for you, majesty, waiting for you and Hélène."

Lubbock toppled over. Could have suffered a heart attack. The little sisters had heard only a slight slap. They stood over Lubbock and examined him. He had an arrow sitting on his eyebrow. It looked like a carved popsicle stick, a thing that shouldn't have done much damage. It had no feathers on its tail, just a little notch that they caught in the blue haze. It was obscene, an arrow killing like that.

Konstantin didn't get up from the table. He sat in the dark with his solitaire while the little sisters started to shoot. They ripped the bannister rails, loaded and emptied their guns. Simonson fell. She had one of those popsicle sticks in her temple. She barely bled at all. The sisters were disheartened without their head nurse, but they still charged the stairs. Arrows landed on them like a dry kiss. Gwendolyn dropped, clutching Sarah's .45s.

The padre crawled behind the little sisters with Neck's birdgun. He didn't scout for George's eyes on the stairs. He exploded one barrel and listened to the tinker of George's feet. His empire had come down to this. George's feet. He exploded the second barrel and started up the stairs. An arrow dug under his heart. He clutched at it, thinking slyly of Rimbaud. Could have been lecturing now, tracing the arc of Rimbaud's life in a couple of lines. But it wasn't Rimbaud he saw in the ceiling. And it wasn't George. It was his own brother, Carlo Peck, like a gnome in the ceiling, eating the wood of the Chanticleer. Carlo's teeth were red. Ah, the magician was cruel. Albert wouldn't have dreamt of his brother without an arrow near his heart.

He crashed into the stairs with his eyes open. The little sisters tossed their guns away and fled into broom closets and other sanctuaries. Even with all the damage around him, bodies on the floor, Konstantin wouldn't give up his game of solitaire. If he ran from the house, the Davidoffs would tear him to pieces. He preferred not to be mutilated by women in high heels. So he put the cards down one by one while George arrived on the stairs, natural as New Jersey, with blood on his shoulder and a blue face. The bow was strung. George had an arrow for him, seasoned with buffalo shit.

"Lo, majesty. It's quiet around here."

The magician took another step towards Konstantin and Konstantin said, "Good luck. You and Tuan can share Ho Chi Minh until Hanoi catches up with you. Those lads will wonder how two montagnards got so rich. I won't be there to help you."

George wasn't coming down to bargain with him in a shirt soaked with blood. That savage couldn't appreciate the subtleties of Hanoi.

"Majesty, I have enough cash to finance a string of movie houses . . . in your name."

Konstantin shut his eyes like an infant praying to God. God must have been from Leningrad, because someone slid against Konstantin and hugged him, so George couldn't have a good target. It was Henry James, with a pile of gauze on his cheek.

"No!"

"That mother tried to kill you," George said.

"It makes no difference. He's necessary to us."

"Teach, I know Konstantin. He'll beg and kiss your hand and betray us the first chance he gets."

"He wouldn't ruin his own gig. We're partners now."

"I won't be partners with a Russian weasel."

"Cut the crap. It's business as usual. And why didn't you tell me you were in town? Couldn't you touch my lip or something when you left me at the talmud torah?"

"I didn't want to wake you."

"So you brought me from Ho like a zombie and made your own deal with the Davidoffs. Did you explain to Samuil that you're a magician on the side?"

"Didn't have to explain," George said. "He's in love with Albert's niece."

"So you promised him Lulu for dessert."

"I never promise," George said.

Teach was jealous of the king's crossbow.

"What gives with all the arrows? Judith did your fighting. You were in charge of the tribe's kindergarten."

"I'm a warrior too," George said.

"Couldn't you have told me?"

"I'm telling you now. Forget Konstantin. We can do opium without him. Pick another Russian if you want."

"There is no other Russian. It has to be him. And he's the only one who can save Vladi's sisters."

"Why should he care about sisters? He'll abandon us all."

"Abandon?" Konstantin squealed like a wounded boar. "Who's been their father and uncle these ten years? You think I did it for Vladi? I'm devoted to Mashenka. I'm not so fond of the other two, I admit. Irina's spoiled. And Elena's dull. But an uncle has a right to his favorite niece."

George grabbed Konstantin by his collar. "You're nobody's uncle, you piece of shit. Just keep the sisters alive."

Konstantin bawled in his lemon-colored suit. "Kill me. I won't be insulted by a mountain nigger."

"Stop it," Teacher said. The Baroness came out of her room, noticed the corpses, and started to go back in when Teacher curtsied to her, pinching the sides of his pants. "Baroness, we'll clean up. It's business as usual."

The Baroness returned to her room. Teach shifted his head and noticed Vladimir lying in the corner. Teach's old vertigo had come back. His knees pitched. Vladimir's neck was ribboned with blood. Teach found a curtain and covered his friend. He had to smile to keep from wrecking the Chanticleer.

"We have something else to discuss," Konstantin said. "The Davidoffs. You'll have to give me some kind of exit visa."

Teacher held his smile. "The Davidoffs won't harm you. They're with us. They get ten percent of the gross."

"That's impossible. I can't consort with Jews. I'm in a ticklish spot as it is . . . make it five percent."

"Ten, Konstantin, or none of us will leave here alive."

Konstantin howled into his lapels. "I'm beginning to like my new partners."

"Ah," Teacher said, banging his skull. "I forgot. The Davidoffs have cousins in Novgorod. They'll expect you to get them out." Teach didn't know the Davidoffs' family tree. But he suspected there were cousins around.

Konstantin bared his teeth. "We're partners five minutes and already you're fucking me. I don't traffic in Jewish cousins . . . it will cost them thirty thousand. I have a whole department to bribe."

"You'll take it out of their profits. They don't expect cousins for free. They're merchants, like us . . . now excuse me, comrade. Have to find my fiancée."

Konstantin started to panic. He'd have to be alone in the big hall. He couldn't face the snow without Henry James. The Davidoffs might haul him into their truck. "Children," he shouted above the corpses, adopting the padre's tone. "We're partners. Shouldn't I go with you?"

"Stick to solitaire," the king said from his shoulder and followed Teach to the second floor. They quieted patients in their rooms. The old men thought George was an Indian who'd come to entertain them. He had to exhibit his bow.

Grandfathers invited Teach into their beds. Ah, he was still a charmer. He stumbled upon a room with a key in its door. He twisted the key and let himself in. Saigon was sitting on a giant bed, wrapped up in a quilt.

"Hello, Sarah."

She blinked at him. "Have the Russians grabbed this establishment? Then you're Nikita Khrushchev."

"Darling," he said. "I'm your skinny man."

"Go away. You stink."

He looked into her eyes. Jesus, they'd drugged Saigon, put her on a zombie diet. He shouted for the king.

"Do something, George. How'll I ever marry this girl? She thinks I'm Khrushchev."

George had no medicine under his armpit. He opened Sarah's eyelids.

"Lay off," she said. "Mr. Nicholas Lenin."

"She's unconscious," the Teacher said.

George didn't agree. "Help me put her into the tub."

They had to fight to get Sarah out of her quilt. They carried her into the bathroom and sat her down in the tub. Teacher decided it was okay for a sorcerer to see Sarah's tits. George didn't fill the tub. He sprinkled drops of water on Sarah's eyelids and chanted a prayer to all the gods and demons that thrived in New Jersey. Since the demons were much more prolific, he concentrated on them.

"Devils of New Jersey, pity us, and give the Teacher back his fiancée."

Sarah leaned against the rear wall of the tub and growled with a certain recognition. "Teacher, who's this guy?"

"Baby, it's the king."

"All the way from Nam to give me a bath without water?"

"It's one of his cures."

"Well, you tell him to cure me with my clothes on."

They thrust her inside the quilt.

Ah, Teacher thought, home was where Sarah was.

It had nothing to do with a talmud torah. They could have all lived on Dostoyevsky Street, moved in with Mashenka.

The war was over. That much Samuil understood. But where was a sign from the winners? The castle seemed closed to him. At least George had learnt how to dance in a white field. No mean accomplishment for a montagnard. And Samuil? Samuil continued to play. He kept dropping into the snow, dreaming of winters at Sokolniki Wood. He was up to his thighs now, but he wouldn't abandon his violin. He'd fallen in love with that tin box when he heard it being scraped inside the talmud torah on those long nights of cabaret dancing. Found a fiddle with perfect pitch. He'd never mourned the Stradivarius. That violin hadn't been his. It was on loan from the Ministry of Culture. Couldn't enjoy such a violin. A prisoner to his own fiddle, he played on borrowed time. He loved his own disorder behind the notes. Played Mendelssohn like a time bomb. Couldn't reconcile Mozart and Marx. He was his own sort of zhid. He preferred the simple anarchy of Coney Island Avenue, the broken boardwalk at Brighton Beach. He didn't need a private cabana, where women danced with diamonds on their fiddle fingers. The boardwalk was Samuil's tent. He loved to lie under that wooden road, away from the sun, while those few Brighton Beachniks from Moscow and Kiev paid homage to him and his aunts. They would reminisce about some Mendelssohn concert he couldn't even recall.

"Our hero," they said, these refuseniks of Coney Island Avenue. "There'll never be another Davidoff."

Couldn't the refuseniks understand? He had to wait for the right fiddle to come along.

And now he plucked and sawed to a silent castle and couldn't even tell if the king was dead or alive. Lulu sat in the truck with Marvin de la Mare. He did "Dark Eyes" for her and "Gypsy Fiddle Horn" and "Good Wives, Go Home." Marvin was in a funk. He hadn't recovered from his encounter with George. Lulu tried to comfort him. She held Marvin's hand, but she couldn't take her eyes off that redheaded fiddler.

The fiddler began to accompany himself.

'Twas under an apple tree
I saw her white eyes.
Was it cowgirl or demon lady?
Dedushka, I didn't even care.

A swirling form interrupted Samuil. Could have been that demon out of the song. But the demon didn't have white eyes. It was Neck crashing through the snow. "Fucking Davidoffs, I pity you."

Samuil didn't consider the beebee gun. He had his tin box, and he pulled on the string.

'Twas under an apple tree

He'd stop Neck with a fiddle string, charm him out of his pants.

I saw her white eyes . . .

He heard a pop behind him. Samuil turned around. Uncle Izak stood with the family gun. Neck howled into the snow. He ran from Samuil, clutching his head.

. . . cowgirl or demon lady?
Dedushka, I didn't even care.

The fiddler smiled at Lulu in the truck. He intended to marry that little girl.

"Come," he said to his people. "Is time to study a war."

And he went up the castle hill with Lulu and Marve, Izak, and his aunts. Izak held the gun. The old man felt like an *urka*, a crook with a blue tattoo. Stalin had sentenced him to oblivion with thousands of other Jews. But it was still hard not to love your tsar, even if he had a red face and a raw moustache. Izak remembered Stalin's seat at the Moscow Circus. That master of all the Russias, that tsar of tsars, little Koba, the man of steel, sat behind a pole, away from the Party hacks. There was no such animal as a circus bodyguard. Stalin laughed alone. He would pull on his nose to keep the roaring down. His tiny eyes would wake out of a tsar's sleep when Izak danced with the polar bears. Koba clapped. But his idolizers were too involved with Izak's bears to bother about Joseph Stalin . . .

Samuil wouldn't say hello to a castle. He walked right in the front door. He discovered bodies in a big room. And then his aunts started to cry. They'd found Volodnishka under a curtain, with his throat cut. They rocked him in their arms, that big bear both of them would have liked to marry. They didn't talk English to Vladi. They fell into their Moscow dialect, crooning childish songs.

A man sat at a table in the castle's big room. Vladi's Moscow master. Konstantin in lemon pants. He was picking his teeth with the queen of spades.

"Comrade colonel, did you kill our man?"

"No. The other guys killed him. Albert's soldiers."

"Of course," Samuil said. "Is always the other guys."

"We're partners," Konstantin said. "It's been arranged. The Teacher drives a hard bargain. I'm supposed to get your cousins out of Novgorod."

"Is a pity, because we have no cousins in Novgorod. We are last Davidoffs Russia had left."

Konstantin winked at him. "Doesn't have to be a cousin. It could be a friend, or an old music teacher."

"We're not in export business," Samuil said. "You'll do us all your favors in cash. And if you forget, I'll come to Moscow myself and sing in front of Lubyanka . . . now get out of our castle, please, with queen of spades."

"And your aunts won't follow me to the door?"

"My aunts have swollen legs, comrade colonel. Is hard to kick with high heels. Can't you see? They're mourning Volodnishka."

"But who will drive me?" Konstantin said with a certain gloom.

"Hitchhike, comrade, but get out of here."

And Konstantin walked into the snow.

It was a curious business. Dead people and a colonel from the KGB. Samuil opened the door and called out to Konstantin's lemon color.

"Is alive the Teacher?"

"Yes," Konstantin said, bundling himself against the snow.

"What about talmud torah lady?"

"Alive," Konstantin said.

"And King George?"

"George's alive."

"Good," Samuil muttered, "good." But he had yet to find that comrade king.

THE RAINBOW KING

15

Lord is my Shepherd. I shall not want.
He maketh me lie down in red pastures. He
leadeth me beside the mountains and the mad waters.

THE king was a Christian sorcerer. He'd begun to doubt the local devils years ago when evangelists had come to his mountain with bibles, banjos, and songs. The evangelists were scouting the district for Saigon Station, but he didn't mind being instructed into a new religion by the CIA. Christianity had powerful songs, and Lord Jesus was a frail magician, much like the Elephant People. George believed in songs, even though every one of the evangelists had seduced his sister. He couldn't hold that against them. His sister had a shameful love of preachers who played the banjo, but that never stopped her business sense.

Hélène extracted money from the evangelists while she lay with them.

The evangelists made the tribe weep, and the Elephanters converted to Christianity. They loved the stories of kings like Saul, who was sick in the heart and could have been one of George's Cambodian cousins. Some missionaries adopted the king's cousins, brought them to Detroit, and sang to them of Jesus. But the cousins weren't comfortable away from their devils. They couldn't plant a spirit table in the midst of houses and cars. And the little sweet cakes the devils required had nothing to do with shopping malls. George's cousins couldn't prosper in blue jeans and baseball caps. They had nightmares and died in their sleep. The missionaries buried the cousins and forgot about them, because it wasn't so Christian to die in Detroit of bad dreams.

George's own conversion stuck, but the rest of his tribe didn't stay Christian. The Elephanters needed a constant reassurance of banjo music, and when the evangelists stopped coming to sleep with Hélène, the magicians abandoned their crosses and Hebrew kings. Saul became a forgotten shadow, a fugitive who wasn't worthy of sitting under the spirit table. But George didn't need such a heavy dose of evangelism. He could hear psalms in his head. That's why he'd taken to the Hebrew school. It was Saul's place, a home for sick kings. He didn't have much use for the Chanticleer, a mansion that sat in snow. But the Hebrew school continued to haunt him.

He was less of a sorcerer now that he'd gone the Christian way. He couldn't transport a Hebrew school to Ho Chi Minh. He had his seat upstairs at the Richelieu. He had Yankeegirls to slip around the women's militia and deliver Mont Blanc pens to merchants, under the militia's nose. The merchants used their pens as money. They would have been hung by their balls if the women's militia caught them trading in deutsche marks or dollar bills. They had to establish their own secret cash, money that wouldn't inflame the militia. So they acquired every sort of fountain pen, from the Mont Blanc Diplomat to the cheapest Czech model. Anything was better than the fucking dong, that Donald Duck money printed in Hanoi, money that tore in your fist and bled on your fingers like a decal. George would have nothing to do with Donald Ducks. And he didn't have to worship the fountain pen. George was diversified. He had eleven whores near the port of Saigon. He had a few bodyguards with heart disease. He had children downstairs who fondled old men.

George was the spider king. No one starved inside his web. And he wasn't scared of women soldiers. The spider king carried deutsche marks and dollars in his pants.

He had birdshot in his shoulder from the Chanticleer, but that couldn't bother him. He wouldn't sit in his throne room at the Richelieu. He chased old men out of the orchestra and watched *Shoot the Piano Player* in the middle of the afternoon with his child whores lying about. The girls had no money in their pockets. They cursed George and called him a savage. The ville was run by montagnards and lunatic militiawomen with their dragonlady, Colonel Mai-lan, who couldn't be bribed. The children were going crazy. They had to endure a film with so many Long Noses. Their heads ached. And their groans got to George. He shut down the projector, locked his throne room, and restored the Richelieu to these children and their clientele.

He'd had enough of movie houses. The king took a walk in the sun. But Jesus must have fingered George, because infants followed him everywhere. It was his own corporation of brats, his private railroad in Saigon. The Yankeegirls warehoused his goods on themselves. They were movable stores. But they'd grown agitated after the Teacher's visit. They dropped alarm clocks in the alleys, lost precious hordes of soap, insisting Teach was their dad. A monstrous idea. The majority of them had blue eyes, and Teach was a dark-eyed man. But no small point of eye pigmentation could stop them from selecting Teach as a dad.

They sang in chorus. "Biedersbill, Biedersbill, Biedersbill."

The king's junior partner, Percival the Fourth, had been teaching them English, which was insane, because Perce was a wanted man and should have kept off the street.

"King, king," the Yankeegirls said, pulling on the tails of his orange-colored coat. Orange was appropriate to his station as one of the richest poor men in Ho Chi Minh. He'd have been richer without Colonel Mai-lan, who obliged the king to move his goods on a railroad of little girls.

"Majesty man, where Biedersbill?"

George had to slap at their hands. That's how disrespectful they were to a magician king. The little cunts would have died without him. They were only entrepreneurs on account of George. Colonel Mai-lan wanted to hurl them into an orphanage. But they were too old to live in a government building. The other orphans would have mocked their blue eyes.

Mother of Toad, they'd ripped off half a tail, and George began to grieve for his coat. The Yankeegirls scattered with their piece of orange material. The king felt mutilated. It took nine months to import a suit of pastel colors from Milan.

He pranced in his wounded coat like Lord Tiger himself, who was twice as powerful as Jesus. Lord Tiger owned the mountains of Vietnam. But that didn't make George less of a Christian.

He marched out of the sun to meet his sister, who sat over a dish of mountain corn with Percival. They couldn't afford pamplemousse. George tossed a packet of Yankee dollars on the table. Hélène grew skinnier month by month. She would only whore for men she loved, and she was a losing proposition. George dressed her in silk, and customers still wouldn't come to her door. Chinese moneylenders were superstitious about sleeping with the sister of a king.

He spoke to Percival. "Little brother, you mustn't do English with the Yankeegirls. It's dangerous. Mai-lan has many spies. They will hear the Yankeegirls yak-yak, and they'll have proof of your existence. We won't be able to manipulate the courts. They'll sentence you in Hanoi."

"It will give me something to do," Perce said with a smile that was all teeth. He'd diminished since his days on the king's mountain. Perce had begun to twitch like Biedersbill. How many times could George send him to intimidate a Chinese money-lender before Mai-lan guessed a white ghost was in town? Perce had fallen in love, and he would have robbed militiawomen to pay Hélène, but George's little sister had sealed her fate with Percival the Fourth. This white ghost with gums that were getting green was the man she wouldn't take money from. That was true love among the magicians. Whoring for free.

George didn't have the courage to question his sister's economic policy. She'd been a matriarch before the magicians fell. And now she had to borrow her silk pajamas from George. If he mentioned property, Hélène would harp on the fact that his crossbow and all his pants had once belonged to her. So he discussed his nights and days in America.

Hélène interrupted him.

"Did you go to the Statue of Liberty?" she said in that masterful English she'd acquired from Percival the Fourth.

"Sister, who had the time?" George gnashed his teeth. "I wasn't a tourist. I had people to kill."

"Then you're a dunce, my brother, to make such a long journey for nothing."

The bones cracked in the king's head. His eyes filled with a fury against his sister. He would have torn the silk from her body if Perce hadn't been there. He blamed those Billy Christians who'd modernized him with banjo music. He'd grown miserable around Lord Jesus. And he was ashamed to strike his sister in front of a Christian commando like Perce. He'd never beaten his sister before. She'd have stolen his pants and he would have gone before the council of matriarchs without his clothes. He begged Lord Tiger to do away with sisters. George demanded a world of men.

"Did you see the Fifth Avenue, my brother?"

"No."

"Did you worship the Christian gods in a big cathedral?"

"No," he said, his mouth churning with spit. "There is only one god, Lord Jesus."

"More than one," said Hélène. "There is mother, father, and all the Christian ghosts. Ask Percival." But Perce was chewing corn. "Did you climb the Chrysler Building?"

"No," said the king.

"Truly, brother, you are a dunce. You have visited a Christian city without being there."

"I waxed the padre," he said. "That's enough." Hélène sneered and Perce wouldn't take his nose out of the corn.

"Such a Christian that you murder your priests," she said.

He gathered up his wounded tail and got the hell out of his sister's hut. Didn't have a clear path to Quay Street. An American jeep leapt out at him with Mai-lan behind the wheel. She had her own curious battle dress, fatigues and a silk scarf. She was Tuan's age, and had once been in charge of nursery schools in the North. Ho Chi Minh ville would have fallen into chaos without her women's army.

"Ça va, monsieur le majesté?"

Mai-lan always spoke to him in French. She wouldn't consider that a savage could learn Vietnamese.

"Ça va, madame la colonelle."

He climbed into the jeep and rode out of the alleys with Mai-lan. The attention she got on the boulevards was ridiculous to the king. Traffic stopped. Old men waved to the colonel. Militia-women stood in stiff salute.

She could donate the king to a firing squad if she wanted, hang him by his balls. Pirates and profiteers were at the mercy of Mai-lan. No one would have missed a montagnard king.

She put a small bundle on his leg. George undid its newspaper covering. Fountain pens rolled into his lap like an offering from Santa Claus. Fat black mothers with a gold trim. Mai-lan must have raided the merchants again. But there was more to Mai-lan's bundle. A bar of French almond soap sat on his leg.

"The soap is yours, n'est pas?"

"Oui," he said, because he wouldn't deny his merchandise to a trader like Mai-lan.

"Majesté, our hospitals and orphanages require soap. I will need a thousand bars by Monday."

"But madame could requisition laundry soap."

"And the stevedores would steal it for themselves. Almond soap will do."

"And how shall we make delivery, madame la colonelle?"

The dragonlady laughed. "You bargain like a French whore." She had tiny whiskers that must have sprouted with each war she'd gone through. "Don't be frightened, majesté. I wouldn't trap you and your brother with bars of almond soap. You'll be my agent in this affair. I will supply a list of institutions and you'll deliver the soap yourself. That way nothing gets stolen."

"But can you trust the hospital managers?"

"With my life," she said. "I've informed them, majesté. If even one bar is lost, they will wander our city . . . like your brother-in-law."

"My brother-in-law?"

"Oui. The blond ghost."

She took the bar of almond soap and dropped the king in front of Tuan's headquarters. He entered the old schoolhouse where Tuan had his secret offices away from the clutter of policemen. No montagnard could think among strange men, not even a fallen magician like Tuan, who'd been a Communist general so long, he would have been lost around a little poisoned arrow.

Tuan came rushing out of his children's closet, collar undone. "You brought the dragonlady here to insult my headquarters. Why didn't you invite her in for tea? We could have told her all our business."

"She's already aware of our business, brother Tuan."

"I'm your king," Tuan said, shoving his fists together. And George bowed at his brother's knee.

"Forgive me, Frédéric."

"She knows what we feed her, nothing more."

"But she mentioned my little brother, Percival, this afternoon. Called him a blond ghost."

"Did she refer to him by name?"

"No," George said.

Tuan allowed his brother to rise. "She won't get Percival."

"She found me at sister's doorstep."

"That's because we've led her to Hélène. Otherwise she would tear the ground searching for sister. We put ourselves in the middle of her surveillance. Her orchestra is ours."

"She might have an orchestra behind that orchestra, with instruments you haven't touched."

"That's difficult," Tuan said, "when all her instruments come from us."

"You sound like Uncle Albert."

"Albert was my first teacher."

Uncle Al had visited the magicians years and years ago as a philosopher and teacher of French. The king couldn't recall the exact date. Montagnards didn't keep Christian calendars and clocks. But he remembered the padre's magic tricks, half a mile of handkerchiefs out of a medical bag.

George's teeth started to chatter. It was the noise of civilization in his skull. He'd fallen into time, a Christian montagnard in love with *Shoot the Piano Player*. He'd had a brother once, a slave like himself, King Frédéric, who'd carried George on his back and shielded him from the matriarchs. Now he had Lord Jesus.

George sniffed with one nostril, a sign of contempt among the montagnards. "I hope Albert enjoys preaching to the worms."

"Don't ridicule the dead."

Tuan was touchy on the subject of Albert's leap into the spirit world. Teach had been scheduled to die, but Tuan knew that King George wouldn't permit little Howard to be dispatched in Ho Chi Minh. So he had to choose between his American

316

Uncle and his rat-tailed brother, who ran a bordello from a projection booth. Tuan chose George. Not because of sentimental reasons. It was more like a military decision. The time had come to shed his American Uncle. That's how it seemed to George.

The king couldn't have gone to America without General Tuan. It was Tuan who bullied the harbormaster and charted that voyage from ship to ship, with Howard in the hold, losing blood.

"Frédéric, the dragonlady has agreed to support our flow of fountain pens."

"Is that what you talked about in her cab?"

"She'll let us have the pens for bars of almond soap."

Tuan produced a dry cough. "She must want to be very clean."

"The soap isn't for her."

"Of course not," said Tuan. "We'll have to supply all the nurseries in town . . . was it fifty bars she asked for?"

"A thousand. By Monday."

Tuan cackled deep in his throat. "Where will two retired magicians get a thousand bars of soap?"

"We'll steal them back from the merchants who bought them from us."

"But a thousand bars?"

"We'll repackage them, cut every bar in half. And what's missing, we'll make up with laundry soap. You'll contribute this month's quota from your police stations."

"Impossible," Tuan said. "My pathologists can't work without soap."

"They'll have to. For a little while."

"Brother, you've come back from America a ghoul."

"I'm just a businessman," George said. "You'll close a couple of noodle shops and arrest the cooks . . . in case we're still short of soap."

"What if she asks for another thousand next week?"

"The dragonlady isn't unreasonable. She'll understand that we've exhausted our quota of miracles."

"I'm glad," the general said, buttoning his collar. He was finished with the king. "Good-bye, little son. I have work to do."

Little son. The king had an itch to tear his brother's collar off. Christianity had made him murderous. No, it wasn't banjo music that heated his blood. It was an old, old anger, a feeling of neglect. Frédéric was a French king, and the French king had abandoned him, run off to Hanoi. The Elephanters were under French dominion long before the Billy Christians arrived. He couldn't play the little savage. He'd spoken French in his cradle. Christianity had come from that cradle music. He'd lied to himself. The Elephanters always had calendars and clocks.

Tuan returned to his closet. He'd pretended, for Uncle's sake, that Myriam Foucault was his mistress. But he had no mistresses or first and second wives, no daughters and sons. He was a shriveled ex-king in a closet. Rode on ideologies all his life, Uncle's ultimate disciple, a policeman in a schoolhouse.

George wasn't eager for that kind of shit. He'd forgotten that King Frédéric knew how to laugh. Frédéric had flirted with the matriarchs once upon a time, fondled their tits. The village troubadour. He'd delivered songs to the prettiest mamas. Frédéric was the one who first wore a rainbow under his mouth. It was considered the sign of his prowesss as a village stud. He slept with women of property. The women adored him. He brought his rainbow into their huts. He didn't have shriveled eyes and a stooped back. The French had declared him king of the montagnards. He carried gold in his ear. He smoked the women's best silver pipe. The rainbow would thicken when he smiled. And then the Viet Minh seized Frédéric. And the Elephanters sank back into the oblivion of a frightened village without its rainbow king. The gold was torn from Frédéric's ear. The rainbow king grew into General Tuan.

"Majesté."

318

George looked up. He'd stumbled into a ghostly market that was on the run from tax collectors. Old women held out their hands to him. He stood amid the rubble of barbecued pork. Vendors were lacquering the chickens they meant to sell. George didn't eat pork or poultry. He existed on a diet of popcorn at the Richelieu. Popcorn and wet noodles from the wandering soup kitchens. The old women's hands were all over him. They weren't petitioning him for Yankee dollars. They wanted to touch a montagnard king.

"Majesté."

He drifted through the market in his orange pants, the last bit of royalty that was left. He got to Pasteur Street with a dread in his heart. George was frightened of Myriam Foucault. She was his own reluctant mama, disguised as Tuan's mistress so she'd have all the protection of the government. The king had other safe houses in Ho Chi Minh. He could have slept near the old Presidential Palace, or in Cholon, or even in the country-side, with any whore of his liking. But he went to Myriam.

Her bastard boy, Jeanick, was in the garden. George wasn't fooled about the boy's father. Myriam had lived with Uncle Al in the old days. Uncle sentenced her to the Four Hundred Blows and flushed Myriam's head with dreams of taking her and the little bastard to Nice. George knew Nice would never come. He'd pursued Myriam, courted her and guarded the bastard while she had Nice in her mind. George was a temporary respite for Myriam Foucault, her fling with a mountain savage. She disapproved of orange pants, but she didn't hesitate to kiss him in the dark. Until she learned that the savage had killed Uncle Al. Now she wouldn't sleep with him. And like a fool he gravitated to her garden.

He was half a father to Jeanick. He showed the boy films at the Richelieu, built up the boy's collection of fountain pens, and taught him the English language. Jeanick was starved for English phrases. His mother would only talk French to him.

319

"How are you, big boy?" Jeanick said to the king.

"I'm good," the king answered.

"Jeanick is also good."

"Did my little man do his homework?"

"Homework not so good," said Jeanick. And he had to shut up, because his mother was lurking about. He was as frightened of Myriam as the king was.

His mother came into the garden. She'd heard the palaver in English. She wore a black turtleneck that had once been standard beanie clothes. It was beautiful against her amber skin. She had the power to make a king shiver. She was George's wound.

She warbled to the boy in French and he ran inside the villa without another word.

"Majesty, why do you delight in contaminating him?"

"How come I'm majesty all of a sudden? I thought I was George."

"Kings are cruel. They declare love and soon become betrayers."

"I didn't betray you."

"You robbed my child of his future."

"I'll get you to the Long Noses. You'll have your Nice."

But Myriam said nothing. She stood there, building up beauty in her black turtleneck. And the king understood. She wasn't interested in Nice with her mountain savage. Jeanick might not prosper with a montagnard dad.

"Where are you going?" she asked.

"To the Richelieu."

"So you can supervise your children's traffic?"

"It's better than hearing bitter songs from you."

"Majesty, do you demand love for destroying the father of my child?"

"He was a son of a bitch. I did him before he could do me. You wish I was the corpse, not Uncle Albert."

"I didn't say that."

"Well, I'm what you've got, the old savage from the highlands, a goddamn Yard with a career in a movie house. Does it matter that I love you and the boy?"

"You're a king," she said. "You don't have to love. You could possess me. Your brother is chief of police."

He slapped her with the smallest portion of his hand. The boy was at the window. Jeanick had witnessed the slap.

"That proves you're my king, doesn't it?" she said. "You treat all your mistresses that way."

"You're not my mistress."

"Then what am I to you, chéri?"

"My intended," he said.

She didn't laugh. "And who will come to our wedding? Lepers and halfbreeds?"

"They're welcome," the king said. "I'll feed every mother in Ho Chi Minh."

And now she laughed. Lord Jesus, she bloomed above the turtleneck. Amber flower on a black stem. She took his arm and led him into the house. They passed Jeanick, who'd gone to his writing desk and scratched at a parcel of homework. They entered Myriam's room. She shut the door and placed the king's hands under the turtleneck. He held her breasts like a lifeline. He kissed her, explored the bones in her cheek. He danced to Myriam's bed, trembling like a king.

But he couldn't stay all night. Climbed over the pillows while Myriam slept like a gorgeous child, her breasts heaving slightly to the wind in her throat. His majesty had another appointment. Got into his ruined orange coat and examined his teeth in the mirror. He might cause a ruckus washing his mouth. He didn't want to wake Myriam. He crept out of her bedroom and visited the boy for a moment. Jeanick slept in his own little room, clutching random chess pieces and fountain pens. Those were his comforters. George had a strange attitude towards the boy.

He couldn't rid himself of the notion that Jeanick was his child. It was nothing but a king's fantasy, and yet the fantasy held. He had a love for the boy that was outside any tribal loyalty. Jeanick wasn't a montagnard. Jeanick was Albert's son. But curse the Christian gods and all their ideas of devotion. He felt like the boy's father.

Kissed him on the cheek and then he took off, leapt like a savage into the dark. The women's militia had their searchlights out. The ville was ringed with shafts of blue light that were like razors in the sky, looking for infinity rather than Chinese bombers. Was infinity where Jesus lived with all the good angels? What if George needed a bad angel on his side?

He avoided Mai-lan's checkpoints. He was like a ghost strutting through the ville. He followed the canal north of the zoo and arrived at the riverbank. There was a fog on the water that rolled around the king, protecting him from the women's militia. He had his flashlight dangling at his belt, but he didn't dare use it. The fog would have curled the light back onto him. So he trilled out to the water, gave a long coot, like some bird of the highlands, and waited there. He saw the ship's castle float toward him and then heard the bump of the *Viceroy* against the river-bank. The engines were idle. The Russkis were feeling the water with their long poles.

It was like George's personal ferryboat. He went aboard the *Viceroy*, and the crew pushed away from the shoreline with their poles. He was on a ship that had no legal existence in Vietnam. The *Viceroy* was a moneymaker, but it was never talked about. If Mai-lan had ever seized the boat, she would have found Hanoi a little deaf to its phantom run. It was a floating barge of currency, an alternate state bank. But Mai-lan still would have arrested the whole ship. It stank of capitalism and special favor. So Konstantin had to pick up George and whatever moneyed guests he had and hide from the women's militia.

George was sorry he hadn't finished Konstantin at the Chanticleer. The Russki was a liar. He cared only about himself. But he was the Rothschild of the Hanoi regime. That mother made himself a millionaire while he kept the country afloat.

He wasn't in his little office. The king found him on the bridge. Konstantin was walking in the fog.

"Spassky-Fischer," he said to George. "I was replaying their third game."

George couldn't understand how you could play chess on the foggy bridge of a phantom tub. Chess required chessmen at least, a board, and a couple of onlookers. But he had no fondness for such a game. It was like a war of little people, won and lost in the head. It had only the merest resemblance to real fighting. The rules were arbitrary. A commando wouldn't have survived two minutes if he could only leap in one direction.

"Forgive me," Konstantin said. "We Russians have a madness for chess. Ten times worse than football in America. I always play on the bridge. I divide it into the squares I need and hop like an idiot. Spassky-Fischer. I made thirty thousand on that match. Dollars, your majesty. Not rubles. From half a dozen generals in the KGB. Ah, why should that interest you, my comrade king? You can't forgive that I'm alive. But you would have gained nothing from an arrow in my chest . . . almost nothing. What do you have for me?"

George removed deutsche marks from his different pockets.

"Ah," Konstantin said. "I can't count in this weather. Come with me."

They went down into an underdeck where the lighting wasn't so irregular. Konstantin smiled at the rip in George's coat. It was the Russki who shopped for George in Milan, selected the king's style of clothes. Konstantin didn't count the deutsche marks. He was much more involved in George's orange suit.

"Off with it, man. I'll give it to my tailor in Hong Kong."

The king had to remove his coat. He felt ridiculous until Konstantin provided him with a sweater pulled off some hook in the wall.

They always met in the middle of the month. Konstantin might be in Leningrad tomorrow. The *Viceroy* only functioned when the Russki was around. It sat in the weeds during the rest of the year.

"Majesty, what can I do for you?"

"Lend me some soap."

The Russki laughed. "I thought there was plumbing at the Richelieu. But you're welcome to my private stock. Our soap comes from Finland. You'll like the smell."

"It's not for me," George said.

The Russki winked. "Ah, a business deal. Are you supplying the black-market butchers with something to wash their hands? Zdena will give you whatever soap we have on board. I'll take my usual twenty percent of the profits."

"This isn't a twenty-percenter. I'll need much more soap than you can carry. It's for the dragonlady. She's put the squeeze on my brother and me. A thousand bars of soap, she says, or she'll cut our traffic to pieces. We won't be able to move a fountain pen through the ville."

"That bitch," Konstantin said. "She's into profiteering now."

"No. It's for her nurseries."

Konstantin scratched his arms and his back. He was like a smooth blond bear. "That's worse. She muscles you for her own charities. She's a clever bitch. She knows you and the general can't come up with a thousand bars. It's Mai-lan's way of striking at me."

"Maybe not. She's hungry for soap."

"Good. Then we won't disappoint the bitch. She'll have a thousand bars of Finland's best. I'll borrow what I can from the pleasure boats in Macao and fly in the rest.".

"By Monday," George said. "Mai-lan can't wait."

"I'll have the soap delivered to her door."

The king was only a pimp in orange pants. Konstantin ran the local economy. He was the absolute lord of Ho Chi Minh.

"Majesty, what else?"

"I'm worried about Biedersbill. How can he run the Baroness's estate without cash?"

"He'll have his cash. Didn't we form a partnership?"

"And the Davidoffs?"

That blond smile went mean. "I don't provide for Yids. Henry James will have to take care of the Davidoffs out of his own pocket."

"But I have to know. Is the Teacher all right?"

"God's my witness," Konstantin said, placing a hand on his heart.

"Commies don't believe in God."

Konstantin neighed like a horse. "You shouldn't listen to all the old wives' tales about us. We have our own chapel inside the Lubyanka. The KGB can worship however it likes."

"But would the Christian gods endorse a boat such as this?"

"Why not? We're as Christian as any tub on the water. Aren't we getting Mai-lan her soap?"

The king was without recourse to Russian arguments.

"No one understands us," Konstantin said. "No one. The West had a perfect opportunity to sting us without all that nonsense of a missile gap. Spassky-Fischer was the key. A hermit from Brooklyn takes on a country of grandmasters and knocks it off its ass. That was America's victory. But did America push? Soviet science was nothing compared to Fischer's eccentric game. But America went to sleep over the board. And our own grandmasters have absorbed Fischer's game. That's the foolishness of America. What's Fischer now? A monk who should have been a millionaire."

George was lost. He couldn't follow chess and Bobby Fischer. He'd been to America, but he'd only met ruins and one farm.

The Russki put his hands behind his back. "What's the use? Majesty, go to the girls. You distress me." And he climbed back upstairs to replay Spassky-Fischer for the thousandth time.

George went looking for Zdena's bungalow. He knocked on several doors. Blonde women peeked out at him, with nothing but their boots on. He was a king, yes, and a montagnard, but he couldn't keep his eyes off those splintered trees of hair between the women's legs.

"Zdena?" he asked. But the women wouldn't answer him. He knocked on another door. Zdena stood inside her cabin, tall, blonde, and naked except for her boots. He wondered if Polish women lounged this way. Zdena drew him into the cabin. There wasn't a language they could share between them. But Zdena was kind to the king. She admired his warrior's scars, the birdshot in his shoulder. She tossed a Polish record onto her flimsy machine. Zdena wouldn't move with him until his majesty took off his orange pants. He danced with her in his underwear.

"I love," she said, the only two words of English she'd ever spoken to George.

"I love," he told her back, and it was partly true. Because he was more at peace with Zdena than he could have been with Myriam. He was almost a happy man. He'd fulfill his obligations to the dragonlady. A thousand bars of soap. He could still murder the Russki if Teach was left an orphan at the farm. Then he'd mail deutsche marks to America.

He had this insane wish, as he stood belly to belly with the Polish dancer, that she might bear him a boy like Jeanick. A future king of the Richelieu.

"I love," Zdena said. And the king stepped out of his underwear, kissed Zdena's face until all the images he'd ever had of Myriam was scalded out of his eyes. Past, present, and future fell from him. He had neither sister nor brother nor orange pants. He'd never bossed a revolution. He was the tail inside that burning color the rainbow left in the sky. He was gas and heat and disappearing design. Dust on Mai-lan's searchlights. But still a king.

"I love," he said to Zdena without his underpants.

16

AH, it was like a hundred Henry Jameses had registered at the Chanticleer. The old men Teach had captured were haunting him now. They didn't gripe about their destiny or demand to see a lawyer. The old men were resigned to their stay on the farm. But they floated by the Teach like the master might have done. Teach was caught in an epidemic of Henry James.

"Biedersbill, you don't look so hot."

It was Nika Nikolayevich Troubnoy in golfer's pants. He'd prospered inside the chateau. And Teach began to wonder if the nurses were supplying Nika with some tail.

"Ah, I'm hassled all the time, Uncle Nick. I didn't expect to be the captain of a retirement colony. I dug up mines in Vietnam."

"But you have talent as a peacemaker."

Peacemaker, that's what he was. He had to steer around the Davidoffs, who were in residence at the farm, and all the nurses and old men, Lulu, Marve, Sarah, and the Baroness. The Davidoff women didn't get along with old Sarah. Zoya and Adelina tried to turn the Chanticleer into their own bakery truck. Bossed the old men and imposed a diet on the farm. The Chanticleer was becoming a house of blintzes.

And then there was old Izak, who'd entertained Stalin, Nika had said. Been the murderer's clown. Played hockey with polar bears. Izak didn't bother with blintzes or borscht that went from green to blue. This old guy was the master of chocolate cake. Loyal as he was to Sarah, Teach would have strangled Stalin himself for a lump of Izak's cake. Soft in the middle, plump on the outside, with wiggles of mocha near the heart. Nika stole a big piece for him every morning, and Teach had to chew it on a back porch, far from Sarah. But he still had to contend with his fiancée.

I'll shoot their lights out, Sarah had told him, Izak and all, and Teach kept an eye on her .45s.

"I could use a vacation," he said to Nika. "I think I'll rent the room next to yours."

"Biedersbill, you're too late. The room is occupied."

Teach winked at Konstantin's old spy and walked into a wall of nurses petitioning the Baroness for a pay check.

"Sorry," the Baroness said. "It is Monsieur Howard who keeps the books."

The Baroness went into her office and bolted the door, having perambulated enough for one day. And the nurses descended upon the Teach.

"We're quitting," they said.

328

"Quit, but don't put me down as a character reference. Who will hire you? Desperado nurses is what you are."

"We haven't been paid in a month."

"And what about me?" the Teach said. "Am I walking around with silver and gold? We're a struggling institution. We have problems with our cash flow."

Uncle had neglected to explain the finances of the Chanticleer before he died. And the Baroness was inarticulate on the subject of money. No checks or cash had come in since the Teacher took control. He'd used up all the talmud torah's funds and had to borrow from the Davidoffs, who considered their loans as a lien on him and the institution.

"Go on," he said, rattling his teeth. "Back to work. You'll be paid."

He was expecting money from Konstantin, but he wasn't sure of the particulars. How could he track a double agent? He couldn't even tell if the Chanticleer was a CIA farm. The mothers had left him in the dark.

But he was shrewd behind his helplessness. Teach had an inventory of dead people in the cellar and no one had bothered to shut the Chanticleer. Not one visit from the FBI, or a few questions from the Jersey police. The farm was a favored nation, immune from arrest.

And with all his cash problems, he had to play cupid. Couldn't leave Marve to flounder at this hotel, caught between Sarah and Lulu.

Teach took a chance. Stole into Marvin's room one morning with a washcloth and wiped off the rainbow and the blue eye crescent and collected the gold nubs from Marve's ear.

Marve woke with a washcloth on his nipple. He leapt in front of his mirror and started to scream. "I'm warning you, Teacher. Don't fuck with my head."

"Christ, I'm cleaning you up."

"I want my rainbow back."

"Nix. You're Marvin of Murray Hill and I'm taking you home."

"I live here," Marve said, twitching like the Teach.

"Kiddo, you have a wife in the big bad ville."

"I'm not a kid. I'm older than you are."

"You're still my kid. I'm captain of this farm."

Teach dressed Marve in a gray suit the padre had kept at the Chanticleer. And then he sneaked Marve out the side door, sat him up front in Sarah's stretch limousine.

"Lliana doesn't want me, Teach. I couldn't be a husband again. I've grown wild. I'm not fit for anything but the Avenue C gang."

"That's the trouble, kid. We're gone from Avenue C."

They rode out of New Jersey and Marve mourned the absence of color on his chest, felt deprived without his rainbow.

He winced at the sight of Murray Hill. "The doorman won't let us in."

"We'll see."

But the doorman was polite and pretended not to recognize Marve. "And who should I say is calling, sir?"

"Biedersbill. And Marvin de la Mare."

Lliana agreed to let them up. Marve twitched on the elevator, but Teach grabbed him and performed a little montagnard magic. Pulled Marve's shoulders back until he heard a couple of bones pop into place. Then he shook Marve's scalp so the blood could travel to his ears and flush out whatever poison was left. Meantime Teach was working on a game plan. He knew Albert would have warned Lliana away from the police, but he wasn't sure how much Uncle had told her. Should he romance that beautiful blonde cow with spy stories?

Lliana hugged Marve at the door, nearly swallowed him into her chest, and held out her hand to the Teacher.

"You're Albert's associate, aren't you?"

330

She prepared mint tea and couldn't keep her eyes off Marve. She giggled a lot and bit her fingers out of nervousness.

"Albert said I'd have to wait a few months . . . and you're here, ahead of schedule."

Improvise, Teach muttered in back of his throat.

"Mrs. de la Mare . . ."

"Darling," she said to Marve, clutching both his hands. "It must have been torture for you."

Ah, if only Teach could uncover the line Uncle used on her. He might have fed into the line, sweetened Uncle's narrative, like a chapter out of *The Beast in the Jungle.* He worried that Marve would give them away, because you could never tell about a man who'd swallowed Elephant sauce. It was lucky Lliana kept talking.

". . . dangerous for both of you."

"Lady, it was," Teacher said, trying to glean a hint from Lliana's words. But she wasn't listening. Lliana only had eyes for Marve.

"How was Albert's crossing?"

"Terrific," Teach said, and now she looked at him.

"Has he settled in one spot? Albert always had a fondness for Nice . . . he wanted to follow Nietzsche's wanderings."

The Teacher felt betrayed. Sure, he'd heard of Nietzsche. And he'd known of Uncle's plans to retire to Nice, where the Baroness had a slew of cousins, but Uncle should have been loyal to Henry James.

"Yes," Teach said. "Nice is on the agenda. But I couldn't swear Albert has arrived."

"And Jonah?" she said, with a tiny ruffle of her nose.

"Jonah's with him. Definitely."

Lliana paused to fiddle with her hair, her fingers like a long, trembling musical instrument. "I thought Jonah's under wraps and can't be found."

"The situation's being resolved," Teacher said.

331

"You can tell Albert he's a pig for not writing. I won't do another word on Rimbaud."

"Ah, that would dishearten him, Mrs. de la Mare. He gets a kick out of your scholarship. Isn't that right, Marve?"

"It's a conspiracy," Lliana said. "You're flatterers. The both of you."

It was time for Howard to leap. He could afford a show of sentiment. Pecked Marvin between the eyes. "You shouldn't be a stranger, Marve."

Teach walked out and Marve began to feel brittle, all alone with his wife. A king without his rainbow, he started to cry, because he loved Lliana and he'd missed her body. He had a brother somewhere. Niles. And he'd been to Dartmouth. But he was Sarah's child. She'd nursed him on a nipple, soothed that scream he carried around in his head.

Could never scream at his mom and dad. He'd endured their silences and couldn't save Niles. Escaped to New Hampshire and found Carlo and Lliana through his Dartmouth connections. He clove to Lliana, but the screaming wouldn't go away. He edited books with an ache in his ear. And then he fell into Alphabetville, vanished from society, and the howling stopped. He'd been graced by a rainbow. He was the rainbow king and he danced for a cabaret of mamas. Part of Sarah's war machine until Samuil introduced him to that other George. He'd discovered his twin, but Marve felt like a candy king. His twin could duck a birdgun, shoot arrows from a toy bow, and Marve was only good for entertaining mamas. That king rescued Sarah and never said good-bye. Couldn't he have talked about his rainbow a little, what it was like to be a montagnard? Marve survived without that conversation. Had his own room at the Chanticleer. But Teacher spanked him with a washcloth and returned him to polite society. Marve was scared.

Lliana moved her mouth. "My poor darling, when I think what you must have suffered . . . and sworn to secrecy. I hope the Russians rot in hell."

Her mouth went to his. Her eyelashes tickled his head. He screamed inside her throat, but his tongue got caught, and the scream turned to a kiss.

Teach could have swung the limo around and gone right home. But something nagged at him. His life as the cash-poor captain of a retirement colony. He wasn't into holdups. And what could he have gotten from robbing some ice-cream parlor? Besides, Baskin-Robbins didn't carry gook ice cream. He drove down to Indian country, parked at the rim, and went into Alphabetville on foot. If Capa was around Avenue C again, why shouldn't Teach collect from the supermarkets? It couldn't have mattered much that Uncle was dead. He'd forgotten his blasting caps, but at least he had the stethoscope, and it wasn't Capa's business what Biedersbill was packing under his cuff. First he'd have to find that Bolivian mother.

He drifted from building to building, shell to shell. Where were all the johns in their Cadillacs? What had happened to the coca people? There were no retailers around. And then he spotted the baby bandits coming out of a garden. They didn't crank their Colts at the Teach. "Caballero," they said, "how you doing, man?"

"I'm looking for old Capablanca."

One of the banditos touched the hairs on his chin. "Follow us."

And they brought the Teacher back into the garden and around the shell of an apartment house. Teach dreamt of garbage bags stuffed with dollar bills. He wasn't greedy. He'd take a smaller cut from Bolivia now that he was alone.

The children led him up a flight of battered stairs to Capa's home base. Capa was running cocaine in a little railroad flat, but he wasn't Monte Cristo this morning. He didn't have his cape. That conservative prince wore a dark suit. His new generals looked like ushers out of Radio City Music Hall. They had gold buttons and dark braids.

"Ah, my little man," Capa said, kissing Biedersbill on both cheeks. "Would you care for a little rum?"

"Thanks, Capa. Another time. I need some coca money."

"Naturalmente," Capa said. "Our little man is back in line. And what would you say is fair?"

"Five percent."

"You're modest," Capablanca said, loading Teach with packets of hundred-dollar bills. "It's hard without Uncle, eh?"

"Yeah. I can't solve the riddle of cash flow."

"And how's your synagogue in New Jersey?"

"It's not a synagogue," Teach said. "It's a retirement farm."

"But it's long on Hebrews, aint it? I hear the Russian Yids have colonized the place. You're part of the borscht belt."

"And you?" Teach said. "Still waiting for Boliv to fall?"

"Politics don't matter to me, little man. Capa wins whoever is in power."

"Aren't you worried about the poison you might breathe?"

Capa laughed. "I'm immune to poison. I can drink any kind of shit."

"Then why were you hiding at Uncle's farm?"

"A precaution, that's all," Capablanca said. "A temporary rest. But I think you owe me something, little man."

"What's that?"

"An apology. You slandered El Nobel."

The generals grabbed Teach and carried him across the railroad flat into Capa's office and held him out the window by his ankles. Teach saw sky and moon in Capa's garden. He watched his stethoscope fall. The generals shook him and all the packets of money flew out of his pants. He could feel his life spill. He was thirty years old and what had he accomplished? An impotent mother, he'd never be a dad. Ah, I'm going to die again. His teeth were knocking, but he longed for another ride through hell. If he floated far enough, his mind might clear of money. Sarah, his mouth said.

Capa leaned with one foot on the windowsill. "Now tell me, Teacher, who is the greatest writer in the world?"

"Henry James."

A general let one of his ankles go and Teach swung in a narrow arc, like a pendulum outside a brick clock.

"I'm deaf," Capa said. "So tell me again."

Teach would have shouted Henry James, but the wind stuck in his throat.

"El Nobel," he coughed into the bricks.

"Who?"

"Gabito, Gabito Márquez."

Capablanca smiled. "I recommend all his other books. *The Autumn of the Dictator. Leafy Storm. The Colonel and the Letter Box.* Do you swear by Santa Maria that you'll read El Nobel?"

"Swear," Teach said, bitter about himself, because he'd betrayed Henry James to the Bolivians.

"Can we drop him now?" asked the general who was clutching Teacher's ankle.

"Are you loco?" Capablanca said. "The twitch has his own little godfather. Marlon Brando lives in his house. Or is it Burt Lancaster? Caballeros, we have to let him go."

And the generals hauled him back inside the window. Teach tried not to shiver too much in front of Capa's men.

"Where's this godfather of mine?"

"Ask Albert."

"Wish I could, but Albert's dead."

"That's your problem, little man."

Teach wandered down the stairs, wondering if Brando or Burt

335

Lancaster would make a better dad. He found his stethoscope in Capablanca's garden. Packets of money were near his feet. But the Teacher couldn't pluck them out of the grass. Baby bandits were standing guard over the hundred-dollar bills.

"Adios," the banditos said.

Couldn't find much peace at the farm. Women fell on him. Zoya and Adelina ragged his ear. They were tall as the Teach in their high heels. Their crayoned eyes closed like metal shutters. Their arms were thick. They could have destroyed Biedersbill.

"No paella," the two sisters said. "Gives indigestion."

Ah, Sarah had put together a pot of yellow rice behind his back. And the Davidoffs considered it gross interference in their reign as cooks. They demanded satisfaction from a farm that hadn't produced cash. Teach was yearning for Izak's chocolate cake. He wanted to dig his head into the mocha and die there. Because what else did he have?

"The gun lady is not welcome in kitchen," Zoya said. "We will throw her out."

Teach had to be judicious. The Chanticleer was living on Davidoff money. "I'll tell her. No yellow rice."

But Adelina was looking at him funny. Her blinkers didn't seem so metallic all of a sudden. Her nose puffed in and out. Teach wondered if Adelina was constipated until Zoya took him aside.

"She is loving you," Zoya said.

Teach had to hear it again.

"My sister, she is loving you, Mr. Poison Man."

"But I'm engaged," Teach said, defenseless against Zoya's pleas.

"Is no problem. We will buy off fiancée."

"C-c-can't," Teach said. "I gave my word."

"Is a terrible mistake."

Zoya returned to Adelina and Teach pulled shrapnel out of his hair. Ah, he was fond of the two sisters, but he wasn't their type. He had a lick of poison and went up to Sarah, who sat with Herman Fish, .45s tucked in her belt, like some mistress of the shore patrol.

"You haven't said hello to my dad."

"Hello, Herman."

The old man blinked from behind his blue blanket. He was wise to be rid of ordinary business at the Chanticleer. He carried a truck of memories, Teach could tell. And the truck stayed inside. That was the glory of Alzheimer's. You could sink into a long boat trip in your head.

"Biedersbill, I've been talking to dad about you."

Teach pulled shrapnel again. "You can't fool me. Herman doesn't talk."

"Yes he does," Sarah said. "I ask him questions and he blinks out the answers."

"What's he been saying?"

"That he shouldn't have kept me from marrying you. I told him he was wrong. I said you're a snake in the grass, and dad finally agreed."

"How am I a snake?"

"You kidnapped Marve without a thought of us."

"I unkidnapped him, you mean."

"He wasn't yours to give or take. That man was communal property."

"Didn't you ever hear of Lincoln? We don't keep slaves."

"Then what would you call the old people on this farm?"

"Men in early retirement."

"And who retired them?"

"Wish I knew," the Teacher said. "I followed Uncle's orders."

"Did Uncle order Russians into the kitchen?"

"Sarah, I have to stroke the Davidoffs while they're paying the bills."

"Have you been stroking Zoya under her quilt?"

"God forbid."

"Then why the hell are you favoring her family? You can tell that high-heeled witch I'll do paella whenever I want. Dad can't digest Russian blintzes."

"Honey, I'll set up a little kitchen on the second floor. You can cook for our side of the house."

"I can't cook for ghosts . . . with Vladi dead and Lulu in love with the beebee-gun boy. Why couldn't you let Marve stay?"

"It wasn't fair to his missus."

"I don't give a damn about that blonde bitch."

"They love each other."

"Love can take a crap," Sarah said.

"What about all your poems?"

"I'll renege on them."

"You can't renege what's written down. Ask your dad."

"Why should I write poems when you love your Russians more than old Sarah?"

"That's ridiculous," Teacher said.

"Prove it."

He kissed her high on the mouth, with the .45s digging into his groin, and Herman blinking at him. He couldn't go on kissing like that with her dad around. He was crazy for Sarah, but he didn't have the slightest tickle in his pants. Ah, he'd have to give up chewing poison one of these days.

"Sarah," he said. "Herman is watching."

"Who cares? He'll have to suffer a little for keeping us apart."

So they kissed away a quarter of an hour in front of Herman Fish and then Teach had to look to his chores. His face hurt where Konstantin had cut him in Ho Chi Minh. Ah, love was a knife wound and a kiss to beat the clock. He wondered if he could sell that to some valentine company. There were enough valentines in the house. Lulu and Samuil were holding hands

on the stairs. She never even asked about Marve. Love was the
blindest mother in the land.

Teach heard a taxicab rumble onto the lawn. Looked out the
window. He would have recognized a Jersey cab. This was some
yellow mama out of Manhattan. What was a yellow cab doing
in the wilds of Passaic? A woman with long ankles stepped out.
Long ankles and a sexy strut. Teach could tell it was Corinne.
He beat her to the front porch. Didn't want trouble between
mother and daughter. Lulu hated Corinne.

"Either you walk to your taxi," he said, "or I'll carry you.
Lulu's in love with a Russian fiddler and she doesn't want you
on her hands."

"Lulu?" Corinne said. "Lulu's at the farm? Since when? I came
for Connie."

"Jesus Christ. Konstantin's lost in Africa or Asia somewhere."

"I don't believe you."

"Corinne, would I lie when he owes me thousands? That
mother has left me with a charity ward."

"I still don't believe you. He's hiding from me."

"You'll have to take my word," Teacher said.

"I'll scream," she threatened. "I'll wake up all the spies."

Ah, he let her into the house. Zoya sniffed at her once and
grew bored with Corinne. Izak came out of the kitchen, examined
her beautiful legs, and offered Corinne the mocha heart of his
cake, without a word of English. And then Lulu arrived. "Don't
you feed that bitch, Uncle Izak."

But Izak was already enthralled. "Who is lady?" he managed
to ask.

"My goddamn mom."

Izak danced like a polar bear.

"But she's a cunt," Lulu said, watching Corinne cry. "Oh
mother, say hello to my intended while you're here."

Teach could have sworn they were bits of a single tree. One
had escaped from Carlo, and the other hadn't.

"Intended?" Corinne said, her eyes searching for Konstantin.

"Yes. My intended. Samuil, come down and meet my mom
. . . we're getting married next year."

"How will you support yourselves?" Corinne asked, searching
over Samuil's shoulder.

"Please, madame," Samuil said. "I am baker, violinist, and
clown, like my Uncle Izak . . . I won Tchaikovsky second
place."

"Congratulations," Corinne said, rocking into a dream. She
stared at the Teach. "When is Connie coming?"

"Wish I knew."

"You're not holding him with the other spies?"

"You ought to go. Carlo might get suspicious. He knows you
wouldn't travel this far for a literature lesson."

"You'll tell me the minute Connie comes?"

"On my life," Teacher said.

Corinne walked around Samuil, took Izak's offering of cake,
kissed him on the mouth, and returned to her yellow cab.

And Teach wondered who was captain of this farm. That old
baker or him? Lulu and Samuil went upstairs. Izak started on
another mocha heart in the kitchen. And Teach was all alone.

He found Doris Quinn wandering in the parlor. Quinn had
gone totally gray at the Chanticleer. She was making scratches
in a notebook as she walked. Sneered at Biedersbill. "You killed
my Gwen."

"Not me, Doris."

"Yes. It was your party."

Quinn stopped scratching. She looked at the front door and
began to cry. "Was that Carlo's witch?"

"Not a witch," Teach said. "And I can't bring back Gwen."

"Gwen can rot in the cellar for leaving me," Quinn said, her
eyes on the door. "Teacher, promise me I can stay at the Chanticleer."

"You're our honored guest, the old Manhattan Spy."

"You won't send me to Singapore?"

"Not a chance," the Teacher said, catching the hint of a man's face in the door's thick glass. The man had enormous eyebrows, like some Poseidon of the South China Sea. Wasn't Henry James. It was Carlo. Had he come in his own yellow cab, looking for Corinne? Teach would have to furnish an alibi, swear he'd been doing Gabito Márquez with Corinne. Two hundred years of solitude at Uncle's farm.

Doris had written books for the old man, but she wouldn't greet him. Quinn withdrew from the parlor and Teach opened the door and blinked, wondering if he should ask Carlo to join the Chanticleer's league of old men.

"Mr. Biedersbill, aren't you going to invite me in?"

"Naturally," the Teacher said, thinking fast. He was always glad to see Carlo. Poseidon wore the whitest shirt in America. His suit was pearl gray. He couldn't have been seventy-five. His back was straighter than Biedersbill's.

"Funny coincidence," Teach said, trying to steer Carlo onto a neutral topic. "Troubnoy is living at this establishment. Would you like to ask him about the Lubyanka?"

"Not today," Poseidon said. "We'll have a quiet talk, you and I."

"It's a madhouse, sir. Traffic in every room."

"What about the Baroness's office?"

"She's not partial to guests."

"Try her," the publisher said.

Teach knocked on the Baroness's door.

Ah, the old girl agreed to contribute her office. She fled in her shawl and Teach sat behind the Baroness's desk and offered Carlo whiskey from the Chanticleer's dwindling stock.

"Thank you, Mr. Biedersbill. We'll drink another time."

Teach had a suspicion the old man knew his brother Al was sleeping in the cellar. Carlo hadn't come for Lulu or Corinne. He was after the Teacher's throat.

He scribbled out a check from the old publishing company.

It was to the order of Howard Biedersbill, Chanticleer Convalescent Home, fifty thousand dollars, payable in cash. Marlon Brando, Teach mumbled to himself. Now he knew what Capablanca meant about a godfather.

It wasn't the signature or the sum that alerted Teach. It was Carlo's scribble pen. The publisher had inherited Konstantin's black beauty. Ah, the Mont Blanc didn't grow on trees. It was passed from one spying mother to the next. Gallatin & Peck was a laundering operation. Carlo had been Albert's financier.

"This ought to hold you for a while," Carlo said. "Call it petty cash." He capped the old fountain pen and dug it into his pocket.

Teach felt he was on a canoe ride, facing a waterfall with his head stuck under the seat. He had to paddle blindly with his hand or sink into the falls.

"Sorry about Albert," he said.

Carlo's eyes stayed a merciless blue. "It's not your fault my brother was such a romantic. Albert put Rimbaud into whatever he did. You don't have that disease, do you, Mr. Biedersbill?"

An anger built inside the Teach. He'd been a cockeyed mother all along. Albert was just another soldier who'd gone to his grave.

"You're our missing dad. Gallatin & Peck is a piece of Saigon Station."

"Good God," Carlo said. "I'm not a Company man. I'm a major in the reserves. Run a tiny school for army intelligence command."

"I'd love to see the graduation list."

"Why?" Carlo said. "You're on that list. The beanies were a branch of army intel."

"Now I know how Konstantin got to the Nam. The CIA wouldn't have had the balls to throw a Russian spy in with the beanies. It was an army op all the time. But what's your pull on Konstantin?"

"Money," the old man said. "Our boy has lavish tastes. He

342

kept stealing from his own till for whores and clothes. But he couldn't destroy the KGB's accounting books. He had to come to us . . . and he didn't fall. We gave him a very long leash."

"I chewed on that leash in Ho Chi Minh."

Points appeared in Carlo's blue eyes. "That wasn't my idea. Albert got careless. He panicked over you."

"Was it panic that put out Jonah's lights?"

"Jonah's a different story."

"But I'd like to hear," the Teacher said. "I'm a loyal son of a bitch."

"Then you wasted your loyalty. Jonah was my personal carrier pigeon. The poor boy started eating his feathers. So in love with Lliana, he couldn't fly. He wanted to finance his silly affair with a little blackmail."

"So I captured him for you, and Konstantin poisoned the dumb mother with merchandise from the jars I mixed."

"Biedersbill, be fair. We couldn't have asked you to finish the job. You didn't know about our existence."

"That's the trouble, sir. I'm still not sure about your existence."

"But it's simple to explain. I'm in charge of a counterintelligence op. We call it Rainbow Room."

Ah, those romancers loved to pick neat little names. Carlo should have bought himself a valentine company. "That's nice poetry, sir. Did you borrow it from George?"

"Not George," the old man said. "Rainbow Room has been around since the time of King Frédéric."

"I get the picture. Tuan is all yours."

"No. He simply inspired the name. Tuan was Albert's man, and Albert kept him in the dark."

"Like he kept all of us," Teacher said. "All of us dancing in the dark. And what kind of magic is Rainbow Room about?"

"Not magic, Howard. Arithmetic. We ferret out Russian operators in New York and elsewhere . . . all over the world."

343

"How do your agents keep in touch?"

"Through Doris Quinn," the publisher said.

"Ah, the old Manhattan Spy."

"I fed Doris information, fed her line by line. Turned each of her editions into a code book."

"And Marve was the dunce who edited a spy manual without knowing it."

Teach might have been wrong to let go of Marve. Montagnard mud was more powerful than an editor's crayon. But he'd have had to kidnap Lliana, and it would mean one more lady in the house. Sarah couldn't have lived near a beautiful blonde cow with slim ankles.

"Sir," he said, "was Brighton Beach also in your code book? Did Konstantin recruit Vladimir for the KGB or Rainbow Room?"

Carlo twirled his fingers. "A little of both."

"Then Vladi was your parlor trick."

"Parlor trick? There were KGB men planted among the refuse-niks that arrived in America."

"The Davidoffs, I suppose."

"It's not impossible," the old man said, and Teach was considering how he could strangle Carlo Peck with the least bit of noise and bury him next to Albert. But the old man had some stinking telepathy.

"I'm your angel, Mr. Biedersbill. Don't spoil that. If you hurt me, your people will starve to death."

"Wouldn't dream of touching you . . . you're the fucking tooth fairy. You watch after old men at the Chanticleer. Only what about Lliana? Will you have to pay her off? She'll wake up and realize her husband isn't a counterspy."

"I had two generals visit her last month. They told a convincing tale. When she starts doubting, they'll visit her again."

"And Marve? What will the generals say to him?"

"Nothing much. He'll sit inside his fog, thanks to you."

Peck was the goddamn magician of the United States. He was

much more than that. Frédéric and George were only tinsel in the Teacher's skull. Silver pipes and Elephant sauce. Peck was the rainbow king. He fished a letter from his pocket. "Some news of Dostoyevsky Street. Konstantin thought you might be worried."

Teach crumpled the letter in his hand. "What about the Bolivian coup that failed? Was it an Army op?"

"Don't be absurd. There was no coup. That was more of Albert's romanticism. He wanted a revolution . . . like King George. He turned reckless in his hotel room. Sent two of his soldiers into Boliv. I had to get Lubbock and Kroll out of there before they started gunning the locals and put Capablanca out of business."

"Then why the hell were all those corpses flung around Capablanca?"

"There was a little war going on between the traffickers in Colombia and Boliv. Capa's own cousins were out to betray him. We couldn't afford that."

"No wonder the narcs didn't come down on Capablanca. He was helping to finance Gallatin & Peck. But how come Renata had to die? Did she have Bolivian cousins under her dress?"

"No. Poor girl, she was connected to Konstantin and our own little cell. But the Russkis were on her trail. Half the world knows Konstantin's a double. That's his singular advantage. Moscow treats him like a special clown. He's tolerated as long as he can declare a profit for the KGB. But Renata might have linked him to us. Konstantin was supposed to have a bit of CIA in his blood, but if the Russkis discovered he was part of Rainbow Room, that would kill our op. Renata was showing her hairy legs to too many people."

"So you made it seem like I had murdered her."

"We didn't have a choice. You were Albert's little son. We had to point her death in Albert's direction. She was another victim of the coca wars."

"Yeah," Teach said. "Everything depends on coca . . . and Konstantin's boat. Is the *Viceroy* your tub?"

"That's a little more complicated," the old man said. "It's Konstantin's baby."

"What about his other baby?"

"Ah, Corinne," said the rainbow king without the slightest twitch. "I saw her taxi on the road. I'm not the adoring husband, I'm afraid. Hardly a husband at all. I tired of Corinne years ago. Never looked at her much after Lulu was born . . ."

"All in the family, eh? First you doubled Konstantin, and then you gave her to him. Albert wasn't the pimp. He was following orders from his older brother. And I was the delivery boy. Did you have to talk about Tolstoy all the time?"

Carlo stood up to go. Then he danced on his heels for Biedersbill. "Almost forgot . . . I think we'll have to dispose of Quinn. She might decide to publish with another house, and it would be an embarrassment to us."

Teach looked into the publisher's eyes. "There's no point in cluttering the cellar, Carlo. I'll burn whatever she scribbles."

Teach held his stare. He was battling with a rainbow king over who would rule the farm.

Carlo laughed without lending his blue eyes. "If you say so, Biedersbill. But she's your responsibility." He wouldn't let Teach walk him to the door. "Less conspicuous if I leave alone . . ."

Teach sat among the Baroness's things: an old lamp, a tray of pens, a calendar from Nice. Her inroads into America. He sniffed Carlo's check. The paper was slightly perfumed. He opened the letter from Dostoyevsky Street for signs of Vladi's three sisters. He would have to ask Adelina's help . . . not her. Troubnoy. Sarah wouldn't be so jealous if Troubnoy translated a heap of Russian words.

He had money for milk and cheese. He'd build Saigon a kitchen on the second floor and the hell with King Carlo. The mothers could dance in their Rainbow Room. Teacher had a home.

A fist clutched at him. "Where's my other man?"
It was Lulu and her redheaded minstrel, with Teach's violin.
"He's gone," Teach said. "Marve's gone."
"I saw you," she said. "You were mumbling with my dad."
"He was worried about you," Teach said, trying not to bite
on his own fib.
"Why didn't he tell that to me?"
"He's afraid of Samuil."
The redhead hummed to himself and pulled on the fiddle.
"Is Marve coming back?" Lulu asked, about to cry.
"Old Marve'll be back," Teach said, and how could he swear
it wasn't true?

'Twas under an apple tree
I saw her white eyes.
Was it cowgirl or demon lady?
Dedushka, I didn't even care.

Sarah was in the linen closet getting extra pillowcases for her
dad when she heard Samuil's balalaika song. The monkey was
serenading Lulu, and Sarah sort of wished she were the one
with white eyes. Samuil's voice was like honey on a wire.
She didn't know whether to shoot him for disturbing the pri-
vacy of a linen closet, or bless Samuil for bringing songs to the
chateau. She felt useless around so many Russians. They stuffed
Lulu with blintzes and chocolate cake. The girl was getting fat
without Marve. But Sarah wanted to drown in Lulu's old lemon
water. She was engaged to an entrepreneur. He palavered with
the nuns and didn't seem to mind if Lulu lived in sin with a

balalaika artist. She wouldn't have tolerated that kind of shit at the talmud torah. She'd have laid down the law: the redhead couldn't sniff Lulu until he presented her with an engagement ring. And then she looked to her own fingers. She had no ring from Biedersbill. There wasn't the least little record of their engagement. If she died tomorrow, people wouldn't have known that Howard had promised himself to her sixteen years ago, under the Bayonne Bridge . . . before he married Hélène of the hills.

Looked up from the linen and Howard was there. "Damn you, Biedersbill, sneaking up on a girl like that."

"Wasn't sneaking," he said.

"Then what would you call it?"

"Saying hello."

She laughed and pulled him into the closet, but she couldn't escape Samuil. That song about white eyes seeped through the wooden door. She didn't care if Teach was short in the pants. He could still kiss and hug her a little.

"Biedersbill, you'd better look for a marriage license."

They sank into the pillowcases, and all that white material felt to Sarah like the underpinnings of a canopy.

Old men bellowed on the other side of the door. Teach emerged in half an hour, with a face full of spit. Nurses glared at him. Old men clutched his pants. "Biedersbill, our sink is broke."

"I'm not a plumber," he said, but he fixed the old men's sink. The army was his landlord and the Russians owned New Jersey, but he was getting good at kissing in a closet.

"Biedersbill!"

It was Sarah calling. She didn't worry about any old bride. She'd recaptured her little man from that sorceress Hélène. "I'd like my dad to marry us."

"But Herman's not into marriages. He does things inside his head."

"He'll marry us if I ask him gentle."

And Sarah dragged Biedersbill up to her father's room. Herman sat under a red quilt, chewing his tongue. His eyes were fixed on the woodwork. His pajama jacket was royal blue. Snow burned from the windows near his bed, and the room was deep in a white blaze.

"Dad," she said, "will you marry us, dad?"

She put her own hand and Howard's into her father's paw. Herman must have been attentive to his daughter's touch, because his fingers closed around the two hands. He never looked at Sarah and that new son-in-law. Wouldn't take his eyes from the wall. But his mouth pulled in another direction. "The Biedersbill boy," he said, "the Biedersbill boy," before he went back to chewing his tongue.

17

NIKA Nikolayevich Troubnoy was back inside the Lubyanka. He didn't have windows or a river under his feet. But there were no colonels to bother him, no guards. Nika walked among the catacombs. He'd heard from some revoltnik that if you burrowed far enough, you'd come to Detski Mir, the giant children's palace which was across the road from the Lubyanka. Detski Mir, the largest kiddie shop in the world. What did Nika have to lose? The colonels could take away his caviar.

Nika marched. He passed other dead souls, like himself.

"Evening, comrade."

"Nika Nikolayevich, where are you going?"

"To Detski Mir."

They laughed at him, considered Nika a fool. "This is the Lubyanka, not the House of Pioneers."

But Nika wouldn't be discouraged by dead souls. He marched. The gangs of men began to thin until Nika was alone. He climbed out of the catacombs. He laughed, because they were the fools, not Nika Troubnoy. He'd entered Detski Mir. He saw cradles and balloons and mechanical starfish that sang and crawled. He saw miniature firetrucks that shot streams of water, a Lenin doll that could talk.

"Ilych," he said to the doll. "What a revolution! Never mind the gangsters and bureaucrats who are in your chair. It's not too late. We'll win."

The doll smiled and went around the corner of Detski Mir.

And Nika Nikolayevich was happier than he'd ever been in his life, happier than his cradle years, happier than his first months of marriage, when he was Moscow's real estate king. What did it matter that he was the only customer at Detski Mir? He had every single toy to choose from, and no clerks with their beads to count up his sales. And then he felt a hand on his shoulder, like a skeleton that had reached out of the Lubyanka itself.

"Troubnoy."

Nika moaned.

"Troubnoy, I give you three minutes to get out of bed and brush your teeth."

It was little Davidoff. Nika's heart slapped with bitterness. Davidoff had stolen him from Detski Mir. But Nika got dressed and ran tooth powder along his teeth. "Where are we going?"

"On a day trip."

"Yes," Nika said. "That tells me everything. A day trip."

They went downstairs without disturbing a soul.

"I'm hungry," Nika said. "Please, a little of your uncle's chocolate cake."

"We don't have time," Samuil said.

"I'm not moving without the mocha."

And Samuil had to give in. They had coffee and cake in Izak's kitchen fortress. Then they marched out into the snow. Samuil brought a hammer along, and Nika had to chop at the ice around the Davidoffs' wheels, while Samuil started the truck.

"Get in."

Nika climbed into the cab of the truck, Samuil's own pilot house. "And why did you bring me?" Nika asked.

"I wanted companionship."

Which wasn't untrue. Samuil preferred to drive into Manhattan with his own assistant baker. He could fall asleep on an icy road, and Nika would be there to wake him. He wasn't used to chauffeuring himself. But he wouldn't take his aunts on this trip. He was going to visit his future father-in-law, Carlo Peck. He'd heard the conversation Carlo had with the Teacher. He'd stood near the Baroness's door like a common *shpik*. And he hadn't been wrong. There was an American Oprichnina, a house of spies. And Carlo was the head of that house.

The conversation troubled him, because he didn't believe Carlo's clever explanations. And suppose Samuil was wrong? He'd have to meet his father-in-law sooner or later. Why not now?

Nika was Samuil's plum. Hadn't Carlo met with Nika at the Brown Bear and talked of a book contract? Why shouldn't Samuil continue the negotiations?

They stared at the city's spires from the Jersey marshland. For a moment the Empire State Building seemed to sit on the Statue of Liberty. And then the moment passed. That tall building moved to the other side of the world.

They parked next to a farmers' market, at the back of Union Square, and walked to Gallatin & Peck. Samuil liked the glass doors and the receptionist's nook.

"Mr. Carlo Peck, please."

"Do you have an appointment?" the receptionist asked. "Mr. Peck doesn't usually see people at this hour."

"Tell him his son-in-law and the famous critic, Nika Troub-noy."

The receptionist whispered into a telephone and Carlo came out of his office in a pair of blue socks. "Yes, yes. Davidoff and Troubnoy."

He welcomed them into his office and shut the door. Offered them mints and a cup of tea. Samuil and Nika chewed the mints, but they couldn't drink poisonous American tea.

"Coffee, perhaps?"

"Please not to beat around the bush. Nika Troubnoy has a book to sell."

"I've already heard about his book. And I've declined it, thank you."

"Is a different book," Samuil said.

"Really? And the subject matter?"

"Espionage, American-style."

"What the devil do you mean?"

"Apologies," Samuil said with a bow. "I am terrible eavesdrop, and you will have to forgive. Was necessary. We couldn't have survived on the boardwalk without extra ears."

"You have my sympathies," Carlo said, "but what does your eavesdropping have to do with me?"

"I listened to your conversation with Comrade Biedersbill."

The old man plucked at an errant eyelash. "Now it's clear. You're looking for a bit of blackmail. And your vehicle will be some phony book."

"Not blackmail," Samuil said. "Survival money, yes. But more than money. Comrade Biedersbill is vulnerable fellow because you told him too much. He is assassin, no? And hotelkeeper. And you sing to him on your mandolin all your government secrets. Is a little dangerous to have a simple assassin know your affairs. You could decide to kill him, yes? And bury his castle. But my aunts are inside with my uncle Izak."

"That's hilarious," Carlo said. "Why should I hurt Biedersbill and your aunts?"

"Comrade, please. I am not your child. I didn't sit in castle to collect real estate. We have no interest in property. I was waiting for you."

Carlo brushed his silver eyebrows. "I'm flattered that you'd wait for a man you'd never met."

"But I saw you, comrade, at the Brown Bear. Why would such a big publisher talk to Troubnoy? He has no talent."

Nika, who understood nothing until now, had to complain. "I have plenty talent."

"Only as a shpik," Samuil said. "But publisher sits with you and then you vanish from bakery and reappear at castle on the hill. Carlo's castle."

"You're almost as romantic as my late brother," Carlo said.

"Not romantic, comrade. I do not want my aunts to die. You've heard of the Oprichnina, yes?"

"Of course. They were Moscow's assassins until the Kremlin cooled them off."

"Then is curious you should have chief assassin like Konstantin on your list."

"Good God, man. Moscow doesn't take him seriously. He clowns for the Ivans and clowns for us."

"But clowning is serious business," Samuil said. "And I do not believe in your little undercover agency. Comrade, you misrepresented yourself. Rainbow Room is a lie."

"Delicious," Carlo said. "Go on, Mr. Davidoff. Tell me who I am."

"I do not think you capture Russian agents. On the contrary. You have small partnership with KGB."

"Ah, so I'm a turncoat now, a bit of a traitor. Benedict Arnold and all that."

"Who is Benedict Arnold?" Nika asked.

"Quiet," Samuil said. "Not a traitor. You have approval of your government. You make deals, you wear many uniforms, like the old Oprichnina. I am not sure if you are army, navy, or marines, and why would you tell? You kiss KGB when is suitable. You run cocaine."

"And how did you learn all this?"

"From your shpik, Jonah Slyke. Why should he concern himself with bakers from Brighton Beach? He puts our apartment on fire and sends us into Alphabetville."

"He was acting on his own," Carlo said. "He wanted you to guard the talmud torah, so Marvin couldn't move uptown."

"Is possible, comrade. But I have better script. Your shpik was jerking everybody. You, Konstantin, and the Davidoffs. You tried to get us out of Brighton Beach as a favor to Konstantin. He had his network of shpiks on boardwalk, scared little men like Nika, and if we shook all the shpiks too much, it could make trouble in Moscow and call attention to Konstantin. But Jonah decided to use my family as private policeniks. He asked us to sit on Alphabetville. But comrade, we're Davidoffs. We don't sit in darkness. We saw the cocaine. And we recognized the KGBniks from Brighton Beach who were driving special taxis on Avenue B. Alphabetville was a wedding between Moscow and United States. No so big. But still a wedding."

"And you'd like to crush that wedding. Is that it?"

"Not crush, comrade. But I do not want KGB men to appear at castle some afternoon with a lot of blowtorches. It could interfere with my uncle's baking. He can't produce mocha with fire all around."

"And what does this preposterous story have to do with Mr. Troubnoy's book?"

"Comrade Carlo, we've gone into business of samizdat. We have manuscripts lying around in many places. And if my aunts should be harmed, or Biedersbill loses a leg, or castle suffers a catastrophe, our manuscripts will start to circulate. You'll feed us, comrade, you'll write the Teacher a monthly check, but you'll leave us alone."

Carlo smiled. "You ought to come and work for me as a scout."

"Comrade, I'm not a shpik."

Troubnoy was troubled on the drive back. He'd sat through a whirlwind in the publisher's office, and he couldn't understand such a storm. A book he hadn't written was circulating where? If only he could harness little Davidoff and get him to agree on a concert tour. It wasn't too late. Nika could produce a Stradivarius somehow and a coat with tails for Samuil's introduction to Carnegie Hall. He scribbled a sign in his own head.

SAMUIL DAVIDOFF

BAKER AND HUNTER

FIDDLER FIRST CLASS

"Samuil," he said. "We could ensure our lives if you returned to the violin. The Banditov wouldn't dare touch a world-famous artist."

"Troubnoy, eat your tongue."

Nika remained quiet for the rest of the ride.

Samuil parked in front of the castle. His aunts were near the door. Both of them were in love with Biedersbill. But Biedersbill only wanted Saigon Sarah.

"Is all right?" Zoya asked. "You leave without a note."

"Business," Samuil said, because he didn't want to frighten his aunts about the castle's connection with the KGB.

"American business?" said Adelina.

"Yes. I had to find Troubnoy a publisher for his book."

"And you couldn't wake us?" Zoya said. "What kind of book?"

"A fairy tale," Samuil said. "About Lenin."

"Is new to us that Nika is such devoted communist."

"Not communist," Samuil said. "A fairy tale. About Ilych in Manhattan."

"And where is book?"

"Inside Troubnoy. He refuses to write without a contract."

"You are the fairy tale, darling," Adelina said. "Is not such a book."

And what could the fiddler do after Adelina had caught him in a lie? Kissed his aunts and went into the castle.

Lulu looked at him with her big eyes. "Sammy, where you been?"

"I had to meet with father-in-law, no?"

He was hungry for cake. He stole into the kitchen and found Biedersbill with his face buried in the mocha.

"Lo," Teacher said, his eyes full of dark cream.

"Save a piece for Samuil," Samuil said.

The Teacher stepped aside.

Samuil saw a shadow in the window. Mozart's mother! Did the KGB beat him to the castle? Where was his gun? Teacher, Teacher, life is more than one big commando raid. Biedersbill was among the disadvantaged. He'd never sucked on snow in Sokolniki Wood.

Samuil would go against the Banditov without a gun. But it wasn't KGB. Only a branch in the window.

He dug into the mocha with Biedersbill, but he couldn't escape the image of his aunts: wild women in America, involved with leather clothes.

He looked into Teacher's mocha face and started to cry, because all that chocolate reminded him of Zoya and Adelina in Moscow, coming home from their factory in bittersweet masks.

"Davidoff," Teach said. "Don't cry. We've knocked all the mothers down."

"Yes, I know."

And Samuil took another bite of mocha. What could he say

to a commando with a twitch? They had no future here. Sooner or later the Banditov would come, kidnap Lulu for Carlo's sake, but no one else would survive their visit.

"Comrade, you will have to close castle. Too many armies are involved with upkeep."

"Ah," Teach said. "That's what I was thinking. But we can't go back to the talmud torah. Alphabetville is crawling with agents, and the agents are into coca dollars, like everybody else. We wouldn't have a chance."

"Agreed. Talmud torah is not right habitat for my aunts. They can't find husbands in such dark place."

"Then where should we go?"

"Boardwalk," Samuel said. "Comrade, you'll enjoy the ocean."

And Teach started to laugh, because his whole life was turning into a trip from Bayonne to Brighton Beach. "Davidoff, I took the D train to your country. I saw rye breads in the window . . . and lots of agents."

"The agents are everywhere. But is America, no? And not New Jersey. The Banditov wouldn't dare harm us on a boardwalk with so many refuseniks around."

"Fine," Teach said. "But I'm not becoming a baker."

"Who asked for such a sacrifice? You will be our family soldier."

"Just like Vladimir," Teach said with a touch of bitterness. "Davidoff, I have my own family now. The Baroness can run to Nice, but I have nurses to consider . . . and old men."

"Comrade," Samuil said. "Is empty building behind Gastronom Moscow. We will move old men into building and have our nursing home."

That little mother thinks like a general, Teach admitted, watching Davidoff with both eyes. "What should we call it, The Russian Fiddler?"

The beebee-gun boy turned gray. "Please, no violins. Is better to call it The King George."

Ah, that's a title Teach could understand. And he almost blubbered, remembering George. Revolutions had slipped away from
the Teach. "One thing, Davidoff. Sarah needs her own kitchen.
She can't live around blintzes. You'll have to get Adelina to
go along."

"A kitchen, of course," Samuil said, his mind on other matters,
like money. He would have to squeeze Carlo month by month,
or they'd never survive.

"Promise me Sarah can make all the yellow rice she wants."

"I promise," Samuil said with a rattling jaw. He didn't have
a ruble's worth of interest in yellow rice. Where would he find
husbands for Zoya and Adelina? Where, where, where?

"A deal," Teach said.

Both of them clapped their mouths with cake before the Teach
fell into a slight twitching swoon and pulled shrapnel out of
his hair.